## Everybody loves
## the Last Kids on Earth series!

"TERRIFYINGLY FUN! Max Brallier's *The Last Kids on Earth* delivers big thrills and even bigger laughs." —JEFF KINNEY, author of the #1 *New York Times* bestseller *Diary of a Wimpy Kid*

★ "A GROSS-OUT GOOD TIME with surprisingly nuanced character development."
—*School Library Journal*, starred review

★ "Classic ACTION-PACKED, monster-fighting fun." —*Kirkus Reviews*, starred review

★ "SNARKY END-OF-THE-WORLD FUN."
—*Publishers Weekly*, starred review

"The likable cast, lots of adventure, and GOOEY, OOZY MONSTER SLIME GALORE keep the pages turning." —*Booklist*

"Jack is a fantastic narrator . . . Young zombie fans will rejoice in this new series that has all the oozing (by the zombies) and heroism (by the kids) that they could hope for."
—*Bulletin of the Center for Children's Books*

"HILARIOUS and FULL OF HEART." —*Boys' Life*

"*The Last Kids on Earth* is a BLAST."

—Powell's Books

"I would recommend *The Last Kids on Earth* for PEOPLE WHO LIKE VIDEO GAMES because it is equally as fast-paced." —*The Guardian*

"It's hard to find something unexpected to do with zombies, but this clever mix of black-and-white drawings and vivid prose brings new life to the living dead." —Common Sense Media

"The MONSTERS IN THIS BOOK just beg to COME ALIVE." —Parenting Chaos

"One-part SWISS FAMILY ROBINSON, and one-part WALKING DEAD, Max Brallier and Doug Holgate's well-imagined book is sure to appeal to readers with big imaginations."

—The Reading Nook Reviews

"The NEXT HOT READING ADVENTURE for reluctant readers or for anyone looking for a fast-paced, humorous adventure." —Guys Lit Wire

Winner of the Texas Bluebonnet Award

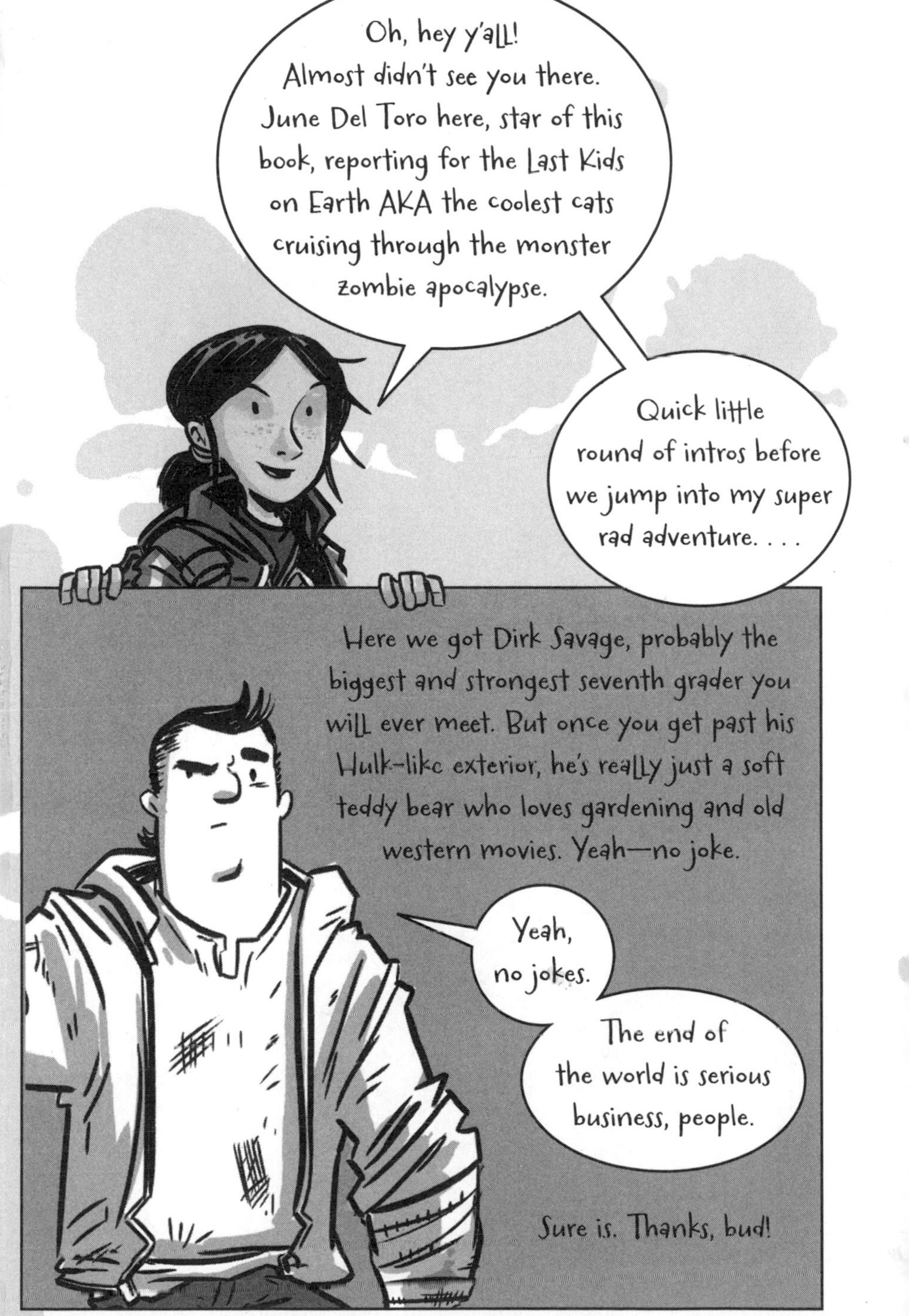
Oh, hey y'all! Almost didn't see you there. June Del Toro here, star of this book, reporting for the Last Kids on Earth AKA the coolest cats cruising through the monster zombie apocalypse.
Quick little round of intros before we jump into my super rad adventure. . . .
Here we got Dirk Savage, probably the biggest and strongest seventh grader you will ever meet. But once you get past his Hulk-like exterior, he's really just a soft teddy bear who loves gardening and old western movies. Yeah—no joke.
Yeah, no jokes.
The end of the world is serious business, people.
Sure is. Thanks, bud!

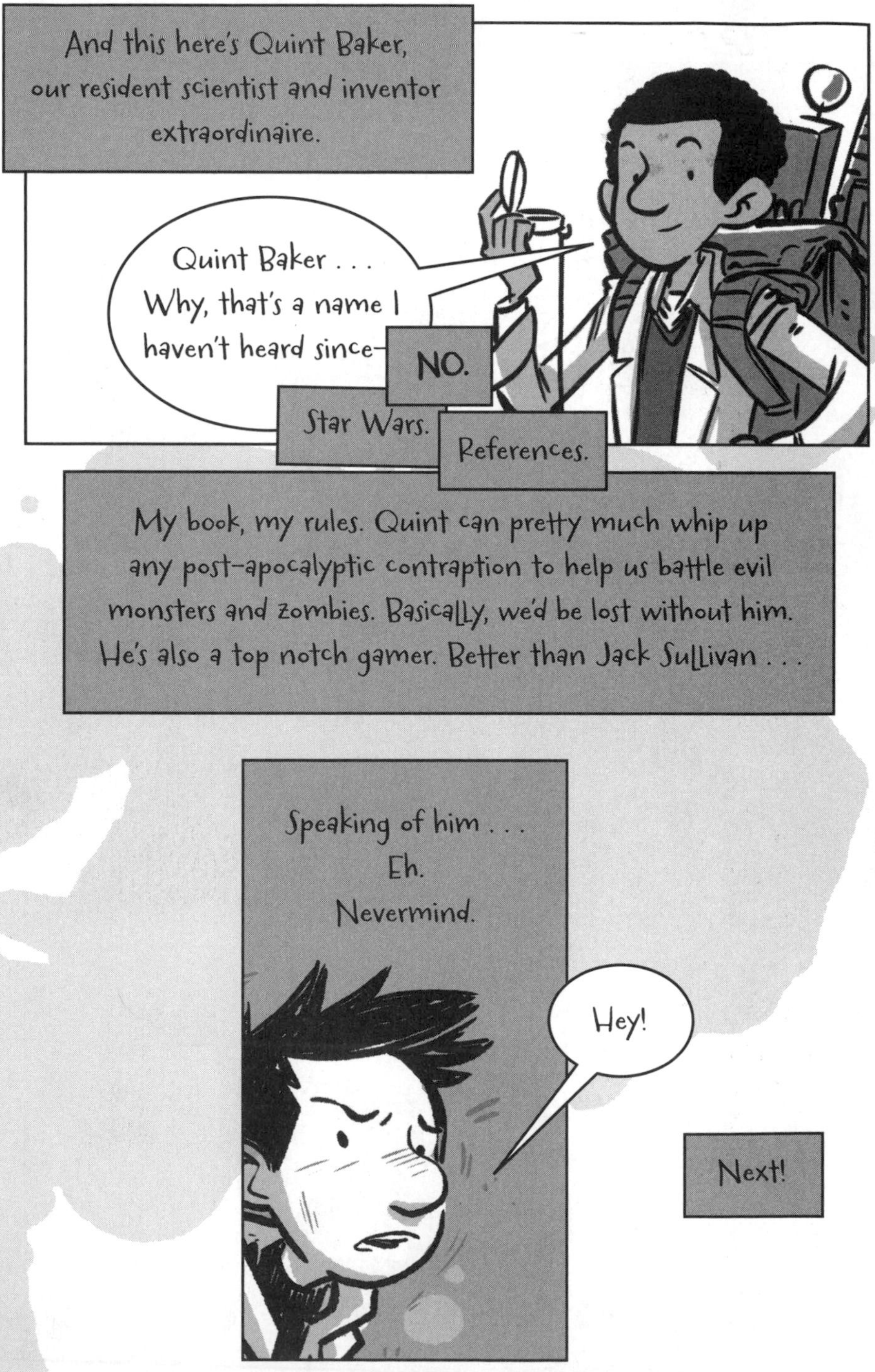
And this here's Quint Baker, our resident scientist and inventor extraordinaire.
Quint Baker . . . Why, that's a name I haven't heard since—
NO.
Star Wars.
References.
My book, my rules. Quint can pretty much whip up any post-apocalyptic contraption to help us battle evil monsters and zombies. Basically, we'd be lost without him. He's also a top notch gamer. Better than Jack Sullivan . . .
Speaking of him . . . Eh. Nevermind.
Hey!
Next!

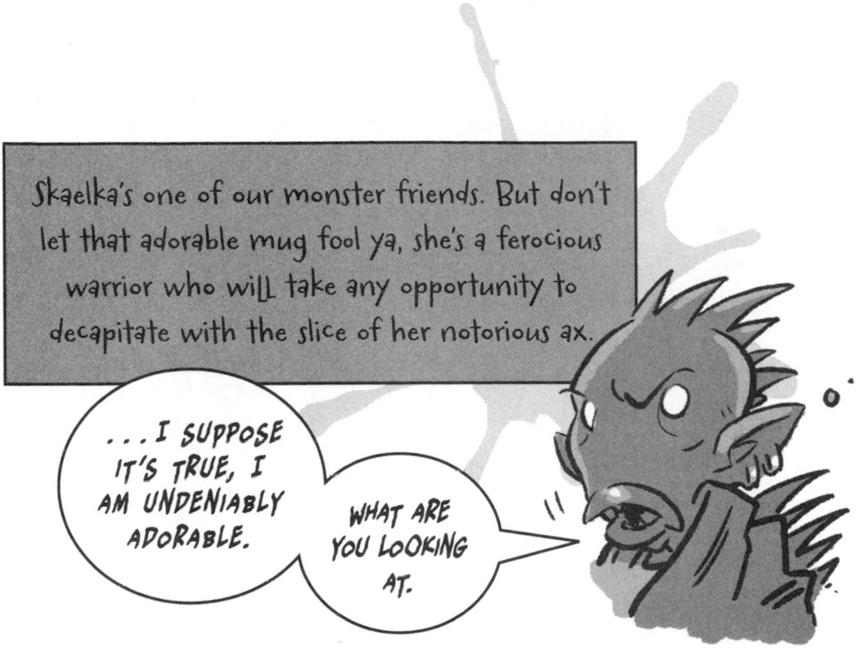
Skaelka's one of our monster friends. But don't let that adorable mug fool ya, she's a ferocious warrior who will take any opportunity to decapitate with the slice of her notorious ax.
. . . I SUPPOSE IT'S TRUE, I AM UNDENIABLY ADORABLE.
WHAT ARE YOU LOOKING AT.

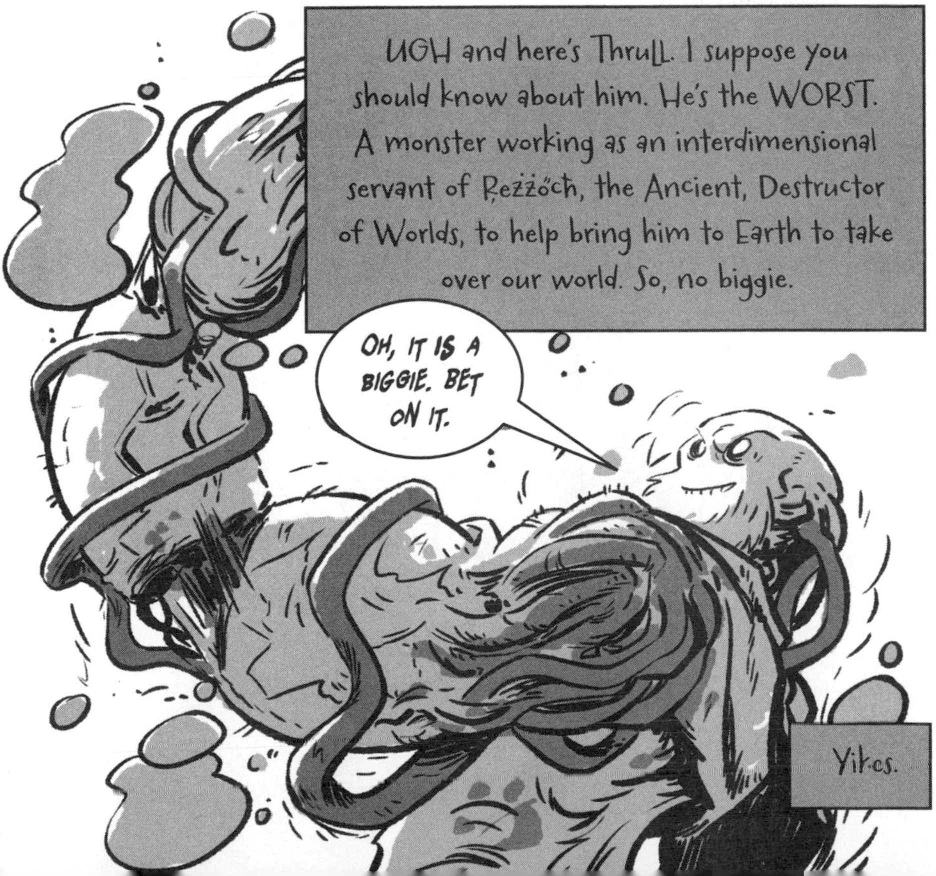
UGH and here's Thrull. I suppose you should know about him. He's the WORST. A monster working as an interdimensional servant of Ŗežžőch, the Ancient, Destructor of Worlds, to help bring him to Earth to take over our world. So, no biggie.
OH, IT IS A BIGGIE. BET ON IT.
Yikes.

That about covers it. You'll meet some of our other monster friends (and enemies) along the way, and catch up on the whole story so far. Plus there will be a zombie encounter or two. . . . It's gonna be a wild ride!
Is it time for me yet?
It is **not.** Page seven, Globlet.
Cool cool cool.
Whatcha doin'? An intro thing?
OK, **bye** now! Anyway—
Buckle up, take a deep ol' breath, and away we go!

# THE LAST KIDS ON EARTH
## JUNE'S WILD FLIGHT

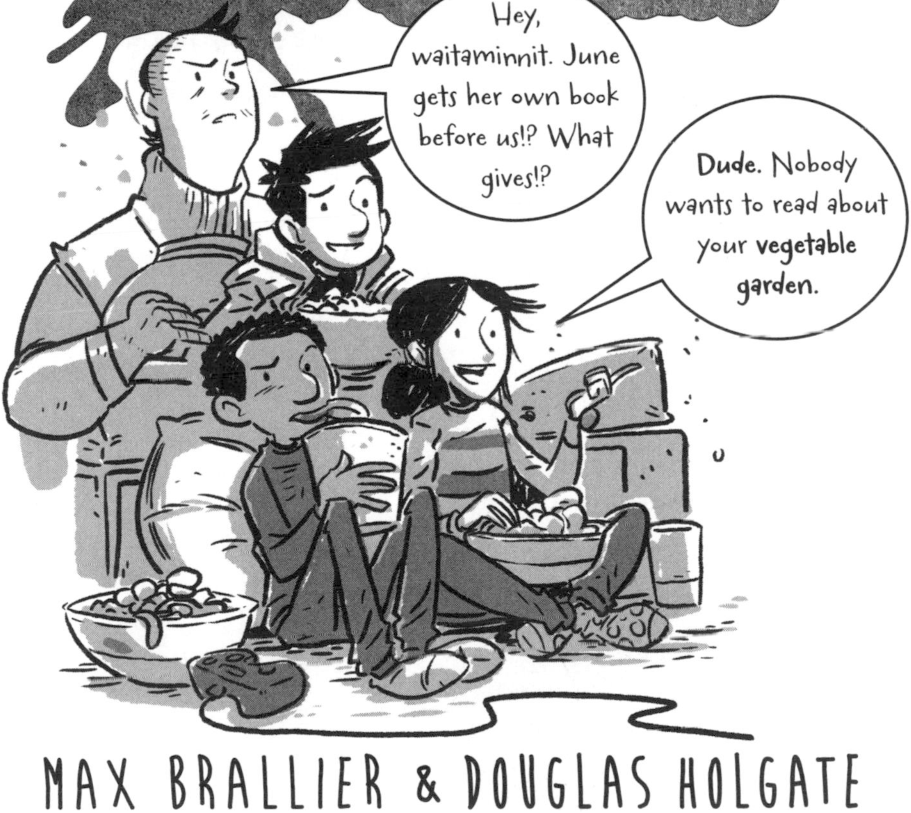
Hey, waitaminnit. June gets her own book before us!? What gives!?
Dude. Nobody wants to read about your vegetable garden.

MAX BRALLIER & DOUGLAS HOLGATE

VIKING

VIKING
An imprint of Penguin Random House LLC, New York

First published in the United States of America by Viking,
an imprint of Penguin Random House LLC, 2020

Text copyright © 2020 by Max Brallier
Illustrations copyright © 2020 by Douglas Holgate

Visit us online at penguinrandomhouse.com

LIBRARY OF CONGRESS CATALOGING-IN-PUBLICATION DATA IS AVAILABLE
ISBN 9780593117187

10   9   8   7   6   5   4   3

Book design by Jim Hoover
Set in Cosmiqua Com and Carrotflower

Printed in the USA

For Sally and Ruby.

—M. B.

For Harriet, Philippa,
Sakura, Elodie, Lilly and
Maggie. The downright
coolest, toughest girl
gang I know!

—D. H.

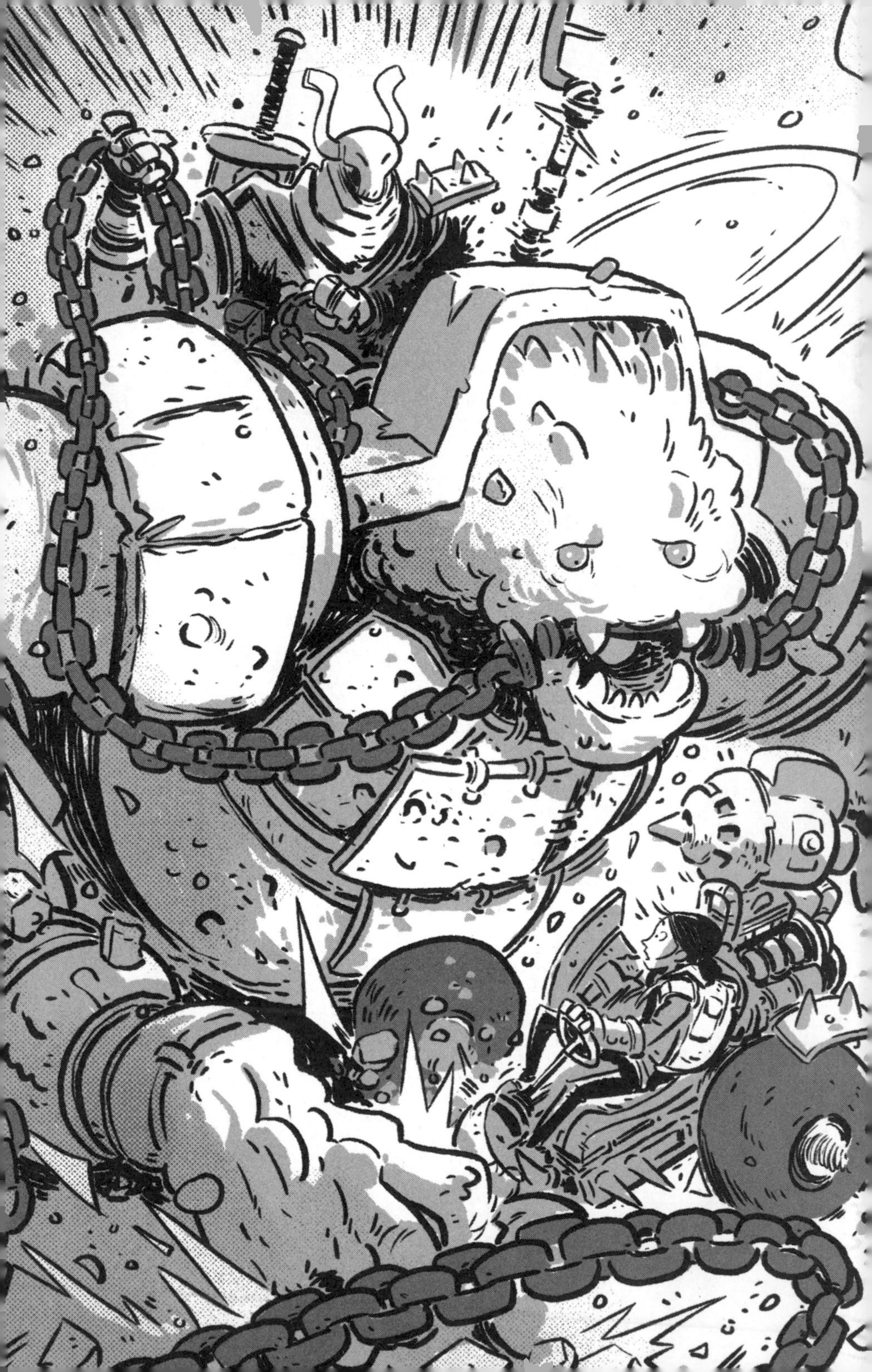

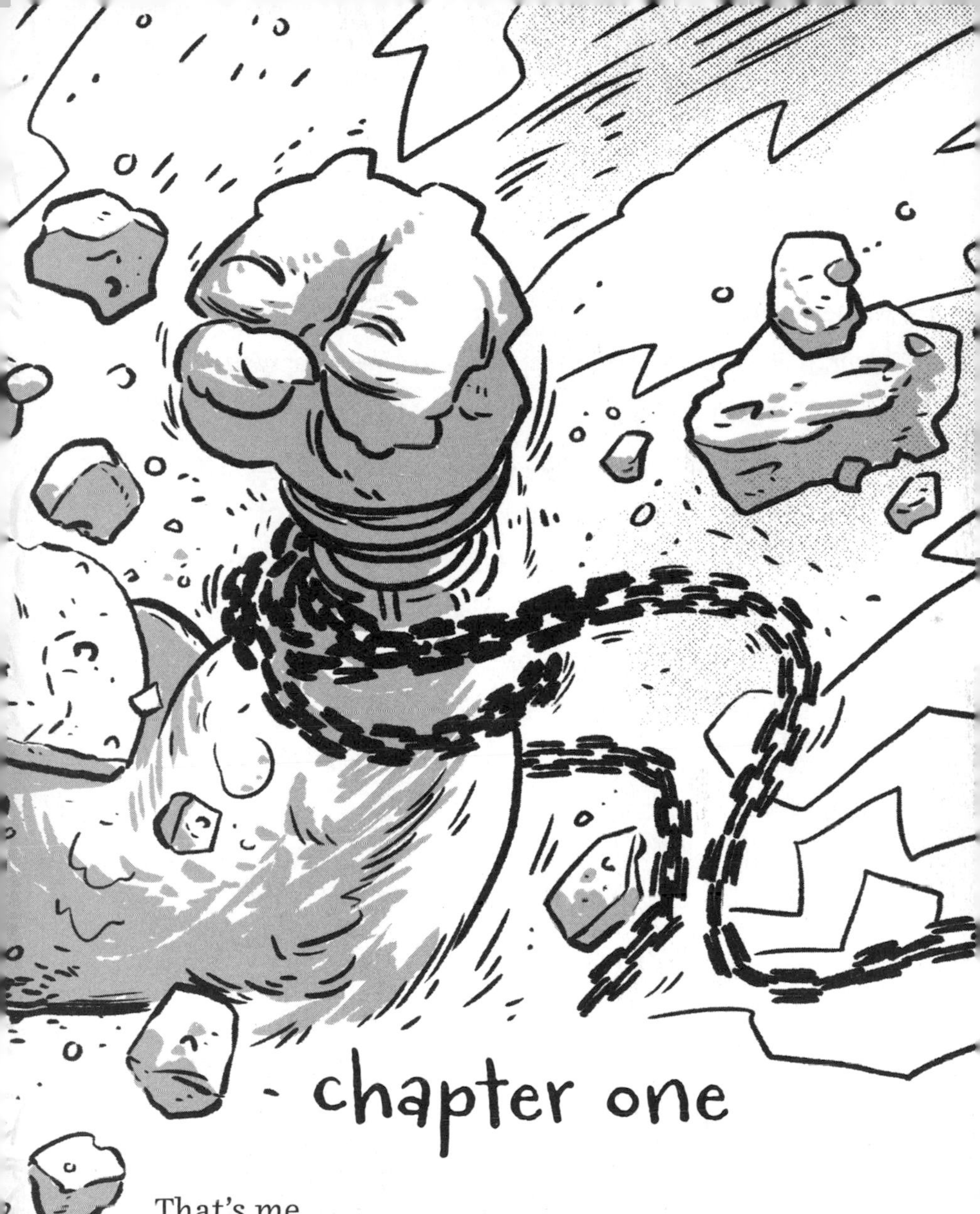

# chapter one

That's me.

Not the giant Ogre.

*Beneath* the giant Ogre. The girl in the driver's seat of the oversized bumper car. The legendarily heroic girl about to get eaten.

My name is June Del Toro, and I had a good life, while it lasted.

For a while, my claim to fame was that I was the first sixth grader to be editor-in-chief of my middle school newspaper: *The Parker Gazette*.

Of course, that was before the Monster Apocalypse. . . . These days, there's no more school, no more newspaper, no more lots of stuff.

Now my claim to fame is that I'm the bravest girl on the block. (To be clear, it's no great achievement: I'm the *only* girl on the block.)

Proof of bravery, you ask? I regularly exchange blows with evil beasts, lock horns with zombie hordes, and make mincemeat out of evil monsters.

And here's the topper—I live in a tree house with three middle school boys.

Yes. It gets gross.

But it's generally pretty rad, because they're also my best friends in the whole world: Jack Sullivan, Quint Baker, and Dirk Savage.

And we have a crew of good-guy monster buddies who live at the local pizza joint next door. We spend most of our time competing in high-stakes lip sync battles, cruising around in our post-apocalyptic pickup truck, and having Nutella-sandwich-eating contests.

Also, battling evil forces from another dimension that are trying to take over our world. And yep—in case you were wondering—that happens a lot.

Like I said, it's been a pretty good life.

I've seen, done, and eaten more weird things than, like, ninety-two kids my age.

But it's not perfect.

I miss my parents—although that's mostly okay, because I know they're alive and out there, somewhere. And I miss getting to break big news stories at school, like ORCHESTRA RECITAL CANCELLED—PARENTS, STUDENTS, TEACHERS ALL EQUALLY ECSTATIC.

The other not-so-perfect bit?

An extreme-evil, power-mad monster named Thrull is assembling an army of skeleton soldiers to build something called the Tower. It's part of his plan to summon the ultimate, endgame evil: Ŗeżżóċh the Ancient, Destructor of Worlds.

Sooo . . . yeah.

That part is lousy.

But not as lousy as being EATEN BY A GIANT BEAST. WHICH IS WHAT'S ABOUT TO HAPPEN!

So y'know what—with the milliseconds remaining before I'm swallowed whole, let me—

***EXPLAIN HOW I GOT HERE!***

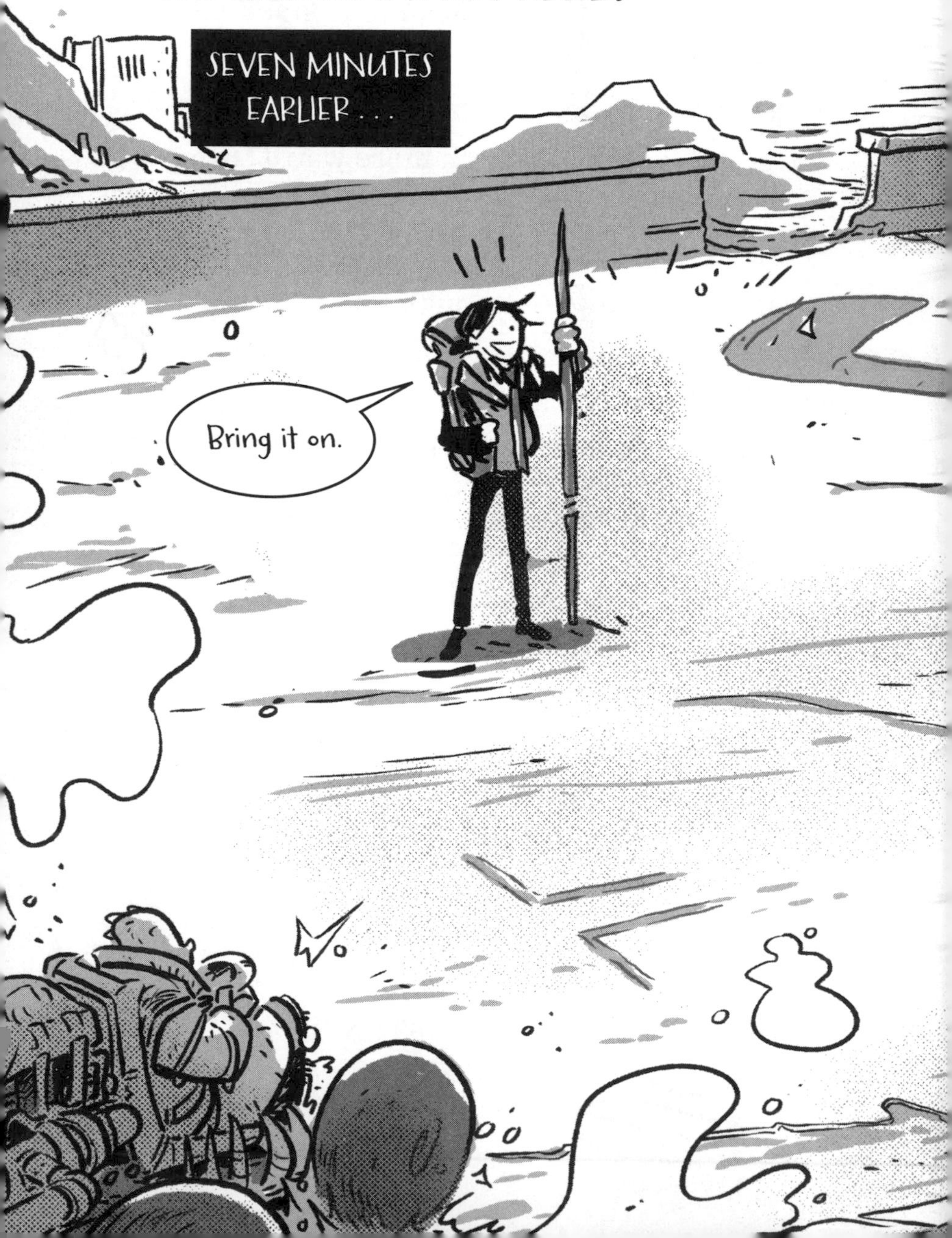
SEVEN MINUTES EARLIER . . .
Bring it on.

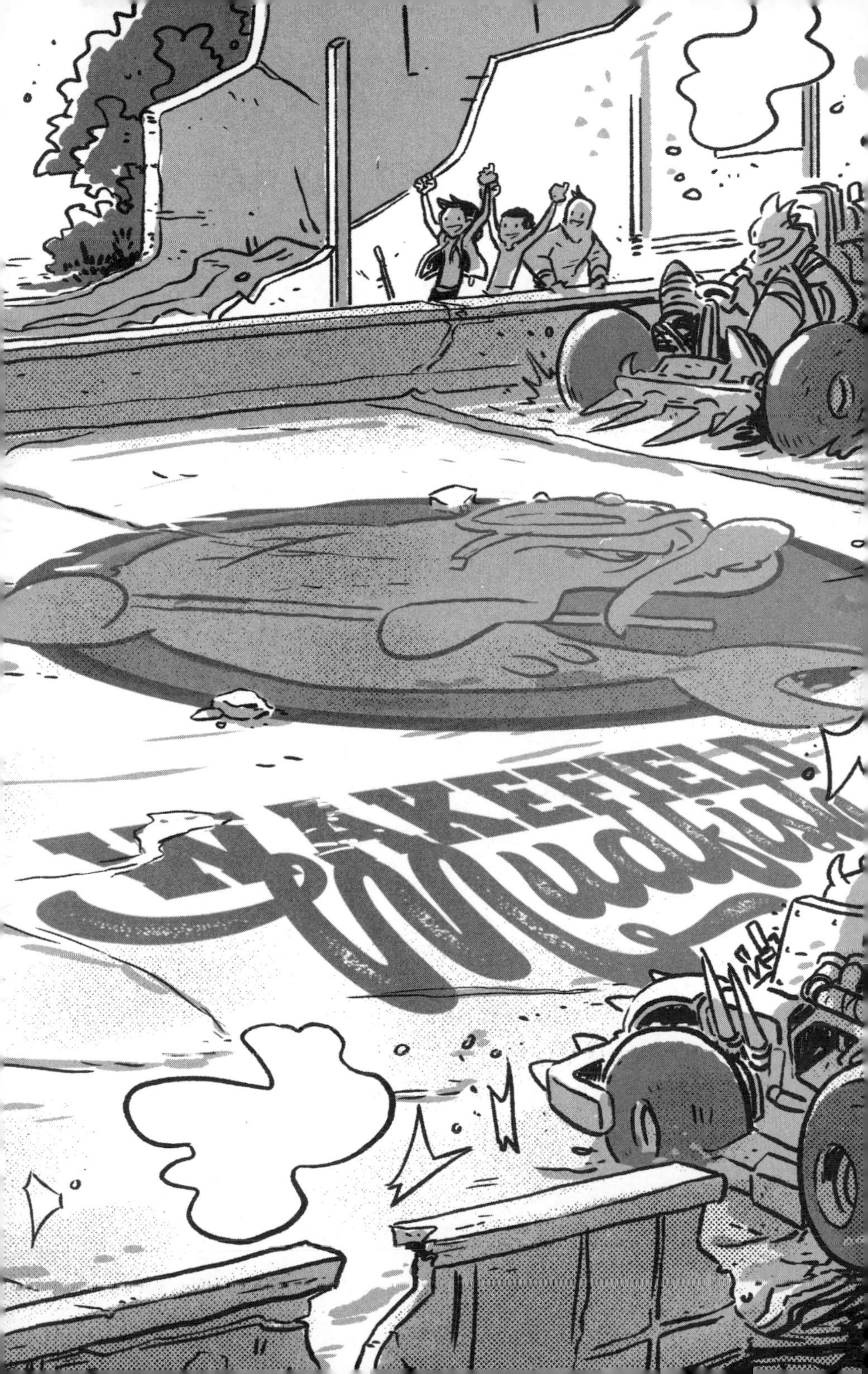
WAKEFIELD

I stood alone at the center of the old Sunshine Roller Rink, tense and alert, ready for action.

Suddenly—

**VA-ROOOM!**

The roar of revving engines filled the air—a dozen DoomKarts: souped-up bumper cars, built to fit monsters. (Like our BoomKarts—but bigger.)

Then I heard the squeal of microphone feedback. It was Quint, in the stands, shouting into a bullhorn: *"LET THE UNNECESSARILY DANGEROUS TEST BEGIN!"*

Jack and Dirk were next to Quint, and they all had a front-row view of the action. I was the guinea pig for this "unnecessarily dangerous test"—which was fine with me, 'cause it was my idea in the first place. Also, I love guinea pigs.

Dirk was gulping down beef jerky, while Jack watched the action through a pair of goofy high-powered binoculars.

If I were writing a news story about this, I'd give it a headline like: LOCAL SKATING RINK HOME TO HIJINKS; **BRAVE GUINEA PIG GIRL TELLS ALL.**

I was just realizing that "Guinea Pig Girl" sounded less cool than I intended when my thoughts were interrupted by—

**SCREEEECH!**

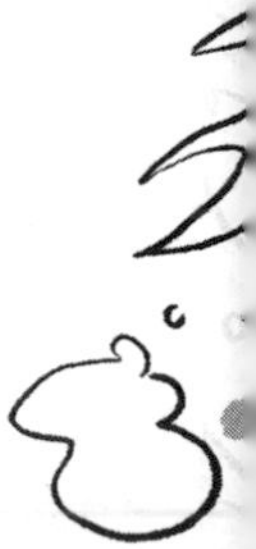

DoomKart tires. Then, from the wings of the skating rink, they came.

Monsters.

Which sounds bad.

But it's only half bad.

They're our monster *friends.* So that was good.

But they had instructions to run me over. So that was *bad.*

I braced myself. Forty monsters atop forty DoomKarts came *roaring at me . . .*

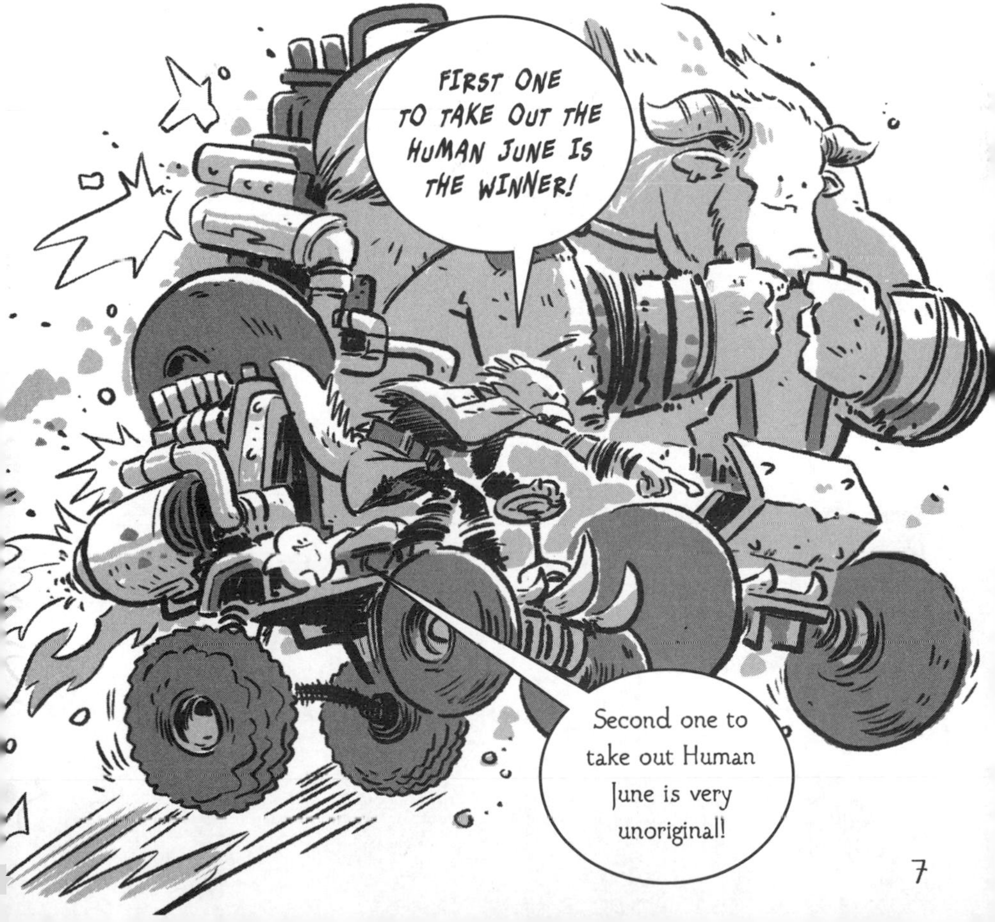
FIRST ONE TO TAKE OUT THE HUMAN JUNE IS THE WINNER!
Second one to take out Human June is very unoriginal!

The monsters were bashing and smashing each other. Two DoomKarts spun out and another nearly flipped.

And I was standing there, waiting. My heart was beating so fast it was like there was an engine in my chest.

Fern was the closest to me, so Skaelka RAMMED into her! Fern shrieked as her DoomKart spun out. Skaelka cackled, "Now I am winning!" and gunned it toward me.

"WHEE!" cried Globlet from Skaelka's passenger seat. Globlet's way too small to drive but she didn't want to be left out.

-Globlet-

Looks like a ball of Silly Putty.

This is more fun than when I got to be the Ping-Pong ball in Jack and Dirk's Ultimate Ping-Pong Championship!

Adorbs.

Lives in the pepperoni drawer at Joe's Pizza.

"Come on," I muttered as the action drew closer and closer to me. "Come ON."

"June!" Quint yelled. "Pull the ignition cord! On your backpack!"

*Nope*, I thought. *Not yet.*

"June!" Jack shouted, sounding a little bit panicky. "If you're trying to be a show-off, DON'T! I'm the show-off! I have all the showing off covered . . . and I'm not even that good at it!"

I caught Jack's eye for a second. He looked ready to rush out and join me. I gave him a quick shake of my head.

*Not yet.*

This was going to work. I knew it.

A dozen monsters were bearing down. I could see the glint of Skaelka's ax, slung over her shoulder. Soon I'd feel the heat of her breath. In the stands, Quint was freaking out. "JUNE! THIS IS NOT GOING ACCORDING TO PLAN!"

But I still didn't move.

Because I didn't *want* this to go "according to plan."

And here's why: to prevent our dimension from falling into the hands of ultimate evil—we need to defeat Thrull and stop the Tower.

And to do that, we'll have to venture out into

the unknown. And I'm pretty freakin' sure that out there, in the unknown, things won't always go "according to plan."

So we're going to need to be ready to improvise.

To handle the unexpected.

That's why I waited until the last possible moment.

Skaelka was nearly upon me. And yeah, Skaelka's my friend—but she's also a ferocious warrior and I'm pretty sure she would *not* lose a combat contest on my account.

But still, I didn't flinch.

I saw everything in what felt like slow motion. I saw Dirk, in the stands, his jerky forgotten, lips pressed in a firm line. I saw Rover next to him, burying his head in his paws. I saw Jack, mouth open, saying the same thing I was at the same time . . .

*"Now!"*

# chapter two

I *yanked* the cord on my backpack, and there was a loud—

# SNAP!
# POOM!

The pack's top exploded open, and a metal *shield* burst out! It was instantly unfolding—a swinging mechanical thing, pieces connecting until it formed a half-moon shield atop my forearm.

I swung the shield *just* as Skaelka's DoomKart was upon me, and—

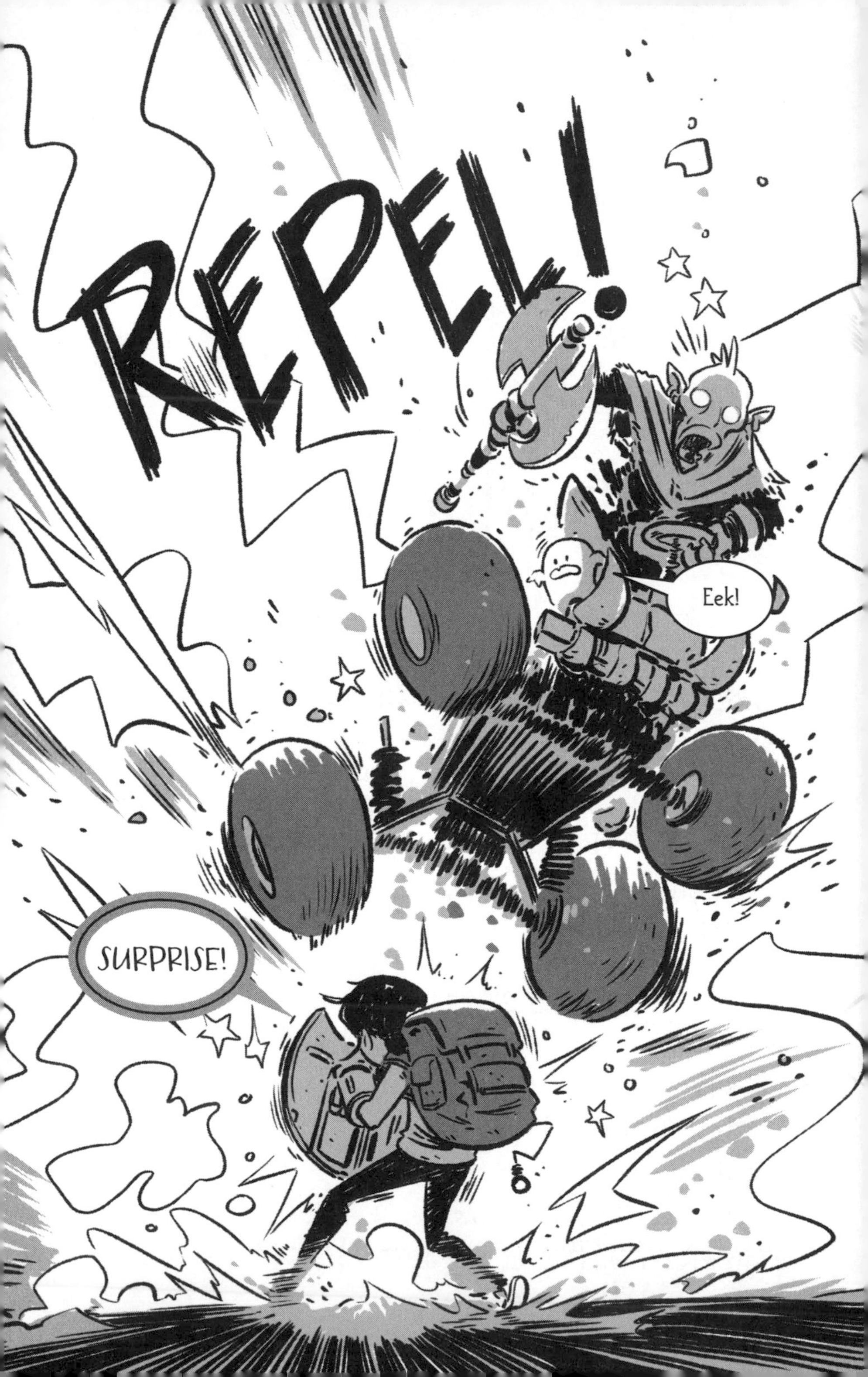
REPELL!
Eek!
SURPRISE!

"IT WORKED!" I exclaimed, gasping and grinning. "THE SURPRISE SHIELD WORKED!"

And, I mean, I knew it would work. But also—HOLY MOLEY I CAN'T BELIEVE IT WORKED and MAN OH MAN I cut that close.

# VA-ROOOM!

I couldn't lose focus. Spinning back around, I saw the next DoomKart nearly upon me. I *slammed* the shield into the ground as I dropped to one knee, and—

# KLANG!

The DoomKart hit the shield and drove up it, straight over my head!

"That's it!" Jack hollered, vaulting over the walls and into the rink. "I'm comin' in!"

Dirk hurled himself into the arena after him and Quint followed.

"Just couldn't watch from the sidelines, huh?" I shouted.

"No way you're having all the fun without us!" Dirk barked as he skidded to a stop beside me. My friends each carried shields, though theirs weren't able to pop out on demand like mine . . . yet.

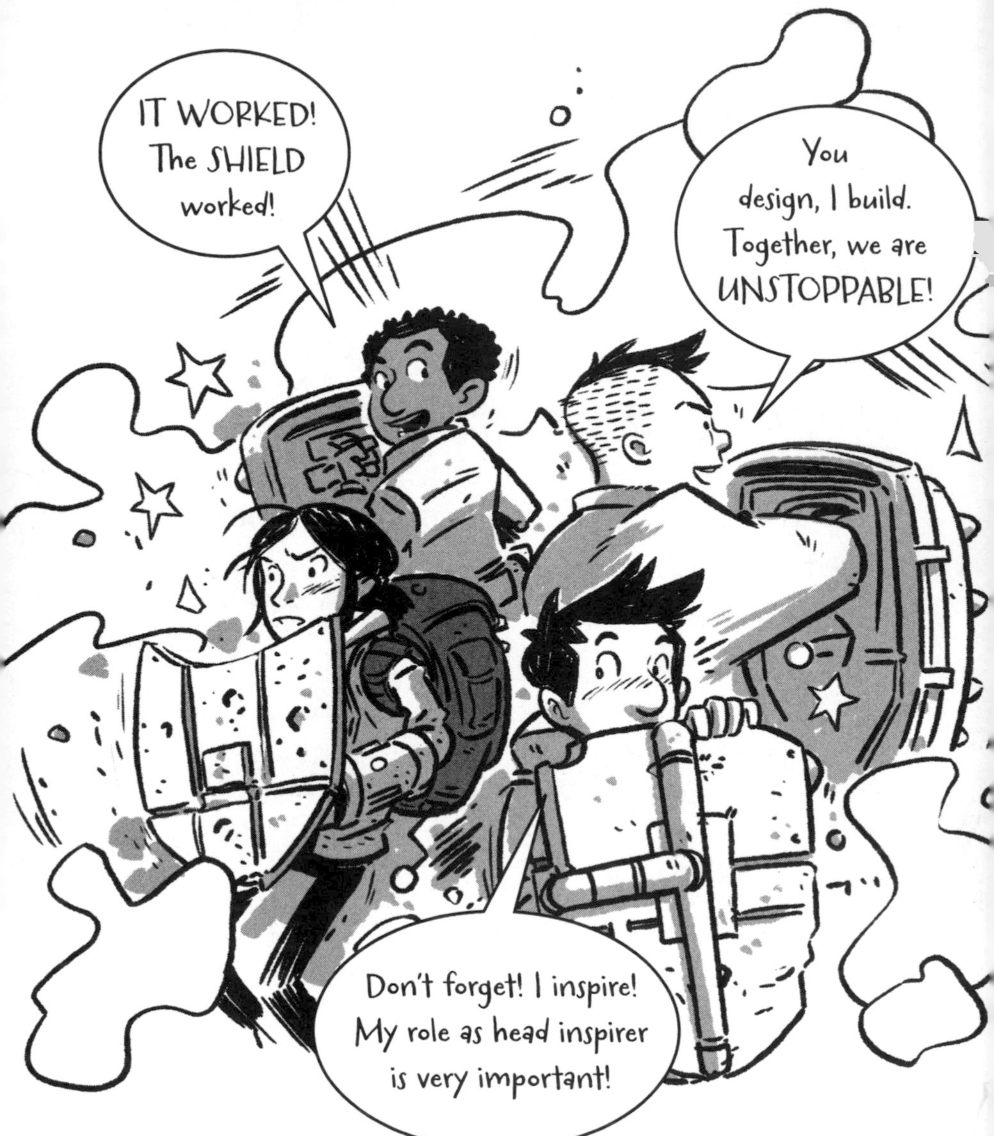
IT WORKED! The SHIELD worked!
You design, I build. Together, we are UNSTOPPABLE!
Don't forget! I inspire! My role as head inspirer is very important!

"We're gonna need more than shields to find the Tower," I said.

"You mean *destroy* the tower," Jack said.

"Uh, friends," Quint said. "We have to *find* the Tower to destroy it. . . ."

"So guess we gotta find Thrull, huh?" Dirk grunted.

I nodded. He was right. We didn't even know—

SHRIIIIIEK!

A high-pitched, monstrous scream! I spun around, just in time to see something *burst* into the arena.

Something fast—

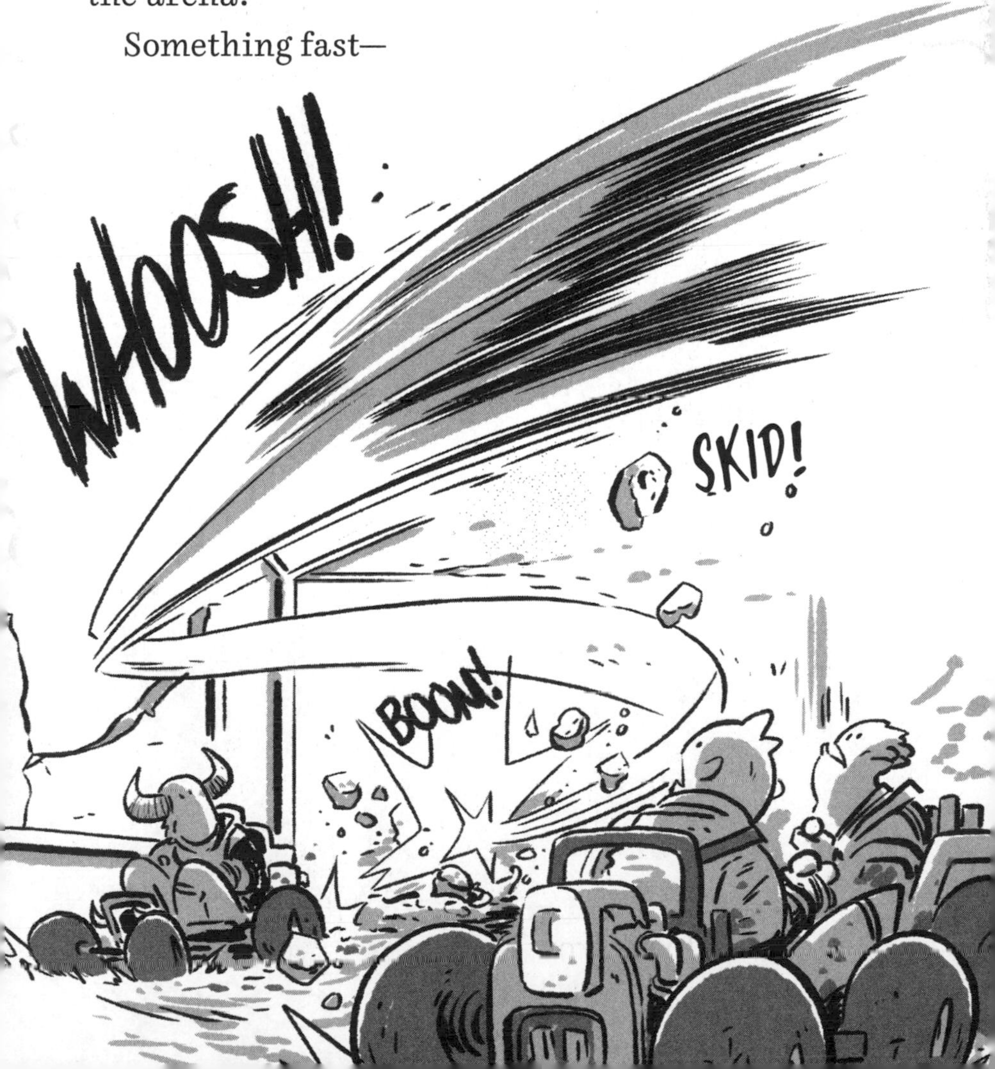
WHOOSH!
SKID!
BOOM!

"What is that thing?" I yelled, ducking down.

"It looked like a living, breathing rocket!" Jack shouted.

The creature was just a speedy blur—like a bee trapped under a glass, ricocheting from one side of the rink to the other.

And then a crashing. And a crumbling.

And Skaelka shouting a word I'd never heard before: "RIFTERS!"

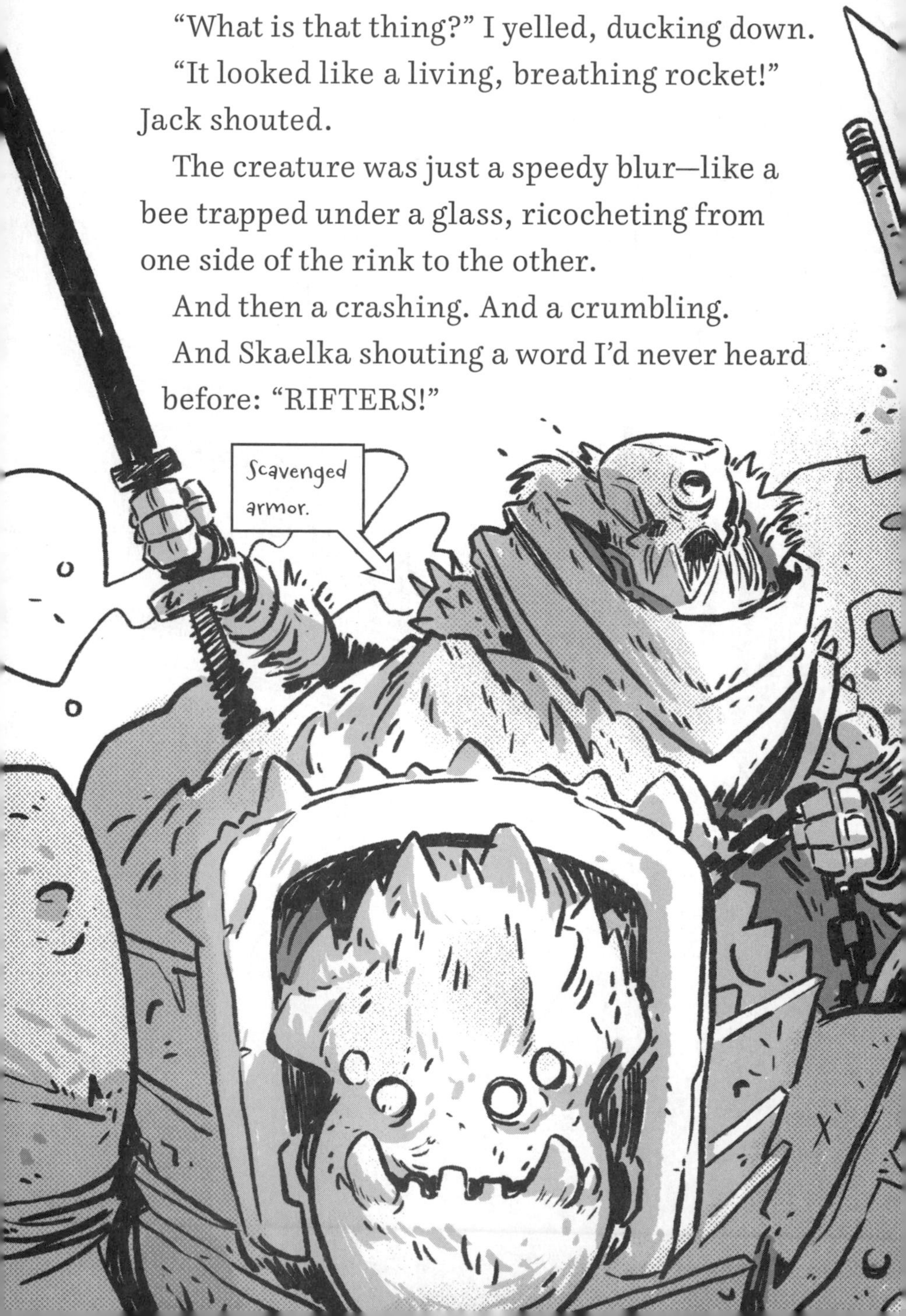
Scavenged armor.

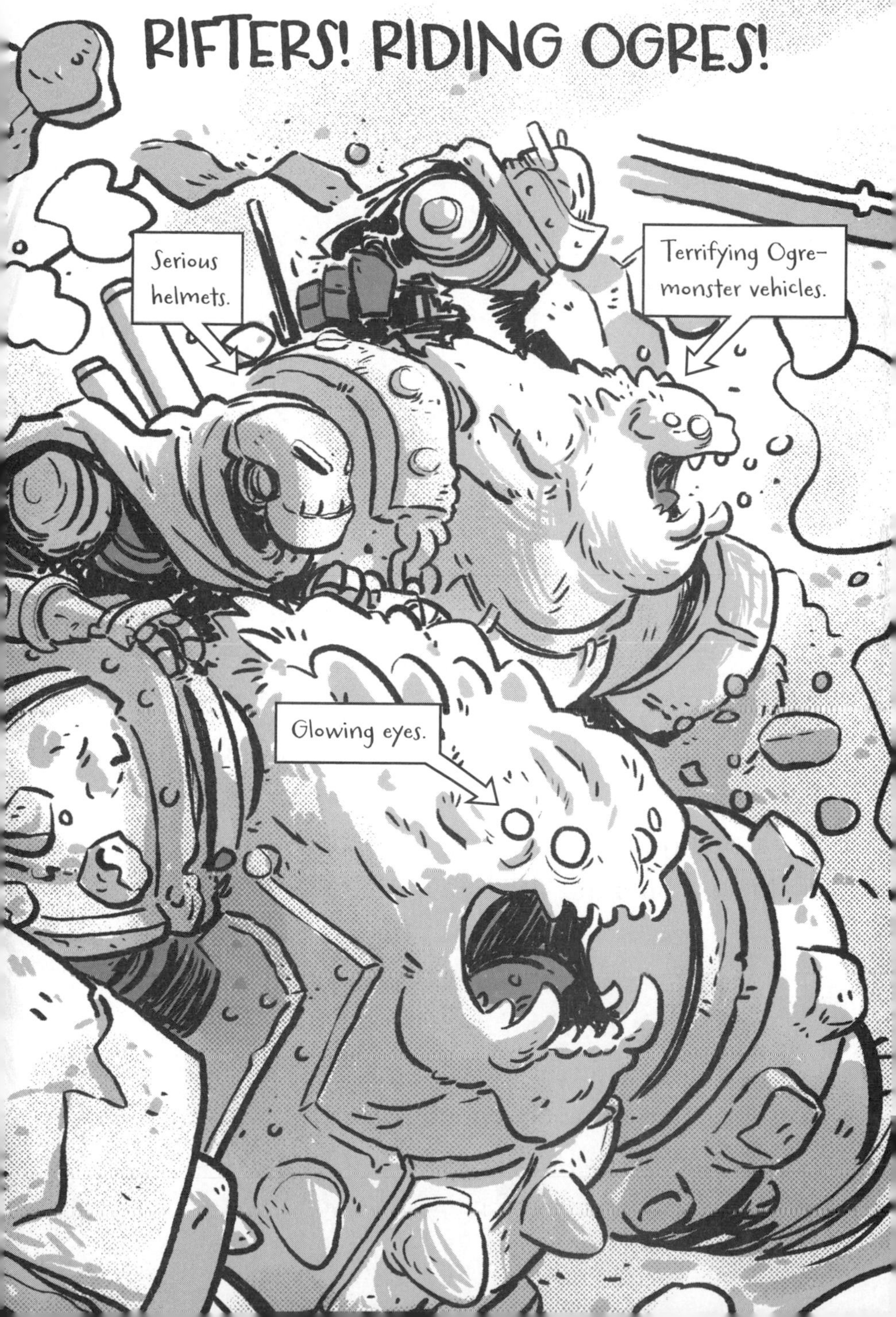

RIFTERS! RIDING OGRES!
Terrifying Ogre-monster vehicles.
Serious helmets.
Glowing eyes.

# chapter three

"RIFTERS!" Skaelka shouted again.
"EVERYBODY! WEAPONS UP! WE GOT
RIFTERS!"

"Rifters?" I cried out. "I never heard of any
Rifters!"

"Quint!" Jack yelled, shaking our buddy by
the shoulders. "What's a Rifter? Tell me about
Rifters!"

"I don't know, Jack!" Quint said. "I don't know
all the things!"

"Hey, monster pals!" Dirk barked, as an Ogre
stomped past. "We need information here!"

Just then, our flying friend Fern swooped
past. She quickly gave us the scoop—

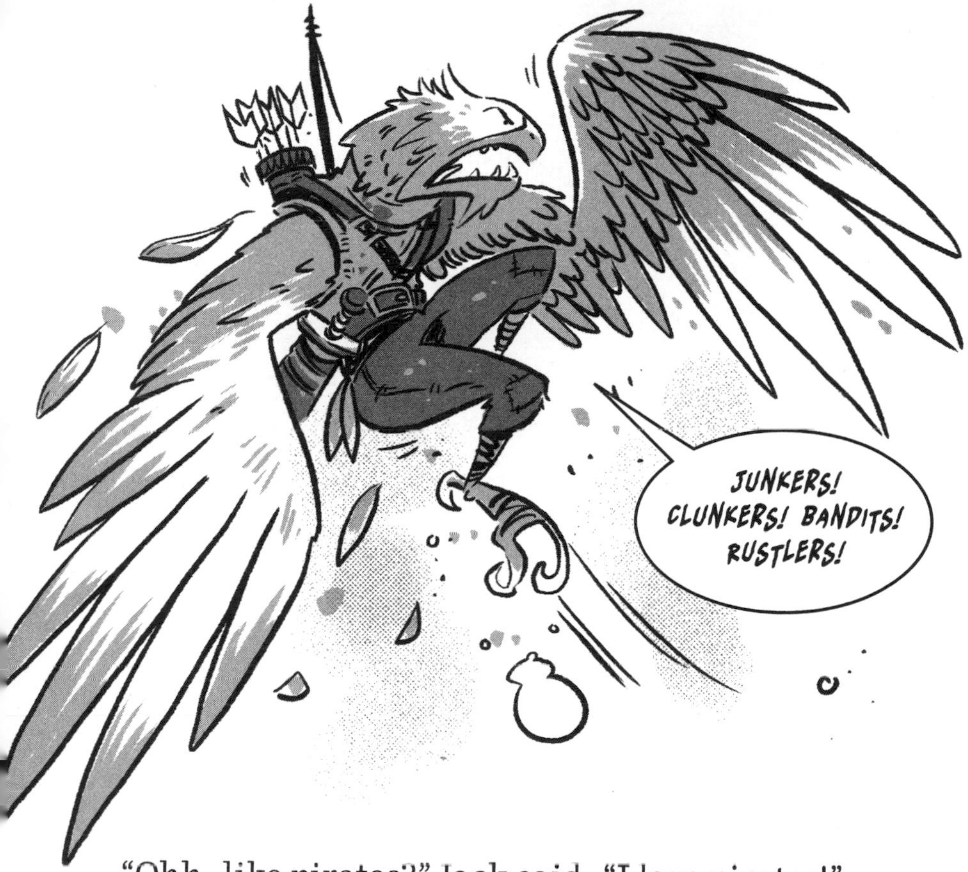
JUNKERS! CLUNKERS! BANDITS! RUSTLERS!

"Ohh, like pirates?" Jack said. "I love pirates!"

Suddenly, a crooked metal arrow came screaming through the air! I *tackled* Jack an instant before the arrow hit him.

"Never mind. Hate pirates," Jack grumbled as—

**WHOOSH!**

A creature zoomed past us. Three more arrows hit the ground in its wake. I watched an Ogre stomp past—and saw the Rifter riding it. He was hurriedly jamming more arrows into a rusty, paint-splattered crossbow.

"I don't think these Rifters care about us," I said. "They're hyper-focused on that neon-colored creature."

The creature was zooming around like a pinball! It made an impossibly sharp turn, causing the pursuing Ogre to slip, and the Rifter atop him cried out as—

EJECTED!

It was pure chaos.

And suddenly—I was at the absolute *center* of that pure chaos.

Because the blur creature was *zipping* toward me. We were eye-to-eye. And in a moment we were going to be head-to-head—by which I mean, *his head was going to be crashing into my head at many miles an hour.*

"Whoa, whoa, whoa!" I cried out, jumping back, then staggering, falling, and finally landing in an abandoned DoomKart.

"June, look out!" I heard Jack call, and I wanted to shout back something like, *Yeah, no kidding!* but I could hardly even breathe.

Right before impact, the blur-creature leapt, springing up and over me. I felt my hair rustle just as—

WHOOSH!

Whoa ...

Next there was a flash of steel—it was a rusty chain, being swung by a Rifter. They were trying to lasso the creature.

"I'm okay, guys!" I called out, but then—

# CHONK!

The DoomKart jerked forward. My eyes shot down and I saw that the Rifter's chain had *hooked on to the cart*.

"Just kidding! Not okay!" I shouted. "NOT OKAY AT—"

# YANK!

The chain *jerked* the DoomKart and we SMASHED into an Ogre's tree-trunk-like leg. It was the biggest Ogre: an enormous, awful thing. And in its saddle was the biggest Rifter.

"Uh . . . hi," I said.

The Ogre's enormous hand came down. I curled up in the DoomKart seat, making myself small, and lifted the shield over my head.

The Ogre just grunted. Its massive paw pinned the DoomKart to the ground. Peering around the shield, I saw the monster's mouth opening wide.

This was it. This was the end. Which brings us . . .

***RIGHT BACK TO THE PRESENT!***

**WHERE I AM SECONDS AWAY FROM BECOMING AN AFTERNOON SNACK!**

**OR AM I?!**

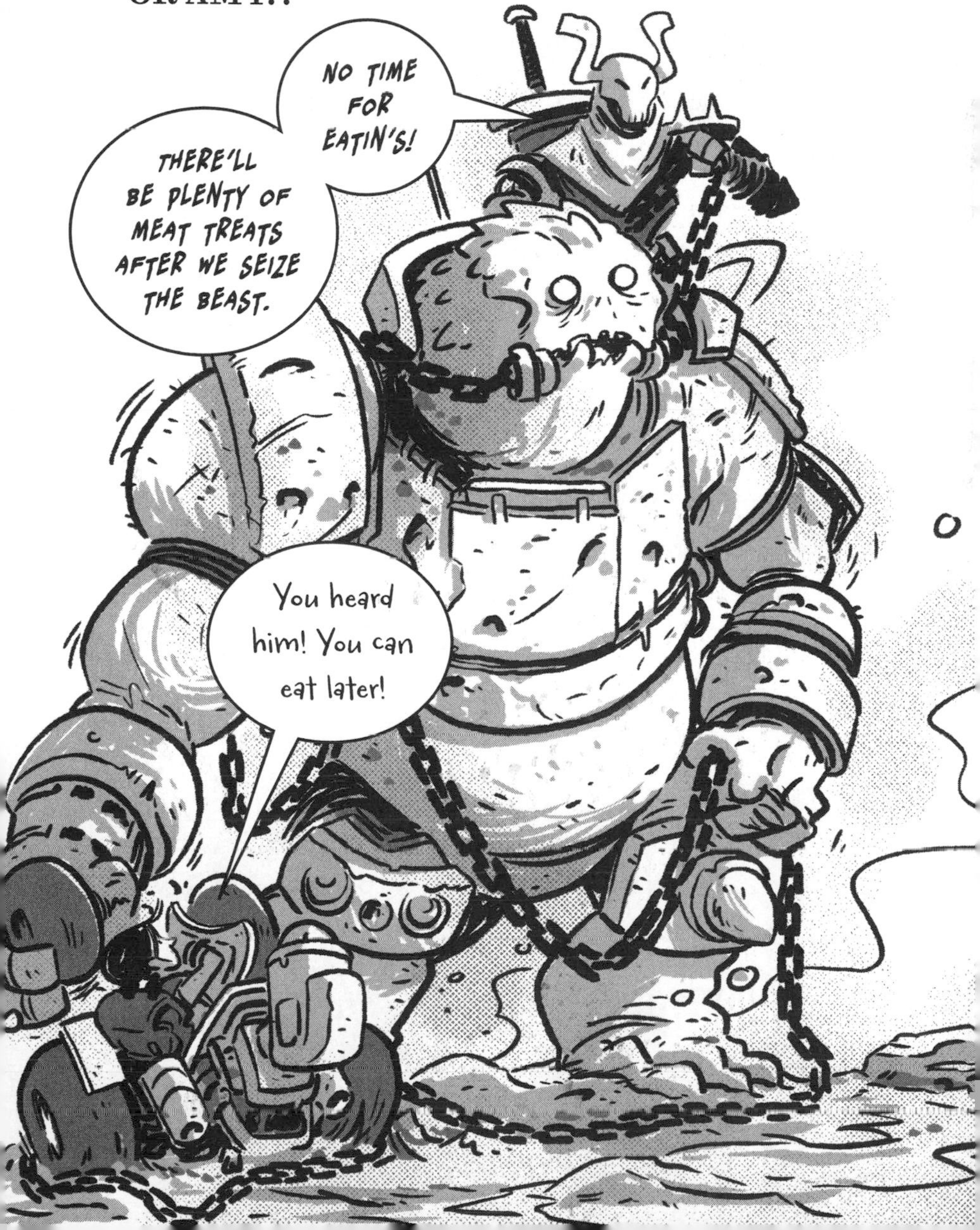
NO TIME FOR EATIN'S!
THERE'LL BE PLENTY OF MEAT TREATS AFTER WE SEIZE THE BEAST.
You heard him! You can eat later!

The Ogre snarls, but does as it's told. The Rifter atop seems to be the established leader of the group.

I come out from under my shield shell, and in the DoomKart's side mirror, I see the speeding blur-creature LEAP over the crumbled skating rink wall.

Gone.

Out of Wakefield . . . and into the unknown world beyond.

"After him!" the Rifter commands.

"Yes, Boss," the others grumble.

The ground quakes as the Ogres move in a stampede, pursuing the creature. I collapse back into my seat, gasping for air, relieved. Then—

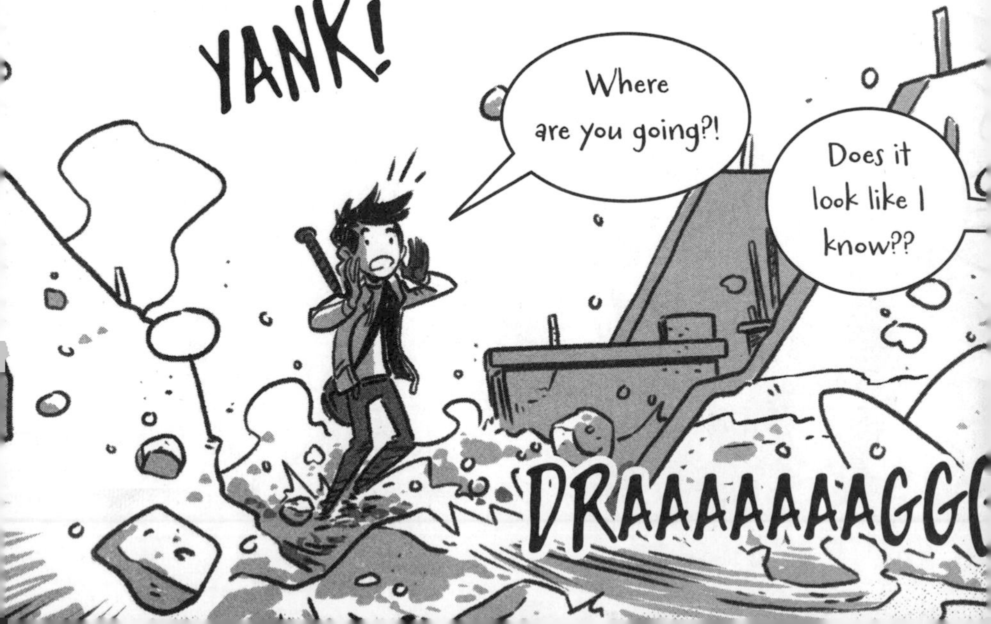
YANK!
Where are you going?!
Does it look like I know??
DRAAAAAAAGG

"The Ogre's chain!" I cry out. "It's hooked to the DoomKart! And my foot is all jammed up in there!"

The massive beast is stomping out of the rink, picking up speed with every earth-shattering step—and I'm being pulled along with it!

"Don't worry, June, we're coming!" Jack shouts.

# BAM!

We explode out of the roller rink.

I grip the sides of the DoomKart as we slice across the parking lot. Cars screech and skid, sparks flying, as the Ogre swats and swipes them aside.

Onto the streets. Long-defunct fire hydrants gush water. Parking meters rain down dimes and quarters.

My heart leaps up into my throat as we start down a steep hill, lined with vine-choked houses, still following that strange, skittery, runaway creature.

This Ogre is squashing cars under its feet, heedless of all obstacles.

"STOP BEING SO HEEDLESS!" I shout.

But the Ogre is so huge, so strong, that it doesn't even notice me hooked on to it. I'm like a piece of toilet paper stuck to a sneaker! And I really hate being like that!

I look behind me, desperate, and spot Dirk, Jack, Quint, and my monster friends. They're all in DoomKarts, chasing after me.

But they can't keep up with the stampeding Ogres.

My friends are quickly growing small in my vision.

Quint shouts something, but I can't tell what. Dirk too. Then Skaelka. Finally, I hear Jack, calling from the top of his lungs, "JUNE! WE WILL FIND YOU! **PROMISE!**"

And that last word, *promise*, fades away as I'm pulled out of sight. . . .

# chapter four

I'm pretty fast.

Not bragging, just saying.

Every grade always has "the fast kid." I was never "the fast kid" but I was "a fast kid."

I used to be able to run from my house to the school bus stop, three blocks away, in ninety-nine seconds.

The bus left at 7:12 a.m., and my dad always insisted I leave the house at 7:00 a.m. sharp. For no reason! I could have left at 7:10 and still made it to the bus stop with thirty-two seconds to spare! More, if the driver stopped off for a chocolate chunk muffin (which he usually did)!

And do you have any idea *just* how much stuff I could get done between 7:00 and 7:10? Give me ten minutes and I'll write you a detailed list.

But, you know what?

None of that speed matters when you are—

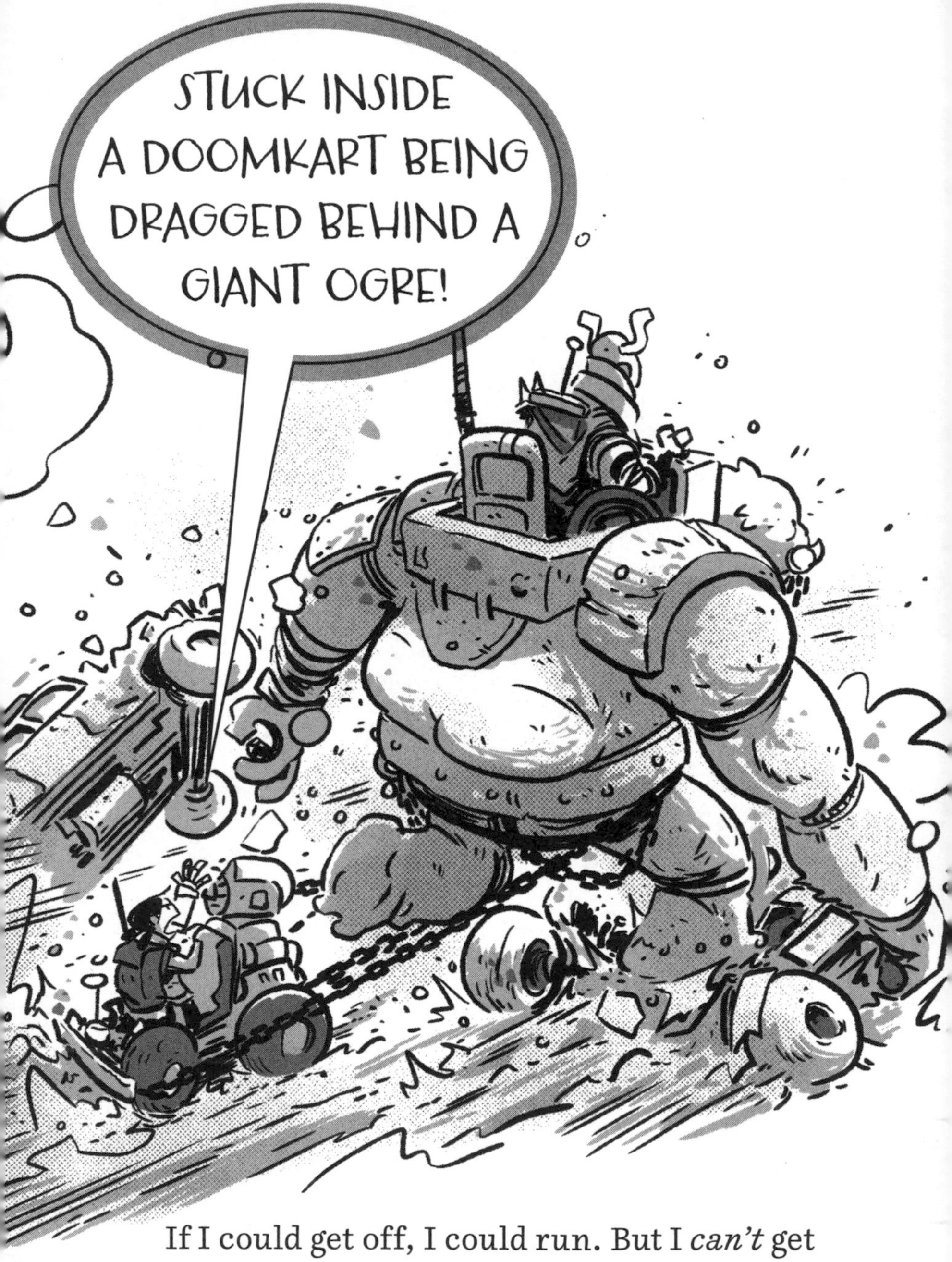
STUCK INSIDE A DOOMKART BEING DRAGGED BEHIND A GIANT OGRE!

If I could get off, I could run. But I *can't* get off because the Rifter's chain has turned this DoomKart into a tiny version of a space shuttle re-entering Earth's atmosphere. Bits and pieces flying off, sparking, screeching, metal nearly melting. And I'm just stuck here along for the ride.

I try to pay attention to where we are, where we're going, but it's all a blurry jumble of scenery. Suddenly—

SHRIEEEK!

The creature's monstrous howl. The Rifters must be closing in. And then, suddenly, a wooden shed ahead. The Ogre is stomping through an overgrown backyard. "YIKES!" I cry out, lifting the shield, just as—

SMASH!

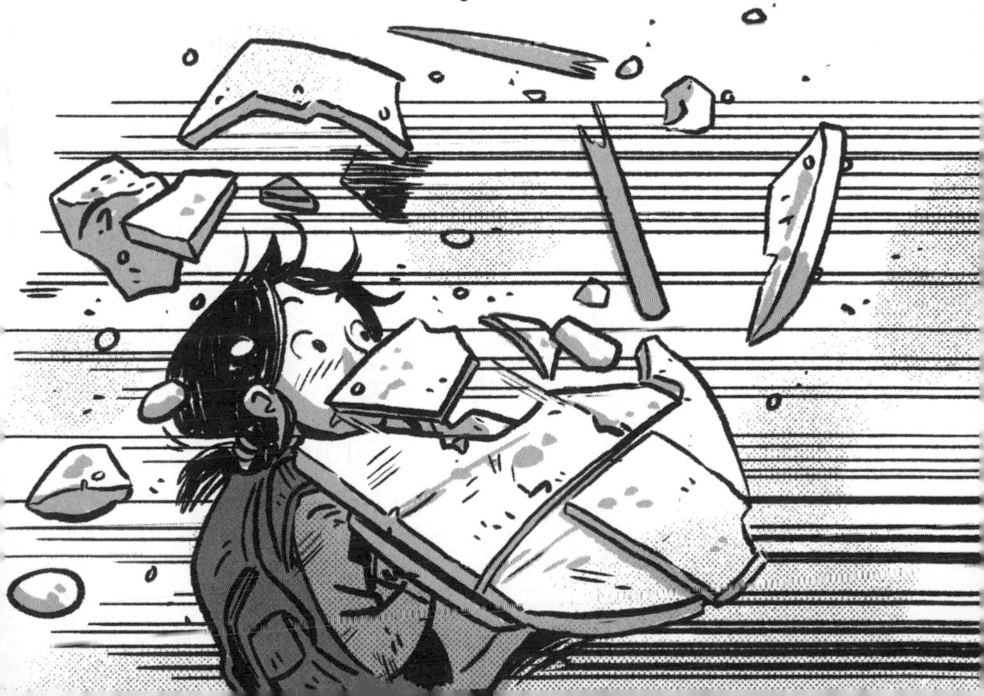

The shed does serious damage.

The steering wheel pops up and nearly takes off my left ear. My fancy new shield is busted up. My spear, slung over my back, snaps in half. But it's not all bad. Looking down I see that—

"I'M FREE!" I shout.

The chain is now hooked to the pedal— not my foot! Sure, I'm still inside a quickly disintegrating DoomKart—but at the very least, I'm not *trapped*.

Now I just need a way *off this thing*. I need something I can jump to—something that will break my fall without, y'know, breaking *me*.

Like a haystack.

Or a bouncy castle.

Or the world's most epic pillow fort.

Unfortunately, within my immediate range of vision, I see no haystacks, no bouncy castles, and no epic pillow forts.

But—*hmm*—I *do* spot something like a mound of oversized M&Ms. Globes of color: oranges and blues and faded greens. I realize it's better than any bouncy pillow haystack fort: "A ball pit!"

*Okay, ya germy pool of plastic*, I think. *Here I come!*

And with that, I *hurl myself* from the DoomKart . . .

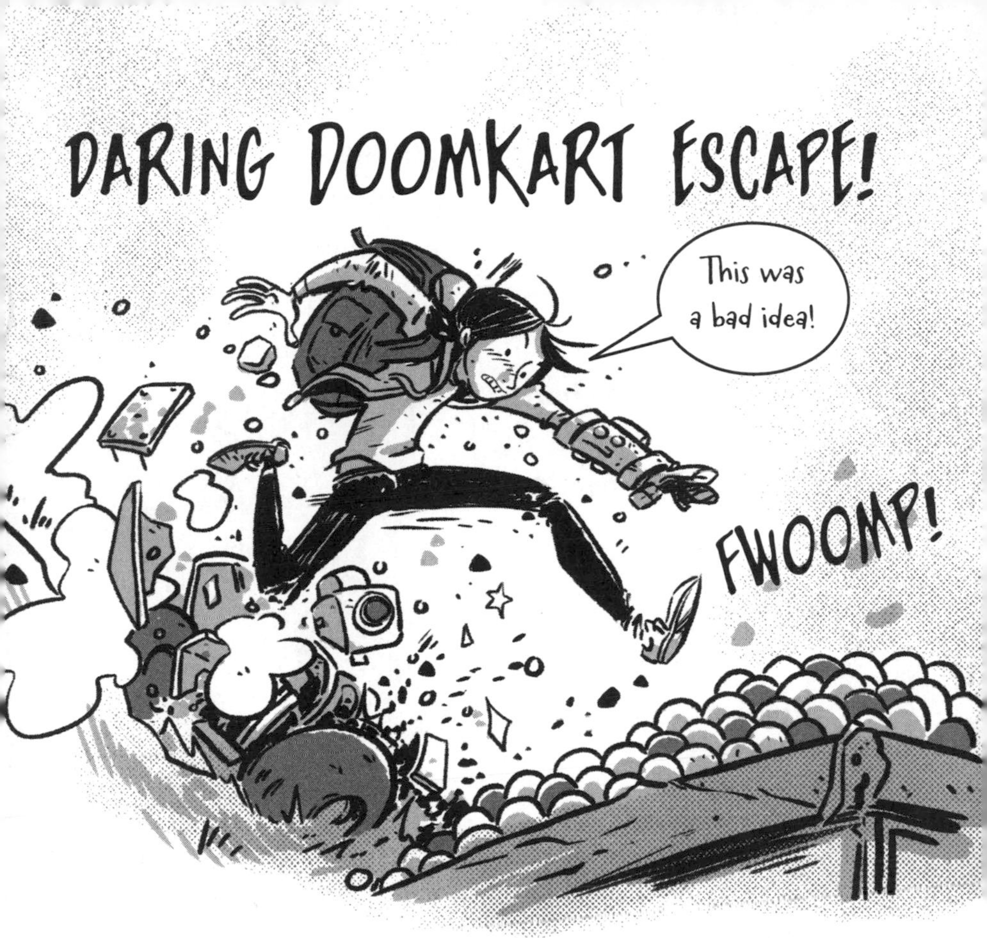
DARING DOOMKART ESCAPE!
This was a bad idea!
FWOOMP!

I land in a heap and sink into the ball pit. I keep my eyes screwed shut, listening to the sound of the Ogres' trampling feet fading into the distance.

My elbows and knees are scraped, my teeth seem to be vibrating, and I'm mostly positive I swallowed a bug . . . possibly a bird.

But that's okay, 'cause. . . .

"I'M ALIVE!" I cry out. "Alive! Alive and . . . I have *no idea* where I am!"

I look around, trying to get my bearings. But I have no bearings.

*Zero* bearings.

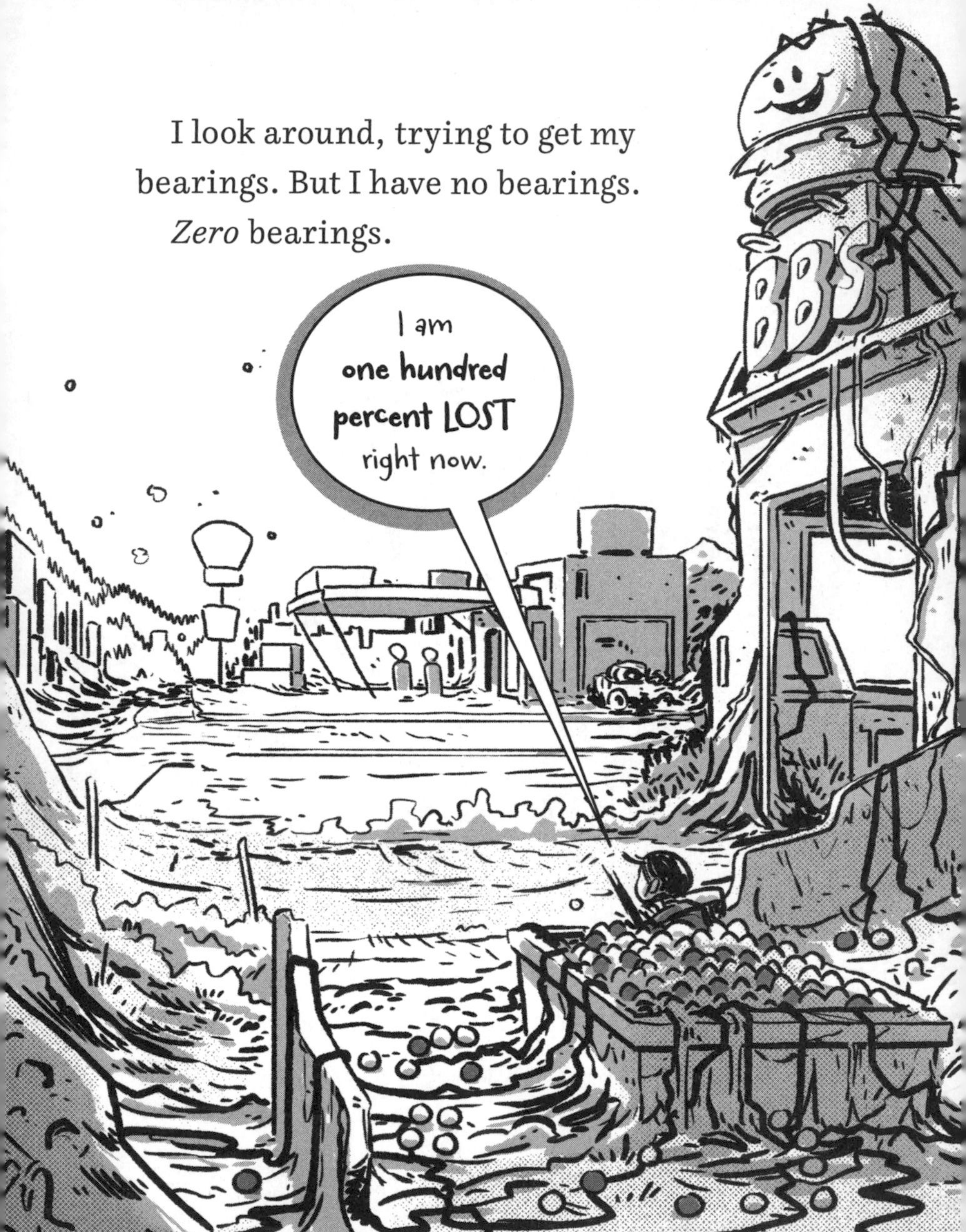
I am **one hundred percent LOST** right now.
BBS

Until . . . a clue! All the balls have the letters "B.B." on them. That means that this is—or *was*—a Blooper Burger.

Looking inside, I see an old jukebox, a soda fountain, and a statue of the big guy himself: Sir Blooper Burger. But his head is hanging off his body and his creepy French fry fingers are broken off.

Although, that's not a huge help—Blooper Burger joints are *everywhere* and they all look *identical*. No joke, their slogan is "It's not a town without a Blooper Burger!"

At least, that's usually their slogan—sometimes the end of the world writes its own slogan. . . .

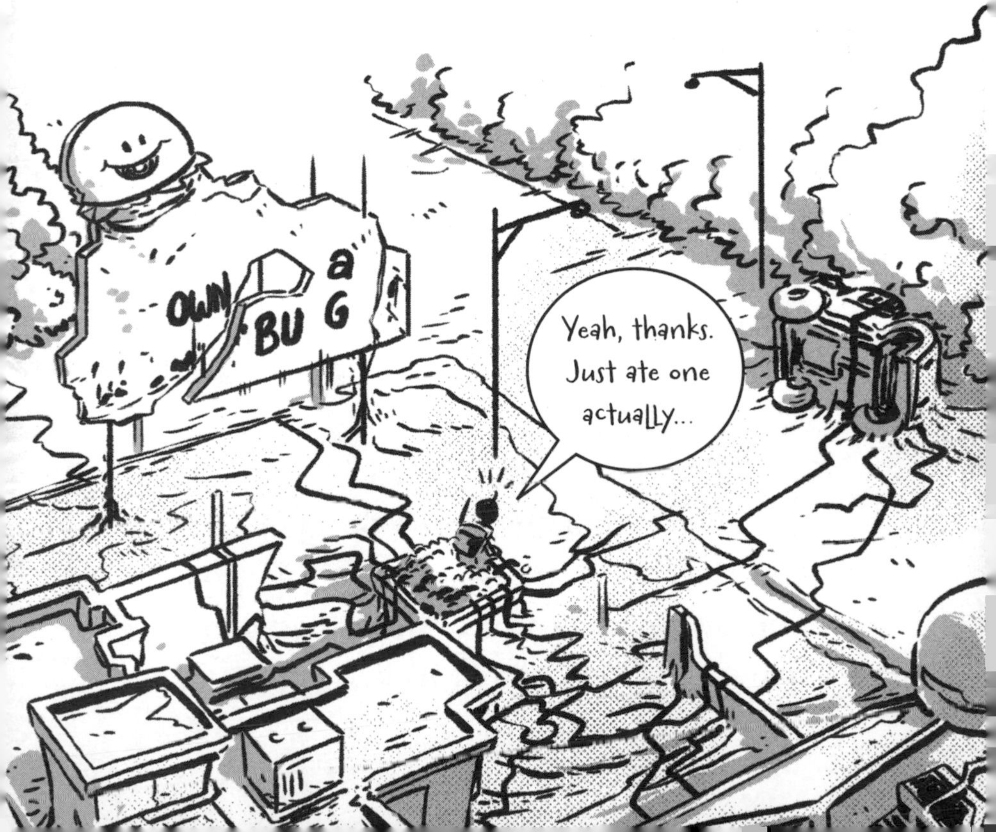
OWN
BU G
Yeah, thanks. Just ate one actually...

I drag my tired, wounded body across the ball pit, which is a bit like moving through rainbow-colored quicksand. I manage to pull myself up and out and flop onto the cracked, broken Blooper Burger floor.

After the sound of bouncing plastic balls stops, I notice something.

It's quiet.

*Extra* quiet.

Over the past year, I've gotten kinda used to constant, nonstop, forever-and-ever *noise*. There's Jack's ***yakkity-yakking***, the ***hum*** of Quint's electricity-sucking gadgets, the ***shrieks*** and ***roars*** of passing beasts, and the never-ending chorus of snores and belches and barks that drift over from Joe's Pizza.

But suddenly, now—it's like someone hit the mute button.

This is silence I haven't known since the months after the world ended. Since I was alone in Parker Middle School.

Back then, I *hated* the silence.

But now it's kinda peaceful—kinda perfect. It's like the silence is telling me, "June, you are on your own. In the mysterious, unexplored unknown that lies beyond Wakefield."

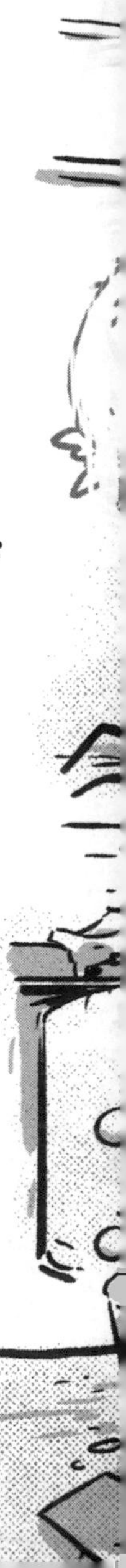

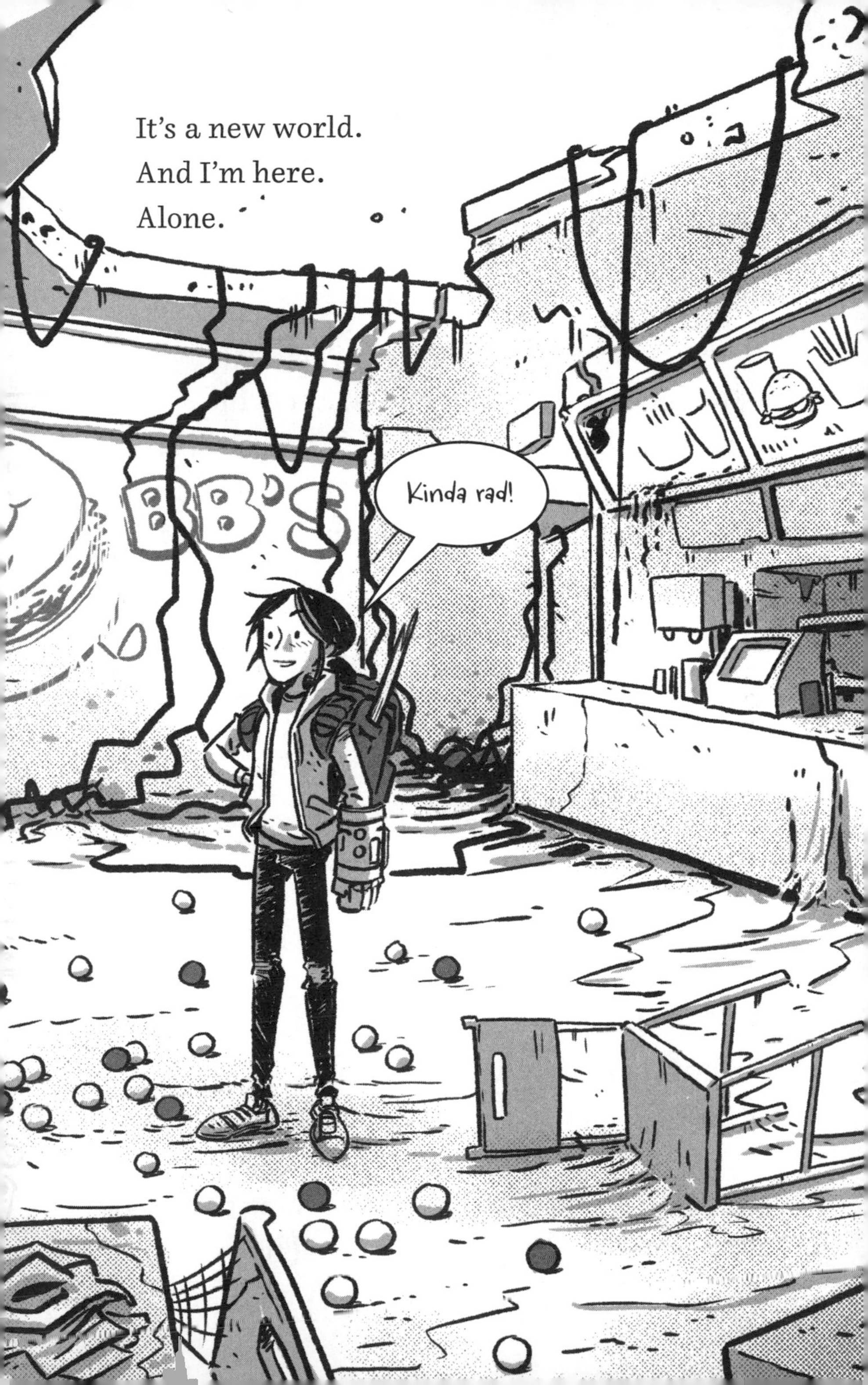
It's a new world.
And I'm here.
Alone.
Kinda rad!
BB'S

# chapter five

This wasteland world beyond Wakefield is strange. It is lush, overgrown, and wild. Greens and pinks and oranges and blues. It's like a warped version of the old world—ripped, stretched, and recolored by some angry kid with a crayon.

It's pretty scary.

But at least it's _pretty_ scary.

In fact, if Jack was here—I'd use his camera to snap a pic of the strange scenery. But like I said, I'm alone.

Without my friends.

Now, don't get me wrong, my friends are rad. But they stink! Like, literally—_their bodies emit foul odors._

And okay, I know, I probably don't exactly smell like the inside of a Bath & Body Works myself. Personal hygiene is nobody's number-one priority during the apocalypse. Plus, washing leads to serious FOMO—what's worse than being in the shower, hearing something _super_ fun going on outside, racing to finish up, hop out, dry off—and then by the time you're dressed, all the fun is over!

But at least I make an effort! I swear, it's like Jack and Quint and Dirk are *proud* of their mussy morning hair, lazy tooth brushing, and ability to "burp supersonically."

But our monster friends are even worse . . .

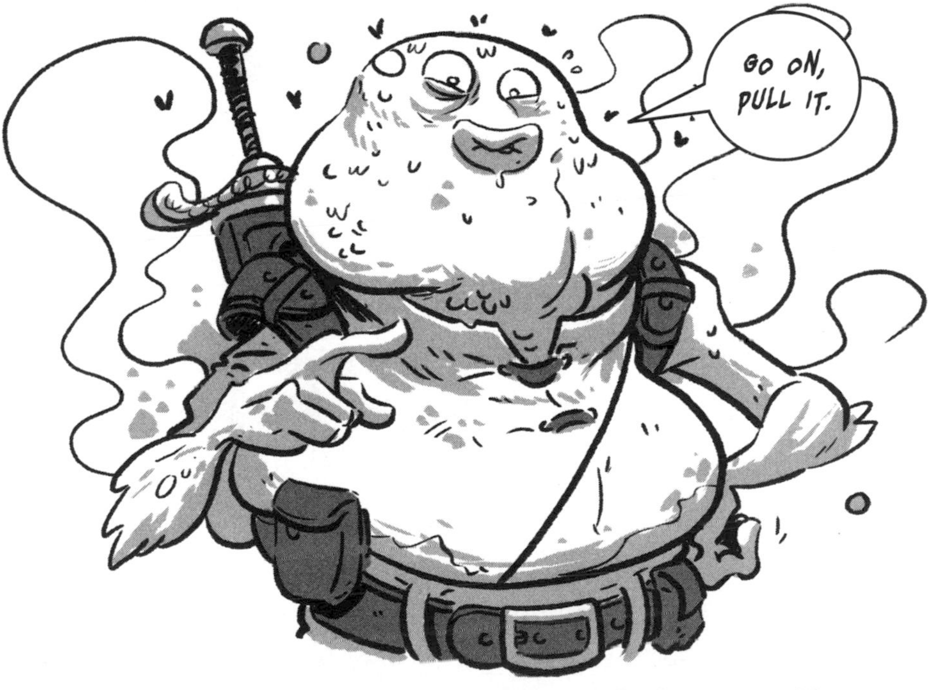
GO ON, PULL IT.

Right now, though, the only stink that I smell is MY OWN STINK.

And I start to grin as I realize . . . *you know what this means?*

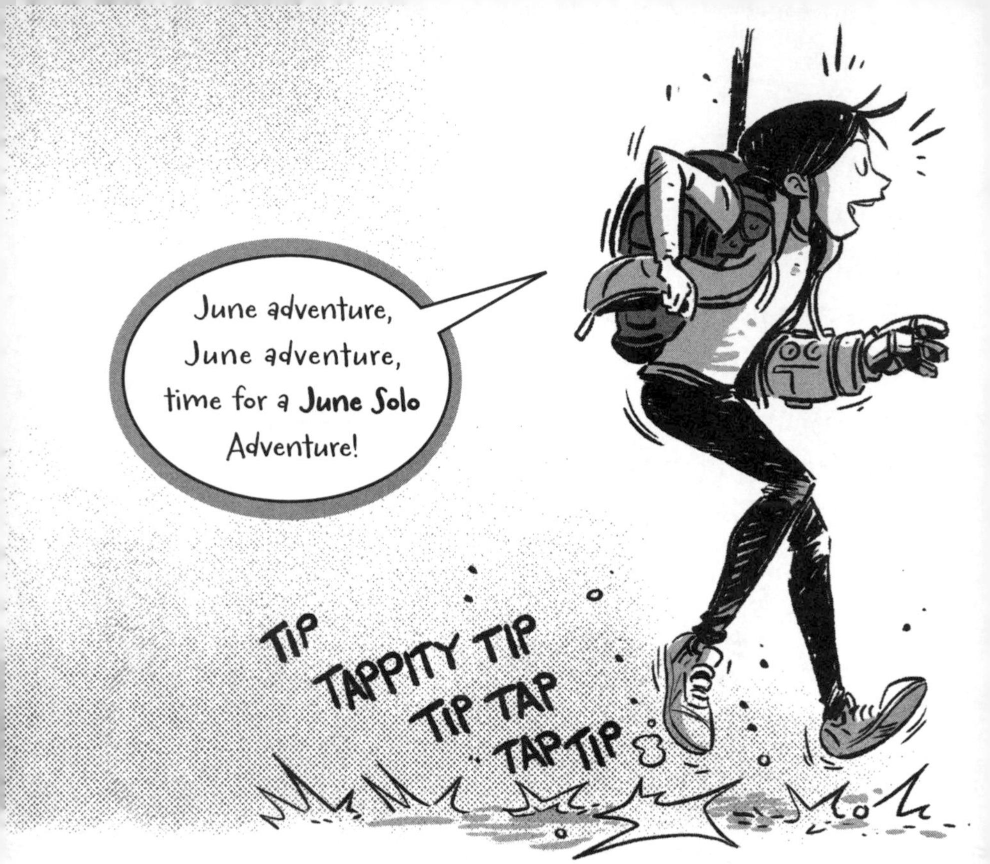
June adventure, June adventure, time for a **June Solo** Adventure!
TIP
TAPPITY TIP
TIP TAP
TAP TIP

Or, wait . . . does "June Solo Adventure" sound too much like a Star Wars thing? Like an adventure about Han Solo's kid sister "June Solo"? I mean, I know Han doesn't *have* a kid sister, 'cause Quint has explained the Solo and Skywalker family bloodlines to me about a dozen times even though I could not care any—

"WAIT!" I exclaim, and I actually exclaim it out loud, to no one. "Quint's not here! I can call this whatever kind of adventure I want! And JUNE SOLO ADVENTURE IT IS!"

And the goal of this June Solo Adventure? *Get back to Wakefield*.

But that's when IT hits me.

And the IT isn't a thought or an idea—the IT is a *thing*. A wet and rubbery and gooey *thing* that hits me in the face at about a thousand miles an hour—

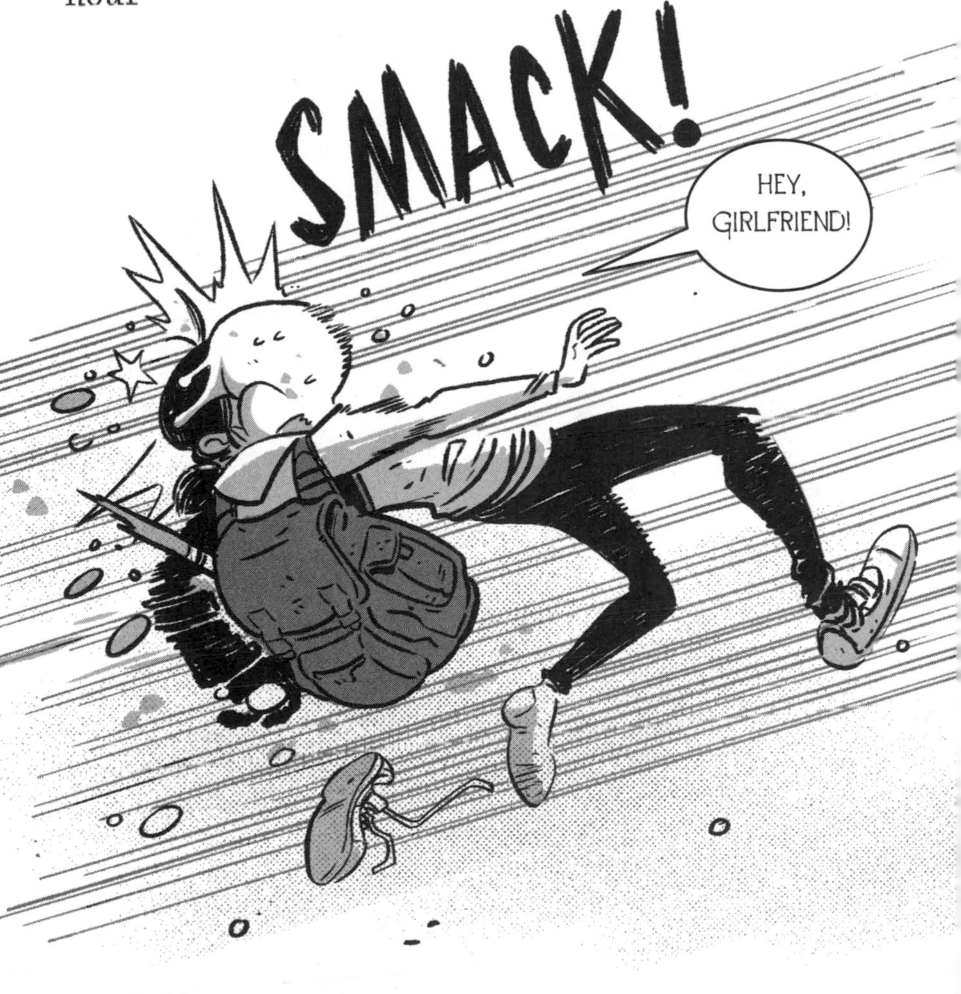
SMACK!
HEY, GIRLFRIEND!

For the second time in, like, three minutes, I sit up—dazed, confused, hurting. This time, the source of the pain is sitting in my lap: Globlet!

"You hit me like a missile made of gum," I say, rubbing my face. "What are you doing here?!"

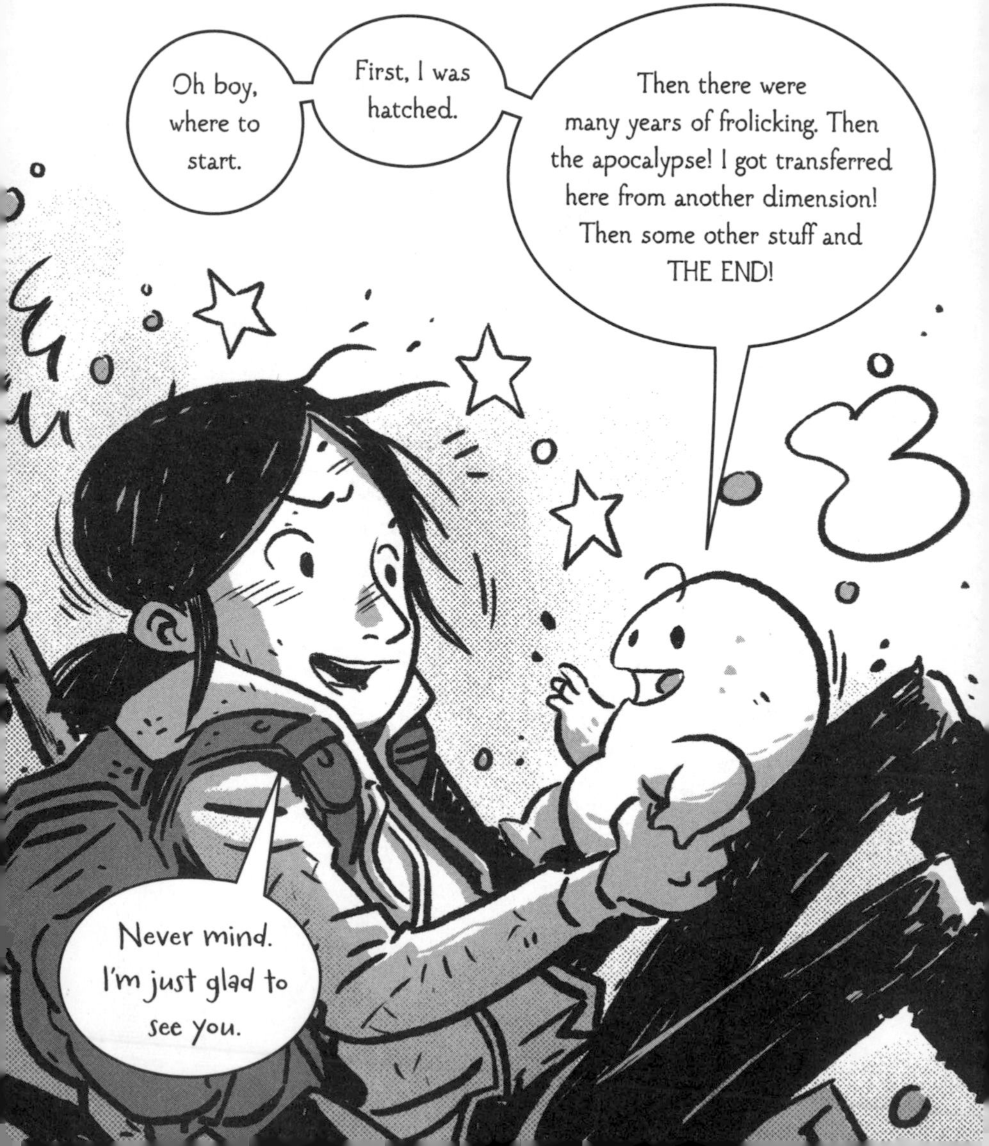
Oh boy, where to start.
First, I was hatched.
Then there were many years of frolicking. Then the apocalypse! I got transferred here from another dimension! Then some other stuff and THE END!
Never mind. I'm just glad to see you.

"But," I say, "guess it's not one hundred percent a June Solo Adventure anymore. . . ."

"Nope. GIRLS' ADVENTURE!"

I grin.

Globlet can glow like a night-light and she thinks that everything I do is terrific. Who wouldn't want an uncharted wasteland companion like—

# KSHHHH!

Suddenly, a cracking, hissing, POP sound makes me jump.

"Hey, your tushy sneezed!" Globlet squeaks.

"My tushy did not *sneeze*," I say, sighing. "It's my walkie . . . oh man, MY WALKIE!"

I snatch my walkie from my belt and squeeze the button. "Quint? Jack? Dirk? ANYONE? Come in, over!"

No response.

Was the walkie damaged during that long DoomKart tumble-sault? Or am I just too far from Wakefield to get reception?

Quint taught me everything there is to know about walkies and radios. And I'm pretty sure mine is A-OK. So it must be the distance.

# YEEAAAAIIIEEEE!

The air is split by a monstrous scream.

"Ooh!" Globlet exclaims. "Someone's getting tickles!"

"What? No, Globlet! That's not a 'getting tickles' scream. That's a 'getting hurt' scream. . . ."

I scoop up Globlet. In a flash, she's on my shoulder, clinging to my neck, and I'm racing through the remains of Blooper Burger.

"Are we going home?" Globlet asks.

"Yep," I say.

"Home is this way?"

"I have no idea which way home is."

"But you said we were going home."

"We are," I say. "Just not yet."

"So where are we going now?"

"Now we're going this way."

"What's this way?"

"We're gonna find out. . . ."

We're racing down some sort of Main Street. This town looks like it's been attacked by a horde of rogue jackhammers: buildings are squashed and torn apart. It's like some vengeful creature pulled the place apart and tried to piece it back together—but *wrong*.

"You're running fast!" Globlet chirps. "Do you have to go Number Two?"

"No, Globlet! I'm running 'cause whatever was screaming sounded scared, and I want—"

"Nachos?" Globlet asks.

"No! I want to make—"

"*Make* nachos?" Globlet asks.

"No! I want to make sure whatever's screaming is okay!"

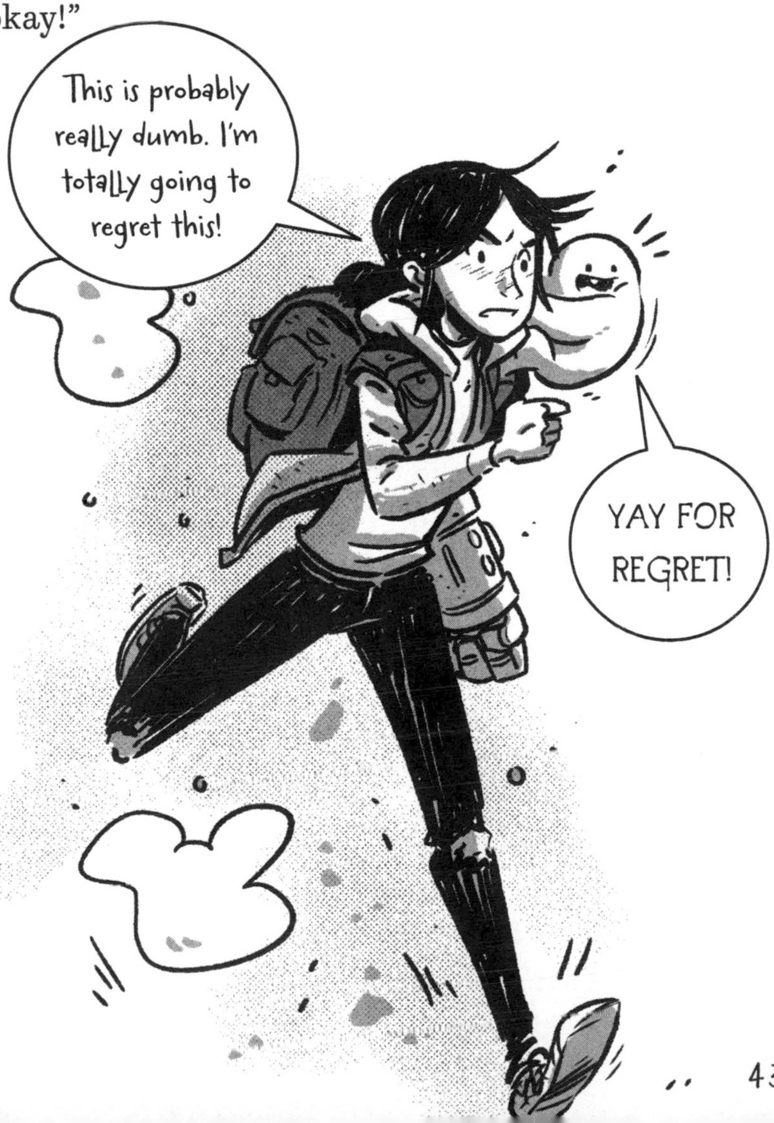
This is probably really dumb. I'm totally going to regret this!
YAY FOR REGRET!

# chapter six

I'm really hoping that whatever made that pained screaming noise is something kind and friendly, who's only, like, *slightly* hurt or *kinda* wounded.

Like maybe a baby rabbit who stubbed its toe?

Or a hamster with a tummyache?

Or a hedgehog who's really nervous about its first day of hedgehog school?

Globlet clings tighter to my shoulder. I scramble up an overturned fire truck that's erupting from the ground like some end-of-the-world Pride Rock.

"Ooh," Globlet says. "Fancy view."

A distant flicker of light catches my gaze: a flagpole. It's jutting out of a strange, vine-choked *forest*. I see bits of wood, yellow plastic, flashes of metal. It takes me a second to realize it's not a forest at all, it's a—

"Playground!" I say.

"YAY! I love playing!" says Globlet. "And I *extra love* ground!"

I pause. "You love . . . *ground*?"

Globlet shrugs. "Duh."

This playground is not one of those swanky new ones where everything is colorful and the ground is squishy. This playground is a sprawling, old, run-down mess of a thing. You could get a splinter just looking at it.

"Whatever made that screaming sound," I say, "it's in there. C'mon."

"You don't need to say 'c'mon,' I'm on your shoulder. I'm coming on regardless."

As we get closer, I see a sign for the playground: WELCOME TO FRIENDSHIP PARK.

That makes me chuckle.

This is about the least welcoming place ever— and also the least friendly. The crisscrossing walkways, ladders, and beams are all rotting. Vines twist and wind around them.

I scramble over a vine-covered fence, then crouch down, trying to be extra inconspicuous.

"Okay, we're in," I whisper.

"Yes, I know," Globlet says.

"Oh. Right. Well . . . whatever."

**YEEAAAAIIIIEEEE!**

The scream again. Louder. We're close.

There is a rusty slide ahead of us. I quietly scale it, then creep to the edge of the climbing tower. Now we'll be able to see what's what.

But when I *do* see what's what, it makes my stomach do a barrel roll . . . .

"The Rifters," I growl.

"And look what else," Globlet says as she stands on her gooey tiptoes. "It's that squirmy creature they were chasing."

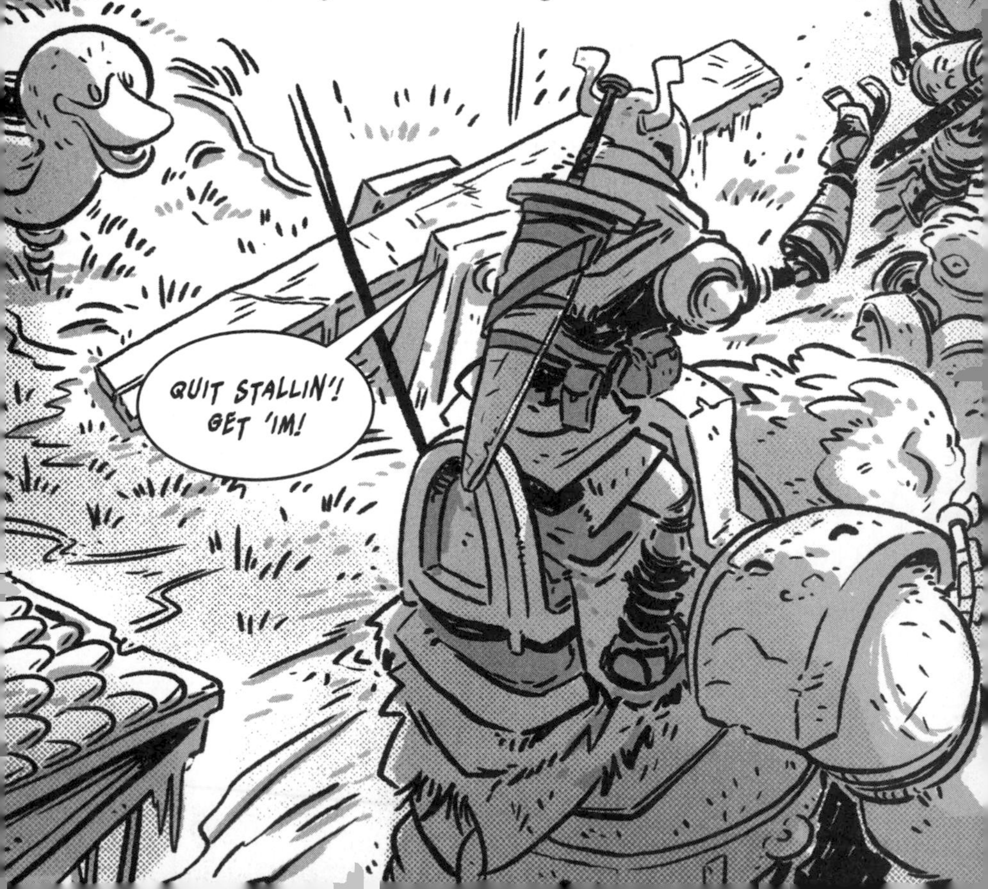
QUIT STALLIN'! GET 'IM!

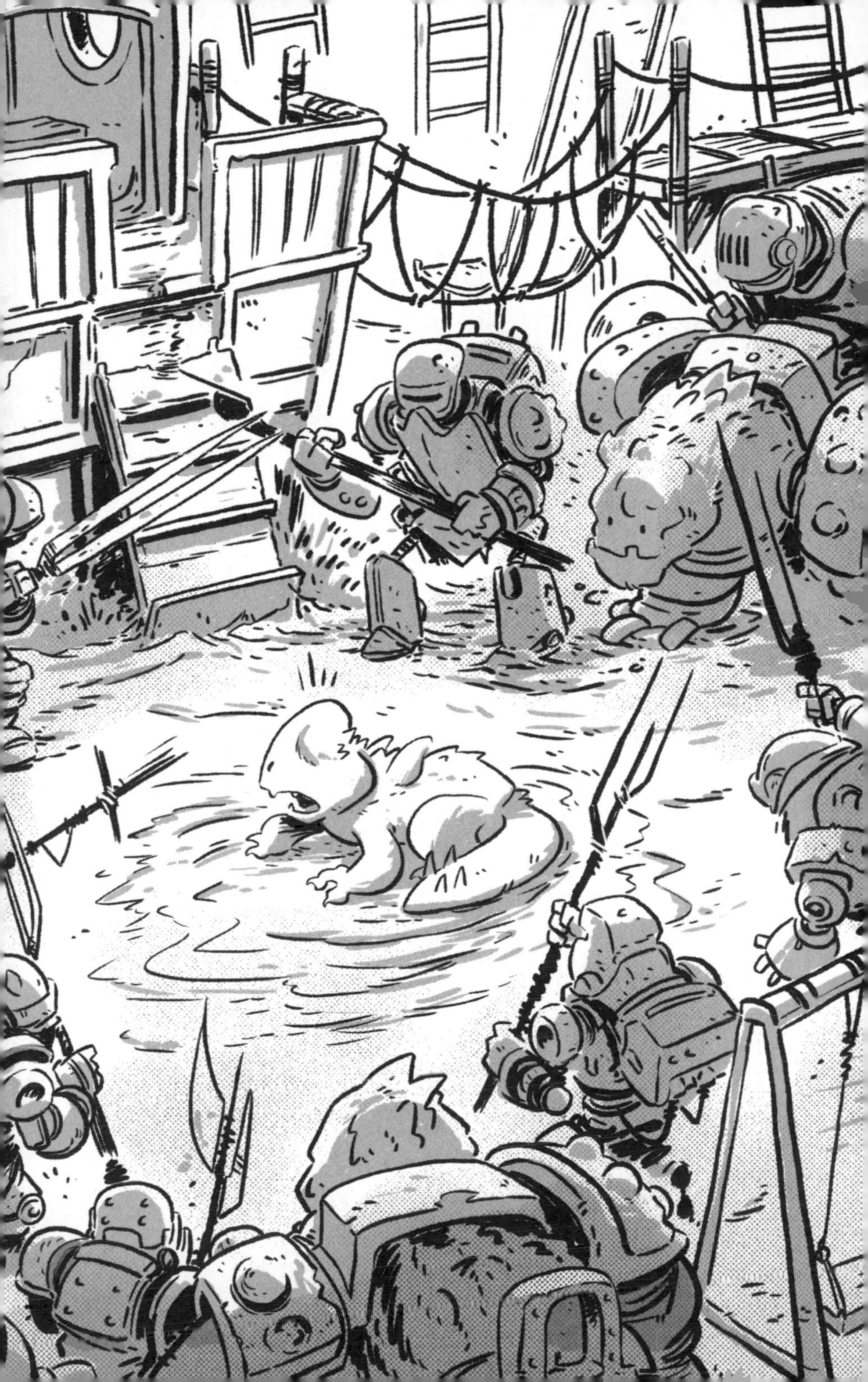

"Sit still, ya dumbin'!" one Rifter roars. The Rifter wears oil-splattered spiked armor—and I can almost smell his monstrous stench from here. He lunges forward and jabs with a hooked blade. But the creature rolls and the Rifter stumbles.

I whisper, "They're trying to *catch* it."

"DO I HAVE TO DO EVERYTHING AROUND HERE?" a loud voice barks.

It's the largest of the Rifters—the previously established Boss Rifter. He carries a long polearm, like some sort of other-dimensional dog-catcher.

The blur creature inches back, but it's too late—

# SLAM!

The Boss Rifter *swings* the polearm down, pinning the creature's tail to the ground!

Globlet's ready to leap over the side, straight into the Rifters' circle, rubbery fists flying. But I hold her back. "Steady, goo-ball," I say. "We're out-numbered, out-sized, and *way* out-weaponized."

"But Jack would just jump in and save the day!"

"Maybe. And then I'd have to jump in and *save his bony butt* like I do half the time anyway. You and I—we gotta be smart. We gotta be stealthy."

"Yesss . . ." Globlet says, "stealthy." She rubs her tiny hands together like a little evil overlord.

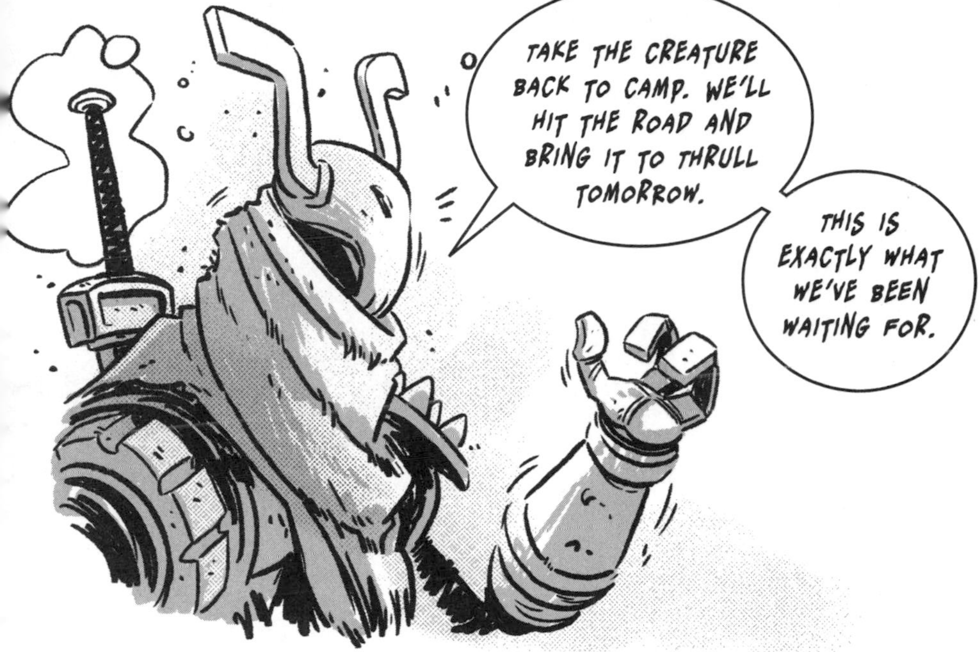
TAKE THE CREATURE BACK TO CAMP. WE'LL HIT THE ROAD AND BRING IT TO THRULL TOMORROW.
THIS IS EXACTLY WHAT WE'VE BEEN WAITING FOR.

"*Thrull*. That big dude said *Thrull*! You heard that, right, Globlet??"

"I heard it all right," she growls. "And also, those other words that he said."

"Globlet, we gotta save this creature. I have zero clue why Thrull wants it, but if I had a post-apocalyptic motto, it would be "DON'T LET THRULL HAVE ANYTHING HE WANTS BECAUSE ANYTHING HE WANTS WILL BE USED FOR EVIL."

Globlet thinks for a moment. "My motto would be that 'Dance like no one's watching' one. It's so profound!"

"Um . . . right," I say. "But y'know—bottom line: if they're trying to take this creature to Thrull, then we *must* help it escape!"

# chapter seven

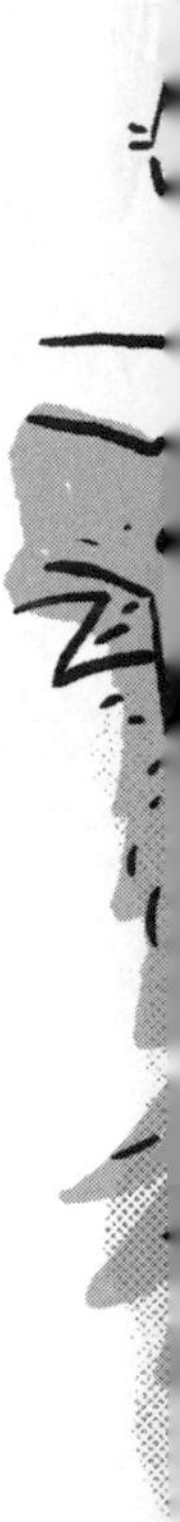

The Rifters are pulling out rusty chains and uncoiling strange ropes made from something like monster hair. They all move forward, about to hog-tie the creature.

Actually, not *all* of them move forward. One Rifter seems more interested in spinning on the tire swing than he does in tormenting small creatures.

"Flunk, quit that swinging and help finish the capture!" hollers the Boss Rifter.

"Sorry, Boss! Coming, Boss!" The Rifter named Flunk tries to get off the tire swing, but he must be dizzy from all that spinning, because he gets one foot out, hops up and down trying to find his balance, and falls flat on his face.

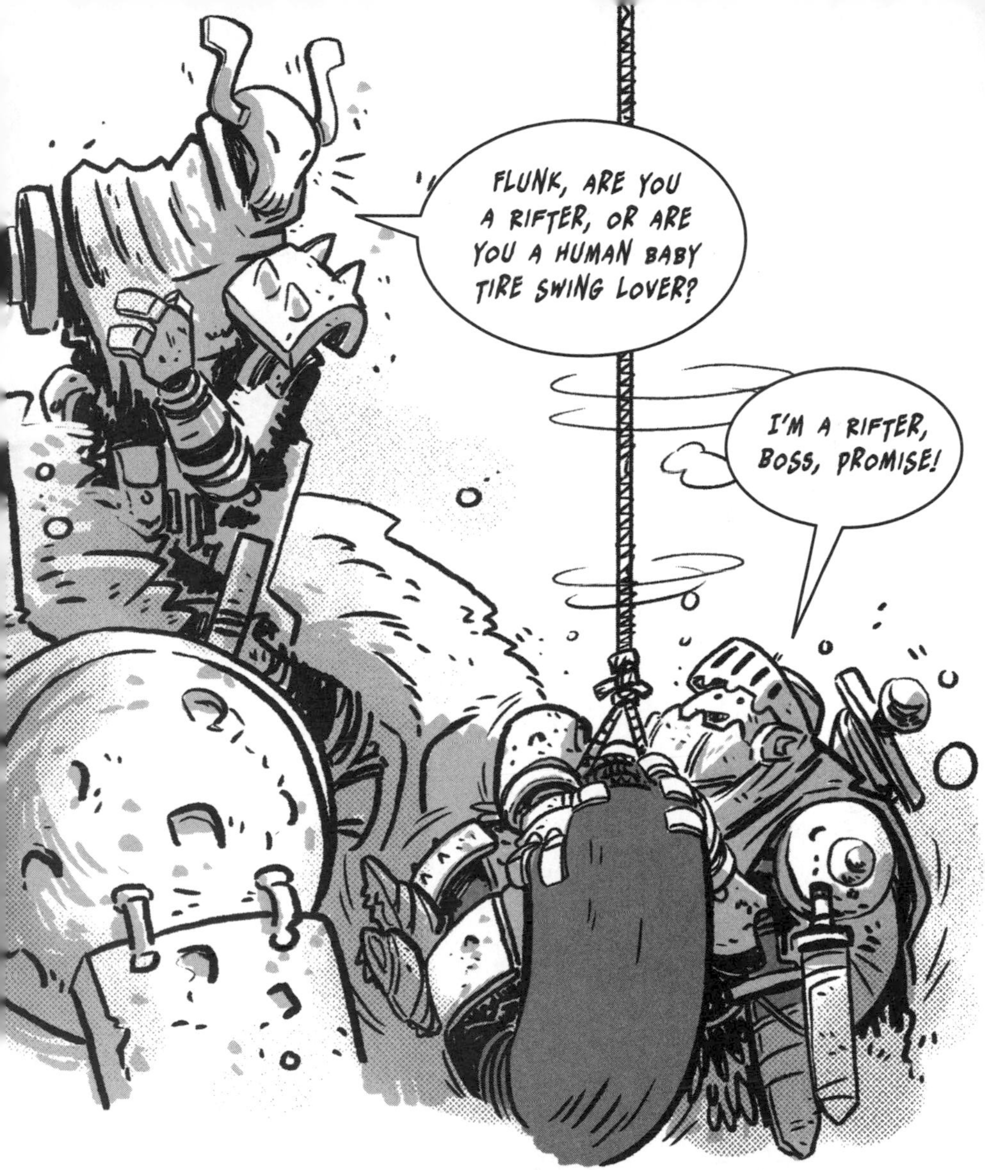
FLUNK, ARE YOU A RIFTER, OR ARE YOU A HUMAN BABY TIRE SWING LOVER?
I'M A RIFTER, BOSS, PROMISE!

I snicker as quietly as I can.

Flunk rejoins the group, pretending to help, but eyes the tire swing longingly.

One Rifter holds the polearm tight, while the others begin tying up the creature.

Things look grim. . . .

"Globlet," I say. "Now is the time to make—"

"Nachos!!" she exclaims. "FINALLY."

"No, Globlet! *Our move*. Now is the time to make *our move*."

"Oh." Globlet is quiet for a moment, then she whispers urgently, "Use the Thing-A-Ma-Blasty Gadget Blaster!"

"The *what*?"

"The Thing. A. Ma. Blasty. Gadget. Blaster," Globlet repeats slowly.

I stare at her, not comprehending.

Globlet huffs, then hops from my shoulder to my wrist. "This!" she says.

"Ohhh. The Gift." The Gift is the multi-purpose weapon that Jack gave me last Christmas.

It's like the Swiss Army knife of monster-battling!

I never take it off—so much so that I'd actually forgotten I was wearing it.

"Yes, 'the Gift,'" agrees Globlet, "except 'the Gift' is a not-cool name and 'Thing-A-Ma-Blasty Gadget Blaster' sounds *super* June Solo Adventure-y!"

Globlet has a point.

"All right. Time for a little Thing-A-Ma-Blasty Gadget Blaster action," I say, sounding like Black Widow if Black Widow had a catch phrase but that catch phrase was the *worst* catch phrase.

I aim for the swing set, a dozen feet from the rifters. I yank a lever on the blaster, squeeze my fist, and—

# ZA-POOF!

A pink Wham-O superball, filled with slices of sparkler, *speeds* through the air, and—

# BOING!

The superball smacks the swing set's top bar and ricochets straight up into the air.

"You missed!" Globlet says.

"Nope," I say. "Just watch."

And then—

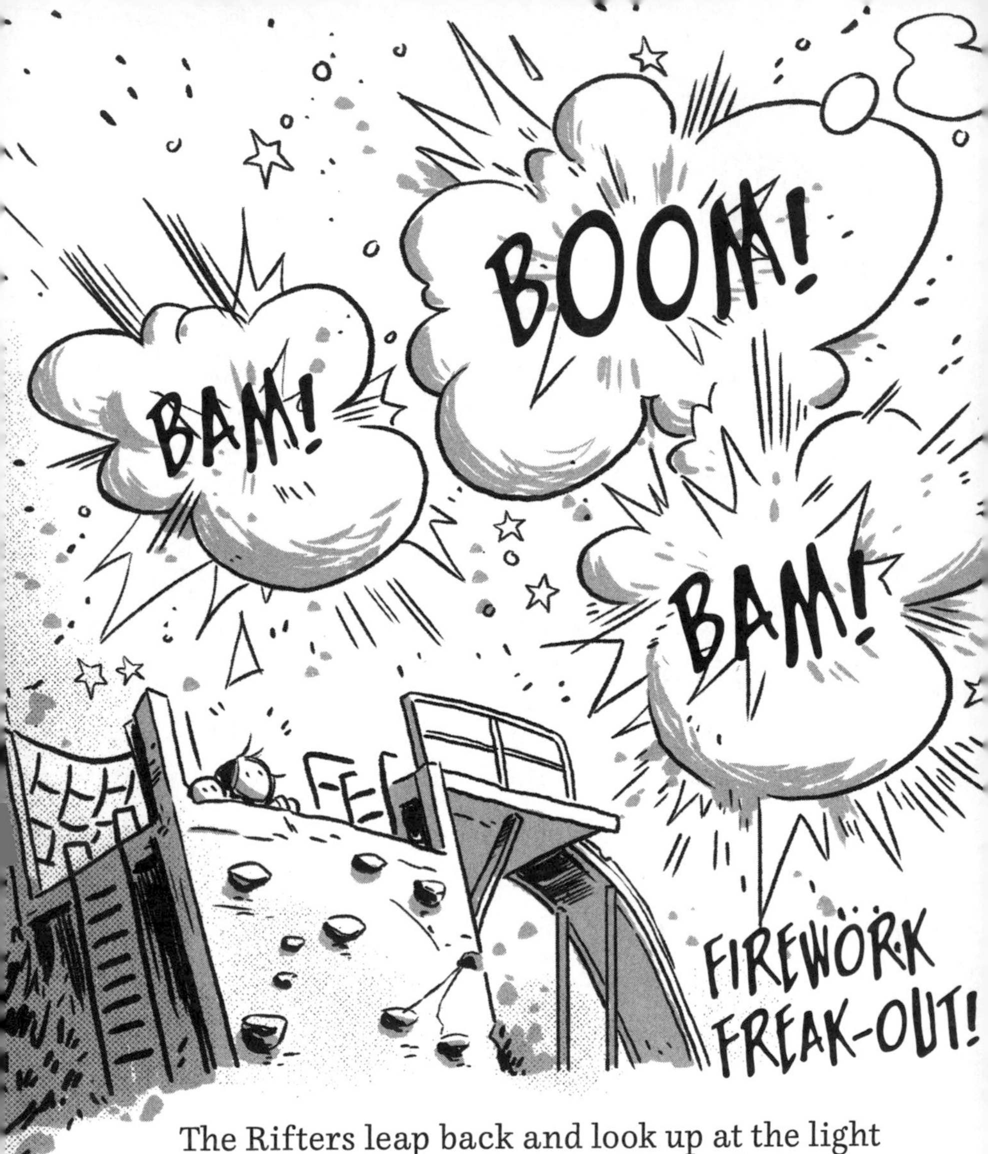
BAM!
BOOM!
BAM!
FIREWORK
FREAK-OUT!

The Rifters leap back and look up at the light show overhead. A whiny-voiced Rifter screeches, "What's that!? WHO DONE THAT?!?"

A smaller, cuter Rifter squeaks, "BRIGHT LIGHT! BRIGHT LIGHT!"

They only have *one moment* to assess the situation, because in the *second moment*—

# FWOOM!
# BOING!

I fire a second superball—and a second round
of fireworks explodes overhead. The Rifters
are spooked, but their Ogres go full-on *haywire
berserk*. There is a deafening, panicked—

# RAWR!

At once: CHAOS! The Ogres are pushing,
jostling, fleeing. Mounted Rifters tumble from
their saddles. Rifters on foot run for cover. The
Ogres stampede from the playground like the
final bell just rang on a half day.

The Boss Rifter's gravelly voice barks:
"FOLLOW ME! WE GOTTA GET THEM OGRES!"

At once, the Rifters give chase. Lucky for
us, these Rifters aren't too bright: they *all* go,
leaving the creature behind . . .

Lying in the dirt.

I take a breath. *We did it. It worked.* June Solo
Adventure (featuring special guest star Globlet)
has just achieved VICTORY NUMBER ONE!

"Now c'mon, Globlet," I say as we hurry down
through the structure. "Let's set this thing
free . . ."

# chapter eight

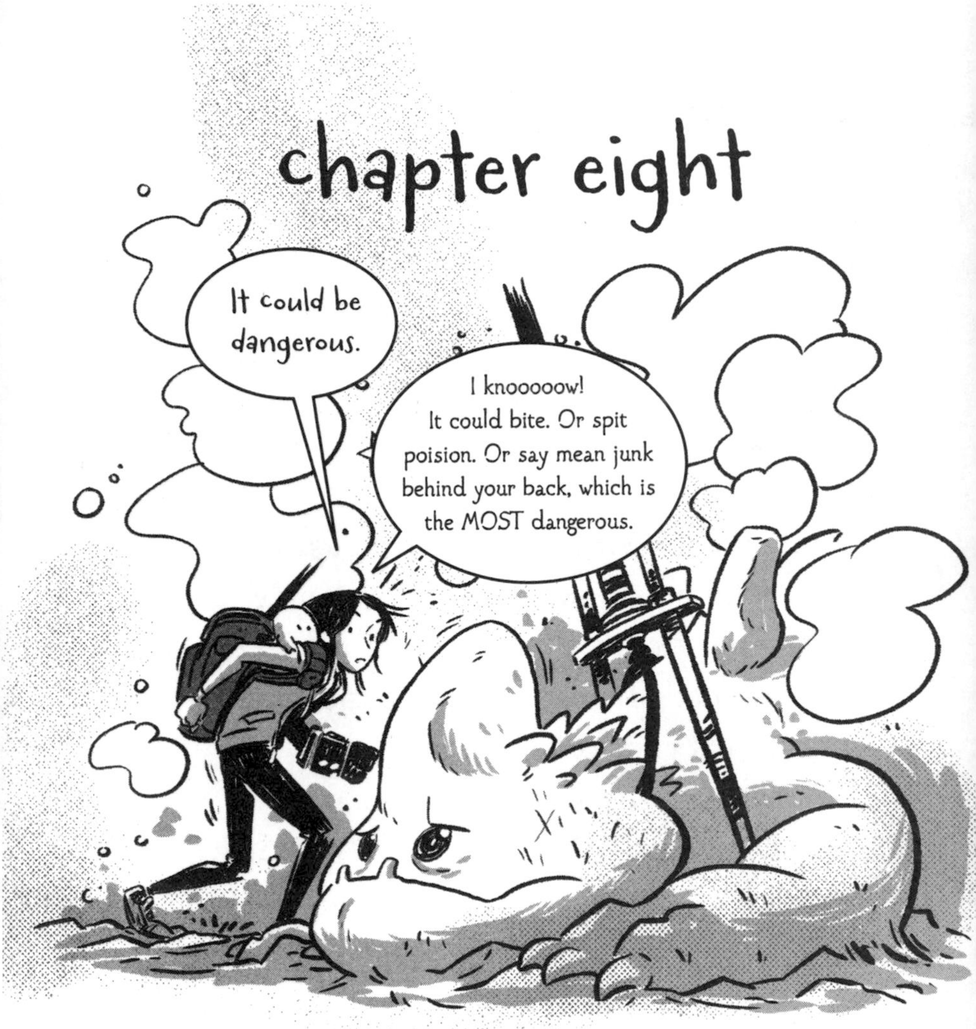
It could be dangerous.
I knooooow! It could bite. Or spit poision. Or say mean junk behind your back, which is the MOST dangerous.

The creature's scaly skin shimmers in the afternoon sunlight. It has short, sharp talons that scrape at the ground. Its long, spiky tail swings slowly. And this look on its face—in its eyes—it reminds me of *something* I've seen before.

But I don't have time to think about that—I

hear stomping and cracking in the distance. The Rifters and Ogres will soon be back.

I take a slow step forward.

I don't want to get attacked by a creature who could easily claw me to death. But I also *can't* let the Rifters deliver this creature to Thrull. If I do that, I'm basically just serving him our surrender on a silver platter. . . .

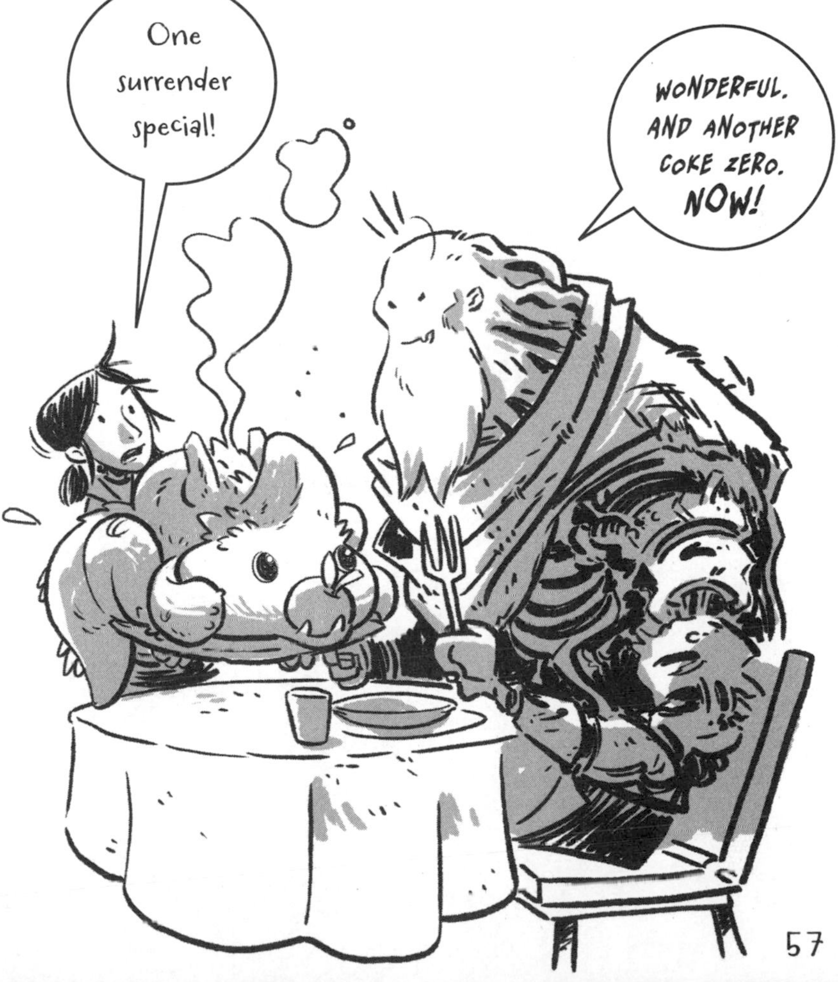
One surrender special!
WONDERFUL. AND ANOTHER COKE ZERO. NOW!

I swallow—and I inch closer. I see nothing evil or cruel behind the creature's blinking eyes.

In fact, the blur-creature's confused, frightened face reminds me of something else entirely: the Wakefield Hound.

Okay, so, quick aside.

The Wakefield Hound was our school mascot. But instead of stuffing some teacher into a big ol' dog costume, our genius gym coach decided to use his *real-life, actual dog*: Mr. Peppers the chihuahua. "For authenticity!" he said.

Well, guess what? Mr. Peppers hated it! Every time they jammed that poor fella into that costume, he'd freak, and then *this* would happen—

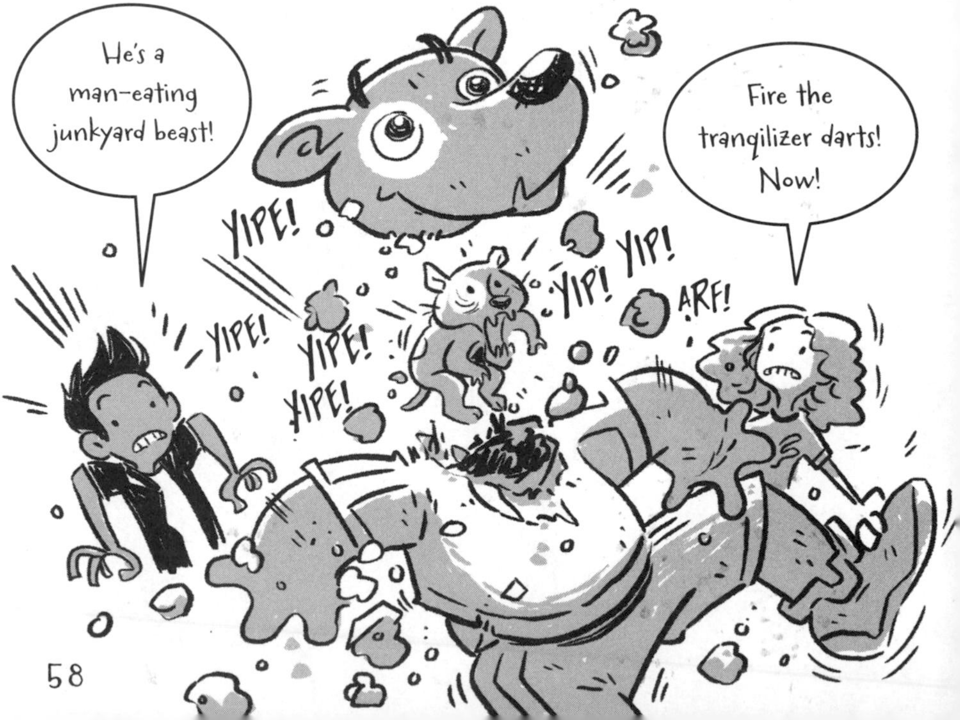

He's a man-eating junkyard beast!
Fire the tranqilizer darts! Now!
YIPE!
YIPE!
YIPE!
YIPE!
YIP!
YIP!
ARF!

But I had a hunch that little pup was no man-eater. It was bunk. So, naturally—as a reporter—I wrote a story about it. The headline was a doozy—

## BARKING NEWS!
### MR. PEPPERS ISN'T MEAN, HE'S JUST PAWS-ITIVELY MISERABLE!

The story was a sensation! Everyone stopped trying to stuff him into a costume, and he went back to being a friendly, happy dog.

What I'm saying is, sometimes being scared and being hurt makes you act like you're mean. Maybe that's the case with this creature.

"Hey," I say, inching closer. "I'm just gonna free you, okay? Then you go your way, and I'll go mine. And you don't let them find you again, cool? 'Cause you don't want any Thrull in your life—trust me."

I stand over the creature and grab the polearm, careful not to get too close.

I twist and turn, trying to wrench it out of the ground, feeling like a postapocalyptic King Arthur.

It loosens.

An inch. Two inches.

The creature is able to move now—but just barely. As I twist again, the creature strains and manages to look back at me.

That's when the weird thing happens—the weirdest thing in a day full of weird things.

As it stares into my eyes, there's a sudden—

**KA-SKAK!**

Like radio static. . . .

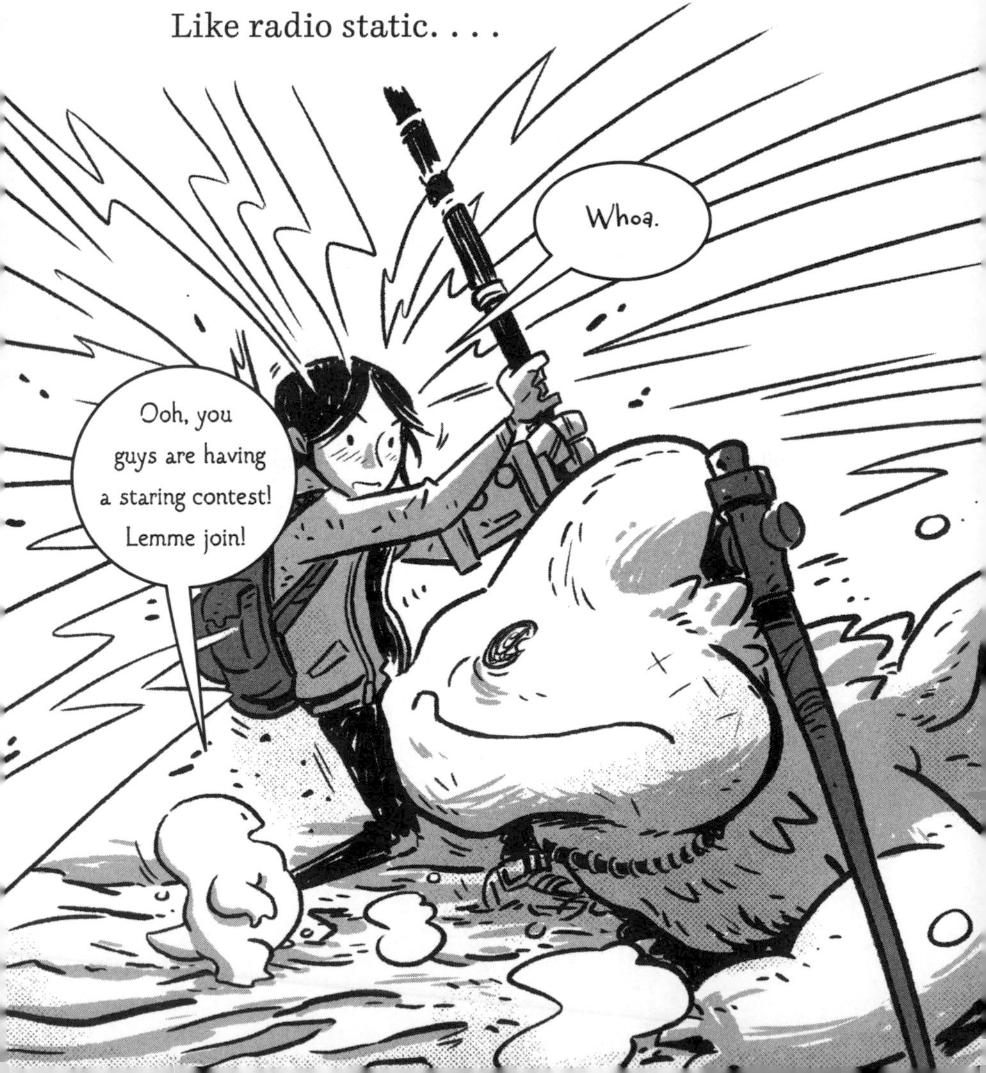

Whoa.
Ooh, you guys are having a staring contest! Lemme join!

A sudden surge of images pass across my vision, like someone's flipping through TV channels at warp speed. I see—

*Something flying through the air.*

*Something that looks like a nest.*

*Something like a glowing tornado.*

And then I just see BLACK. I move my eyes back and forth, but still nothing. Then color and light, and I realize it's Globlet.

"I put my hands over your eyes 'cause you were being weird."

"Uh-huh . . ." I mumble.

My mind is a hazy, speeding jumble. That felt like one of those *tired-beyond-tired* moments at school, where you fall asleep in the back of the bus or in class. It's not like a full *dream*—it's something else. . . .

Like a trance.

I can imagine the look on my face. It's a look I've seen before. Nearly a year ago, back when—

# RAWRRR!

"June! Watch out!" Globlet squeaks.

Too late. My hand is ripped from the polearm!

I'm snatched by a big, butt-ugly brute's enormous grubby paw.

"Let go!" I shout. I'm kicking and thrashing, lifted into the air until, suddenly, I'm face-to-face with the Boss Rifter.

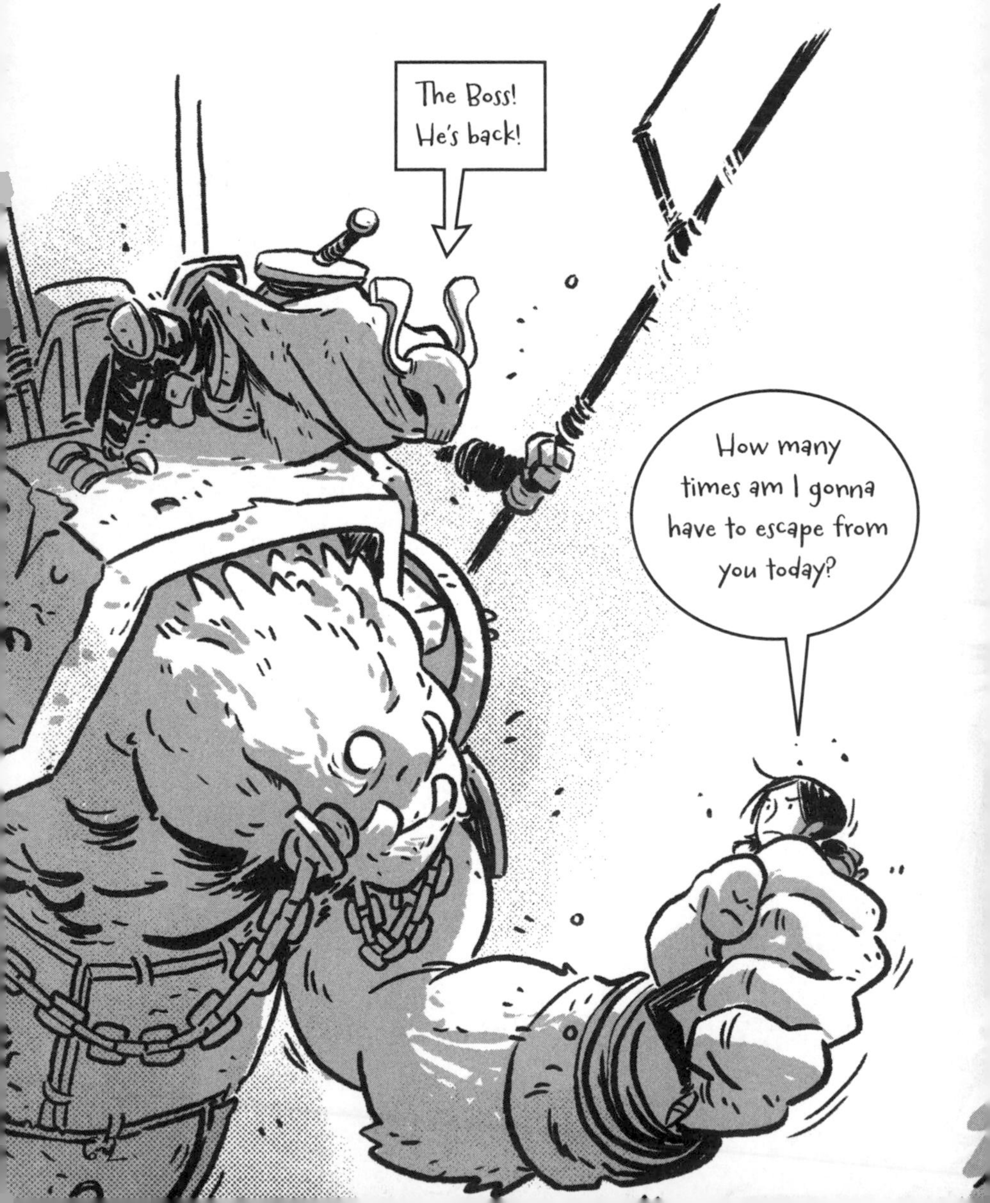
The Boss! He's back!
How many times am I gonna have to escape from you today?

"Interferin' with my catch, is you?" asks the Boss Rifter, though he's not so much *asking* as he's *accusing*.

"No, no," I say. "I would never. I just, um . . ."

*Come on!* I mentally order myself. What would reporter June do? But this Ogre is squeezing so hard I can't remember anything but the first thing I ever learned about news—the ol' who, what, where, when, why.

So, just as it feels like my insides are about to explode, I burst out—

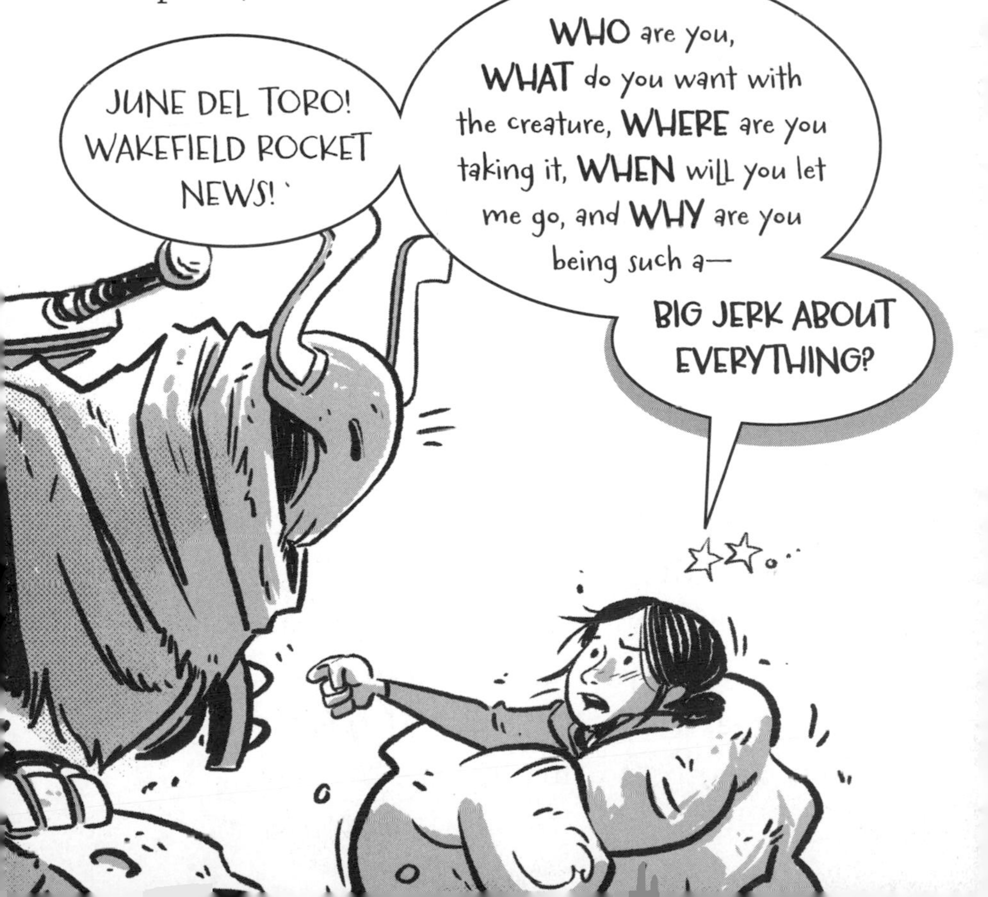
JUNE DEL TORO! WAKEFIELD ROCKET NEWS!
WHO are you, WHAT do you want with the creature, WHERE are you taking it, WHEN will you let me go, and WHY are you being such a—
BIG JERK ABOUT EVERYTHING?

The Boss Rifter cocks his head, confused for a moment—good. Maybe I've thrown him off-guard with my flurry of hard-hitting questions.

But then he leans in—so close I can smell his fetid breath. "I'm doin' the inquirin' here, not you," he snarls.

"Actually," I say. "That's not how I like to operate. Normally, I find an interview goes best if—"

# KA-SLAM!

The Ogre punches the dirt next to me, and I feel the ground shake.

The Boss Rifter says, "You talk a lot. Creatures that talk a lot is usually *up* to something. You plannin' to deliver the wingzer to Thrull, izit? So you and your blubber buddy here gets the credit?"

Before I can get *any* clarification on that, Globlet hops out from behind my back. "HEY! I'M NOBODY'S BLUBBER BUDDY!"

The Boss Rifter snaps, "Silence, jelly ball!"

"Lemme at him," Globlet whispers.

The Ogre's hand tightens and pulls us closer. The Boss Rifter says, "*My* bunch tracked the beast and *my* bunch trapped the beast! And soon, right, it'll be my bunch that gives it to *Thrull*."

"Dude," I say. "Believe me. I'm not trying to give anything to Thrull."

*Except a swift kick in the butt.* In my head, I kick a lot of butts.

The Boss grunts, and I realize now he's suspicious of why I *wouldn't* want to give Thrull a gift. Great, I've really put my foot in it this time.

Wait. My foot. That's it! I spot the polearm still jutting out of the ground and know what I have to do. Just gotta keep the Boss distracted. . . .

"So, what's with the gift for Thrull? Is it his birthday or something?

"Like you don't know what's happenin'. Ev'ry creature in this rotten dimension knows. Thrull is the big boss now," the Boss Rifter says.

He's studying my face, then Globlet's. Finally he notices the Thing-A-Ma-Blasty Gadget Blaster, and grabs at it. "And whadda we have here?"

"IT'S AN OVERSIZED WATCH AND SHE WEARS IT WHEN SHE WANTS TO FEEL FANCY!" Globlet shouts. "NOW BACK OFF."

The Boss laughs. "I think my ogre'll be crushin' you, now. The both of you. Yep, you'll both be crushed good."

My dangling foot can feel the bottom of the polearm. It's close. . . .

As the Ogre squeezes tighter, the top of my foot finds the polearm and I manage to—

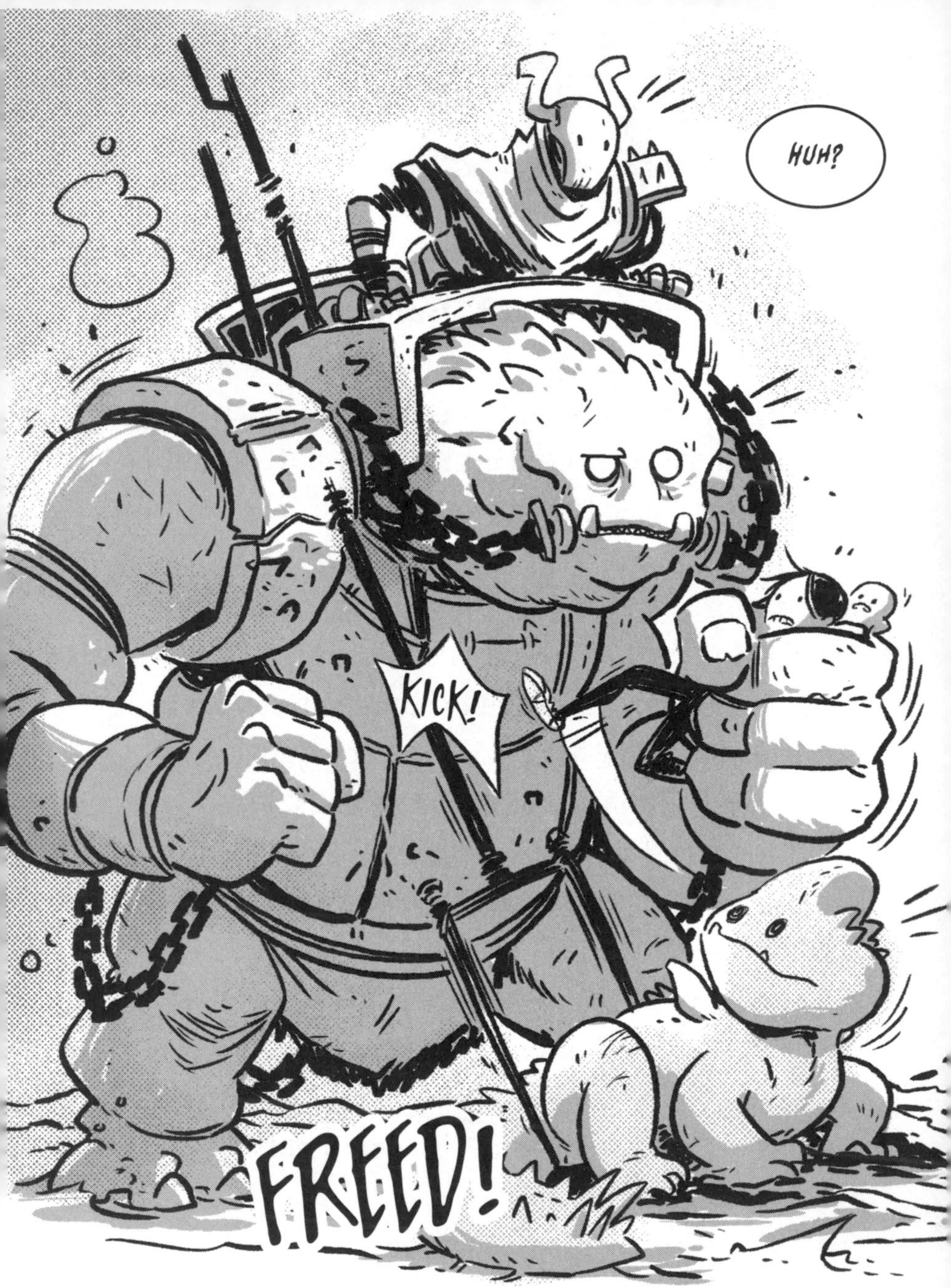
HUH?
KICK!
FREED!

Suddenly, there's a FLASH of movement beneath us. I see a blur of color—a spark of neon light—as the creature darts away!

"GET IT!" the Boss shrieks. The Ogre lunges out, paw opening, and Globlet and I crash to the ground.

The creature speeds across the playground, almost slithering. The Ogre chases after it—squashing swing sets and stomping over slides.

I watch—relieved—as the creature disappears, escaping by diving and drilling down into a sandbox.

"We're getting outta here!" I say.

"Don't narrate it!" Globlet says. "Just do it!"

I grab the polearm from the ground, and then we're racing back the way we came, I spot a half-open manhole cover—just enough room to slip in.

I glance back.

The Ogre stomps his foot in frustration, the Boss Rifter scowls. The creature got away.

But I watch for a moment too long—because the Boss Rifter suddenly turns, locking eyes with me.

He looks at me like, *You won this round, but there will be another . . . soon. . . .*

And then Globlet and I disappear into the darkness. . . .

# chapter nine

"We'll walk this sewer until we're far away from that lousy playground," I tell Globlet. "Then we'll come back up and find our way home."

"Genius! Genius!" Globlet exclaims.

But the farther we walk, the less I like my plan. The sewer is dark and slimy. Dirty water and garbage rush beneath my feet, and sometimes I'll hear a crunch that sounds suspiciously like breaking bone.

Only Globlet's glow guides us. I hold her out like I'm some old-timey, Ebenezer Scrooge innkeeper. . . .

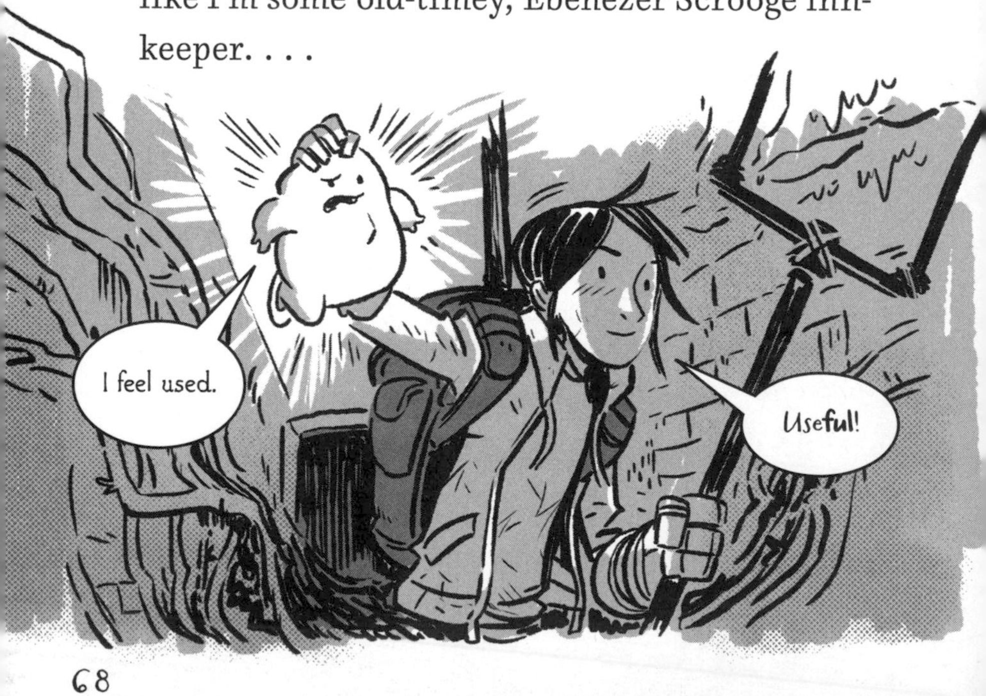
I feel used.
Useful!

When we finally come to another open manhole cover, it's been hours. I'm so eager for fresh air that I don't care where it takes us—I just climb up and out.

"I'm happy to be out of these tunnels!" Globlet chirps. "All that glowing was making me sleepy."

"Only problem," I say, looking around at our new surroundings. "Now I have even *less* of an idea where we are. . . ."

"I know where we are!" Globlet proclaims triumphantly. "This is the place you call Earth!"

I sigh. She suddenly looks concerned.

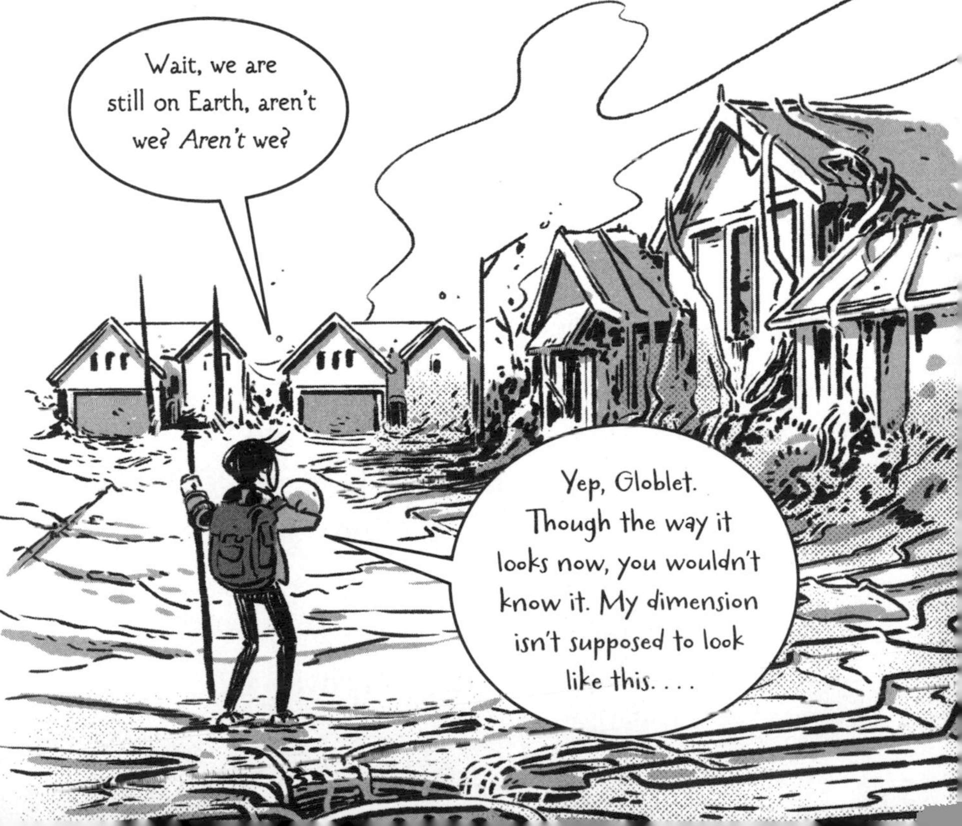
Wait, we are still on Earth, aren't we? *Aren't* we?
Yep, Globlet. Though the way it looks now, you wouldn't know it. My dimension isn't supposed to look like this. . . .

We're in one of those just-built-yesterday neighborhoods, where every house is almost identical to every other house, and the only way you can remember which one is yours is if you plant some tulips or something. Then every time some parent is dropping you off, you gotta say, "It's the one with tulips out front!" But then it snows and the tulips die and nobody knows the difference anymore.

There aren't any tulips here now.

Just an endless web of thick, pulsating Vine-Thingies that weave the houses together.

"I just want to get *home*."

But that'll be easier said than done. We walk. And walk. And walk. And it's not just that every house looks like same. Every *street* looks the same. And they're *all* named after trees!

I go left onto Maple Street, which turns onto Pine Street, and loops us around to Poplar Street. Where even *are* we?

We pass a huge, snaking Vine-Thingy that I'm *sure* we've passed before. The houses are rotting while the Vine-Thingies are flourishing.

"I need a sec, Globlet," I finally say, as I take a seat on the ground. "My legs are like rubber."

"I know the feeling," Globlet says.

Just then, I look over.

And I gasp.

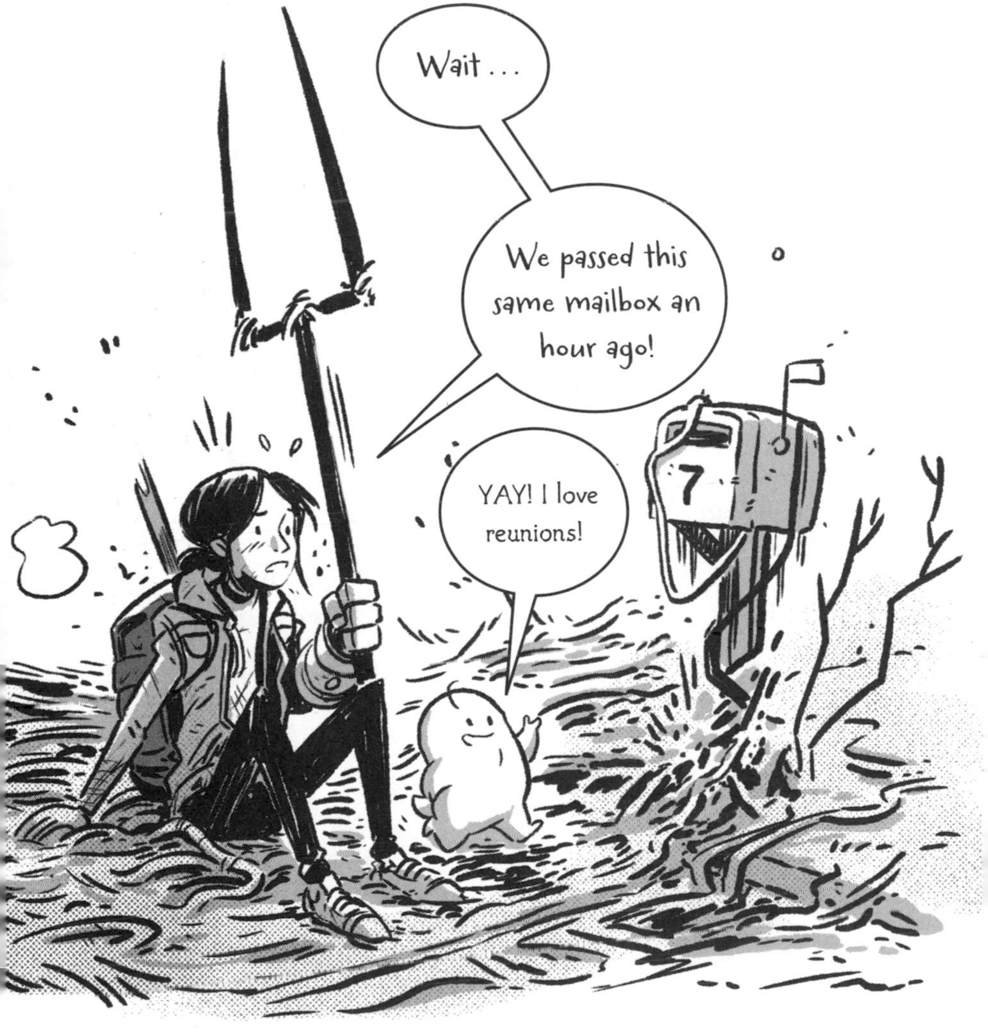
Wait . . .
We passed this same mailbox an hour ago!
YAY! I love reunions!
7

"No, Globlet!" I groan. "That means we're going in circles! We're lost!"

A scary question starts gnawing at my insides.

What if we *don't* make it back? What if we're not just *lost* but we're, like, *lost lost*?

It's like the TV remote. Sometimes you can't find it for a while, but you know it'll turn up eventually—you just have to finally get frustrated enough and go digging between the couch cushions.

But other times you lose something, like my lucky slap bracelet, and somehow you just *know* that it's never turning up. Like, ever.

Is that me? Am I now my lucky slap bracelet? Am I *lost lost*?

My shoulders sag. My legs are throbbing and my feet are on fire. I want to curl up. I want to fall asleep to the cute, soothing sounds of Globlet's bubbly snoring. I want to hear—

# RAWRR

Not that.

That's a roar. A soft, shrill, barely there *roar*.

I look up.

The blur creature.

It's back.

Perched on top of a massively thick Vine-Thingy that is draped *over* a two-story house.

And it's staring at me.

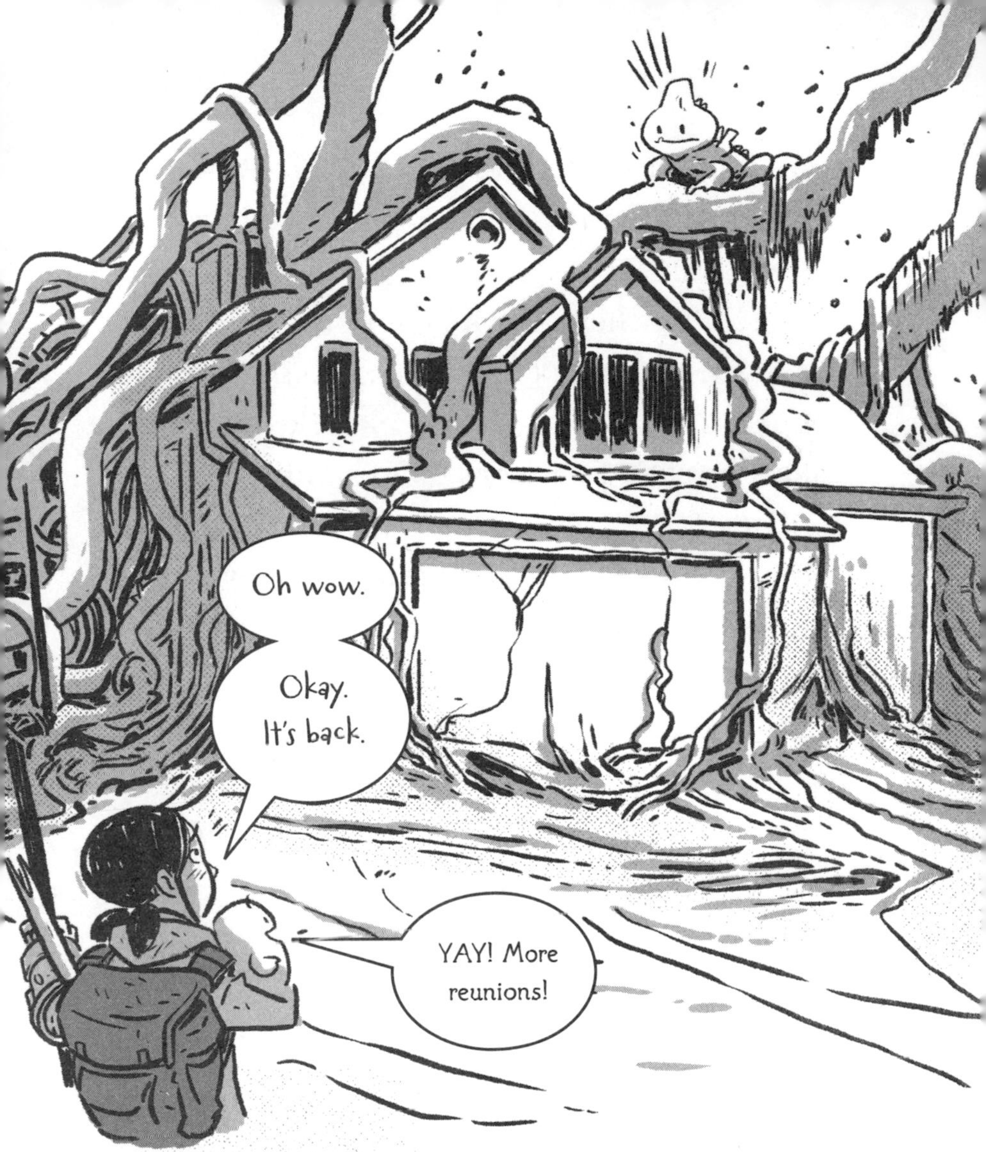
Oh wow.
Okay. It's back.
YAY! More reunions!

"Do you think it wants us to, um, follow it?" I'm partly asking Globlet—but mostly asking myself.

"I don't know what *it* wants," Globlet says. "But I am WAY too hungry to take another lap around this boring tree town. FOLLOW! FOLLOW!"

We cross the street, toward the creature. A smile creeps onto its face. It turns, striding up the wide vine.

And that's when I see its back.

It has fins. No, not fins. *Stumps*. Small remnants jutting out of its back—like a hint of something that was there before. Like . . .

*Wings*.

That's gotta be it. Maybe it used to have wings. And now it doesn't.

I wonder what that's all about—

And right then, the realization hits me with absolute, complete, total, overwhelming *terror*. The way my head felt. The vision. It was just like Jack and the King Wretch.

We learned about the Winged Wretches' monstrous abilities when the most powerful of them—the King Wretch—beamed nightmarish visions into Jack's head.

Bardle told us that all Wretches have that power, but he'd never seen one with the strength of the King Wretch. And I'd never experienced it before today.

All Winged Wretches are soldiers; soldiers that serve Ŗeżżóch. Pure evil. I mean, the last time I tangled with one—it was ugly. . . .

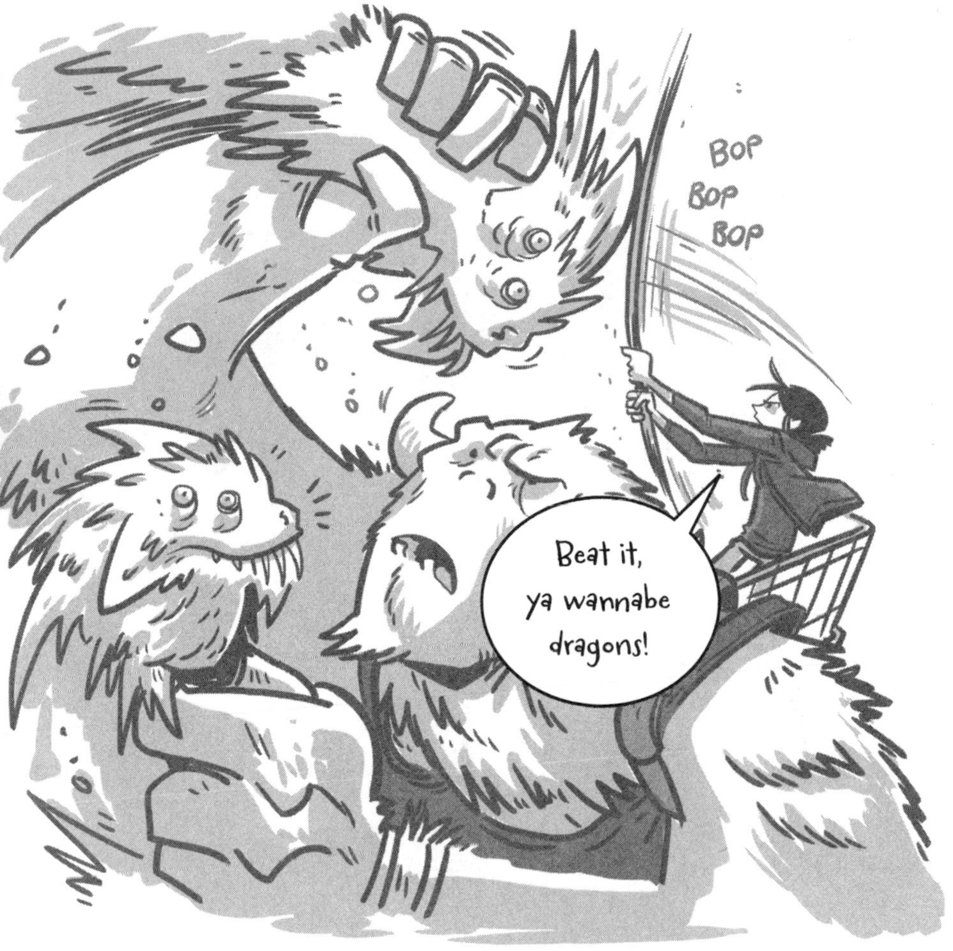
BOP
BOP
BOP
Beat it, ya wannabe dragons!

The creature's lizard-like neck turns. It's looking back at us.

I see little raised bumps above its eyes, like bubbly eyebrows. That's where *more* eyes will grow in. Because Winged Wretches have *lots* of eyes for seeing *stuff* so they can do *bad stuff.*

There's no doubt. This creature is a baby Wretch. . . .

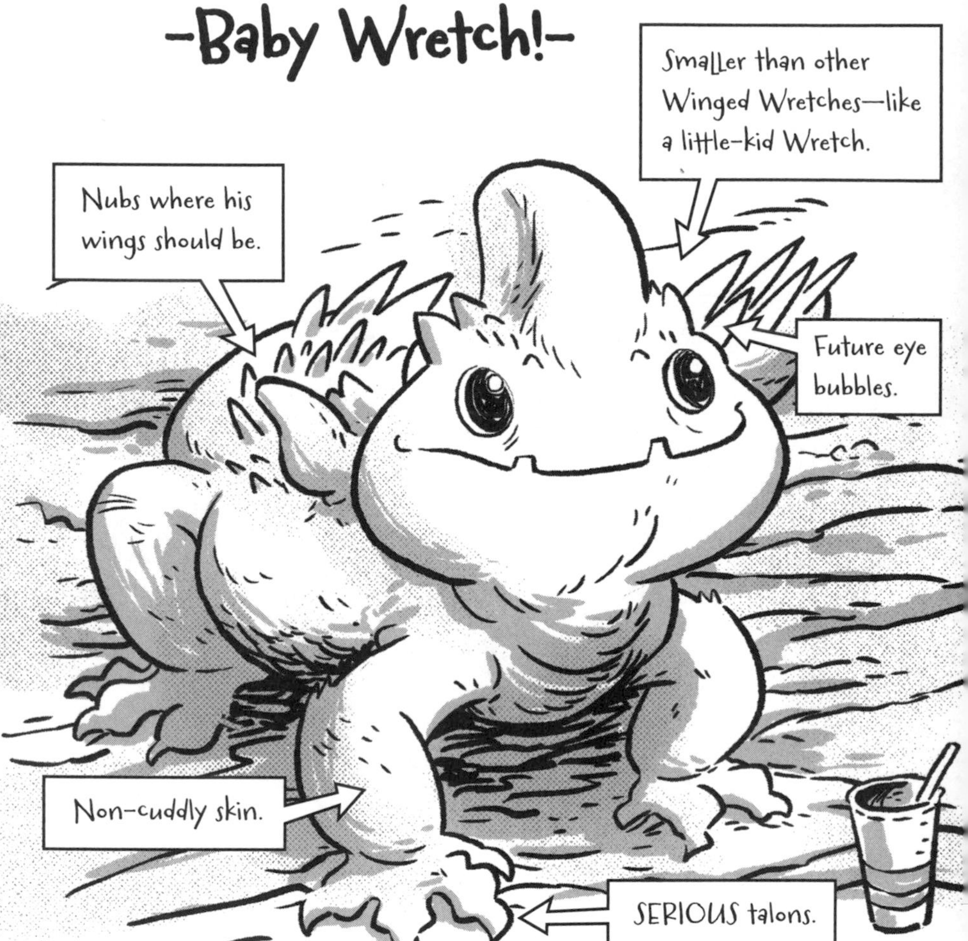
-Baby Wretch!-
Smaller than other Winged Wretches—like a little-kid Wretch.
Nubs where his wings should be.
Future eye bubbles.
Non-cuddly skin.
SERIOUS talons.

I take a step back—not even quite realizing it. "It's a—it's a—it's a . . . baby Winged Wretch."

"Wait, WHAAAAAT?" Globlet asks.

The Wretch's head bobs upward in that classic "C'mon, gang!" nod. Guess that gesture works in all dimensions.

And then my mind is juggling two different scenarios.

Stay where we are—and maybe remain hopelessly lost? Or follow a Winged Wretch—and maybe be eaten?

I'm trying to do what I do best—weigh the pluses, the minuses, the goods, the bads—

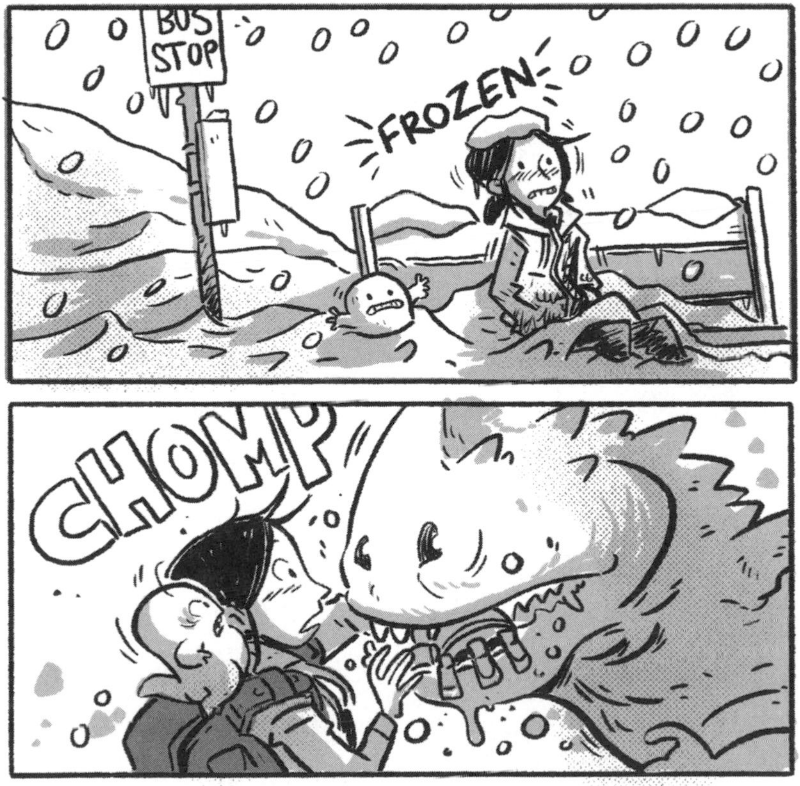
BUS STOP
FROZEN
CHOMP

But I can't think straight, because there is a strange, new noise filling my brain.

Noises coming from all around us. . . .

At first, I think I'm just imagining it. Could just be the fear, causing me to hear creepy things that aren't there. Like that time a few years ago, when I lay in bed and became *convinced* the lacrosse helmet I'd left on my bedroom floor was actually a *human skull* and had to call my mom in to hit the lights. Yeah, that was embarrassing.

But I know it's not just my imagination when Globlet says, "What's that sound? Is it vines?"

"No," I say. "Vine-Thingies don't MOAN."

But that's undeniably what I'm hearing: MOANING. Coming from *everywhere*. This labyrinth of look-alike streets and houses suddenly feels ALIVE. As the moans grow louder, it occurs to me that I only know one thing that moans. . . .

Suddenly—

# SLAM! CRASH!

There is movement everywhere. Doors fall open, windows shatter, and screens rip.

It's like some gruesome end-of-the-world game show, and each house is hiding a terrifying prize. . . .

# LET'S SHOW HER WHAT SHE'S WON, FOLKS!

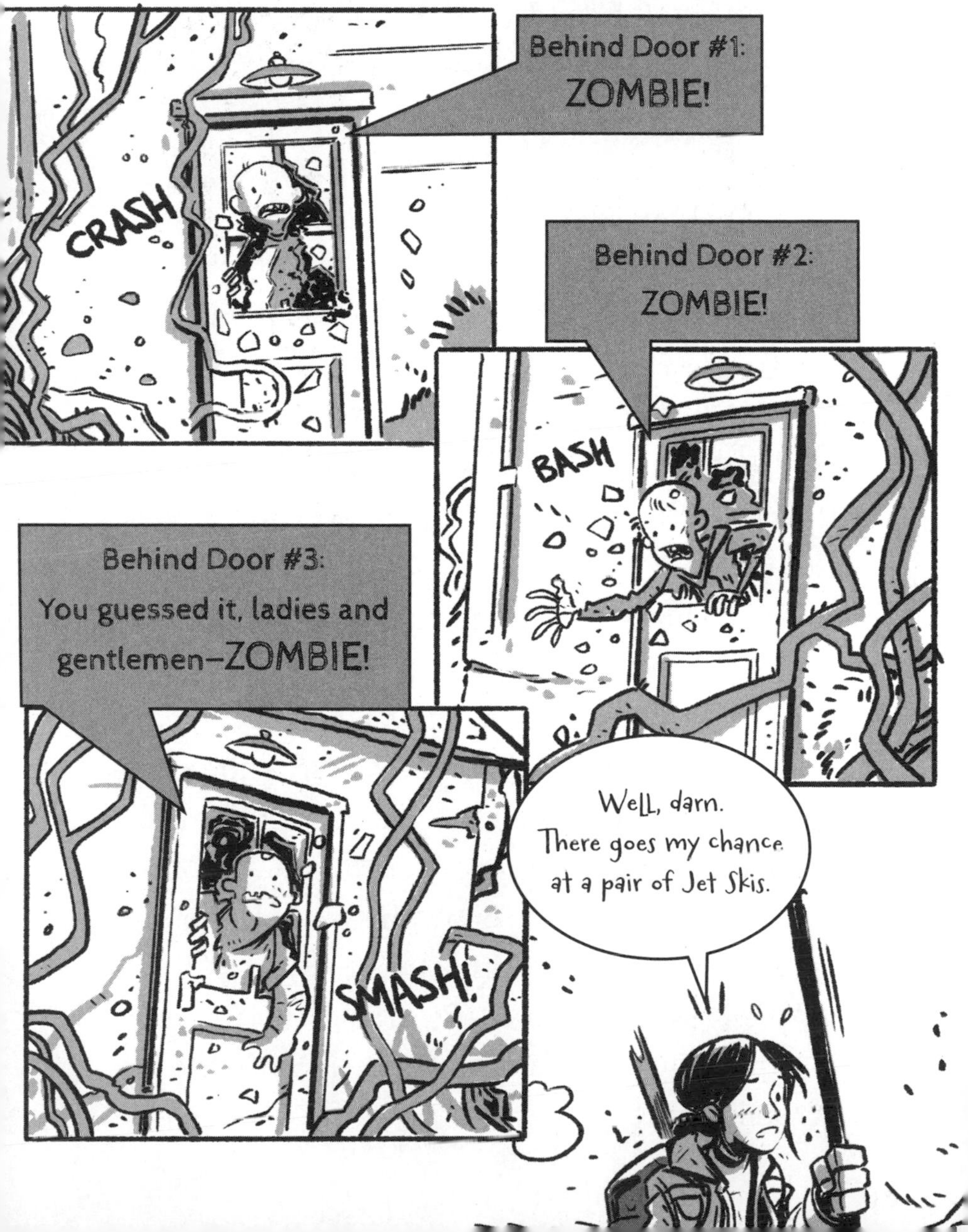
Behind Door #1: ZOMBIE!
CRASH
Behind Door #2: ZOMBIE!
BASH
Behind Door #3: You guessed it, ladies and gentlemen–ZOMBIE!
SMASH!
Well, darn. There goes my chance at a pair of Jet Skis.

# chapter ten

I can't believe I let this happen!

I was too loud! Too careless. Globlet and I didn't check these houses! We did no reconnaissance! We were just loudly bumbling down the streets like eighth graders on Halloween night! With no idea we were traveling through a GIANT MAZE OF ZOMBIE-FILLED HOUSES!

Then, suddenly, there's that *rawr* sound again. The baby Wretch.

It's still there, looking at us with that *Hey, what are you doing, dummies?* expression on its face. Then its head dips and it strides up the thick vine, disappearing over the roof.

I stare at that spot for a split second, though it feels like an eternity. Finally—

"Well, June!" Globlet exclaims. "GO!"

"But, but—" I stammer. "That's where the Wretch went!"

"Uh . . . yeah?" Globlet says. "WENT. Past tense! Which means now it's GONE. Which means that must be a way OUT."

Argh! Now I have to update the math in my head. Stay where we are—and *definitely* be devoured by zombies? Or follow the Winged Wretch and *maybe* be hopelessly eaten?

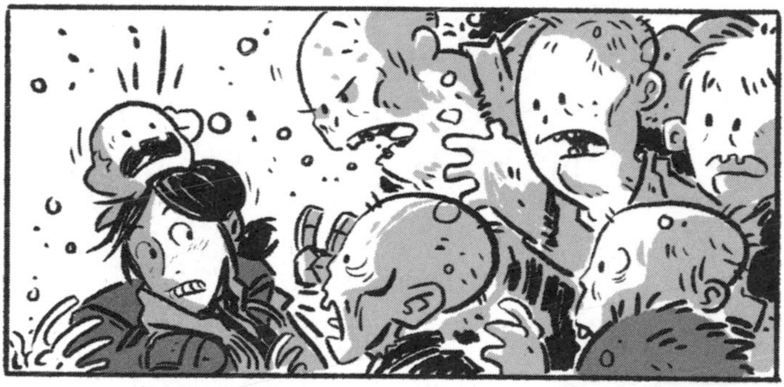

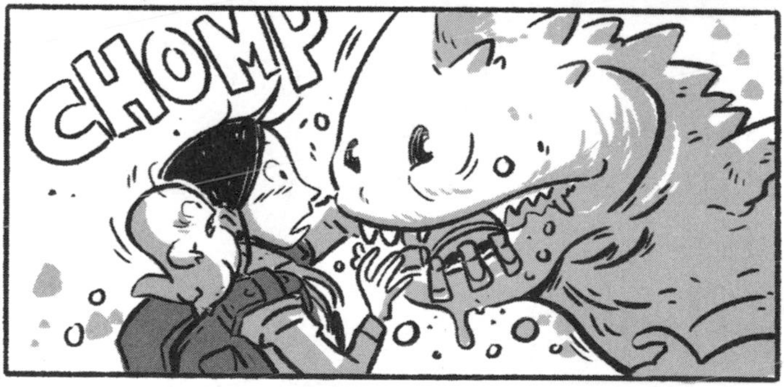
CHOMP

Fine. I'll take the *maybe eaten* over the *definitely devoured*.

But I realize, terror ripping through me, that I may have taken too long to act. Zombies are staggering from the house in front of us.

One enormous zombie, wearing swim shorts and half-deflated water wings, stands in our way.

"Globlet, hang on!" I shout, and I dart forward. Globlet slips off my shoulder, then manages to grab my hair. She smacks, smacks, smacks against my back as I run.

The water-wings zombie lunges toward me. I yank the Rifter polearm from my backpack and skid to a quick stop. Maybe too quick—

"AIEE!" Globlet shouts as she goes flying over my head, still clutching my hair, then *slams* into my face.

"Let go!" I shout. "I can't see!"

"*You* let go!" Globlet exclaims.

"I'm not holding you!"

"Your fur is! Tell your fur to let go!"

"It's not *fur*, it's *my hair*!!"

"I HATE YOUR HUMAN HAIR-FUR!" Globlet shouts.

# MUURGGH!

The swimming pool zombie's moan is loud. I can't see, but I swing anyway. Whacking and slashing and snapping the polearm through the air. But I miss my target every time!

"Where is it, Globlet!?" I bark.

Globlet is less than helpful. . . .

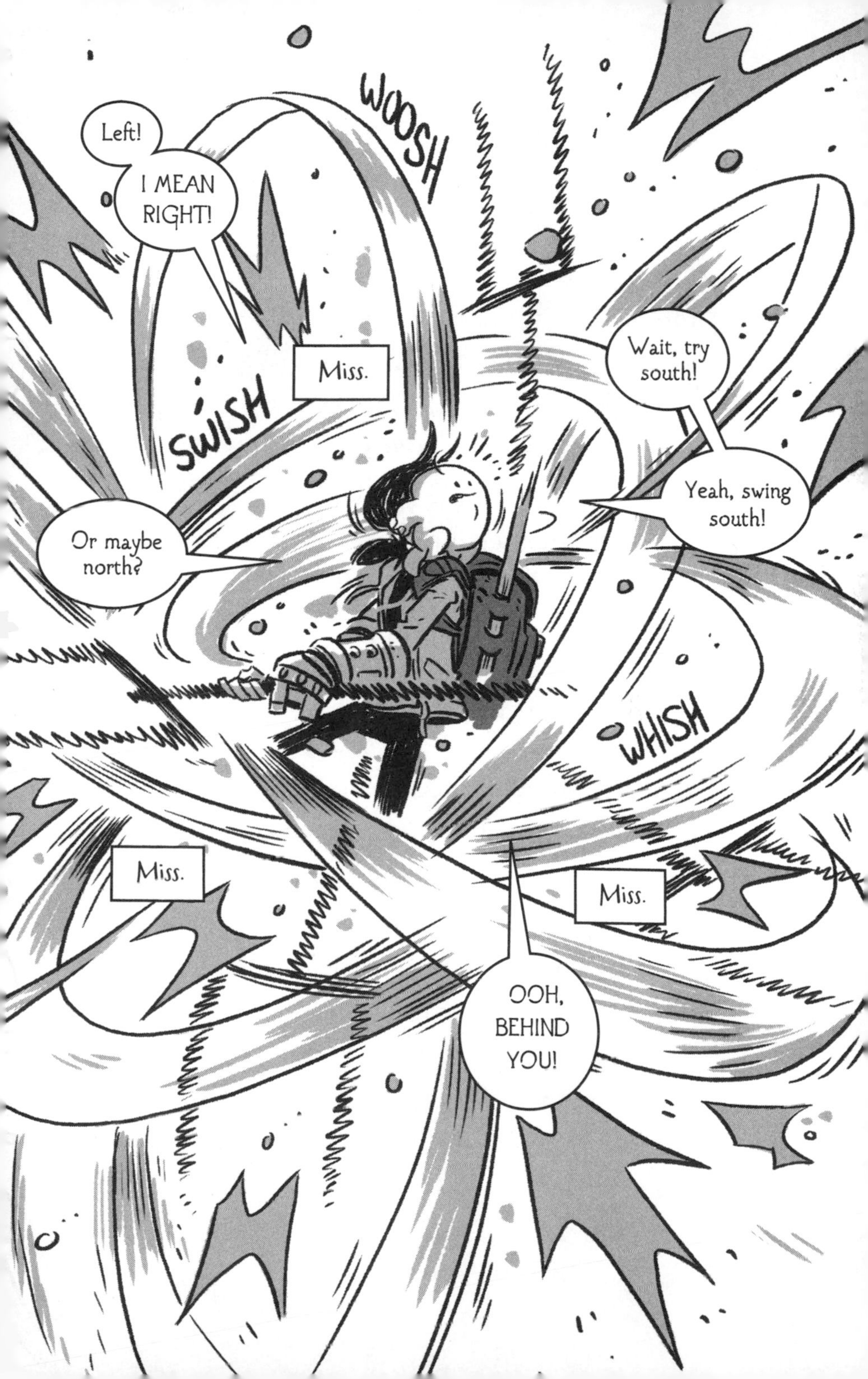
Left!
I MEAN RIGHT!
WOOSH
SWISH
Miss.
Wait, try south!
Yeah, swing south!
Or maybe north?
WHISH
Miss.
Miss.
OOH, BEHIND YOU!

Finally, Globlet says, "LET ME HANDLE THIS!" and she *pounces* from my head, toward the zombie. I can finally see—and I watch, in awe, as—*smack!*

Globlet slams into the zombie's chest, then slides to the ground. She shrieks, "Back off, bozo! This is a June and Globlet adventure play date and you weren't invited!"

The staggered zombie leans down, swiping for her. But she scuttles beneath his legs, grabbing one moldy flip-flop and pulling his feet out from under him. The zombie topples to the ground with a loud—

# THUNK!

I scoop Globlet up, carrying her like a football in the crook of my arm, as I speed toward the massive vine that leads up and over the house.

We scramble up, finally reaching the top— the point where the baby Wretch disappeared. Behind us, zombies are swarming the lawn and pawing at the thick vine. But I don't look back— I just look forward.

"We better not see that Wretch again," I say as we set out.

"Don't worry!" Globlet says cheerfully. "I'm sure we won't!"

# chapter eleven

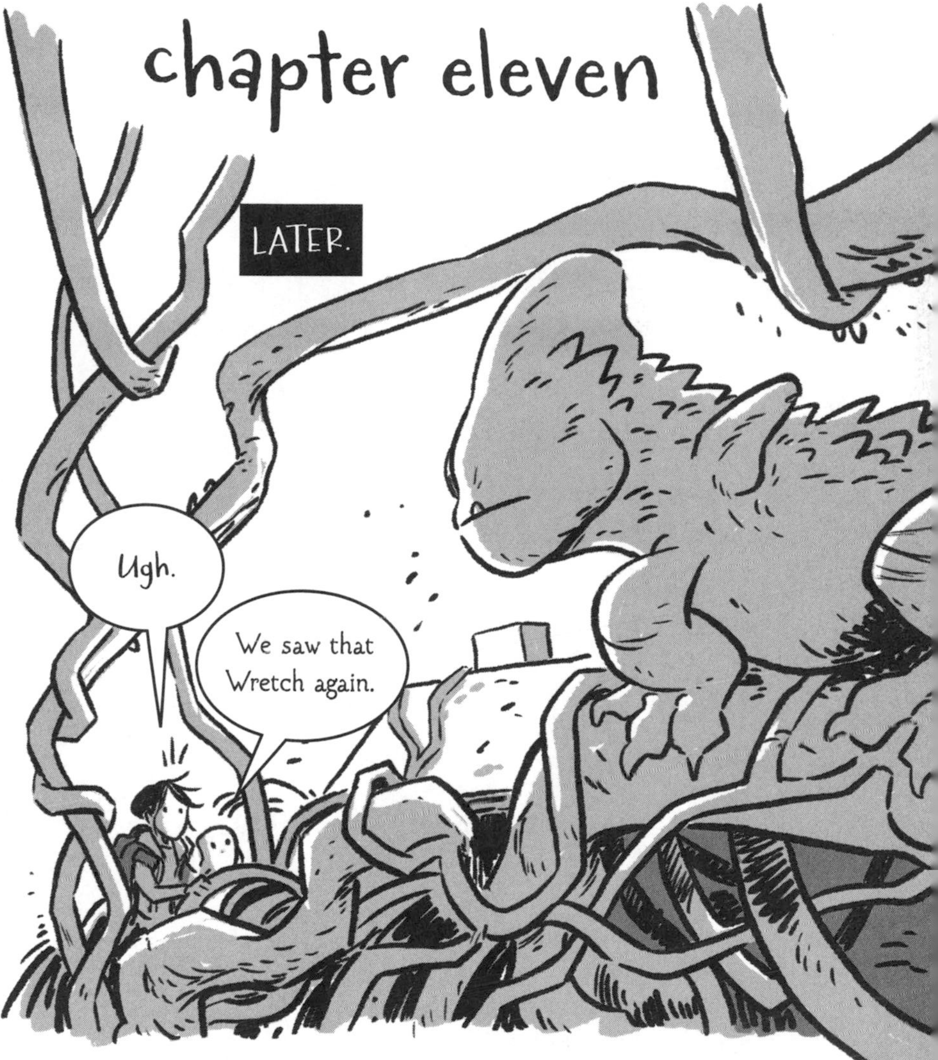
LATER.
Ugh.
We saw that Wretch again.

Globlet and I followed the thick vine, which led us down to a narrow, crooked alley that we *never* would have found otherwise. And from there, we escaped the head-spinning neighborhood maze.

And I thought we left this thing behind us too.

But nope. He's here.

He doesn't bare his teeth or flash his talons or anything. He just . . . watches us.

"Maybe it's like, y'know—when you see a spider," I say. "And it's just as scared of you as you are of it."

"Which is NOT SCARED AT ALL!" Globlet exclaims. "HI, WRETCH! HUG PARTY?!"

"Globlet!" I snap, throwing my hand over her rubbery mouth hole. "Just, like, don't pay attention to him—and maybe he'll leave. Don't look him in the eye or anything. Just be, like, *nonchalant*. . . ."

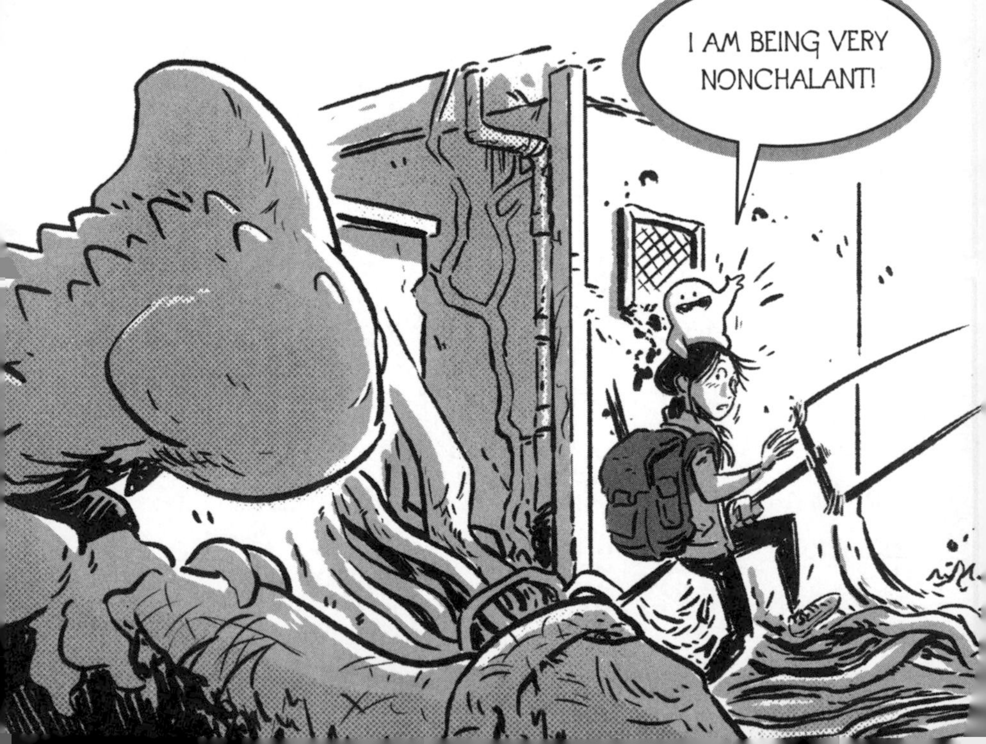
I AM BEING VERY NONCHALANT!

I glance back, just to see if he's still there.

He is.

He's hanging behind, but doesn't get too close. It's almost like HE'S wary of US. Which is *insane*.

He just, like . . . wants to be nearby.

Which would be fine, if he wasn't *evil*. Finally, I'm just too fed up. . . .

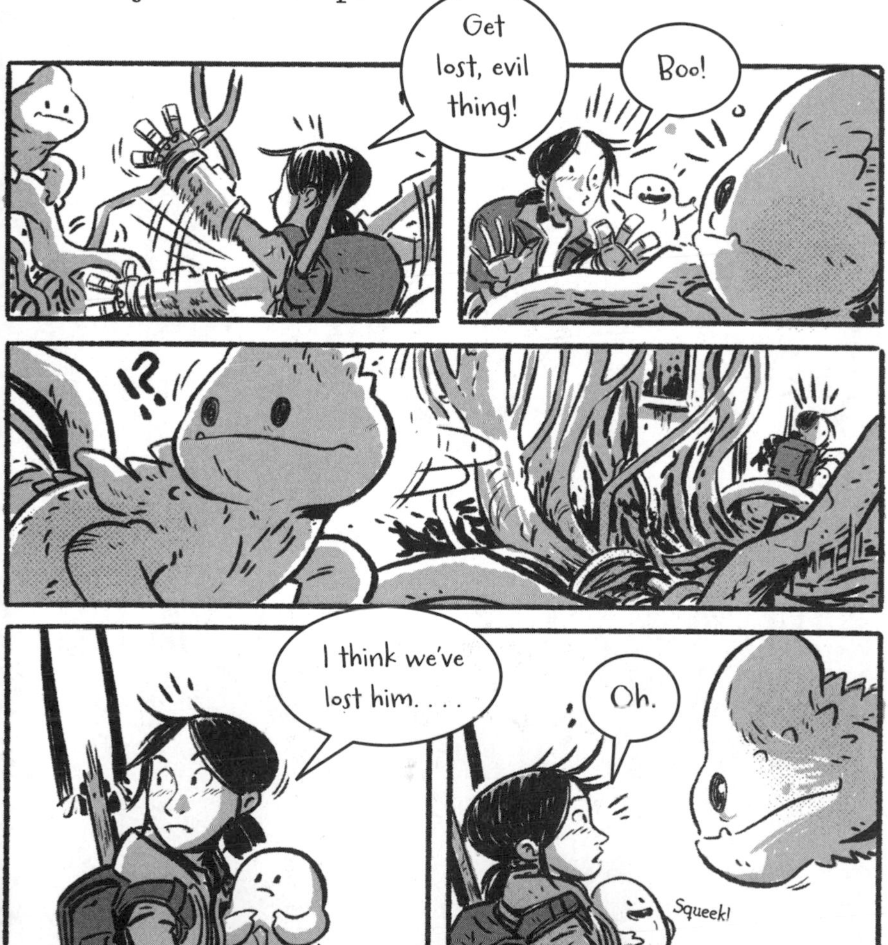
Get lost, evil thing!
Boo!
!?
I think we've lost him. . . .
Oh.
Squeek!

I turn to the Wretch and exclaim, "I don't know what you want—but whatever it is, I don't have it!"

The creature looks at me, and our eyes catch. Suddenly, a brief burst of Wretch-like *vision* appears in my mind.

*A tennis ball hitting the zombie. . . .*

*My locker at school—*

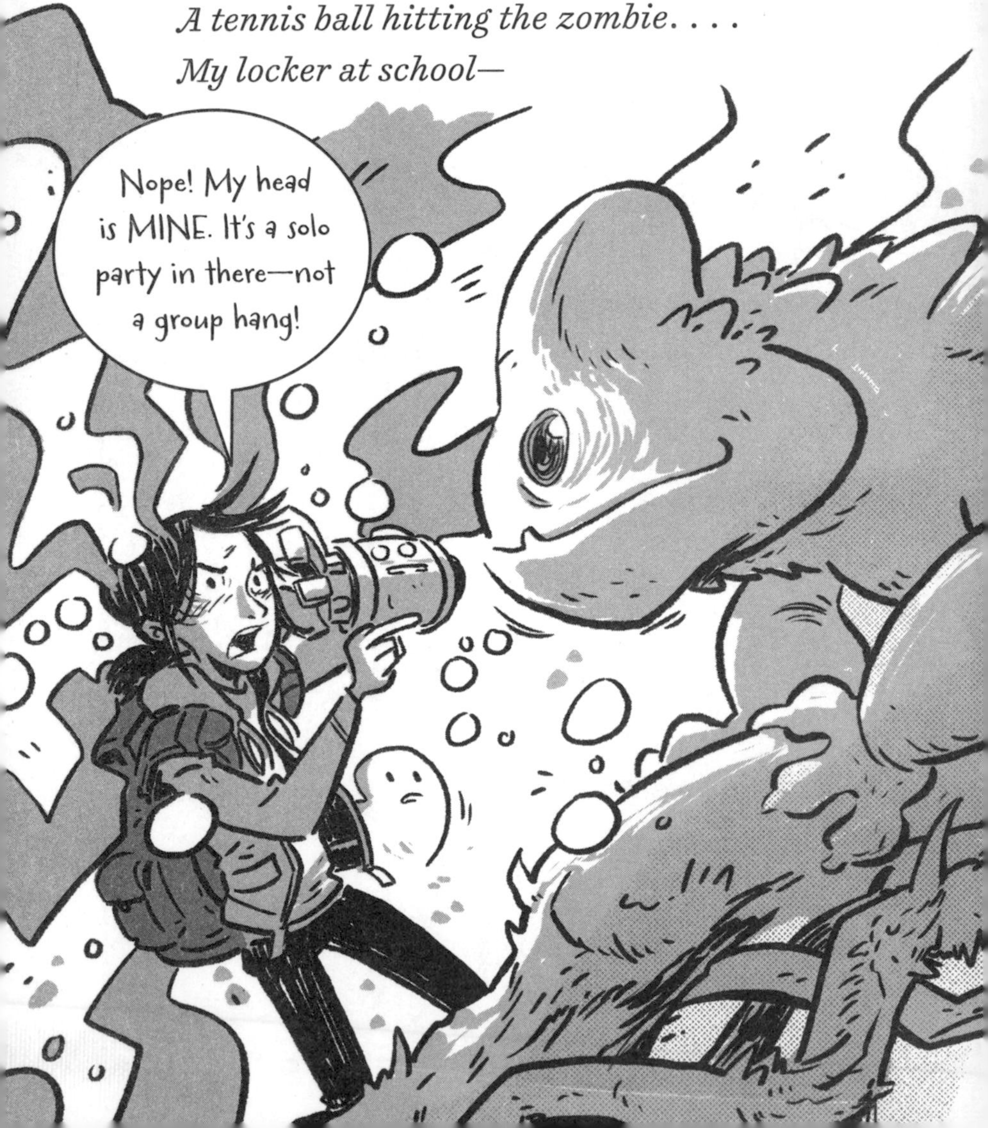
Nope! My head is MINE. It's a solo party in there—not a group hang!

All my shouting works.

The vision, which was just beginning to bubble up, stops.

But as it clears, my eyes catch sight of a huge electrical tower in the distance, and I can't help but think—*TOWER*.

Argh. I look away, shaking my head. My gut is overriding my brain in a big way.

"Globlet," I say softly. "I know what we have to do. . . ."

"Yup." She nods. "Rob a bank!" Globlet says, just as I say, "Get him back home."

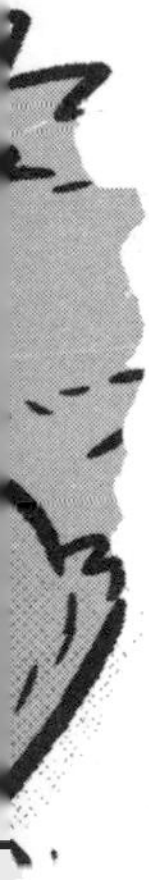

"Nope, Globlet. Not 'rob a bank.' The answer is never 'rob a bank.'"

"Never?"

"Never."

She kicks the ground and mutters.

We need to get him someplace *safe*. Someplace the Rifters won't find him—because if they do, they'll hand him over to Thrull.

This creature is just a baby. A *Winged Wretch baby*, but still. He's alone and he's hurt, and that was why I helped him back at the playground.

I can't just stop helping him now. Solo adventure or not.

"Okay, here's the deal, Wretch," I say. I pace a little bit, trying to find my words. Finally, I set my jaw and tell him. . . .

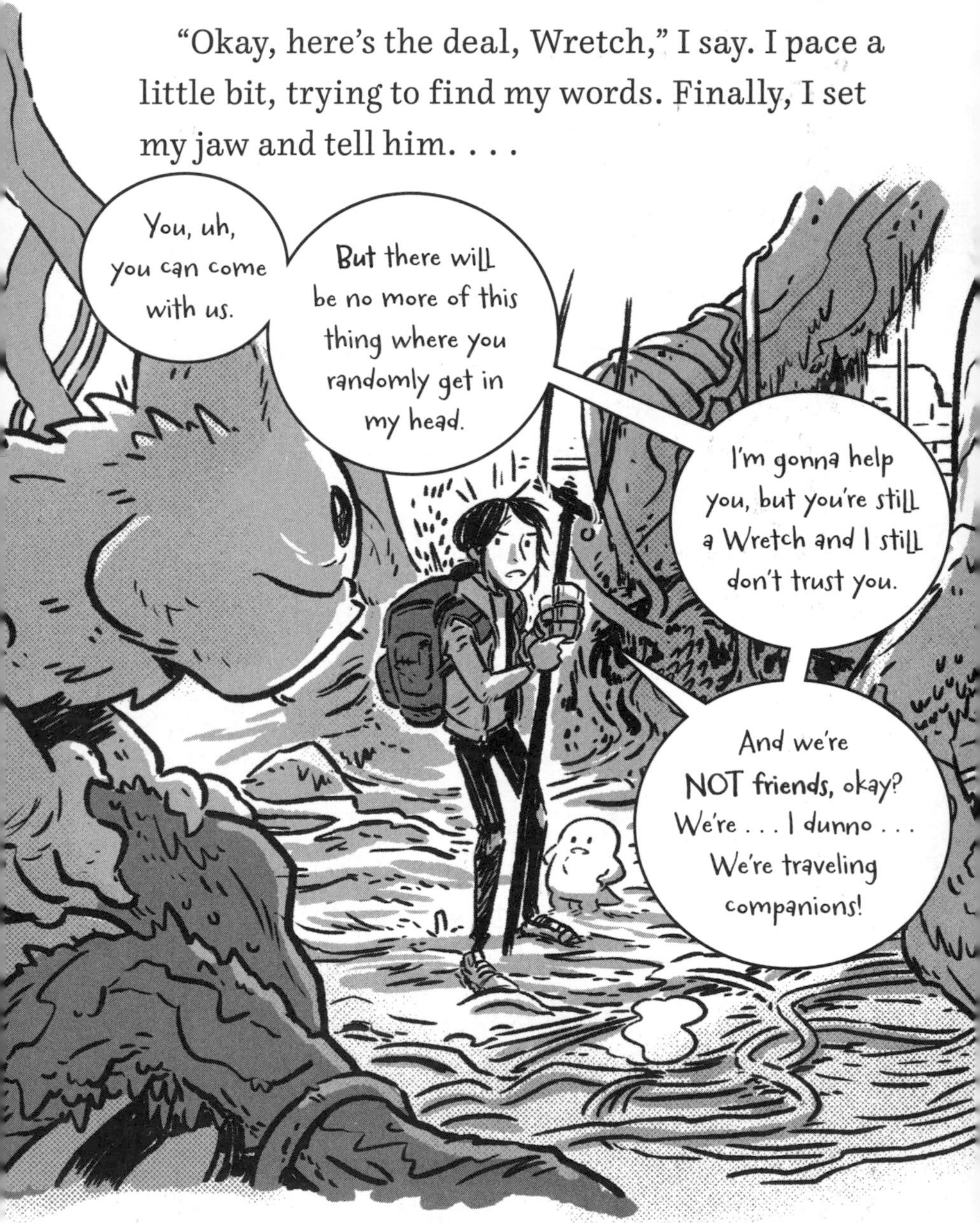
You, uh, you can come with us.
But there will be no more of this thing where you randomly get in my head.
I'm gonna help you, but you're still a Wretch and I still don't trust you.
And we're NOT friends, okay? We're . . . I dunno . . . We're traveling companions!

The creature squawks. I think it's with delight.

"Y'know," Globlet says. "He needs a name, if he's going to be your trusty friendship chum—"

"He's not my 'trusty friendship chum'! Didn't you hear what I just—"

Suddenly, some sort of rat-rodent critter skitters past us, and the Wretch chases after it, like a beagle puppy after a squirrel. All I see is a flash of neon and—

"COME BACK, NEON!" Globlet shouts.

"Wait . . . *Neon*?" I ask. "Where'd you get the name Neon?"

"Helloooo. He's all neon-looking!" Globlet says. "Why? You think it's a bad name?"

"No, it's fine. We just hadn't, like, agreed on it. And then you just started using it. I was just caught off-guard."

And then I'm caught off-guard again: *Neon* reappears, poking his head over a pile of rubble.

"Okay, Neon, so now we get you home," I say, taking a big, dramatic, first-man-on-the-moon sorta step forward. We brave souls are going to *get you home* and *away from Thrull.*

"And where is his home?" Globlet asks.

"Oh right," I say, and stop. "Good question. We should probably know that before we—"

# WHACK!

And the ground beneath my feet SPRINGS open with a loud *SNAP*. I go tumbling back. Wiping dirt from my eyes, I see that the ground I was standing on was not ground at all. It was the *door* to a *port-a-potty*!

First of all, gross.

Second, *who opened the door?*

"Well, hello there, fine gentlefolks!" a voice says. A little monster is climbing from the overturned toilet, like it's emerging from a secret, underground bunker.

And then, half a second later, just as I'm getting a glimpse of this thing—

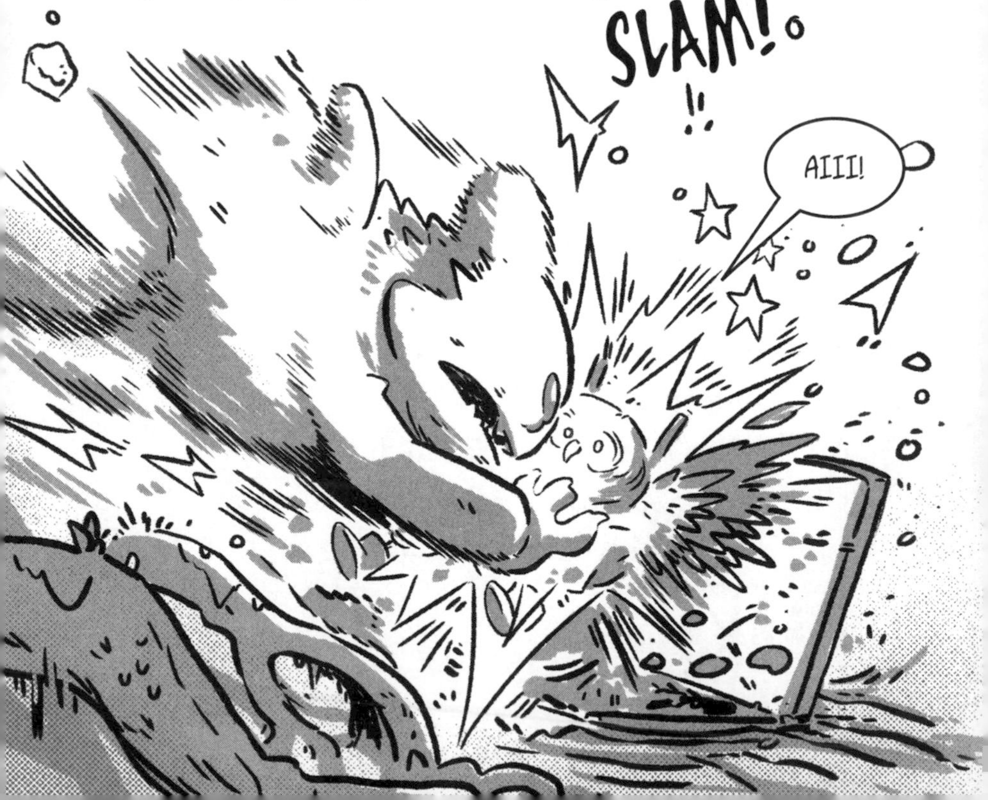
SLAM!
AIII!

# chapter twelve

Neon is on him in a flash, growling, talons
pinning the monster to the ground. Neon's
mouth is half-open, and pink-yellow saliva is
dripping onto the creature's face.

"Whoa!" I cry. "Neon, stop! We don't attack
strangers!"

"We HUG strangers!" Globlet says.

I groan. "No, Globlet! Not that. DEFINITELY
not that. No attacking, no hugging!"

Neon sniffs the creature, then glances over at
me—like he's asking if he can eat the thing.

"That's a hard no, Neon," I say.

Neon reluctantly retreats, allowing the
monster to compose himself. The creature
stands, brushes himself off, and I finally get to
see him—really see him—for the first time. He
vaguely resembles an oversized owl on his way to
a beginner's magic class.

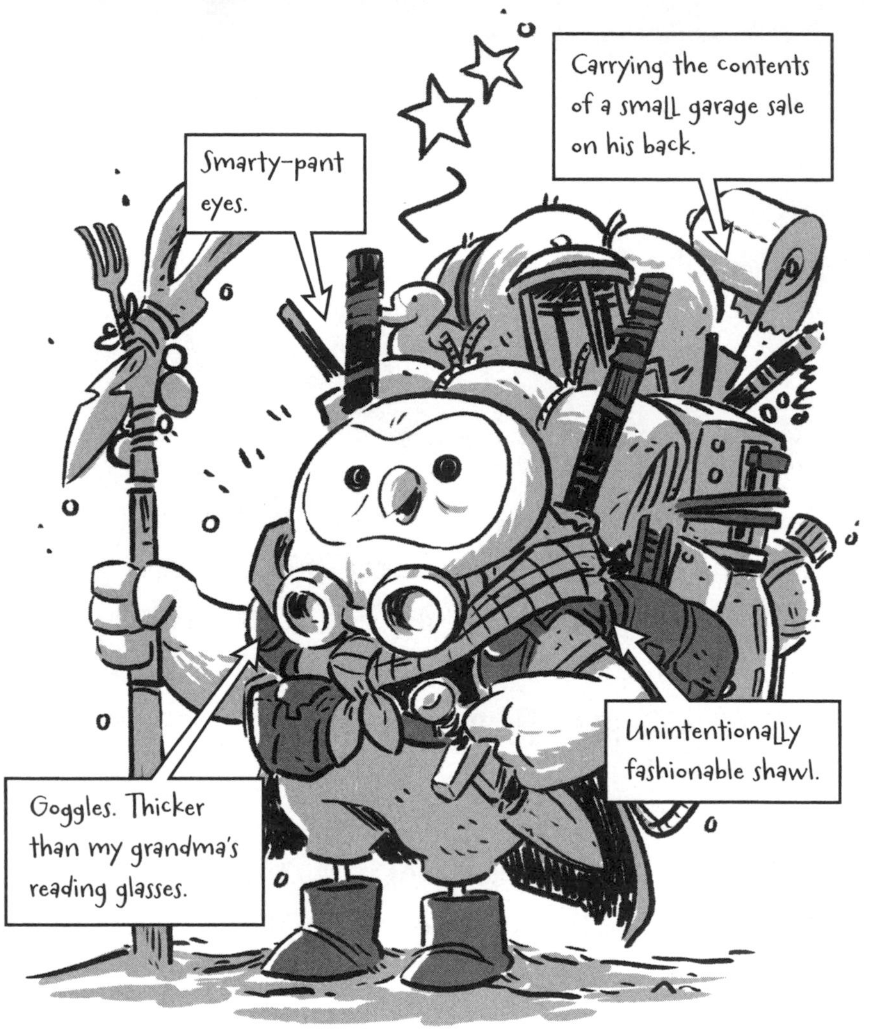
Smarty-pant eyes.
Carrying the contents of a small garage sale on his back.
Goggles. Thicker than my grandma's reading glasses.
Unintentionally fashionable shawl.

Suddenly, this oversized-owl dude breaks into a huge smile. "Oh-ho!" he exclaims, pointing a finger at me. "I know *exactly* what you are!"

"Confused?" I say.

"Please! Remain still while I fetch my publications!"

The owl-type monster dives back into the port-a-potty. I hear crashing and banging, like a bunch of pots and pans are having a wresting match. When he re-emerges, his goggles are on and he's balancing a huge stack of books.

Neon apparently isn't amused by any of this— because he jogs off, sniffing and exploring.

"I know it's in one of these . . ." says the owl dude, pushing the books forward, then lifting himself out of the port-a-potty.

He riffles through the books, then stops and buries his beak in one. "Of course! I know from my expertise of this dimension that you are surely a . . . parakeet and a microwave, two earth-bound creatures known for their closely bonded relationship."

"Nope. Human."

"And I'm Globlet. I'm not a microwave. *Anymore.*"

"Of course!" the owl barks. "That's what I said!"

"You said parakeet and micro—"

"No, you misheard. See, I don't want to brag," he says, in the tone of someone who is *definitely* about to brag, "but I am something of a human EXPERT. However, you are actually the first human I've met *in the flesh!*"

"Ya don't say . . ." I manage. I might be hangry because I'm feeling *extra impatient.*

"Ooh!" he exclaims, suddenly very excited. "Can we do the human thing?"

I blink twice.

"You knowww," he says. "The one with the hands!"

I guess he means handshake? The only non-human I ever met who shook hands was Mr. Peppers, and that's only because we spent like seven months training him. And even then you had to give him a bacon-flavored biscuit as a reward.

I stick out my hand, then pause. "You wash your hands after using your . . . uh, *home*, right?"

Too late—

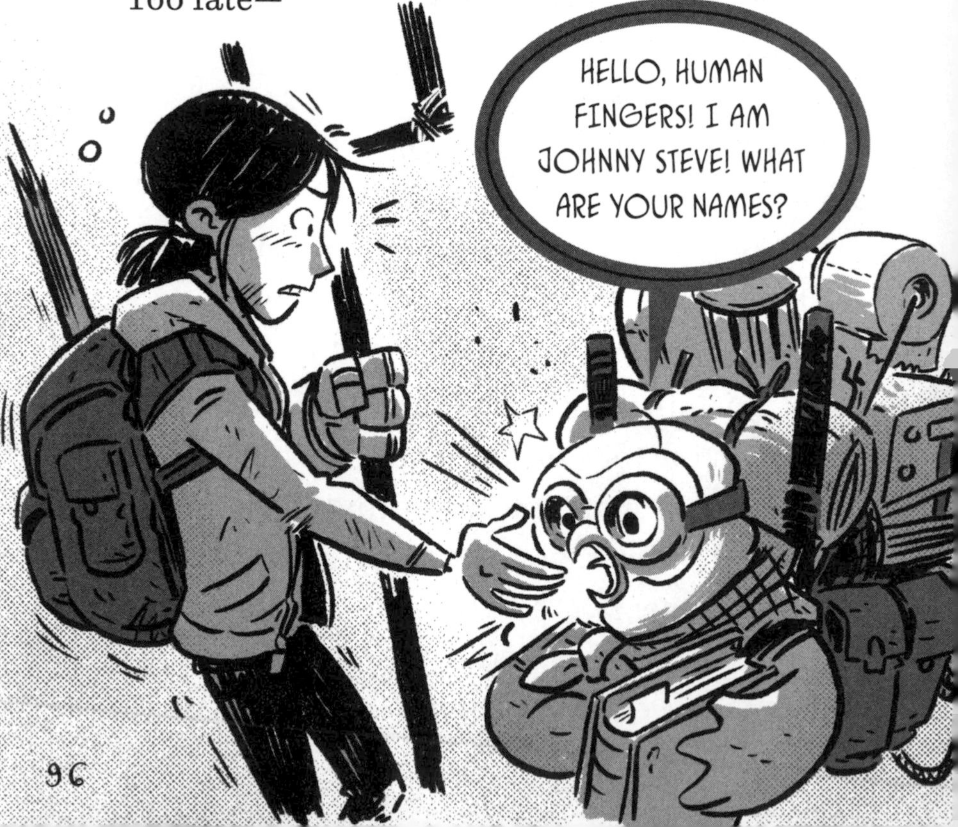
HELLO, HUMAN FINGERS! I AM JOHNNY STEVE! WHAT ARE YOUR NAMES?

"Okaaaay, that's enough of that!" I say, yanking my hand away. "And I'm sorry, did you say your name was *Johnny Steve*?"

The owl-type monster—Johnny Steve—nods enthusiastically. "I named *myself* so that I would fit in with any humans I encounter. I chose a name from your giant yellow books of telephone numbers!"

"Aww man, I wanna name myself!" Globlet whines. "From now on, call me PATTYCAKE HAMBURGER JONES!"

Johnny Steve bows graciously. "PLEASED TO MEET YOU, PATTYCAKE HAM—"

"NOPE! NOPE! Shutting that down!" I say. "Globlet, you're Globlet. And sure—why not—you're *Johnny Steve*. I'm June. And this ferocious weirdo is Neon."

Neon is busy poking his snout around Johnny Steve's port-a-potty. Glancing back, Johnny Steve explains. "You see, being a human expert," he says, "I chose to make my home in the place humans love most . . . THE TOILET. Did you know humans LOVE toilets? Even more than flowers, pizza, or the internet!"

I'm about to explain that he's mostly wrong there. And that, also, you never really know how much you love toilets until all the real ones stop working. But then—

*KRR-CHHHHHH!*

A hiss at my belt!

The walkie!

It startles me, and I do a little leap backward. We must be back in signal range! I'm eagerly reaching for it, yanking it from my belt, when—

*POW!* Neon pounces, snatching the walkie from my hand in his teeth!

"No!" I cry. My hand is grasping the base and we're locked in a tug-of-war. "No! Give . . . it . . . back! Bad Wretch! Bad Neon!"

I pull harder, but that only makes Neon pull harder. He's bouncing happily from paw to paw, like this is the best game ever. His glowing saliva splashes the walkie. My hands are slick and I feel my grip loosening. "Tug-of-war *is* fun," I groan, "but this is NOT the time—"

## GULP!

He swallows the walkie, as my hands slip and I fall backward.

Neon thrusts his chest out and smiles proudly. He seems to think he just saved me from some sort of buzzing, box-shaped bug.

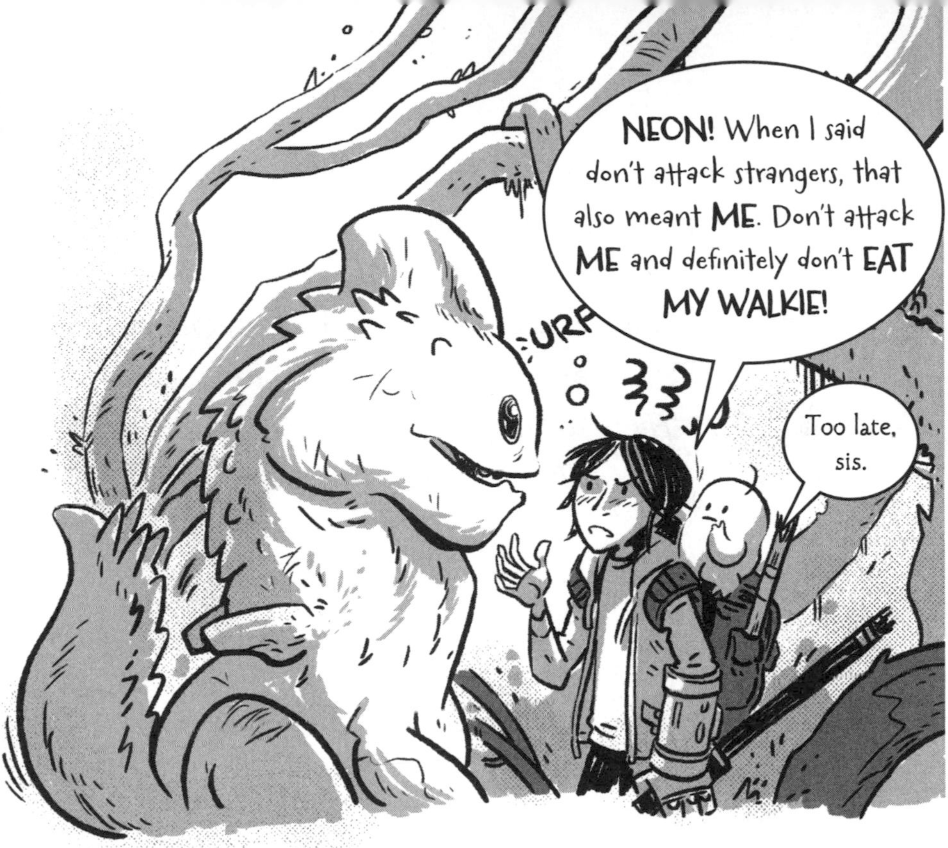
NEON! When I said don't attack strangers, that also meant ME. Don't attack ME and definitely don't EAT MY WALKIE!
URP
Too late, sis.

"Just great," I say with a sigh. No walkie. No getting in touch with my friends. No hope of the cavalry showing up to help me. I plunk down on a nearby rock, shoving my backpack aside, feeling pretty hopeless.

Johnny Steve waddles over. He pulls back his hood and looks me in the eyes. "You look like you have chosen to embark on a grand quest."

"Ehh," I say with a shrug. "Not sure I *chose* to embark on a grand quest. But yeah, me and Globlet are trying to get this walkie-eating monster back to his own kind. Only, I have no idea where to find his kind. Or what I'd even do if I did find them. Wretches are—"

"Evil," Johnny Steve says in a mysterious whisper. "Indeed, the adults of that species are very foul. They serve . . ." He looks around, then whispers, *He Who Shall Be Named a Whole Bunch.*"

"Wait, wait—*what*? He Who Shall—"

Rezžőch! the Ancient, Destructor of Worlds!

Y'know, Rezžőch! The reason we're all here! Don't you know about Rezžőch?!

You call yourself a human, but you don't know about Rezžőch even a bit?! Oh, blammo, Rezžőch is the worst. The most awful, evil, super-Rezžőch-y, just bad news—

"Dude!" I bark. "I know about Ŗeżżőcħ. That's why we're trying to get Neon someplace safe! A band of Rifters are after him and—"

"Ahh, Rifters," Johnny Steve interrupts. "Interdimensional pirates! Bad business. Very bad business. I mean, pirating is a *good business* to be in! Lots of freedom, no pants required. But what you speak of is, overall, a *bad business*."

"These Rifters are trying to deliver that Wretch to Thrull."

"Thrull!" he exclaims, nodding. "The talk of the land! Of course the Rifters would go to him—they side with whoever has the most power."

"Wait," I say. "What do *you* know about Thrull? Do you know about the Tower? And, ugh, did you say Thrull is *the talk of the land*?"

Johnny Steve goes quiet. After a moment, he whispers, "We shouldn't speak of the Tower, human. Leaves a bad taste in our brains. A very bad to-do, it is."

"I know it, duder," I say as I take a tired seat on the ground. "I know it."

Johnny Steve eyes me. Then Globlet. She waves at him. He waves at me. Everything is odd.

Johnny Steve looks like he's considering something major. He paces for a few moments, then suddenly—*whack!*—he taps his staff against the ground. I see that it's both a walking stick and a sword.

"Human June," he says. "I will guide you. I know where there is a Wretches' nest—not so far from here, but not so near either."

I shoot him a skeptical glare. "Why would you help us?"

His little nose pinches inward. "I have explored these lands. I know where you must go, and I know you will not make it alone. Humans are notoriously breakable."

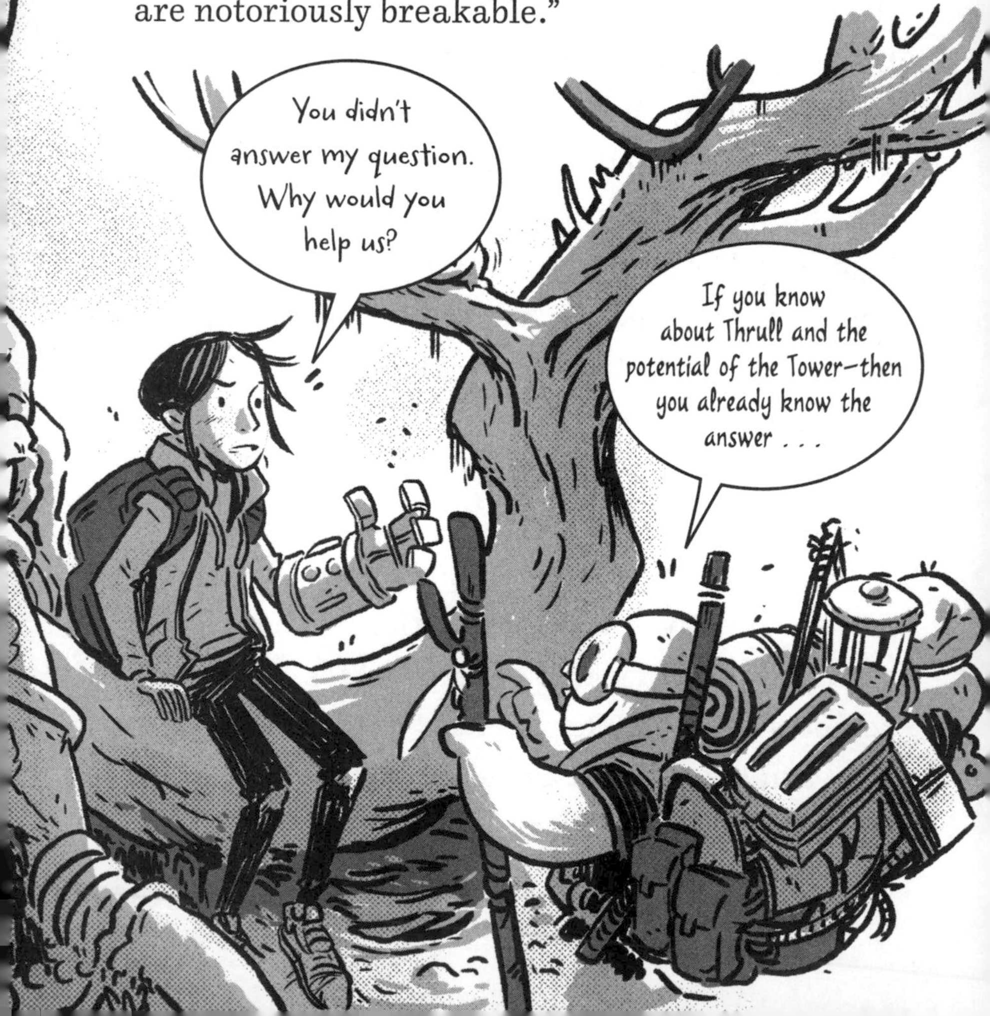
You didn't answer my question. Why would you help us?
If you know about Thrull and the potential of the Tower—then you already know the answer . . .

I look at Globlet, hoping she might offer some sage advice. But Globlet is currently attempting a handstand.

"However!" Johnny Steve says. "I must ask you for something in return."

*Of course. This'll be the part where he bargains for my soul or one of my friends' souls or asks me if I know a place where he can bargain for a soul, quick, no questions asked.*

"In exchange for guiding you," Johnny Steve says, "I request conversation. As I said, I'm a human *expert*—and now that I am in the company of a real human, I am excited to discuss your strange species."

*Not bad*, I think. *Weird, but not bad.*

However, there's one problem. "I'm not super into being led around on a string," I tell him. "I kinda pride myself on being independent."

"Okay, relax, Beyoncé . . ." says Globlet.

I shoot Globlet a look. "How about this, Johnny Steve: you tell *me* where the nest is, and I'll let you tag along with us."

"And we'll talk human stuff?" he asks excitedly.

"You betcha."

"Deal!" he says.

And with that, I tighten my sneakers, jerk my backpack straps, and make sure the Gift is secured around my wrist.

In a flash, Neon is at my side—but I don't shoo him away. I'm ready to get on with this, ready for whatever comes.

And so, we continue our journey—only now, we have a defined destination.

# chapter thirteen

It's a strange, haphazard path.

We cross crumbling bridges that nearly collapse beneath our feet. We march along freeways that have become zombie-filled parking lots. We pass gas stations that are now home to giant, sleeping slugs that sip on gasoline while they snore.

It's a long walk—and Johnny Steve talks the *entire* freaking time.

"I am just *so thrilled* to chat with a bona fide human!" he explains. "My previous attempts at communication have not gone well."

UURRRRM
And what, pray tell, is your favorite pizza topping?

"That was a zombie," I say. "You've been talking to zombies."

It turns out, though, that Johnny Steve doesn't actually much care what *I* think about human life. Instead, HE wants to tell ME about being human. He rattles off a list of his favorite human facts. . . .

1.) Humans can breathe underwater, but they choose not to (because of the odor).

2.) Humans didn't **always** have hair. However, they were cursed by a magical being known as the Hair Bear and humans now have **too much hair.** No more feathers or scales. Also, the Hair Bear lives in North Dakota in a beautiful motorhome.

3.) "The most famous human in the history of human history" is a wizard named Barry Potter.

"Okay, hold up!" I say. This guy can mangle human anatomy all day long—but I will *not* let him mess with HP. "It's HARRY Potter."

Johnny Steve gives me a quizzical look. "Don't be ridiculous," he scoffs. "Harry Potter is a fictional wizard from a book!"

"Wait. But, you said—"

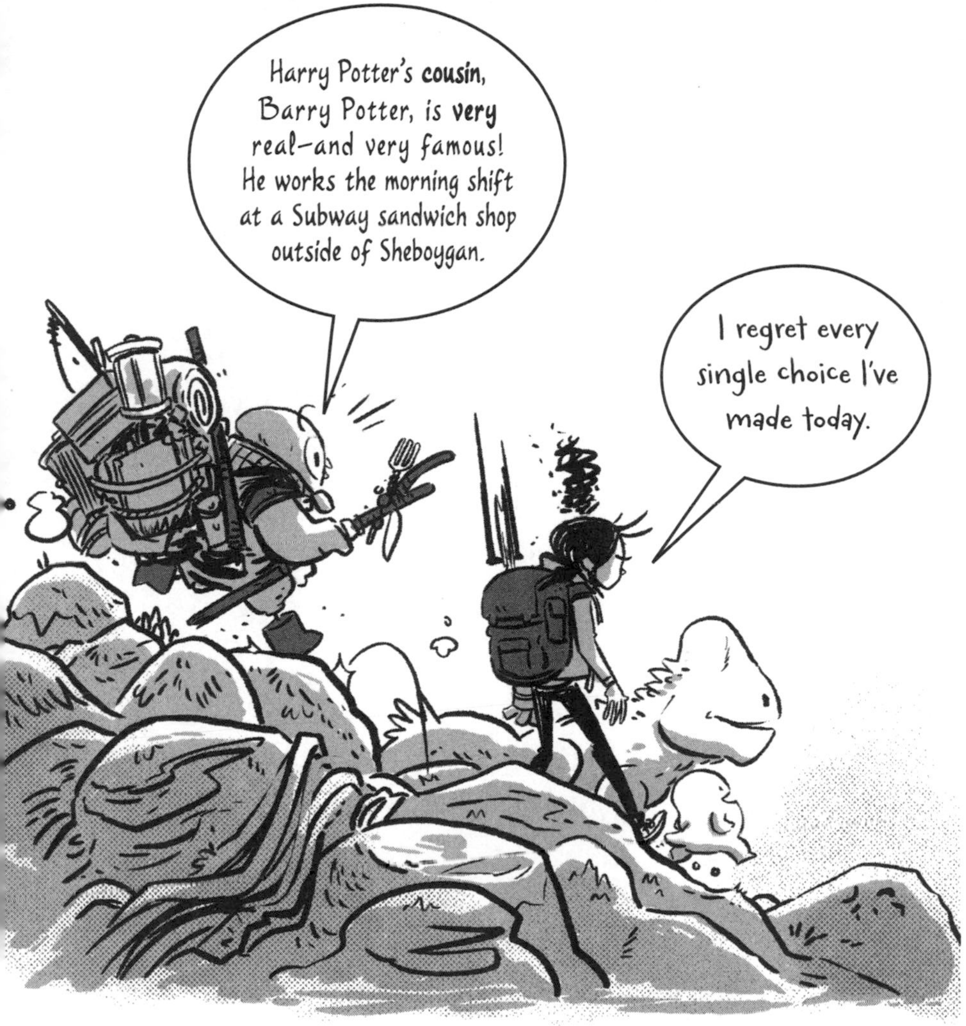
Harry Potter's **cousin**, Barry Potter, is **very** real—and very famous! He works the morning shift at a Subway sandwich shop outside of Sheboygan.
I regret every single choice I've made today.

"Also," I add, getting a little peeved, "I AM a human! So you don't need to explain human stuff to me. Don't you think I'd know if I could breathe underwater? No human can. Except for Kevin Costner. And I don't know what that means, but I heard Jack say it once in his sleep."

"Oh, indeed!" Johnny Steve says. "No one can

breathe underwater like Kevin Costner! He's top-notch! But you're certainly *able*. You just haven't tried hard enough."

For a moment, I wonder if Neon had the right idea when he almost ate Johnny Steve's face.

Now, though—Neon's in his own world. He's like the world's most untrained, out of control, harebrained puppy. He just keeps rushing ahead, eating stuff, breaking stuff, then hurrying back to us like, *See? See what I did there? Did you see me eat that street sign? Wasn't that just AMAZING?*

"There," Johnny Steve says, interrupting my train of thought. He's pointing ahead. "We need to cross *that* to get the creature to his family."

My heart sinks.

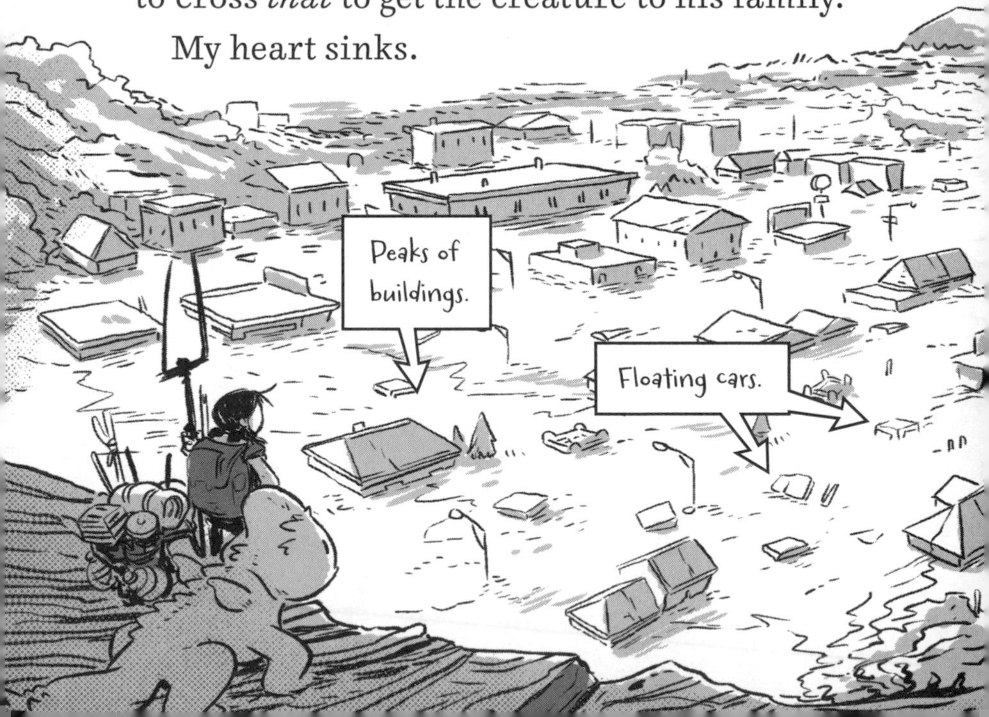
Peaks of buildings.
Floating cars.

# chapter fourteen

Water.

So much water.

It is a town, completely flooded. And there's no way around it. . . .

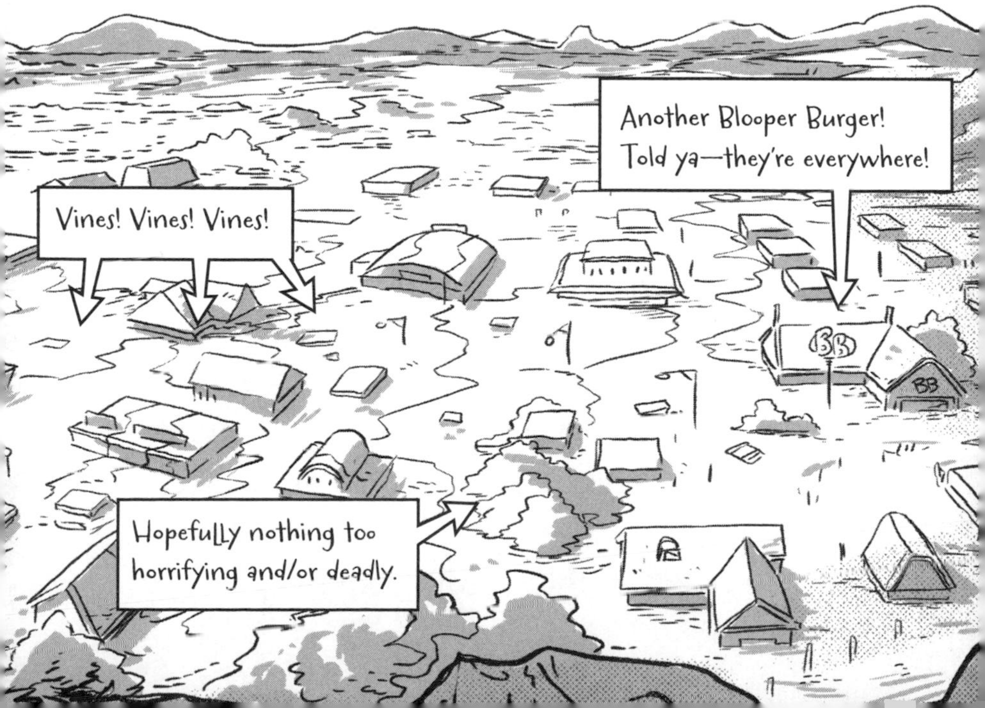
Another Blooper Burger! Told ya—they're everywhere!
Vines! Vines! Vines!
Hopefully nothing too horrifying and/or deadly.

I've got a bad feeling about this. And not just because I didn't pack a swimsuit.

"How are we supposed to get across?" I ask.

"Ooh! I got it! I got it!!" Globlet exclaims. "What if . . . I inflate like a life raft and pull us all across?"

"Wait, you can inflate like a life raft?!?" I ask.

"Oh. Oh, right. Yeah, no. I can't. Never mind, ignore that idea."

I sigh and take a step forward. I evaluate the situation like a reporter, mining the facts for any information we can *use*.

There appears to be enough floating wreckage—cars, trucks, garbage—for us to jump from one to the next. I think, *Just like crossing a stream by hopping from rock to rock. Only way more intense.*

Neon runs to the edge of the water, then looks back—he's eager to cross. "Okay," I say. "I've seen you leap about and launch yourself. Now you're gonna do the same—from thing to thing—all the way across."

I reach into my backpack and pull out my spear that was split in two from being dragged by the Ogre. I hand a piece to Johnny Steve. "We're going to pole-vault. Like the Olympics.

We can make it all the way across without ever touching water."

For myself, I use the polearm I swiped from the Rifters.

Moments later, we stare out at the watery obstacle course. Then I take a deep breath, crouch, and launch, and we're off—

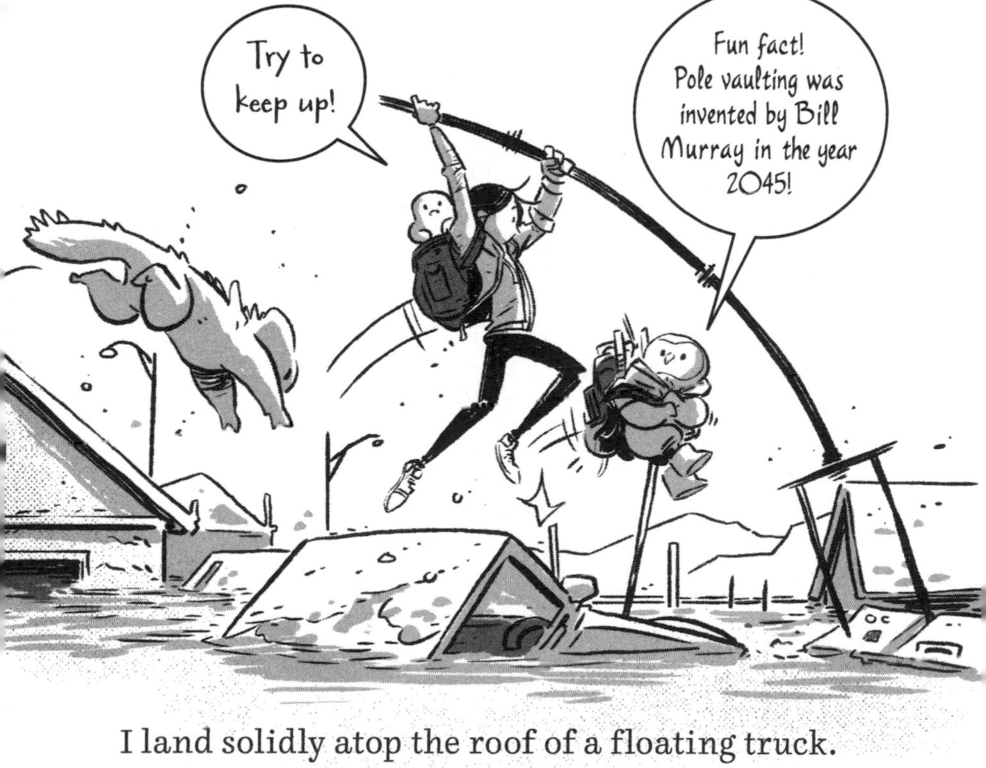
Try to keep up!
Fun fact! Pole vaulting was invented by Bill Murray in the year 2045!

I land solidly atop the roof of a floating truck. Johnny Steve follows—and after a slow, tense moment—Neon jumps, too.

I look around, find the peak of a slanted IHOP roof, and make the next leap.

BAM. Perfect landing.

We continue like this. No talking. We can't afford to lose focus.

We've made it nearly halfway across when Neon seems to be gaining courage. We're standing on the roof of a floating ambulance when Neon gives me this look, like he wants to make sure I'm paying attention.

Then, screwing up his face with determination, he swan-dives off the roof!

I see the moment when Neon would catch the breeze, if he had wings, and find myself holding my breath. It's like I'm hoping maybe extra backup wings are suddenly going to spring out and take him up into the sky.

But . . . nope.

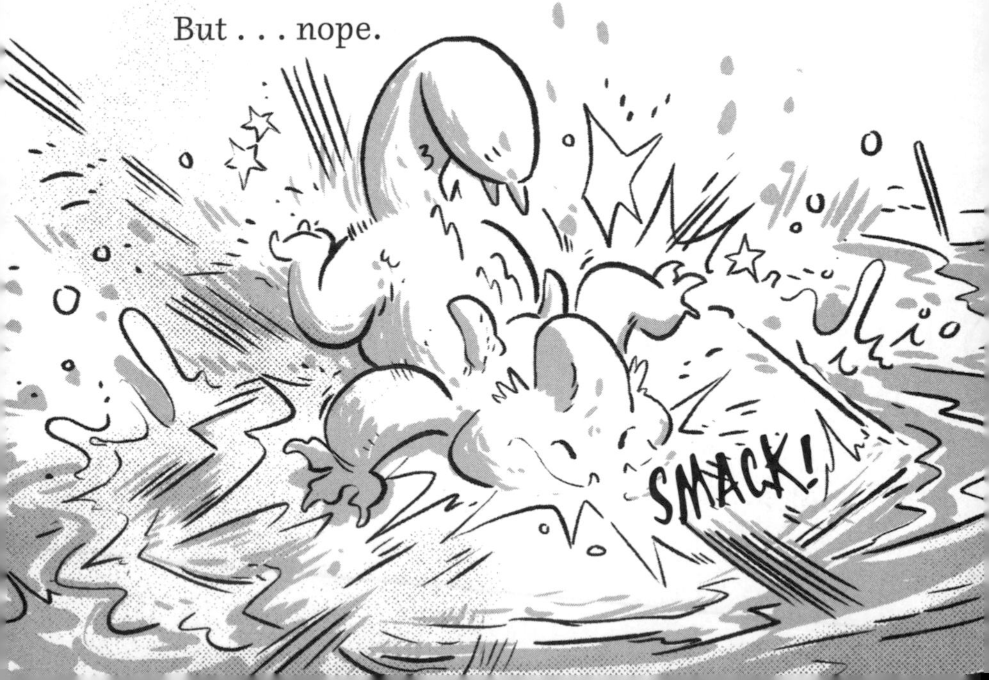
SMACK!

He SMASHES onto our next stop: a tangled mess of floating plastic. He tries to get to his feet, but instead he just lands flat on his belly.

"Neon! What were you thinking?!?" This *is not* the kind of setback we needed. But Neon's the whole reason we're doing this at all.

Suddenly, Johnny Steve is scurrying past me. "Coming, creature!" he says as he vaults off the ambulance and lands on the plastic island.

I'm next, and I hit the plastic surface and slide into Neon. He tries to get up, again, but slips and now he's sliding toward the side. There's a loud *THWACK* as he slams his talons into the plastic.

"Come on, Neon, you can do it! Put a little pumpkin to it!" Johnny Steve calls down. He looks over to me and says, "That's one of my favorite human phrases."

As Neon's talons dig in deeper, I feel the floating hunk of plastic *shake*. Before I can respond, there is a loud—

# BBRRRR-ERRMM

The plastic starts *rising*. I've been in situations like this before, and they don't go well.

"June!" Globlet shrieks. "My tummy's got the flutterbies!"

This plastic is not plastic, I realize. It's *skin*. It's *a body*. And it's rising, coming out of the water, higher and higher.

"EVERYONE, GRAB ON TO SOMETHING!" I shout.

And they do.

*Me*.

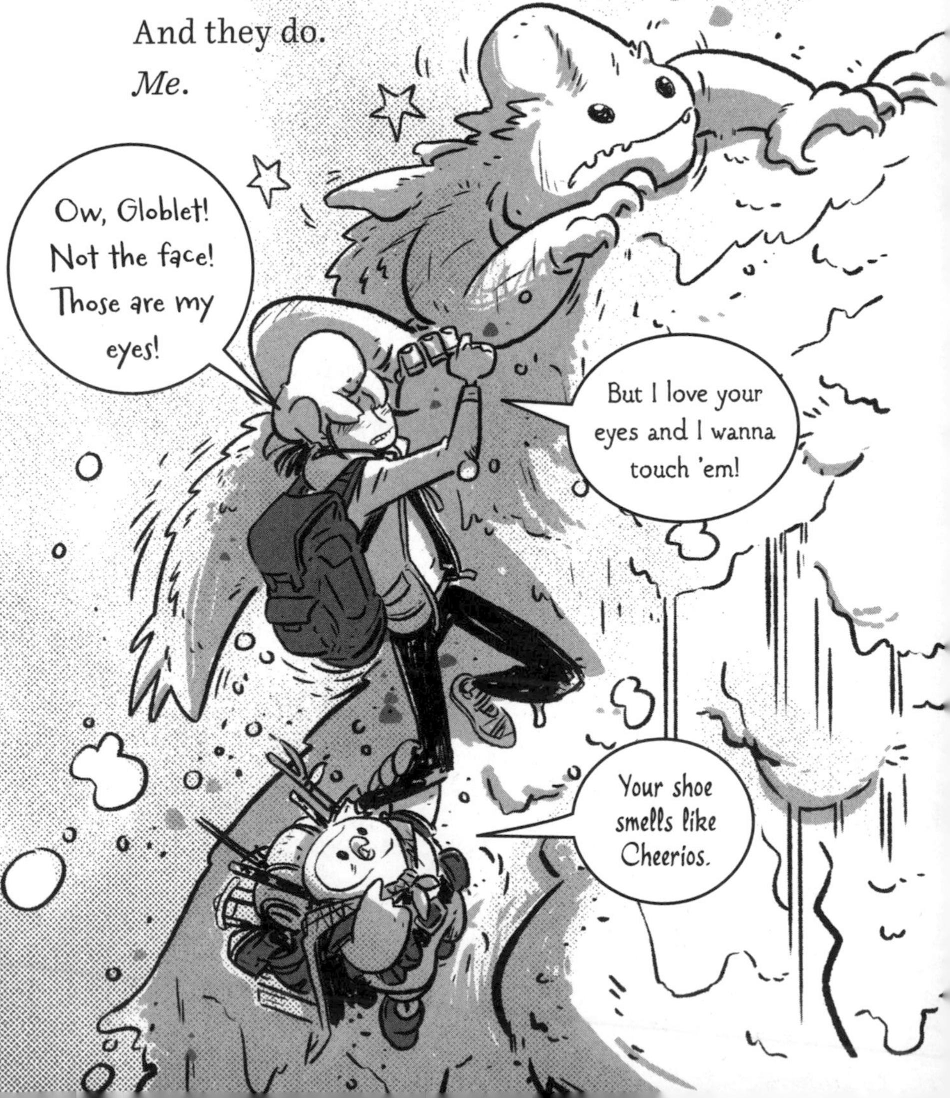
Ow, Globlet! Not the face! Those are my eyes!
But I love your eyes and I wanna touch 'em!
Your shoe smells like Cheerios.

The metal fingers of the Thing-A-Ma-Blasty Gadget Blaster press into this yet-to-be-seen creature's hide.

"YOU GUYS!" I shout. "IF YOU ALL KEEP HANGING ON TO ME THEN NONE OF US ARE GOING TO BE HANGING ON!"

"DON'T WORRY, JUNE!" Johnny Steve shouts. "HUMANS CAN EASILY SURVIVE FALLS UP TO 92,470 FEET!"

"That's not TRUE!" I shout

"In fact, it is! You just don't know enough about—"

"QUIET!" I cry.

Glancing down, I see the floating ambulance below and behind us. It's a big enough target—I think. *I hope.*

Any higher, and the fall will be deadly.

So I'd rather fall now.

"Guys," I manage to spit out. Johnny Steve's claws grip my ankle. "This is gonna hurt. But not on purpose."

And then I jam my sneakers into the creature's hide and kick-push us out, away from the creature, and we're tumbling, dropping, plummeting. . . .

# chapter fifteen

We fall.

And fall.

And then—

**WHAM!**

We hit the ambulance like four tiny comets, crashing to earth. Johnny Steve rolls onto Neon, then I crash into the pair of them, and Globlet flops onto my face.

I shake the cobwebs loose.

Looking up, I see a towering Blooper Burger sign. It's rocking back and forth as the monster rises.

The ambulance is spinning like an inner tube in a wave pool. The sloshing, rolling water grows choppier. The massive monster fully emerges, turning toward us.

And I gasp, because—well . . .

"His face! He's cute!" I blurt out.

"Ermahgerd, SO cute!" Globlet adds.

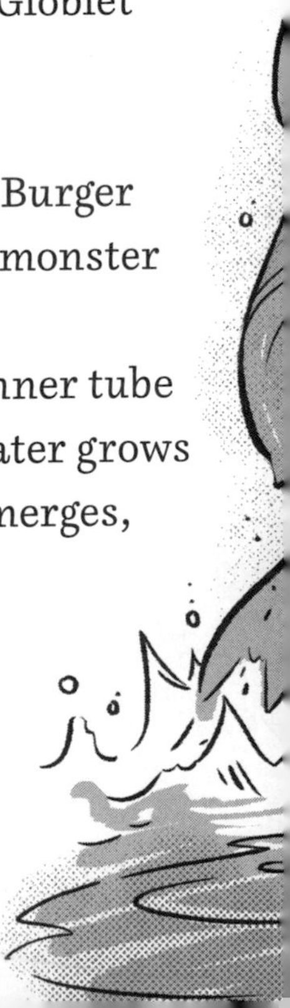

# - Big Ol' Wet Cutie! -

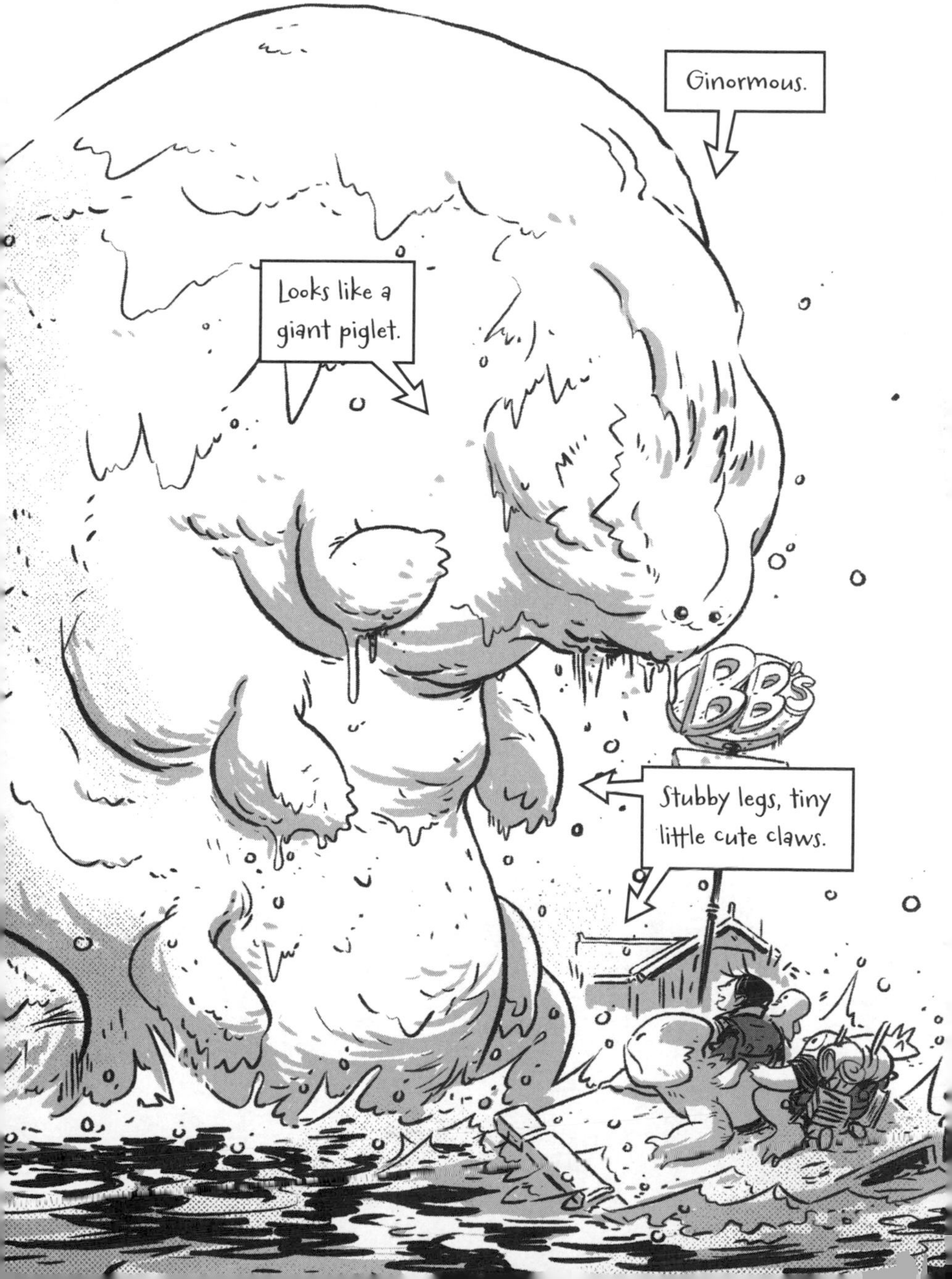
Ginormous.
Looks like a giant piglet.
BB's
Stubby legs, tiny little cute claws.

I hear Johnny Steve staggering to his feet. Neon's talons pierce the ambulance hood, gripping it tight. My back is radiating pain.

"This is all a big giant mess," I say. "But I kinda wanna snuggle that cutie. Is that so wrong?"

"Oh yes," Johnny Steve says. "That *is* so wrong. That is a Ploonk. Ploonks don't snuggle."

Before I can *ask* why—I *see* why.

It happens lightning fast—in an instant, the Ploonk's flesh *rearranges* itself! Bones bend, and its face is splitting, changing, and *opening* like the petals of some horrible, hideous flower.

Its huggable, pig-faced snout is gone—replaced by a face only a mother could love.

And even then, that would have to be one *hugely* big-hearted mama.

The Ploonk's maw opens wide, and a tornado of tremendous, screaming air is unleashed—

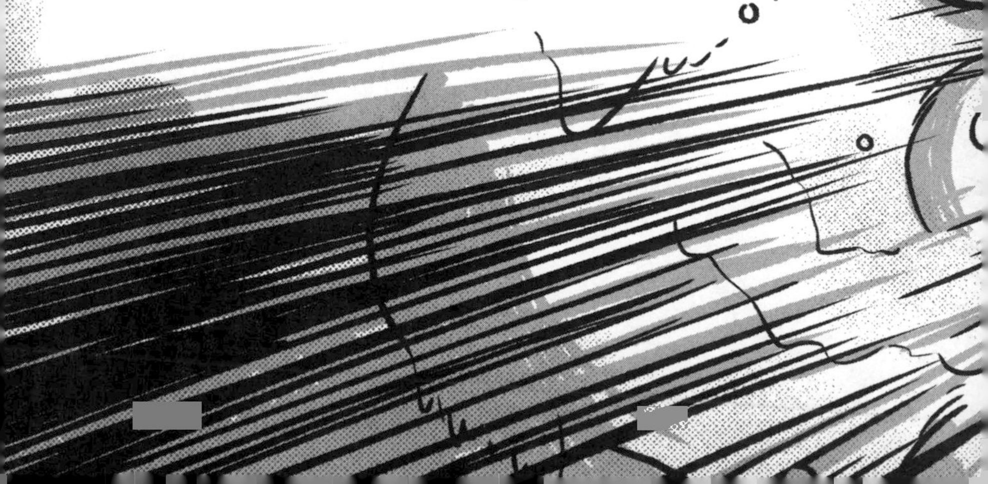

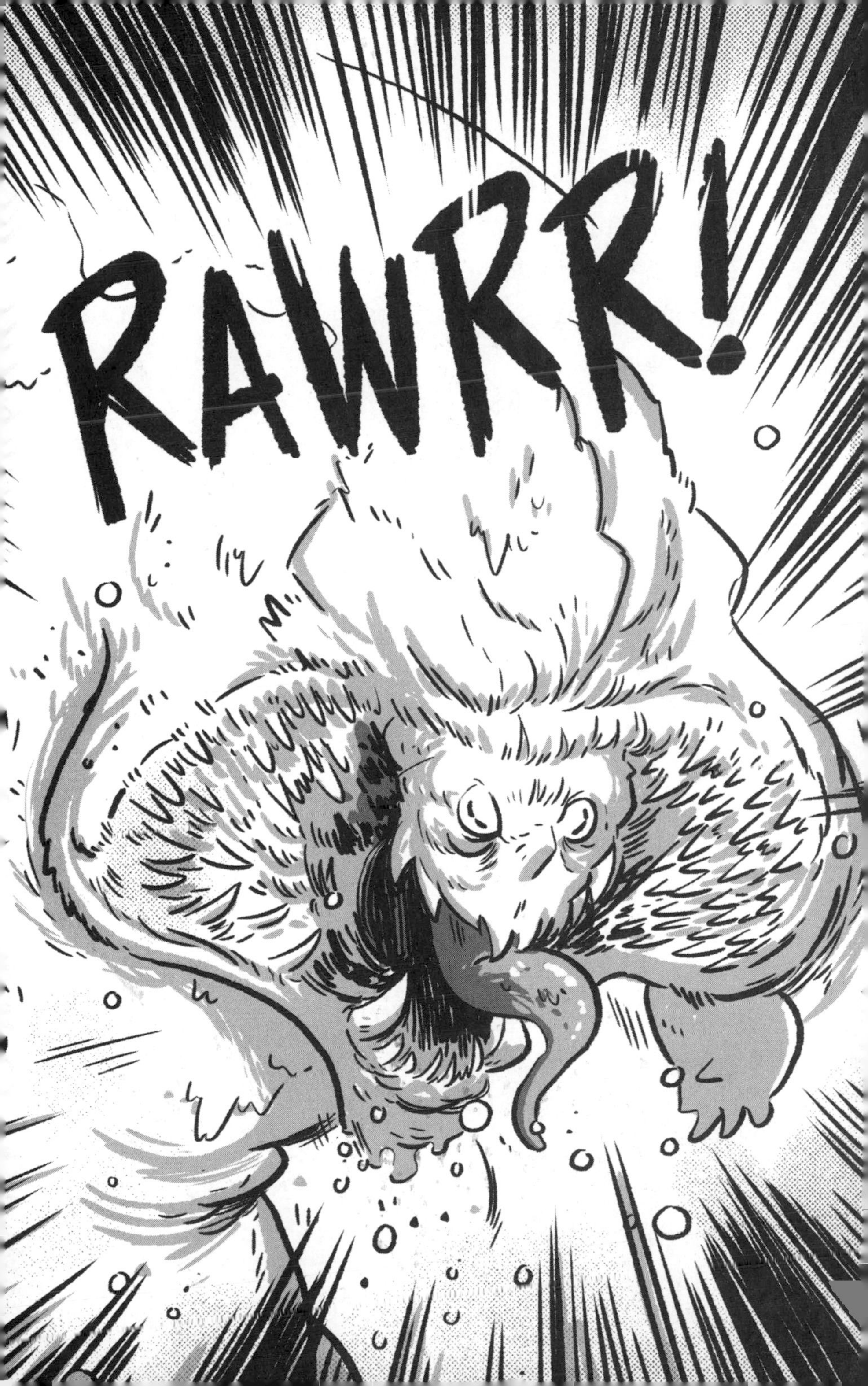
RAWRR!

"HANG ON!" I shout.

A wave roils, the ambulance drifts back, and I do a near-backward tumble. Johnny Steve breaks my fall, seconds before I go toppling into the water. I pin him, he catches me, Globlet cheers. Teamwork!

The Ploonk's short, plump arms extend outward. With slow, deliberate force—the monster *slaps* the water and—

# SMACK!

Two rolling waves splash outward, and the ambulance nearly flips. Johnny Steve is grabbing Globlet by the back like a knuckleball. Neon is on his belly, hugging the roof.

"What a grump," Globlet whispers.

"Maybe it's over," I say. "Maybe it just wanted to show off its ability to switch from cute piggy face to horrible nightmare fuel! And now—"

I stop yapping. I see six purple dots on the Ploonk's hide, dripping purple ooze.

*Monster blood.*

*From where Neon stuck his talons.*

To quote Jack Sullivan, fisticuffs.

"Gang, we gotta get outta here NOW!" I say, whirling around.

But we can't.

Because Neon is halfway in the water! He slides and his claws scrape against the sopping wet ambulance. There's a spark of color as—

**SPLOOSH!**

Neon slips into the water.

"Neon, get back up here!" I shout. "No time for messing around! That giant monster is—"

"Bad," Johnny Steve says. "This is all very bad. Baby Wretches can't swim."

It takes me a moment to process what Johnny Steve just said. And when I do, I spin around.

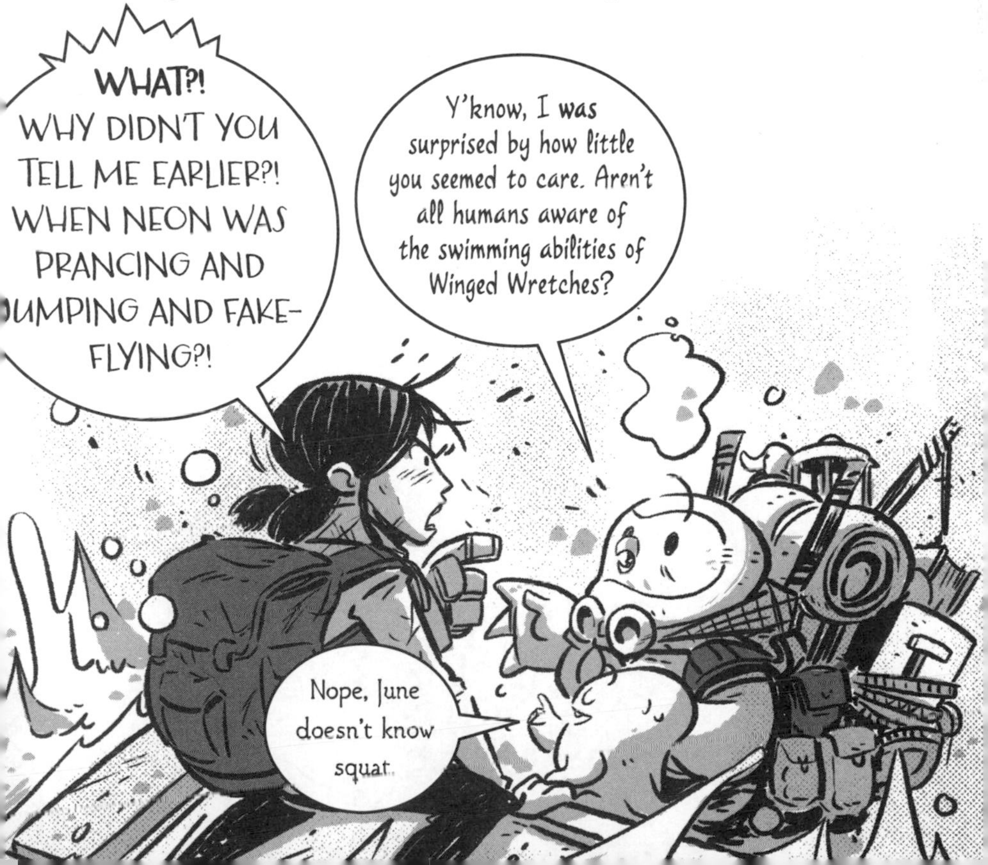
WHAT?! WHY DIDN'T YOU TELL ME EARLIER?! WHEN NEON WAS PRANCING AND JUMPING AND FAKE-FLYING?!
Y'know, I was surprised by how little you seemed to care. Aren't all humans aware of the swimming abilities of Winged Wretches?
Nope, June doesn't know squat.

"NEON!" I cry out.

I slip and slide across the ambulance roof. Looking over the side, I see Neon. He's staring up at me with wide, fear-filled eyes—as he sinks.

Another surge of water.

The Ploonk begins descending back below the surface. It's going after Neon.

"Oh no you *don't*," I mutter.

I narrow my eyes, focusing, aiming the Thing-A-Ma-Blasty Gadget Blaster, then—

POOF!

I fire! A Quint-brand flexi-wire grappling hook rockets through the air, and—

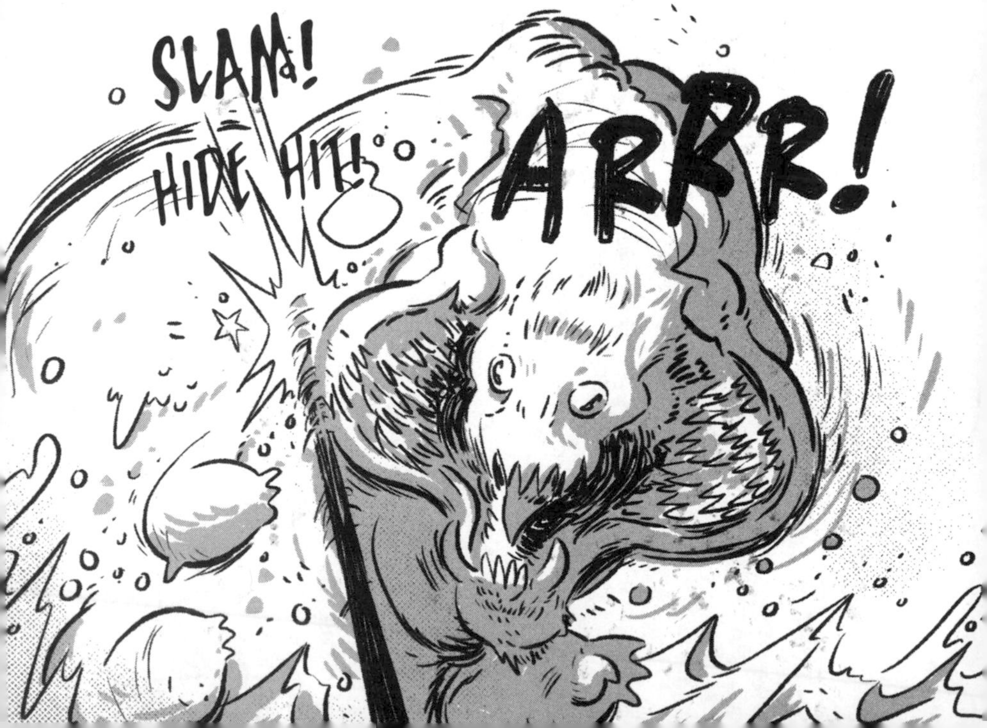
SLAM!
HIDE HIT!
ARRR!

The flexi-wire starts to go taut! The claw-hook is attached to the monster's hide, but the rest of the wire is still inside the Thing-A-Ma-Blasty Gadget Blaster.

The Ploonk snarls, slapping the water. The wire tugs from the force of its weight, and I hold tight to the other end like a fishing rod. But it's not enough to stop such a massive monster—and the Ploonk is on the hunt. It wants Neon.

It descends back under the water in pursuit, and I realize I have to go after it. I have to protect Neon. I quickly glance around, searching for something to secure the wire to. My eyes land on the ambulance's long emergency light bar. With the push of a button, the flexi-wire releases from Blasty, and I tie it to the light before it unspools.

*Okay, Ploonk,* I think. *If you're mad now, just wait until you find out your butt is attached to an ambulance.* "Johnny Steve!" I shout. "Get to the other side! I'm going after Neon!"

And before I can think about how stupid this is, I'm grabbing Globlet, slapping her onto my back, and diving! For a split second, in midair, I think about Saturday morning swim lessons, and silently thank my parents for forcing me to go all those times I didn't want to. And then—

SPLOOSH!

I open my eyes, but all I see is inky darkness. Then—

*FLASH!* Globlet lights up, glowing bright: a shimmering sphere surrounding us.

I'm able to get a sense of my surroundings. Everything down here is eerie and floaty—it looks like a five-hundred-year-old shipwreck except it's an entire modern-day town. . . .

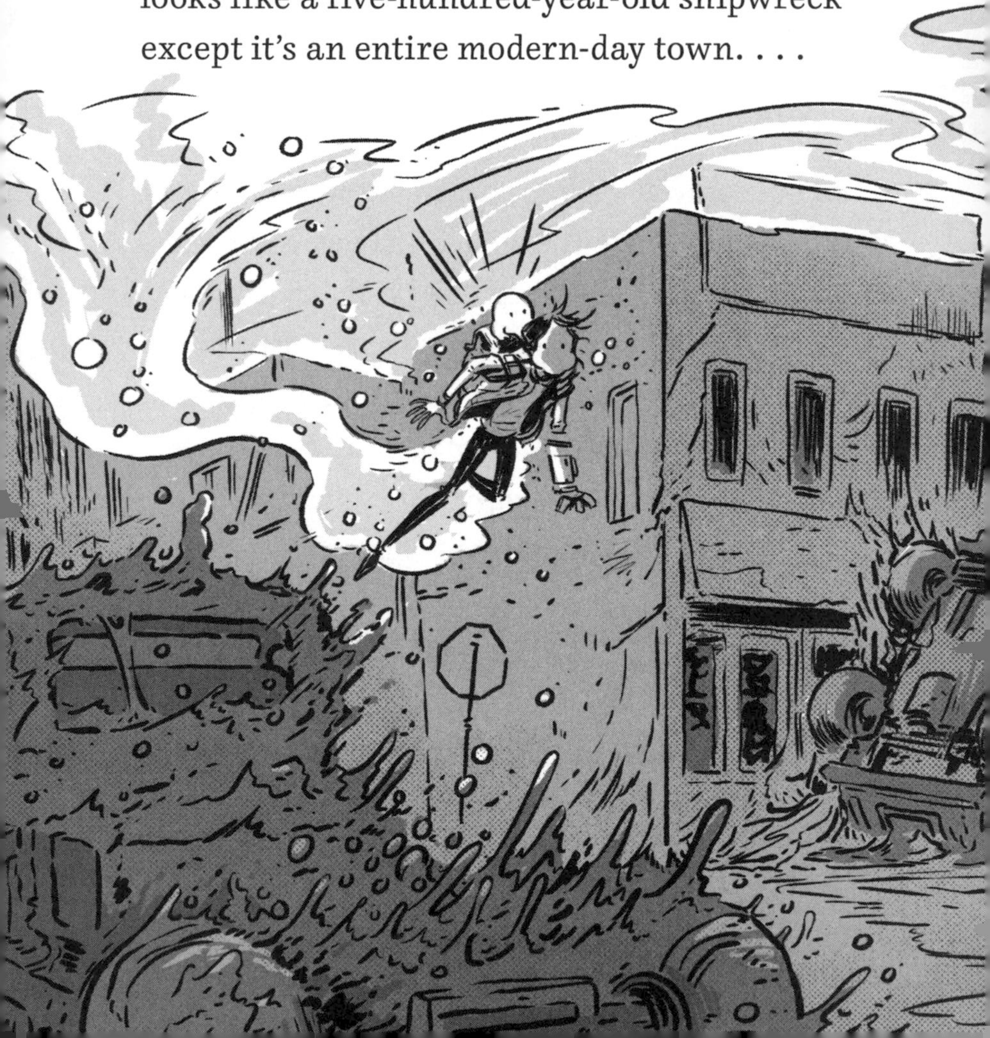

I'm drifting among the cars and buildings, frantically searching the murky waters.

Then, down below, I spot air bubbles.

It's Neon! I've found him!

He is in a complete panic, tail whipping, arms flailing. He does a frenzied barrel roll, scraping the ground, kicking up a cloud of ground dirt. I start kicking my way toward him, but just then his tail *snaps* out and—

# KSSSHH!

His tail cracks the streetlight in half! I watch in horror as the metal pole topples in slow motion. There's a muted, underwater *SMASH* as the streetlight lands, pinning Neon to the ground!

He tries to kick away, but jagged metal presses hard against his back.

I'm losing air. My brain, the survival part, is screaming at me: *It's a Winged Wretch! Winged Wretches are evil! Don't die trying to save something evil!*

And I want to listen.

But I can almost feel my conscience kicking me in the pants, reminding me that the *hard thing* is usually the *right thing*.

*Stupid conscience!* I think as I kick furiously, rocketing toward Neon.

We speed past soda cans and busted laptops, finally weaving around a bent stop sign.

And then I'm there, spinning underwater, bracing my feet against the ground. I pull up on the streetlight.

Neon's eyelids are heavy, fluttering closed. I'm running out of time. . . .

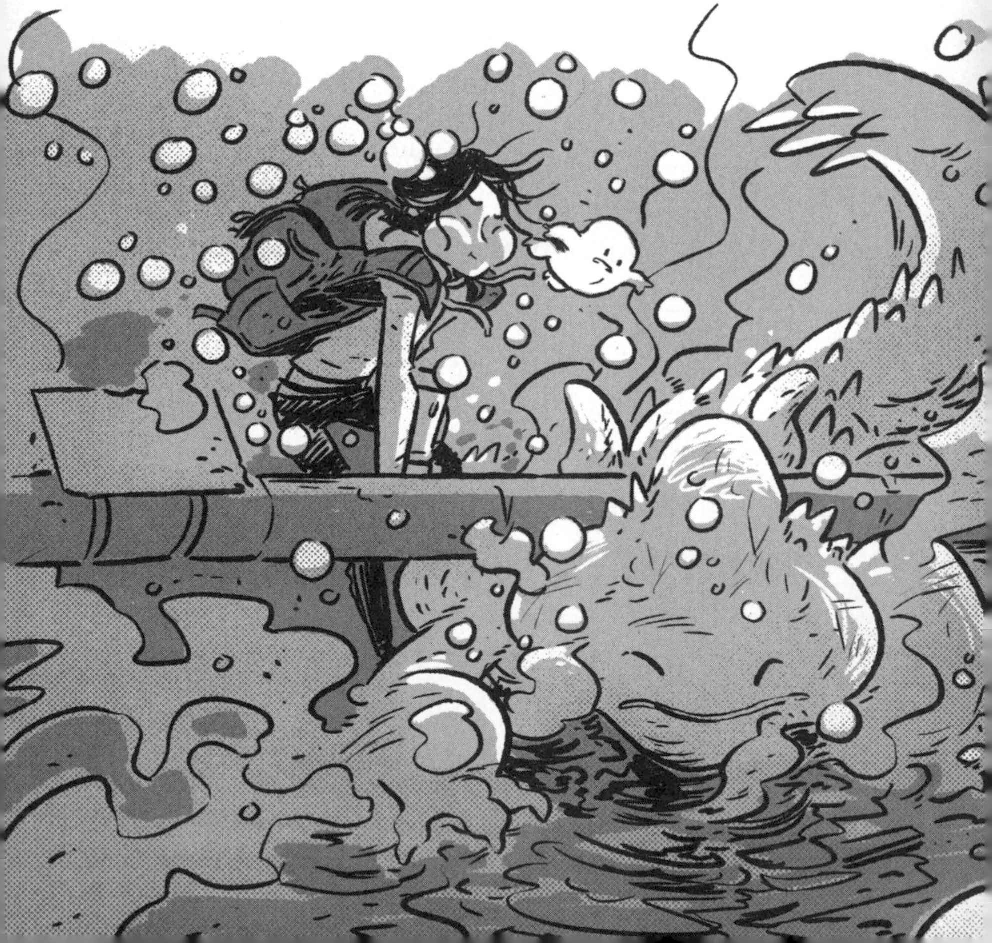

As I'm pulling, my fingers brush Neon's talons. And then one talon begins wrapping around my hand, like in the movies, when you see the newborn baby wrapping its chunky little baby hand around its dad's finger.

I feel a sort of electric buzzing and—

FLASH!

A hurricane of images in my head.

Neon's eyes are dancing. He's not *trying* to do this. It's his mind, racing, losing oxygen—he can't control it.

These aren't visions. These are memories. *My* memories! There are two of them, crystal clear. . . .

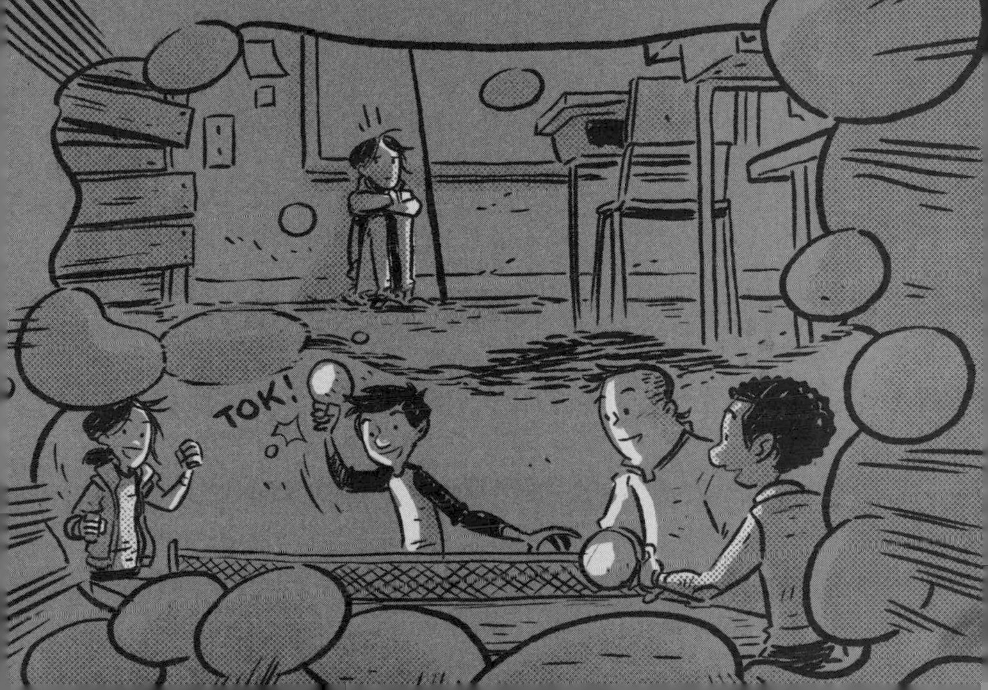
TOK!

I manage to pull my hand from Neon's buzzing talon. As I free myself from his grasp—

ZAP!

The visions end.

I'm back. Where I was. Underwater. I never left. But I do have a lot less oxygen.

I need to hurry.

I grit my teeth and pull Neon as hard as I can. I can't hold my breath much longer, and the Ploonk is after us. But then Neon's eyes suddenly open and—

KRAK!

Again, I'm transported. But these aren't my memories.

This is something else. Something unearthly. . . .

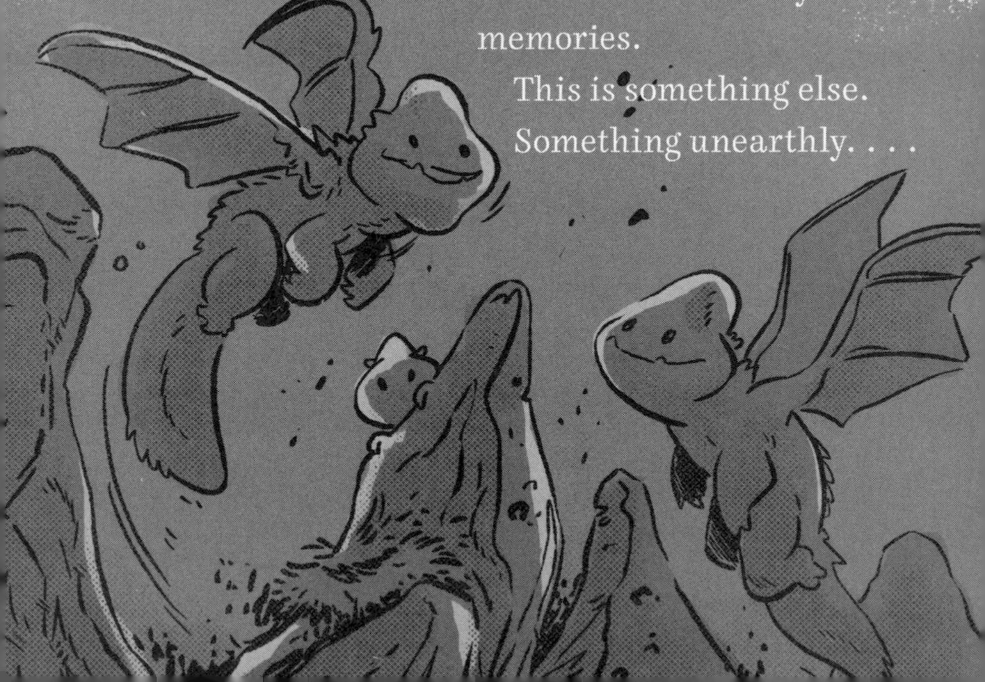

Somewhere at the end of my arm, Neon's talon is suddenly icy cold and gripping me tighter. I can feel his pulse—can feel his blood pumping just beneath the surface of his skin.

It's weird.

But what I see is weirder. . . .

First —

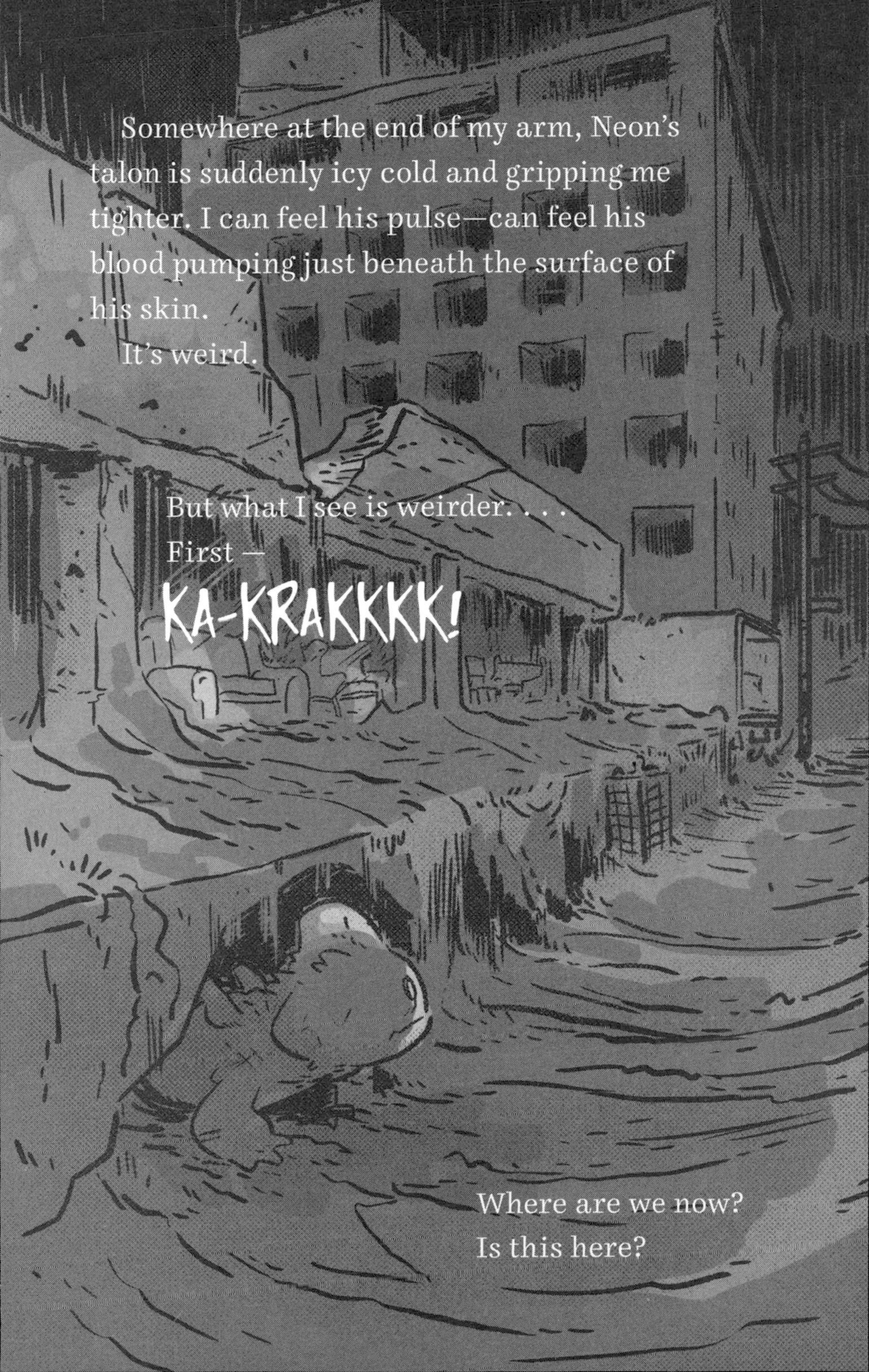
KA-KRAKKKK!

Where are we now?

Is this here?

The vision is interrupted by an enormous—

# SLAM!

The Ploonk! It's back for Neon! The Ploonk swipes at him! I duck as Neon manages to burrow his head, and the streetlight is knocked aside.

*C'mon! C'mon!*

# SLAM!

Another swipe, and now I'm somersaulting through the water. My vision is blurring. Somewhere, either above or below, I see Globlet's faint glow.

My lungs feel like they're on fire.

I want to swim for the surface, but I can't tell which way is up. . . .

Then suddenly—something *hits me*! My eyes pop wide, and—

Neon still can't swim—but one powerful leap and we are *launched* upward. His feet wrap around a crumbled building, and he catapults us upward *again*, beyond fast, *and then*—

**SPLOOSH!**

Neon *rockets* us out of the water! I gasp and finally take in a big breath of fresh air, dangling beneath him for a moment until we both crash down, flopping on the concrete shore at the edge of the lake. Safe for a moment.

I lie on the ground, completely done. I'm hacking up water—in a level of pain I've never had before.

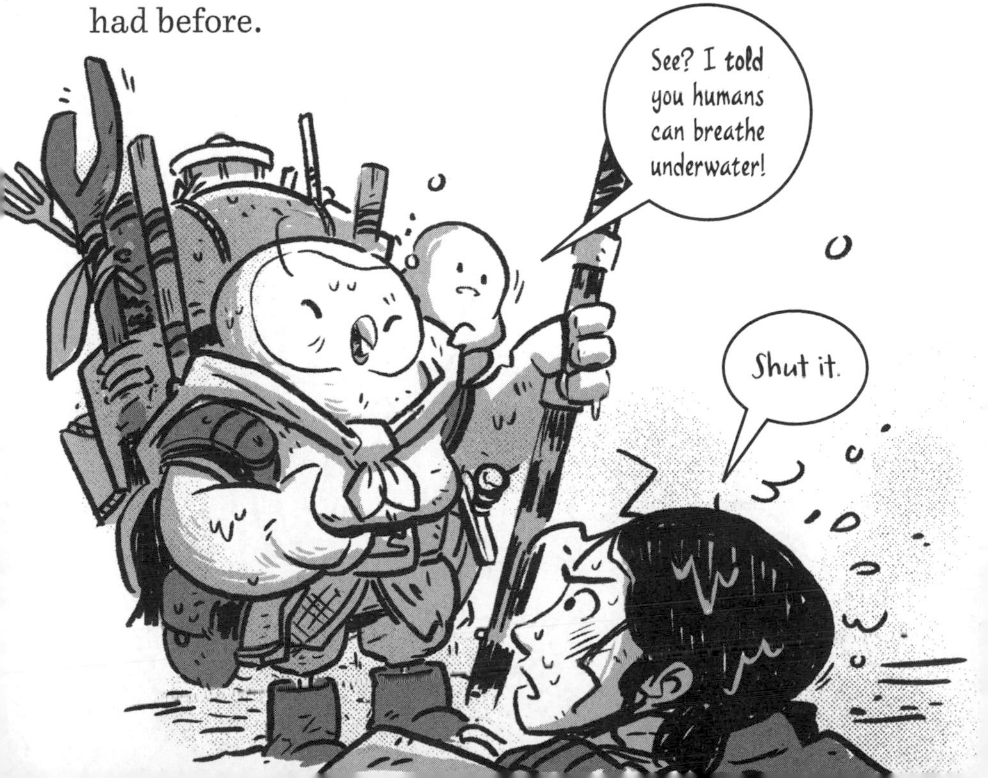
See? I told you humans can breathe underwater!
Shut it.

*I could lie here all day,* I think. *Good a place as any for a ten-year nap.*

But before I can get too comfortable, I hear Globlet's little voice in my ear. "June! Get up! The Ploonk is super extra mad now!"

It's all I can do to roll my head around. And that's when I see the giant Ploonk, the one who started this whole business, angrily stomping toward us. It crosses the strange lake in mere seconds.

The Ploonk's final, furious steps position it directly over us. About to come crashing down, crushing us—

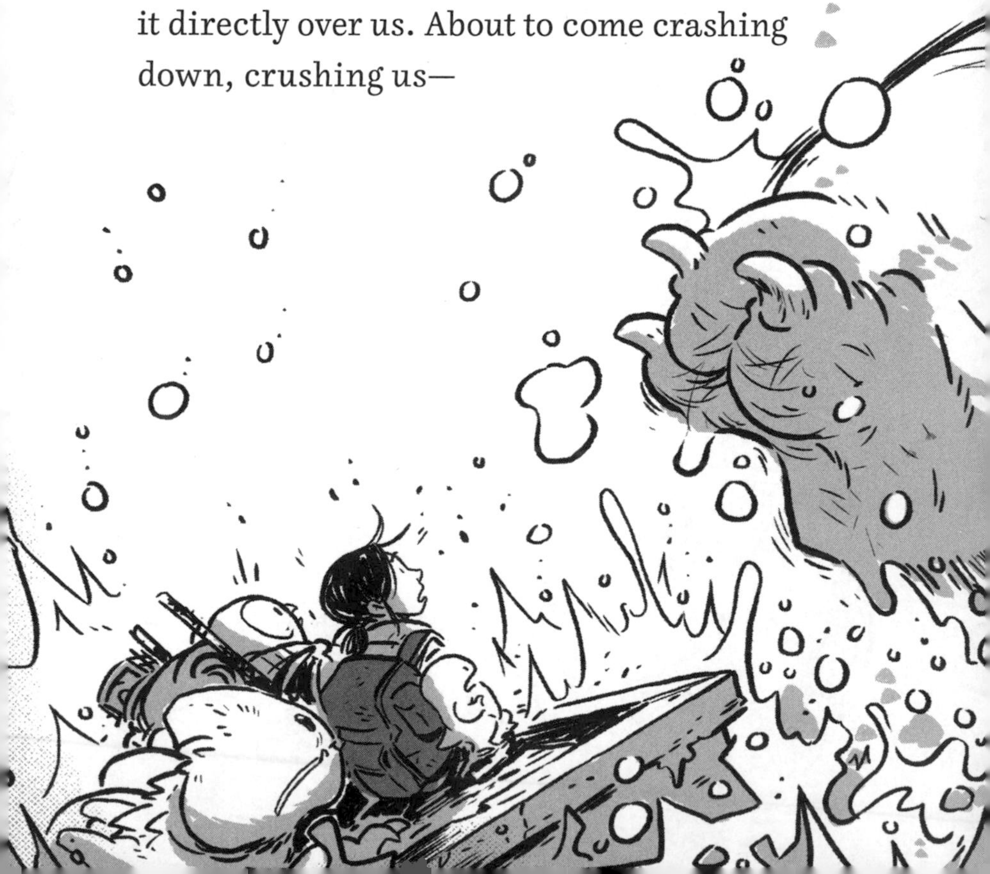

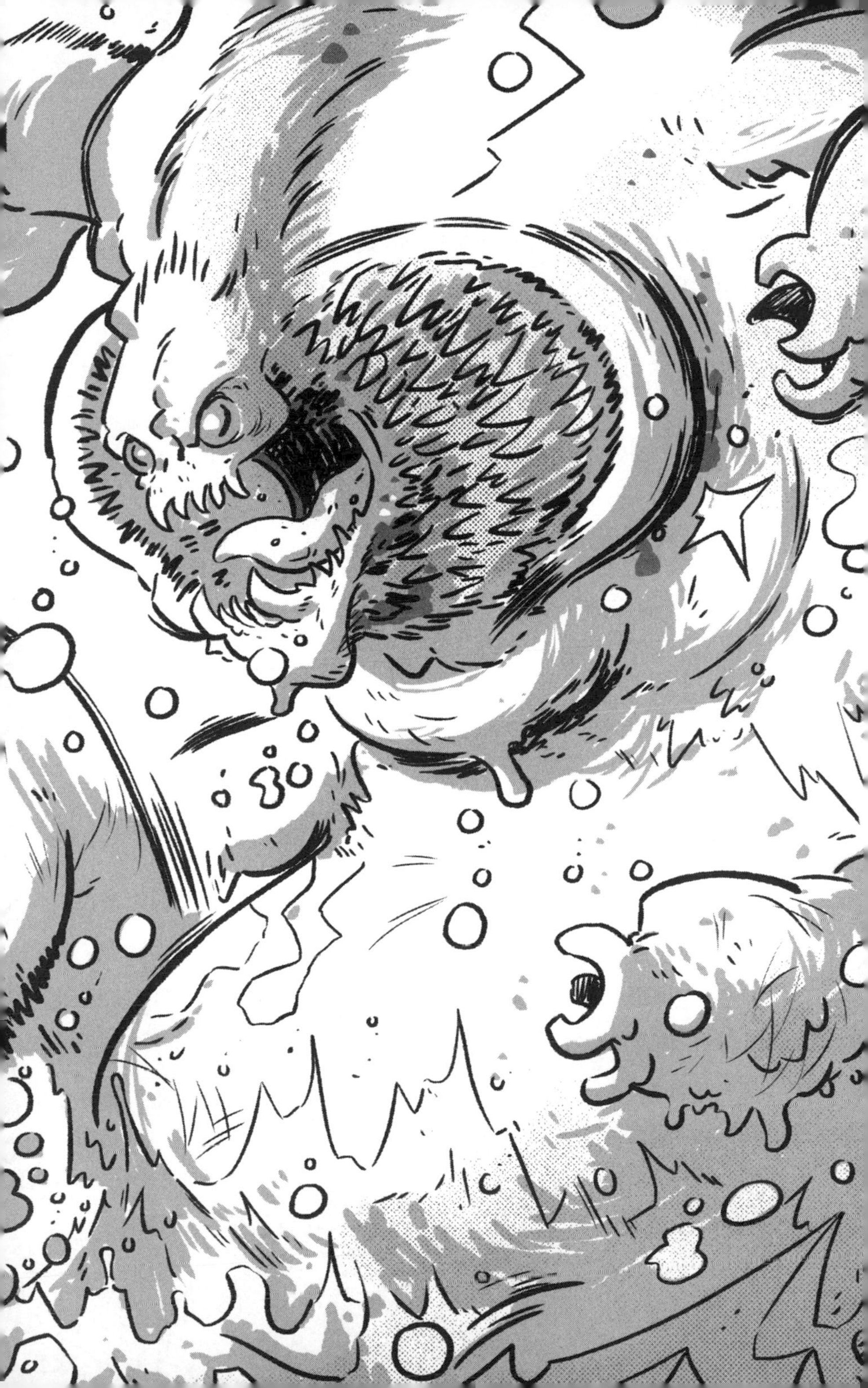

The Ploonk lurches forward and—

**SNAP!**

The grappling hook wire attached to the ambulance is still embedded in its hide! The Ploonk turns and roars in frustration. But as he does, his tremendous strength yanks the ambulance into the air!

It's now sailing, flying, toward the Ploonk, and then—

**SMASH!**

The ambulance slams into the towering Blooper Burger logo!

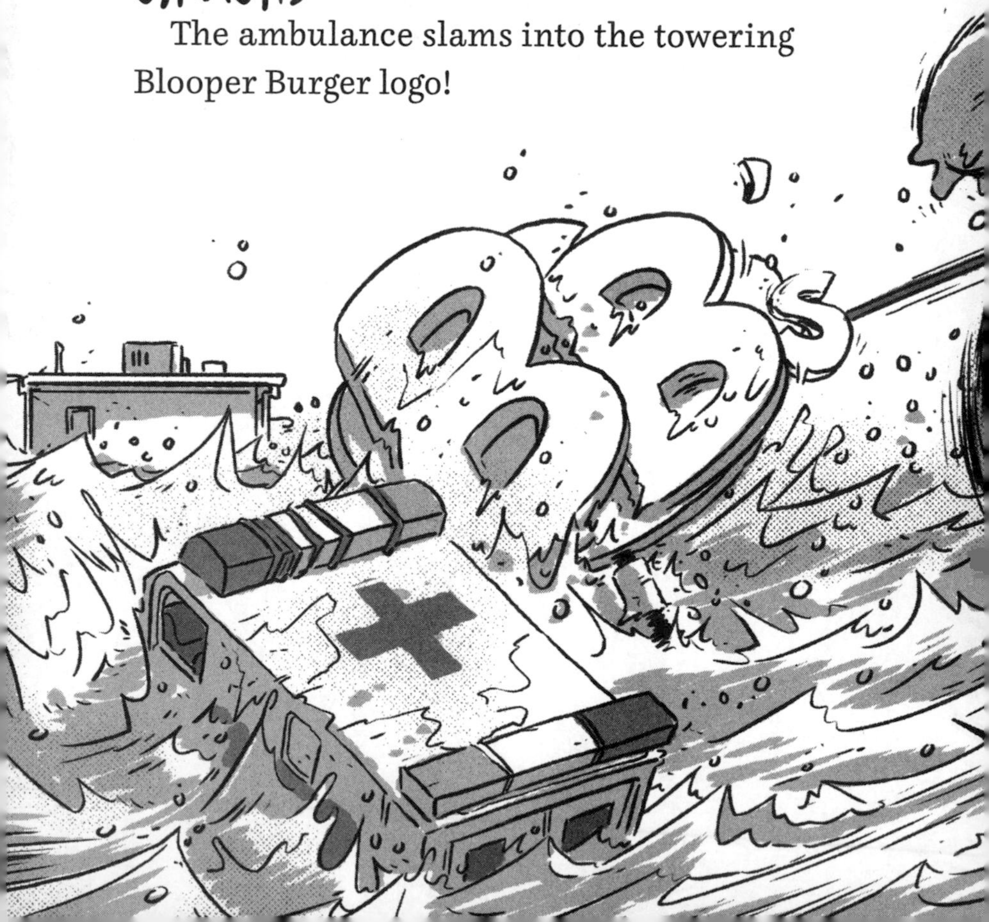

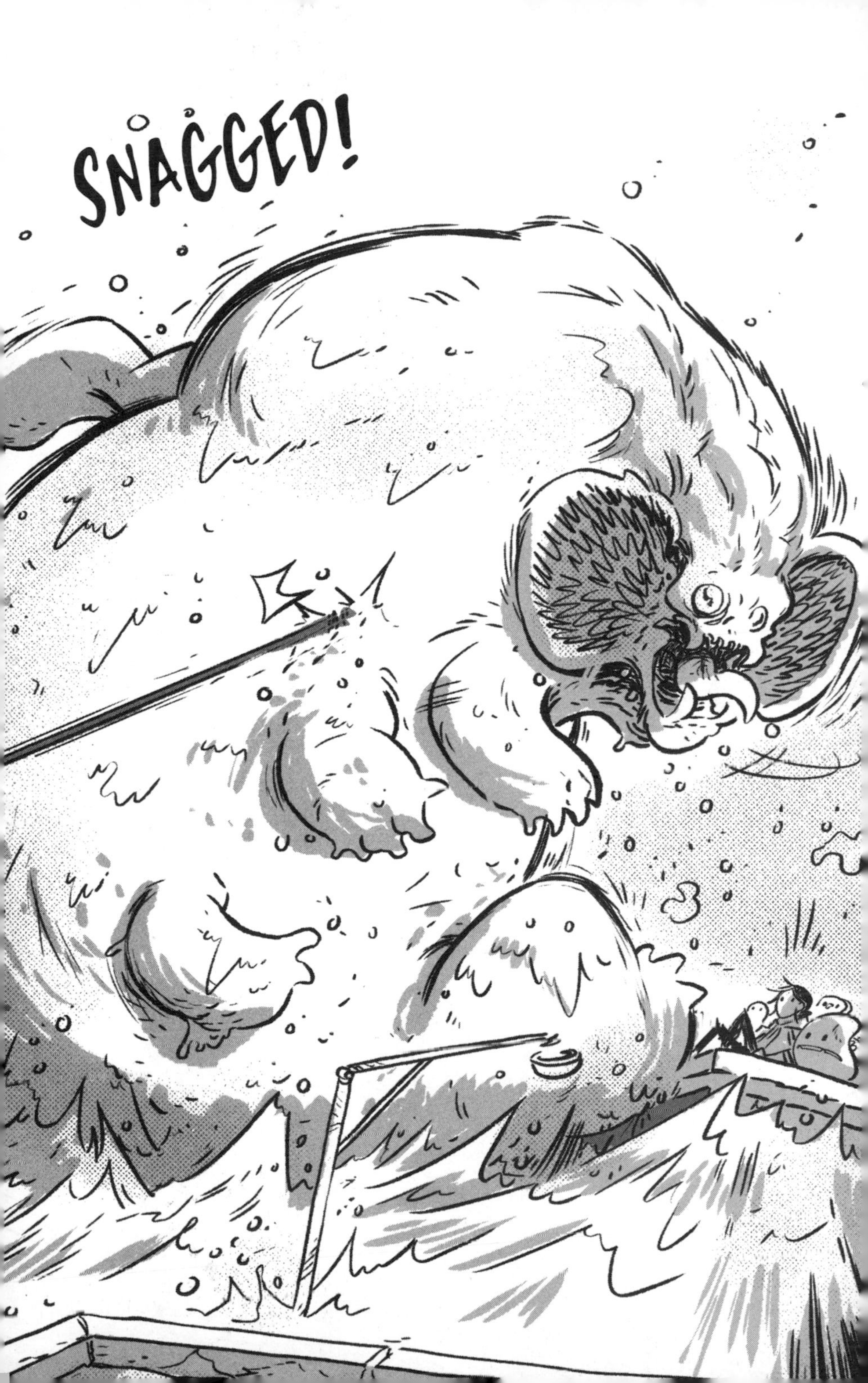
SNAGGED!

The Ploonk gives a final lunge, then turns back. It stomps toward the Blooper Burger tower, whacking the sign as it tries to free itself.

"That grappling wire is Quint-built strong," I say. "But it won't last forever."

"Let's split like tight pants!" Globlet shouts.

Johnny Steve helps Neon to his feet, and then we're all running.

But as we run—it's not the massive monster I'm thinking about. It's what Neon showed me— what I saw inside my head. . . .

# chapter sixteen

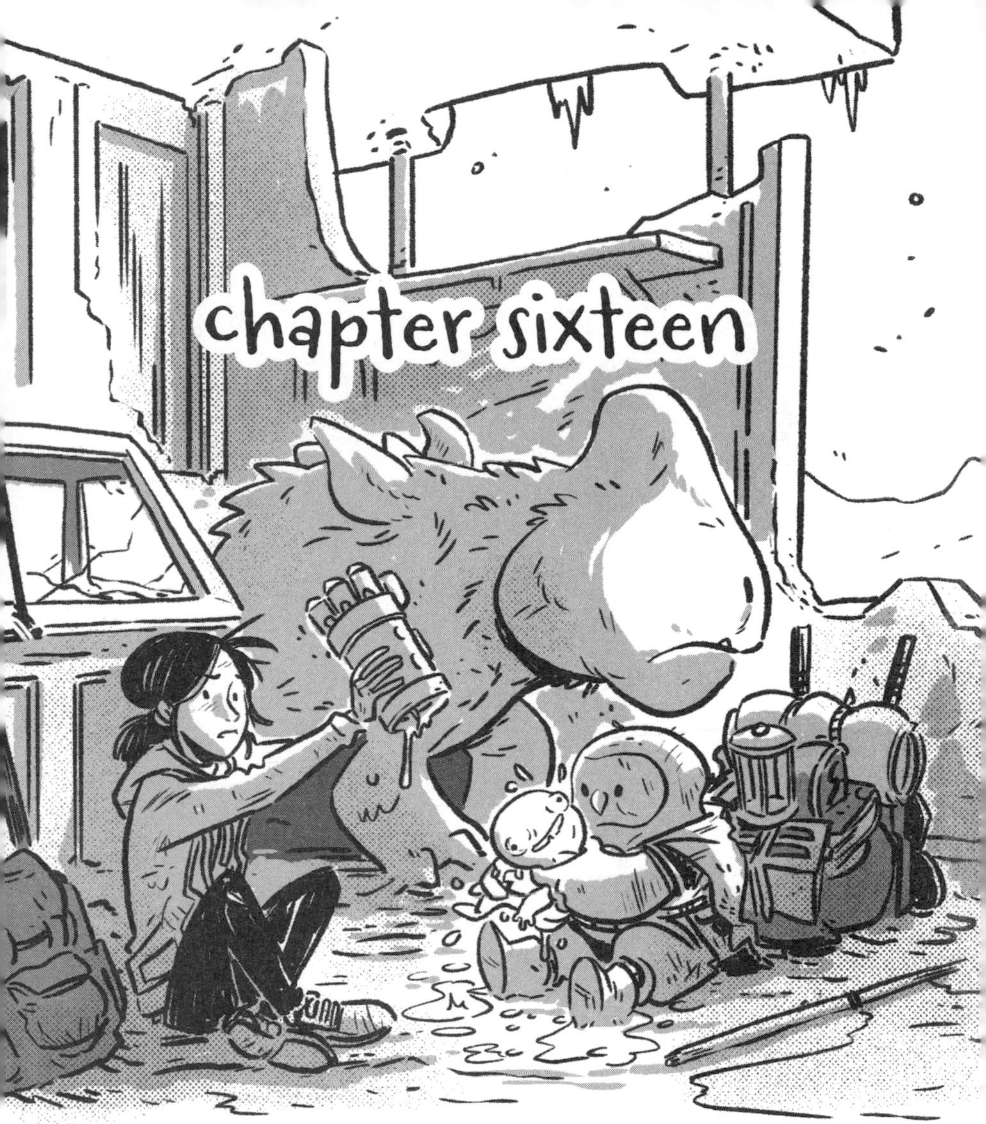

We staggered away from the town square, finally taking shelter inside an old deli. It's torn open from the inside, a vending machine lies smashed on the ground, and everything smells like soda syrup and ham.

Neon is moving slow—like each step hurts. His tail is coiled up, pressed back.

“Hey, Neon, you okay—” I start to ask, but then he looks at me, eyes wet, and suddenly *collapses* to the ground. A heavy thud.

“Neon!” I cry, and rush over—surprising myself by how worried I am. I run my hand over his curled tail. Neon winces and tries to wriggle away, like me at the doctor, trying to avoid a flu shot.

I manage to pull the tail aside—and I see glowing green liquid. It’s blood. There are long cuts atop his wing-stubs. That skin is soft, unlike the rest of his shiny hide. The falling streetlight must have sliced them open.

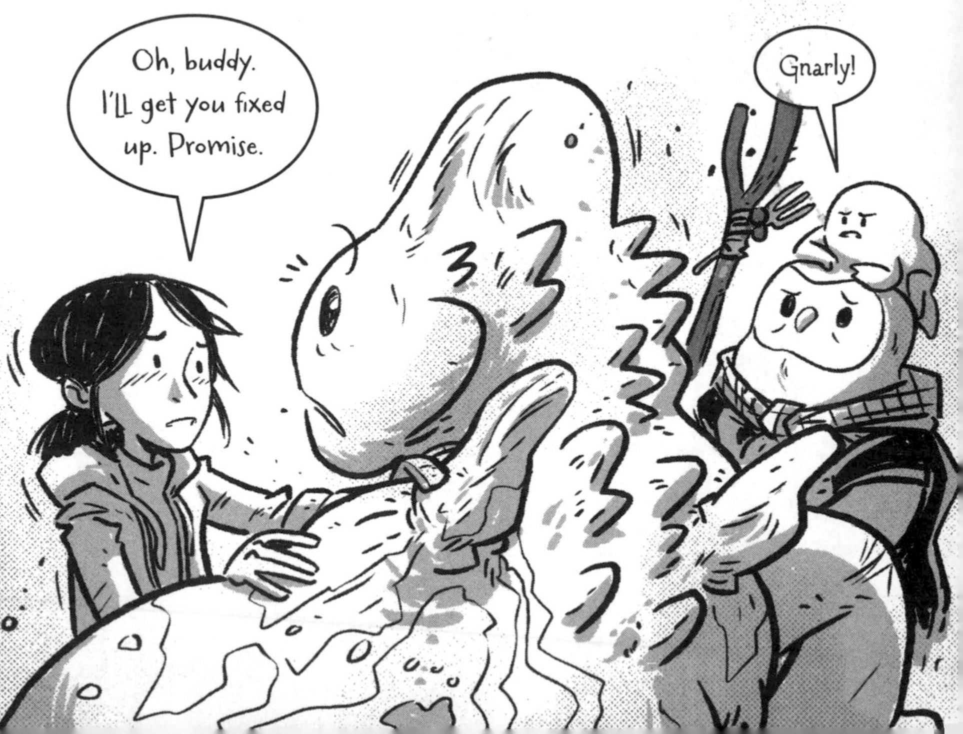
Oh, buddy. I'LL get you fixed up. Promise.
Gnarly!

It's not the first time I've needed a makeshift bandage during the Monster Apocalypse. . . .

The first week I was stuck alone at Parker Middle School, I sliced my leg bad. Worst part, it wasn't even an injury from something cool and heroic, like dodging a zombie horde. I was trying to butt-surf stairwell banisters near the art room. But the metal snagged my jeans, tore them open, and sent me sprawling.

I made it to the nurse's office—only to discover that Nurse Carol was now *Zombie Nurse Carol*. She was stomping around the office like some sort of video game mini-boss. But, I was in luck!

I found an unwrapped Fruit by the Foot in the waiting area.

It made for the perfect bandage, until I woke up at two a.m. in desperate need of a snack. . . .

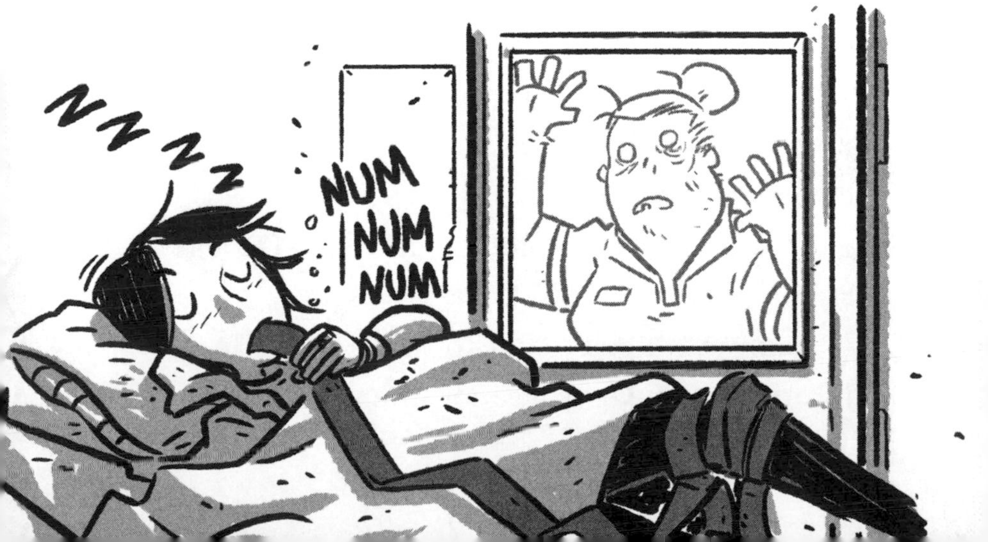
ZZZZ
NUM
NUM
NUM

I learned a valuable lesson: don't use yummy snacks as medical supplies.

"Fear not! I will find something to apply to his wounds!" Johnny Steve says. He gives Neon a gentle little scratch behind his ears, then races off.

I look back at Neon and wonder, again, if I'm just absolutely *nutso* for trying to help a Winged Wretch. I mean, this entire thing could be a trick to lure me to the Wretches.

Or worse—to lure me to Thrull.

No! I won't believe that!

I *saved* Neon.

And *he saved me*. I'd be at the bottom of that flooded town square—*permanently*—if it wasn't for Neon.

Sure, Neon is destructive. And rough. And stronger than he realizes. But after what we've been through, I just can't believe that he's *evil* like the other Wretches.

Before long I hear Johnny Steve. "I found medical supplies!" he says, hobbling around the corner. "Come see!"

"WOO-HOO!" Globlet exclaims. "Medical supply party! C'mon, June!"

Neon manages to get to his feet while Johnny Steve eagerly races ahead.

Two streets over, we find Johnny Steve. I've never seen someone so proud—and so wrong. . . .

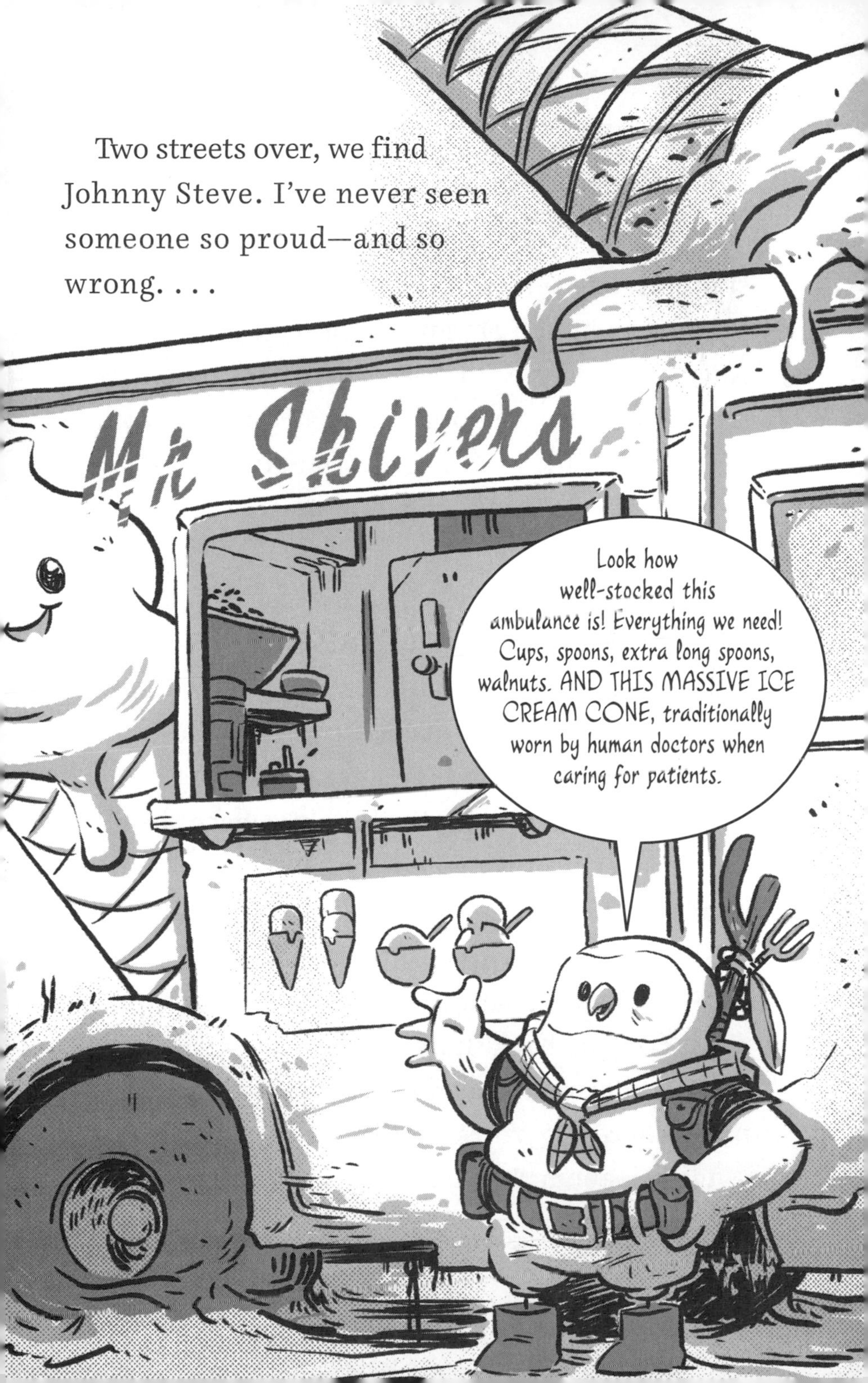
Mr Shivers
Look how well-stocked this ambulance is! Everything we need! Cups, spoons, extra long spoons, walnuts. AND THIS MASSIVE ICE CREAM CONE, traditionally worn by human doctors when caring for patients.

"Johnny Steve," I say with a sigh. "You found an ice cream truck."

But I'd rather not have to keep looking for supplies, so I take what I can from the truck.

I wrap a bunch of paper napkins around Neon's wounded wing stubs, then seal them in place by melting sprinkles like a wax adhesive.

"Don't eat it," I tell Neon. "No matter how delicious it looks. Trust me, I know from experience."

Neon fiddles with his tail, but doesn't so much as lick the sprinkles. He's got more willpower than I do, that's for sure.

Johnny Steve and Globlet climb into the truck. Johnny Steve is saying something about wanting his very own Mr. Shivers mascot head and Globlet's going on about some "Choco Taco hoedown."

Then it's just me and Neon.

"Hey," I say, looking at him. "Uh, thank you for saving me back there."

Neon lowers his head modestly, and I see the nubs where his wings should be.

I think about the vision he accidentally showed me when we were underwater. Neon *used* to be able to fly. Neon *used* to have wings.

Someone, or something, *took them*. It's like a punch to the gut. I reach out to touch the wound, but he pulls back.

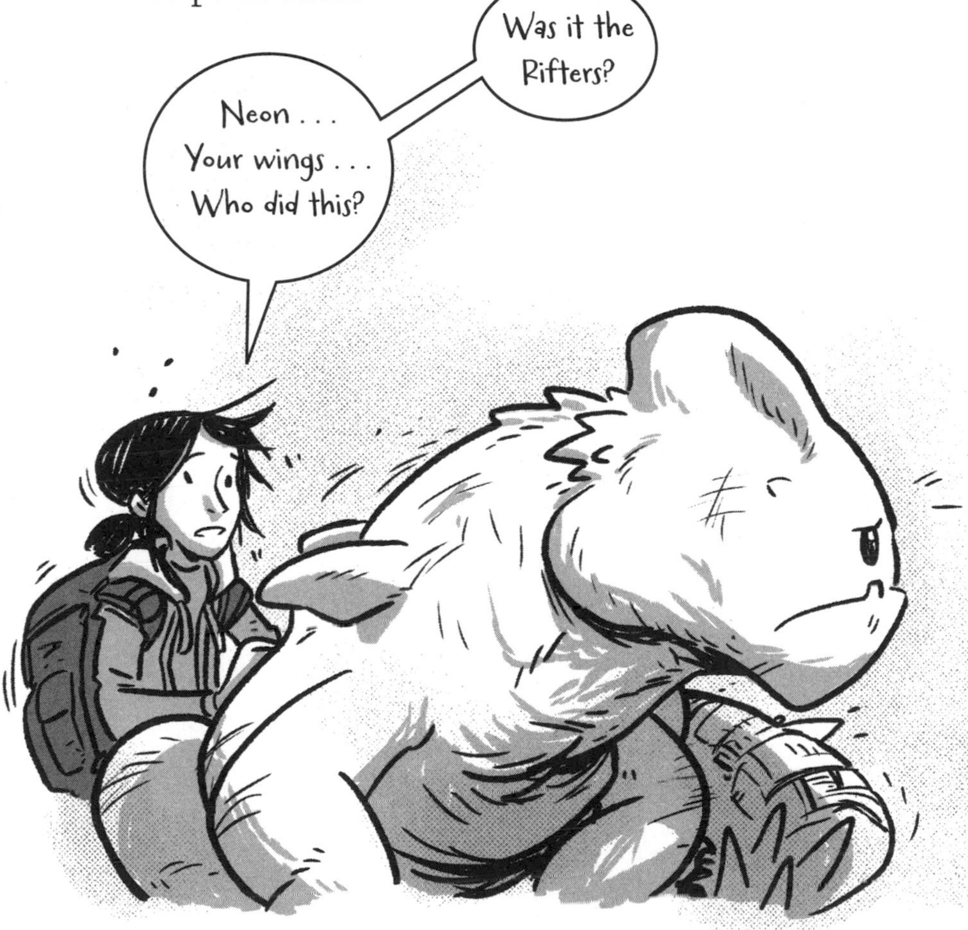
Was it the Rifters?
Neon . . . Your wings . . . Who did this?

He just looks at me for an impossibly long time, then hangs his head.

And I think, whatever happened—it had to be pretty awful. . . .

# chapter
# seventeen

When we finally get back on the road, the sun is starting to go down. Everything is drenched in a soothing, creamsicle orange and even the awful vines sparkle gold.

It's beautiful.

And we all must think so because, for a moment, we're all quiet.

Except for Neon.

Now that he's bandaged up, Neon has a *lot* more spring in his step. I mean, he's practically prancing! It's a whole lotta cute, a little bit out-of-control, and kinda painful.

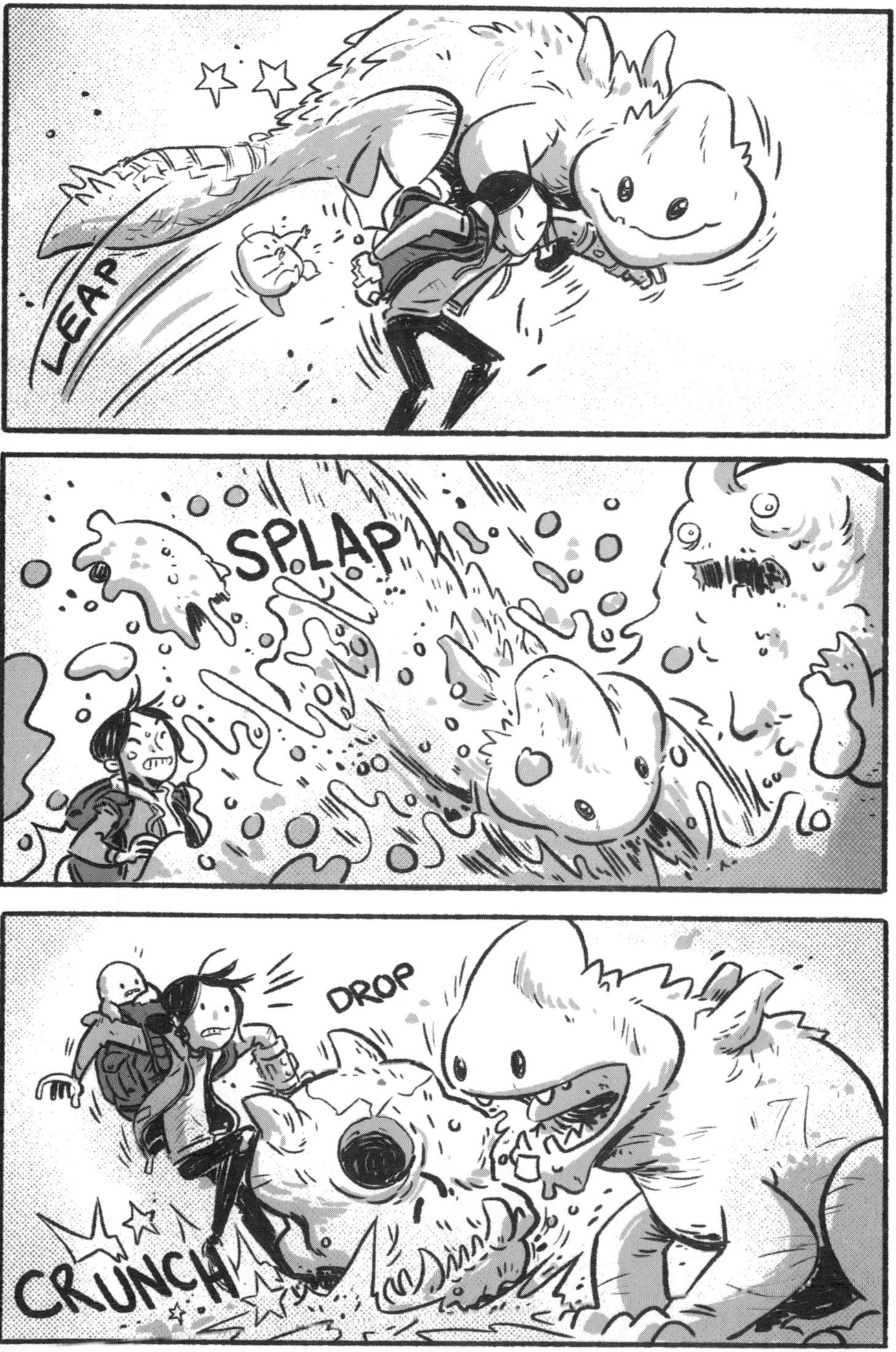
LEAP
SPLAP
DROP
CRUNCH

Neon is *exhausting*—but the longer I'm with him, the more I'm sure that he's not *evil*.

Evil monsters emit a *stench*, always. Blarg, Thrull, Ghazt—they all *stank*. Like how the smell of bad milk tells you "don't drink me!" the odor of evil practically screams "RUN FAR AWAY!"

But Neon pretty much just smells like water balloons and magic markers. What if Winged Wretches *aren't* destined to be evil from the moment they're hatched? Maybe they just *turn* evil because they're raised to *be evil*?

Or . . . maybe they have, like, a big "YOU'RE EVIL NOW!" party when they hit a certain age, like a quinceañera or a sweet sixteen. . . .

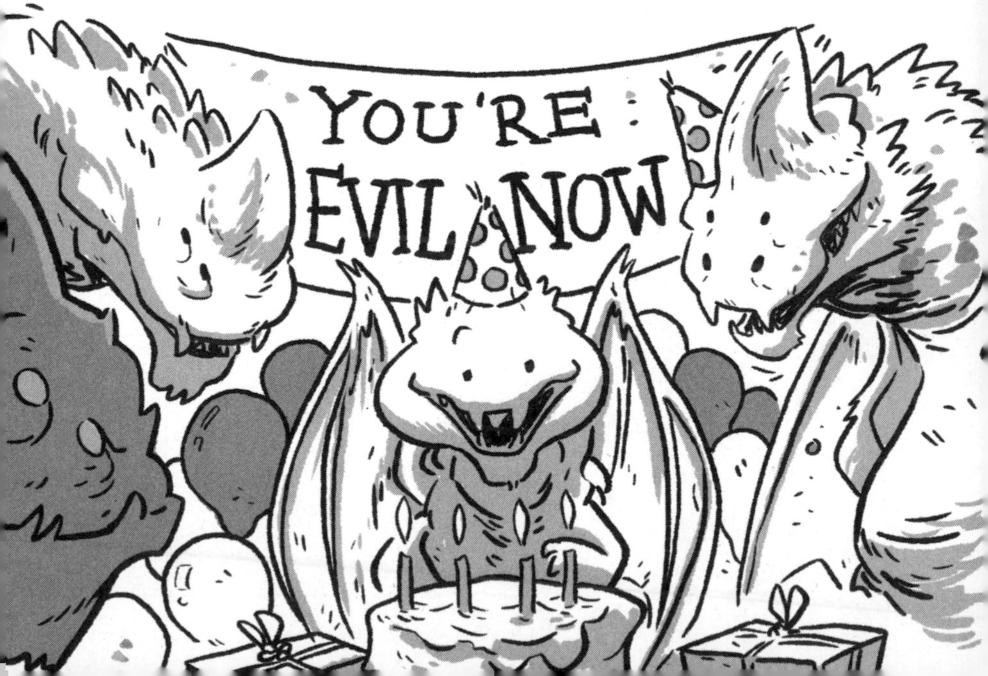
YOU'RE EVIL NOW

I'm thinking about important stuff like birthday parties and the nature of evil when we reach a railroad crossing. The tracks stretch out endlessly to the east and the west.

"Ahh, yes," Johnny Steve says. "Now we are getting close."

"He's right," Globlet says. "Look."

Squinting, I see something in the sky—way, way off in the distance. It takes me a second to realize that they are Wretches—they're so far away they don't look any bigger than seagulls.

There are a dozen of them, lazily circling in the sky, like buzzards.

"We simply follow these tracks," Johnny Steve says, pointing. "Thataway."

I look down at the train tracks.

"Thataway" leads east.

But I have to wonder. . . . Railroad tracks are like man-made rivers—you follow them long enough, and you'll always get *someplace helpful*. And I wonder what *someplace helpful* might lie *in the other direction*.

There is a sign at the crossing. Moss has grown over it, and it's covered in caked-on dirt. I step toward it, reach out, and wipe it off. Beneath the grime, I see the words: *Shady Side. Two miles west.*

Shady Side. That rings a bell. I've seen that name before . . .

Of course. THE MAP! After the Monster Apocalypse, during the months when I was alone at the middle school—I spent endless hours poring over a map of Wakefield and *all* its surrounding towns and cities.

I was looking for places where survivors might have ended up, like army bases. I didn't find any. But man, I looked at those maps for *so* long. I'd *never forget* a single town name.

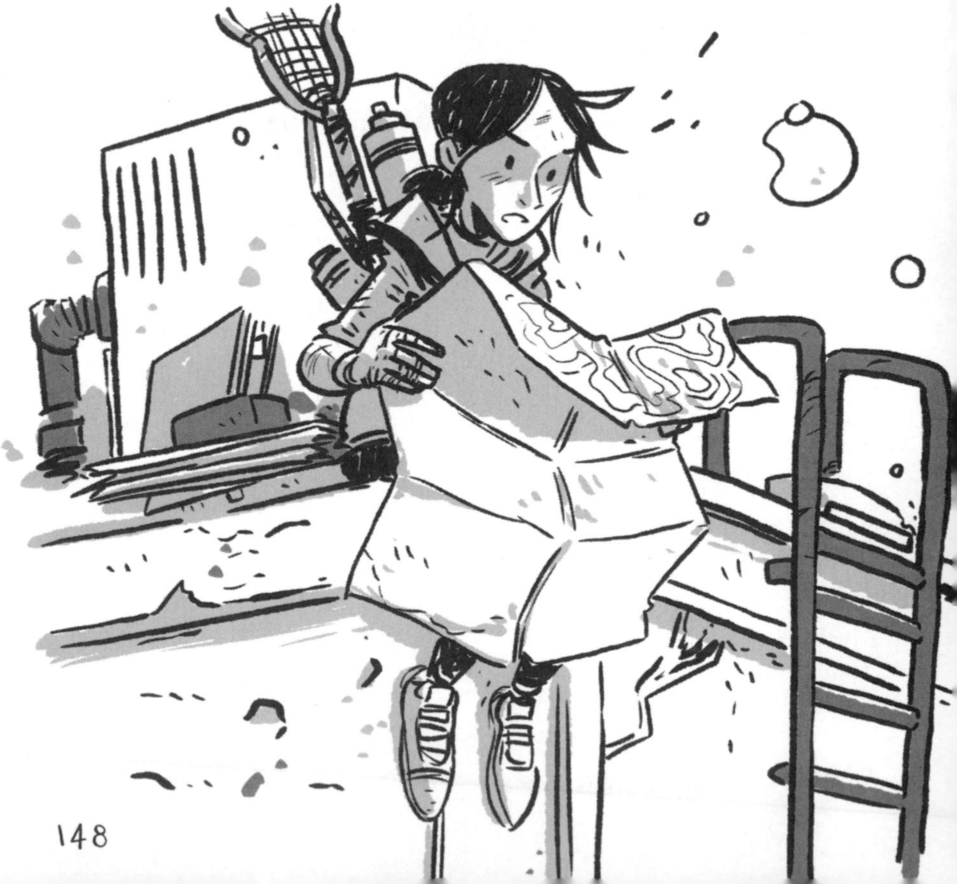

The reason I know the name Shady Side: it's on the same train line as Wakefield! If I follow these tracks west, I *will* GET BACK HOME.

I stare down at the tracks. Home. Wakefield. It's close. And I'm tempted.

It's what I *want to do.*

I could pat Neon on the rear-end and send him off on his merry way. I bet Johnny Steve could get him back to the nest. *Maybe.*

But I look back.

And I see Neon staring at me.

Neon showed me something, when we were underwater. It was a memory. Me and my friends, happy together. And then he showed me another memory—himself, flying with other Wretches.

It makes sense. . . . I want to get home to Wakefield, to my friends.

Neon wants to get back to his family, his kind.

But if I *don't* take Neon back, then sooner or later, the Rifters will catch him. They'll take him to Thrull. And that will be bad for *my whole dimension.*

*But wait,* I think. *What if there's another way?*

We could *all* go back to Wakefield! I'd get Jack and Quint and Dirk! We'd fry up some pretzel-sprinkled watermelon, throw some old-school dance tunes on the stereo. And then, *together*, we could all deliver Neon to the Wretches' nest.

We could finish this mission as a *team*.

Sure, it would take longer. But it's the *smarter* move! The safer move!

And I'm nearly decided. Turning to my companions, I say, "Guys, I'm thinking about a change of plans—"

# REEEARGH!

It is a spine-chilling, goose-bumps-raising roar. "Ogres!" Globlet says, looking over her shoulder like they're right behind her.

"They must have reached the flooded town," Johnny Steve says.

I gulp. "And if they saw the Ploonk strung up, they'd know it was our doing. That would put them right back on our trail."

"NEON!" Johnny Steve exclaims. He hurries toward him. Neon is on the ground—and his entire body is shaking. I rush over, kneeling down. I try to run my hand over his back, where his wings used to be, but he caws and bangs and pushes me away.

"Don't worry, we won't let them get you. We won't let them take you to Thrull."

# REEEARGH!

Another Ogre roar! Louder! Closer!

Neon caws and howls and bangs his body against the ground! I reach down, but he swats my hand away and *runs*!

"NEON! NO!" I shout.

He's racing down the tracks with his head down like a rodeo bull, just trying to get as far away from those Ogre howls as he can.

But he's going the wrong way—away from Wakefield.

I give one last look behind us, toward home—and then I take off, running as fast I can after Neon.

It's dusk when we finally catch up to him. Geez, I thought I was fast, but Neon is like lightning on four legs. He's lying alongside a little creek. The water is covered in glowing green algae.

"Neon!" I cry out. I'm happy to see him—but only for a moment.

Neon shoots up. He was sleeping. He must have worn himself out running.

"What is wrong with you?!" I cry out. "Why did you just run? That wasn't FAIR! I had a plan! We were gonna go—"

And then I just stop, because I've run out of steam. Too tired to yell. Too tired to argue.

"We need to hurry," Johnny Steve says. "The Rifters will not be long."

So much for returning to Wakefield now. So much for finishing this with my friends. I scoop up Globlet, plop her on my shoulder, and begin walking down the tracks.

"C'mon, guys," I say softly, having a hard time hiding my disappointment. "Time to go. Destination: Wretches' nest."

# chapter eighteen

Neon is himself again—mostly. He's not shrieking, not throwing himself into things. But he also knows that I'm angry—and he now seems almost *scared* of me.

And, yeah, I *am* annoyed—but Neon has enough to be scared of without me adding to the list!

I think about Jack, and how—when things get bad—he has this amazing (and amazingly annoying!) ability *to be his most gung-ho.*

Jack might not be here—but I decide to follow his lead anyway. I go *super enthusiastic!* I sing. I skip. I practically dance down the train tracks, belting out some happy pop song that I haven't heard since, y'know, *before.*

Okay, so, the Rifters are still following us? Not ideal! Handing Neon over to a crew of evil, Ṛeżżőcħ-worshiping servants? Don't love it!

But it's gonna be okay!

Because I'm gonna make sure it's okay!

And, most importantly, we *do* have a destination. And a PLAN. And having a plan, even in a lousy situation, can make you feel *OKAY*.

Like back at the middle school. After I saw my parents, on the bus, and I couldn't reach them—I knew I was gonna be alone for a *long time*.

Those were the bad days. My worst days.

I yanked the flagpole off my homeroom wall and used it like a spear. I got really good at popping lockers off their hinges: just a quick stab, a twist of the wrist, and I was in.

That's how I survived. . . .

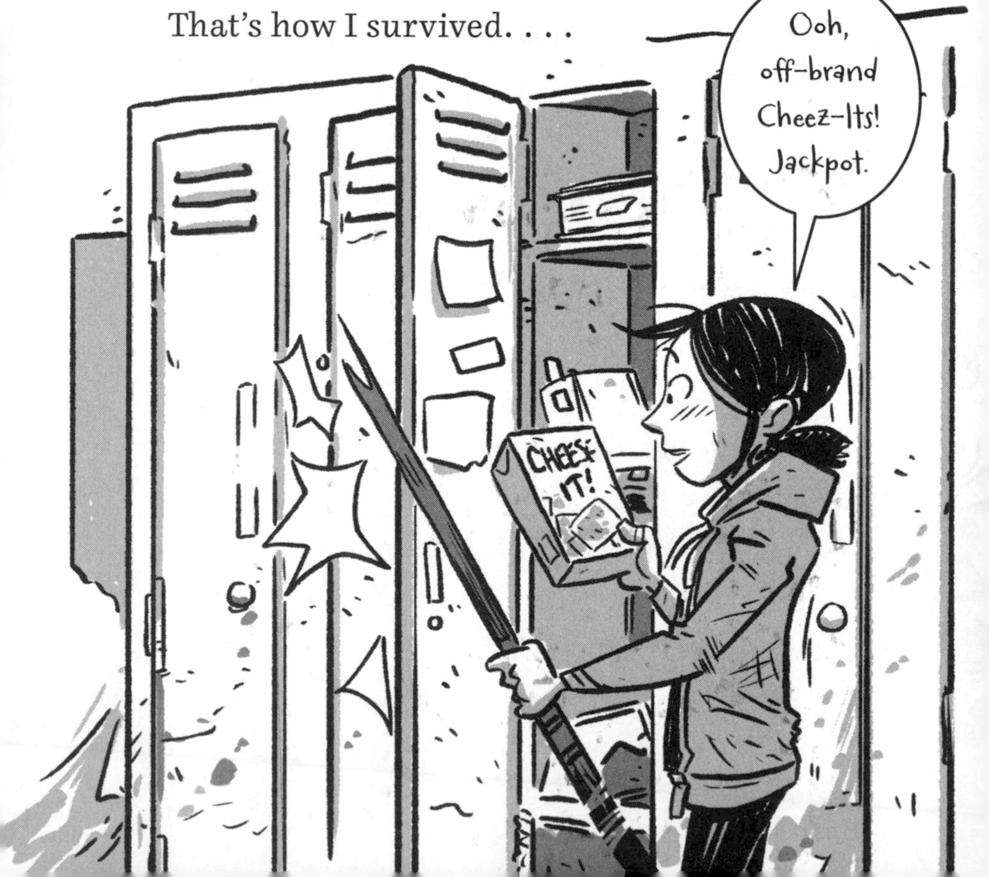
Ooh, off-brand Cheez-Its! Jackpot.
CHEESE IT!

But soon, I was out of lockers. I had eaten my way through the entire sixth-grade wing of the school. Every locker, every backpack, every desk.

And again, I was hungry.

Of course, I knew *where* to get food: the cafeteria. But there were *zombies* in the cafeteria. I spent two full days lying around, scared, until finally I was so ravenous that I came up with a plan.

And that sparked something in me. It forced me to use my brain. I was thinking, planning, training.

I was excited.

Finally, I stormed that cafeteria like freaking Captain Marvel—if Captain Marvel engaged in combat while lunch meat hung from her lips—

WHACK!

KRAK!

I feel good!

After that, I was over the hump—past the hardest part. . . .

And that's how I feel now.

I know what to do with Neon, and I know how to get home. "I know everything!" I shout, hopping up onto the train track, walking it like a balance beam.

Neon trots behind me, his tail swishing back and forth. I don't know if he knows that we're fulfilling his dream of going back to the other Wretches, or if he's just happy because I'm happy, or—

"Ahem," Johnny Steve says, interrupting my train of thought. "I must point out that, technically, you do not know *everything*! I am not even human, yet I know more about them than you do!" He chuckles, shaking his head. "Humans are quite silly. . . . "

I shoot him a look—then shrug. "Y'know what, I'm not even gonna argue. I refuse to let your human-splaining ways annoy me."

"Aha!" Johnny Steve says. He elbows Neon gently in the side. "She admits it, at last!"

"Okay, fine. IT'S ON! You think you know humans? Let's see if you know humans. I'm giving you a human quiz. "Johnny Steve, how many teeth do most humans have?"

"Four," he says confidently. "Well, four during the daytime. Seventy-seven, in the evening."

"Why do humans have belly buttons?"

"For powering down at night! Now give me a difficult one."

"What is *one thing* that *all* humans can agree on?"

"Ha! Nice try. All humans agree on everything."

"What's the most popular human food?"

"Pez. Cherry-flavored Pez."

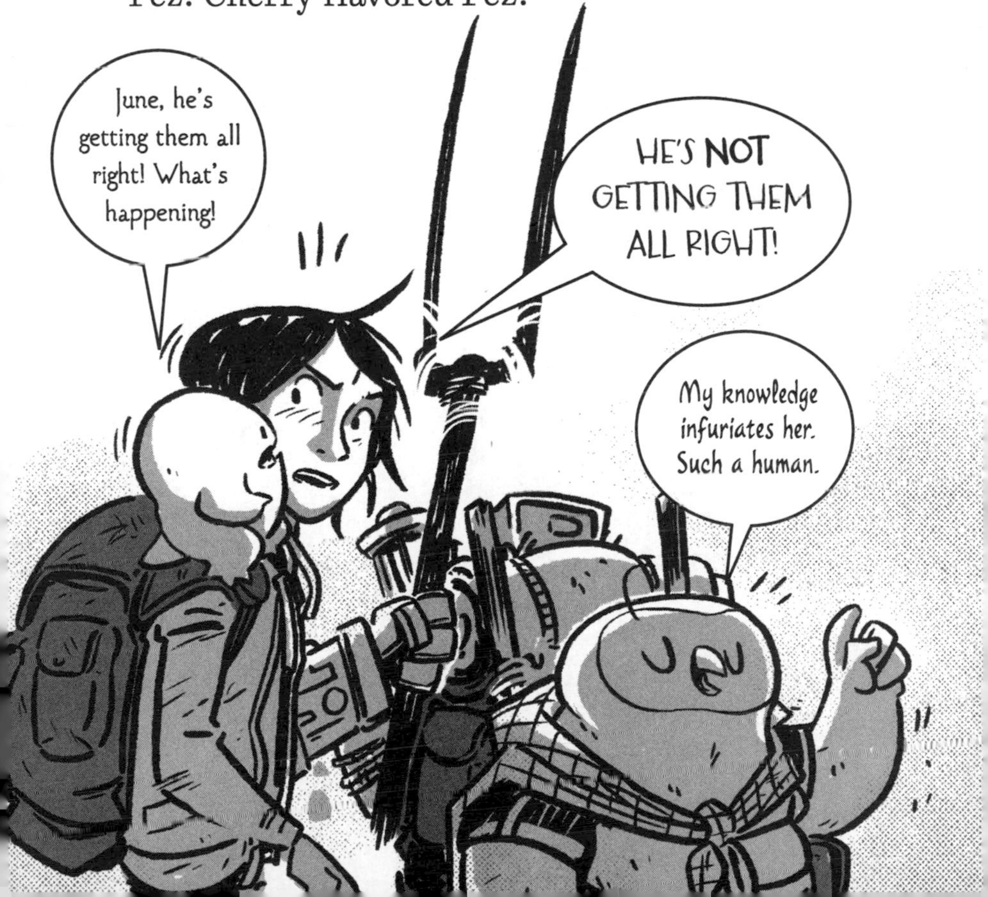
June, he's getting them all right! What's happening!
HE'S **NOT** GETTING THEM ALL RIGHT!
My knowledge infuriates her. Such a human.

# chapter nineteen

We're getting close. I can feel it. I can SEE it. The world is getting stranger. . . .

Our path is overrun with glowing green plant life. Odd, unknown noises burp and chirp from the shadows. It begins to feel like we're on some sort of apocalyptic walkabout. . . .

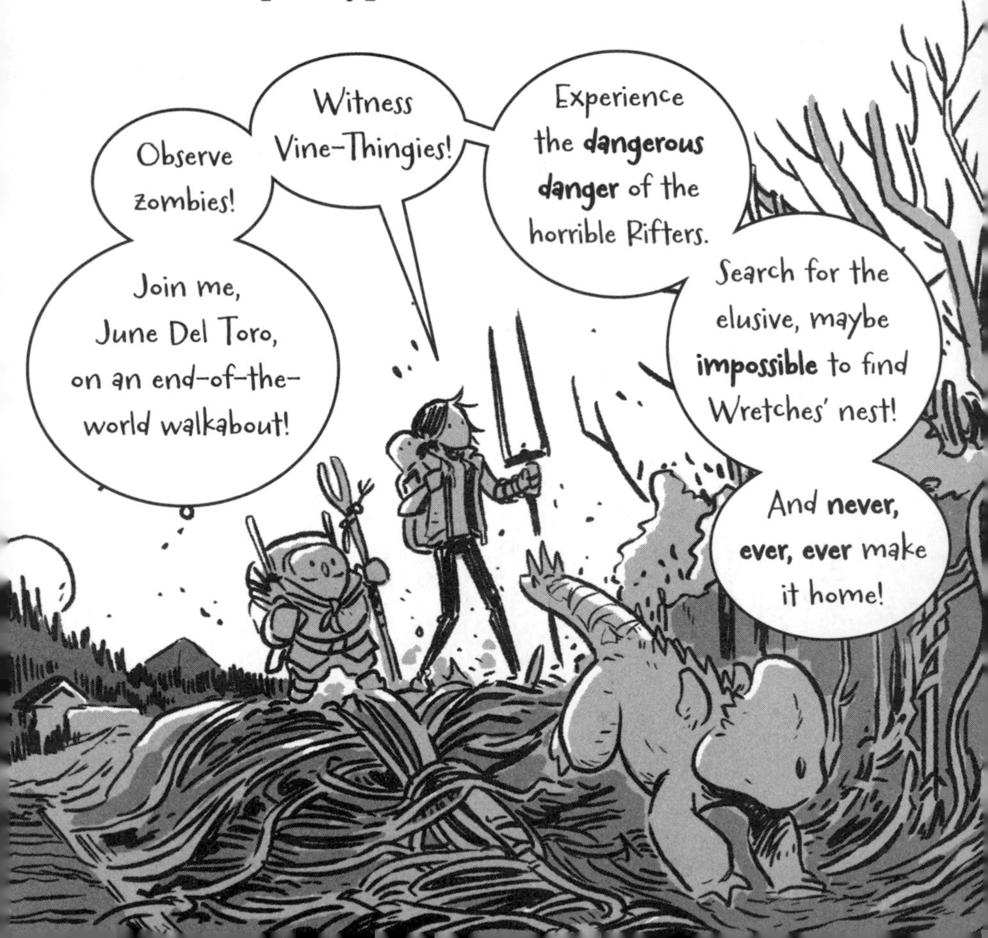

Observe zombies!
Witness Vine-Thingies!
Experience the **dangerous danger** of the horrible Rifters.
Search for the elusive, maybe **impossible** to find Wretches' nest!
And **never, ever, ever** make it home!
Join me, June Del Toro, on an end-of-the-world walkabout!

No one laughs.

Everyone seems to have lost the energy to chit-chat.

We walk on in silence. . . .

I smell the monsters before I see them.

The odor of evil.

The wind carries the scent, unfiltered and raw. It's foul.

And so are our surroundings.

Everything is warped and burnt. Homes lean back, away from where we're headed—it's like if they had legs, they'd get up outta there quicker than you could say "Wretches' nest."

There are huge claw gashes across sidewalks and streets, like the Wretches have been using them as a scratching post.

"There it is, up ahead," says Johnny Steve, sounding a little sad. "Their nest."

I squint into the distance. Moonlight is throwing dark shadows everywhere. I see the nest—a towering silhouette, like some sort of homemade volcano. Then I see the Wretches, in shadow. They look like gargoyles come to horrible, nightmarish life.

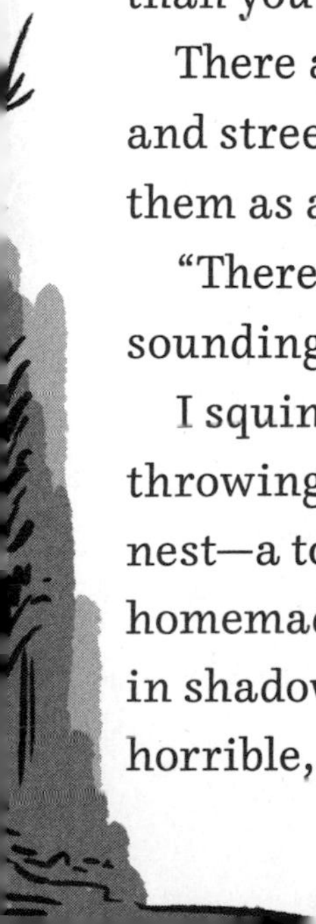

"It's too dark now," Johnny Steve says. "Your slow human legs took too long."

"Well, I *really* didn't want to wait until tomorrow," I say, hoping they don't hear the lie. "But if we have to, we have to."

"HAVE TO, HAVE TO!" Globlet exclaims. "CAMP OUT! Can we watch *Now and Then*? It's everyone's favorite! Please!"

Instantly, everyone's mood brightens. We'll say our good-byes tomorrow.

Tonight, we just relax.

We set up camp. I gather pine needles and kindling to build a fire. Neon "helps" by tearing chunks of siding off of houses and dropping them at my feet.

We huddle around the cozy fire. Johnny Steve hung on to some chocolate drizzle from the ice cream truck, and I show everyone how to make bootleg s'mores.

Johnny Steve is super impressed by the fire. "How did you make that?" he asks, his rubbery lips hanging open in awe.

"Building fires actually *is* a human skill," I tell him. "When I lived in the school, I made a fire using only a science lab magnifying glass and a pile of ungraded quizzes."

"Cool story," Globlet says. "You should brag about it."

I poke Globlet in the side and she squeaks and giggles.

Neon must not have been this close to fire before, because he inches toward it, curious. Ash blows off, his eyes water, his nose crinkles, and then—

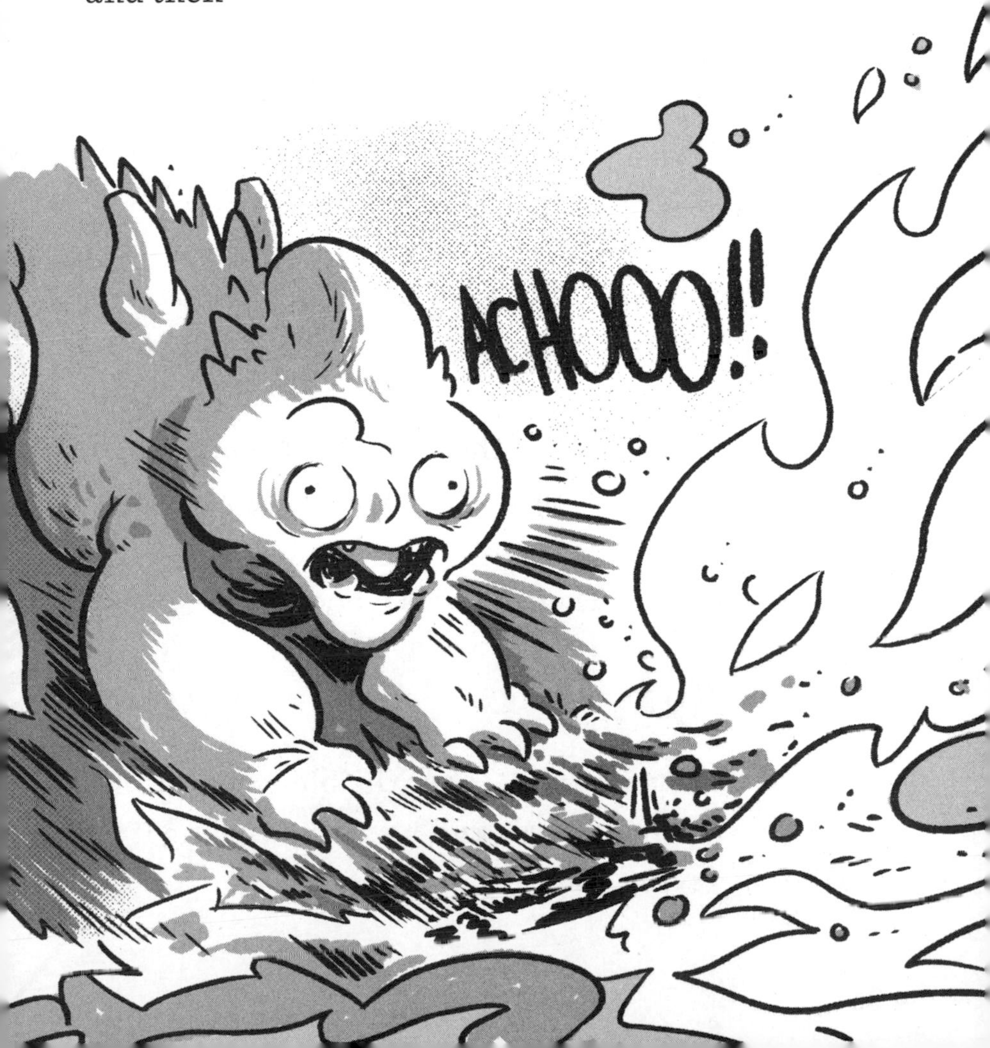
ACHOOO!!

Neon leaps back, confused. He shakes his head and paws curiously at his snout.

"No, Neon. You didn't *breathe* fire. You just sneezed," I say, laughing. "You're not *actually* a dragon. You just kinda look like one."

He brightens at the sound of my laughter. He does it a few more times, sniffing the air until his nose crinkles, then sneezing and making the campfire roar. He looks at us for approval each time, and hops from foot to foot when Globlet giggles.

"Neon's a natural sneezer!" Globlet says. "Way better than *you*, June."

Johnny Steve struts over, swinging his walking sword. "Human sneezes are notoriously lame."

I glare at the two of them, then: "Neon, how about you show Johnny Steve your biggest, *best* sneeze?"

Neon smiles. Then there is a booming—

# ACHOO!

The stream of fire catches the blade of Johnny Steve's walking sword, and he starts waving it around, trying to extinguish it—

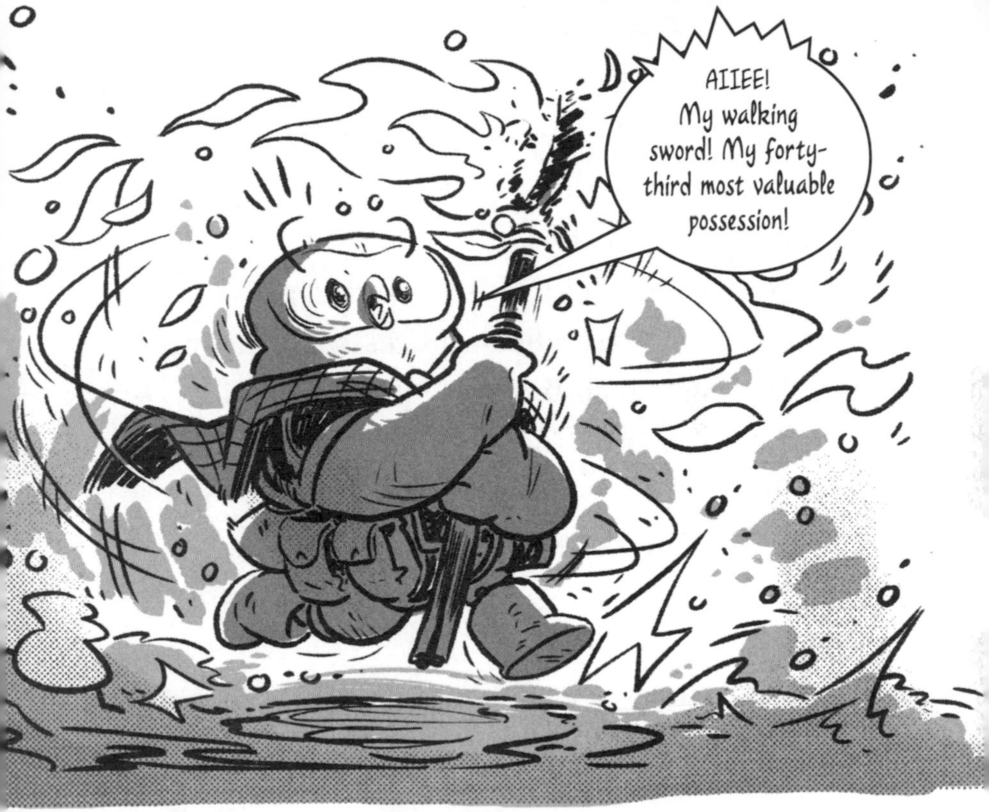
AIIEE!
My walking sword! My forty-third most valuable possession!

Now we're all clutching our stomachs with laughter. When we get ourselves together, Globlet snuggles into my shoulder.

I reach out to rub Neon's head. He finally, reluctantly, inches toward me. I scratch his neck, silently encouraging him to come closer.

"Hey, Neon. I'm, uh—I'm sorry," I tell him. My words are quiet, not much louder than the crackle of the fire. "If I were you, I wouldn't want to hear those Ogres' roars or those Rifters' voices again, either. And you never will. 'Cause first thing tomorrow, you're going someplace safe. I know you don't quite understand that, but it'll be for the best."

Neon yawns and rolls over in the grass. His paw is outstretched and rests against my leg. His body is cold, but it feels okay, with the campfire burning itself down to glowing embers.

And we fall asleep like that. . . .

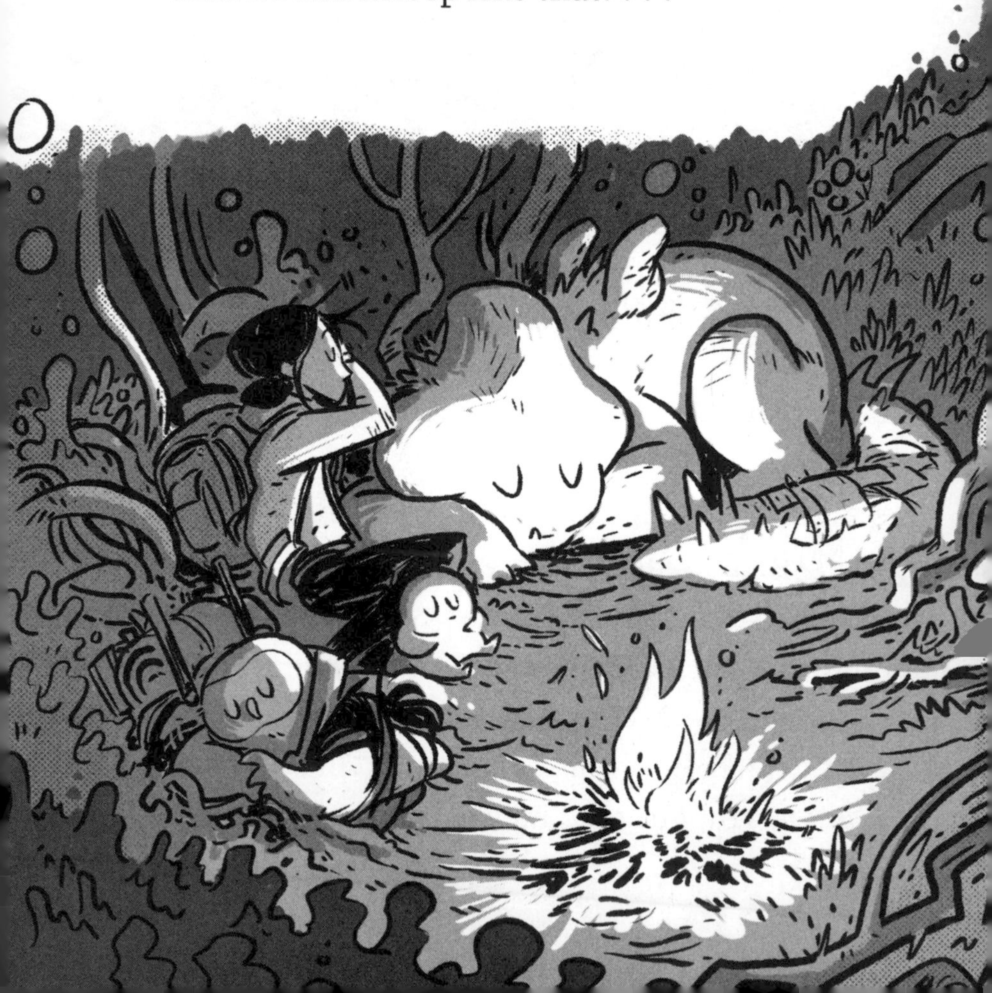

# chapter twenty

I wake, but I don't open my eyes.

I'm not ready for today. I don't want to take Neon to the nest.

So I keep my eyes shut. Like maybe if I don't open them, the day will never actually begin.

But then I hear Neon panting. And I feel him nibbling at my foot, trying to shake me awake.

"Morning, Neon," I say, finally opening my eyes. He's staring at me, waiting, giving me a look like he *knows* things but can't express them.

I sigh. I tell myself this is one of those things you just have to *do*, no putting it off, because that will just make it harder.

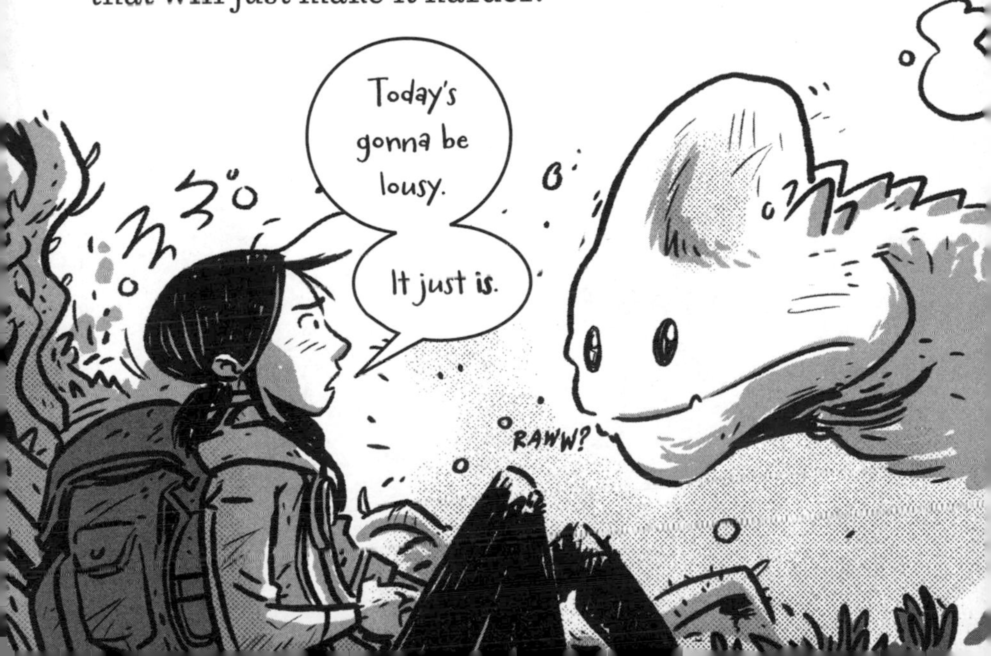

Today's gonna be lousy.
It just is.
RAWW?

I'm going to miss Neon.

*I'm going to miss a Wretch!*

It's the first time I'm genuinely, 100 percent glad that my friends aren't here. They wouldn't understand this.

But that's only because they've never met Neon.

And now, they never will. . . .

Soon, Globlet is awake—stomping around, all grumpy because she hasn't had her morning coffee. Johnny Steve does 196 jumping jacks. "As all humans do each morning," he explains.

Then we get to it. Packed up, headed out.

Cresting the hill, we see the Wretches' nest in daylight in all its terrifying glory . . .

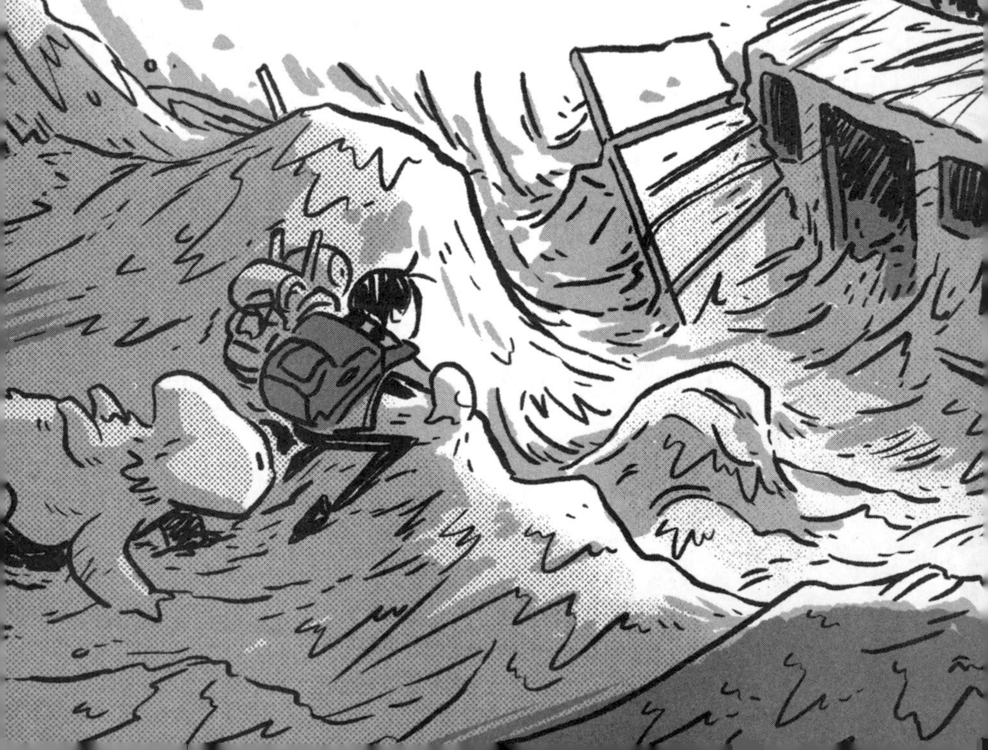

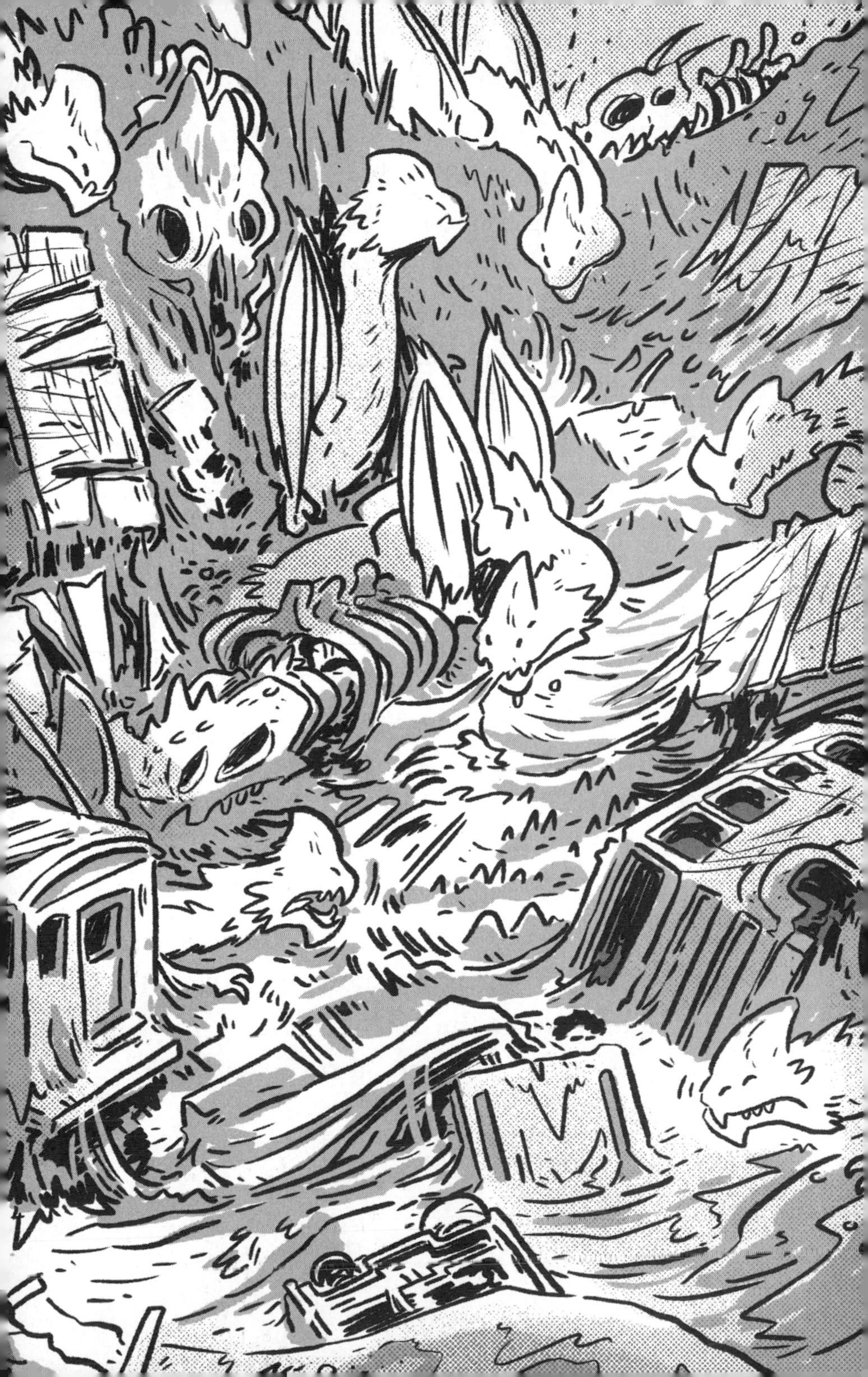

"Home sweet home, eh, Neon?" I say, trying to ignore the fact that I'm staring at one of the more horrifying sights I've ever seen.

"Oh, neat," Globlet says. "They have a corner just for carcasses."

I shoot Globlet a quick glare. *We need Neon to be happy. It might be horrible-looking to us, but it's the only safe place to leave him.*

Near the top of the nest, two Wretches are fighting over a hunk of meat. I wonder, *Will Neon be like that soon? Will he be a ferocious, monster-flesh-devouring servant of Reżżóćħ?*

*Or will he remember that once, when he was very young, he met a girl who told him not to attack strange creatures, not to be evil, and to never, ever, ever eat walkie-talkies without permission?*

I can't think about it any longer—I have to just do it. "Okay, Neon, it's time." I say it quickly, because I feel my lower lip starting to tremble.

I walk halfway to the nest with Neon. Any further, and I'm just about guaranteed to get torn to bits.

Looking into Neon's eyes, I suddenly understand why my parents cried when they dropped me off at summer camp.

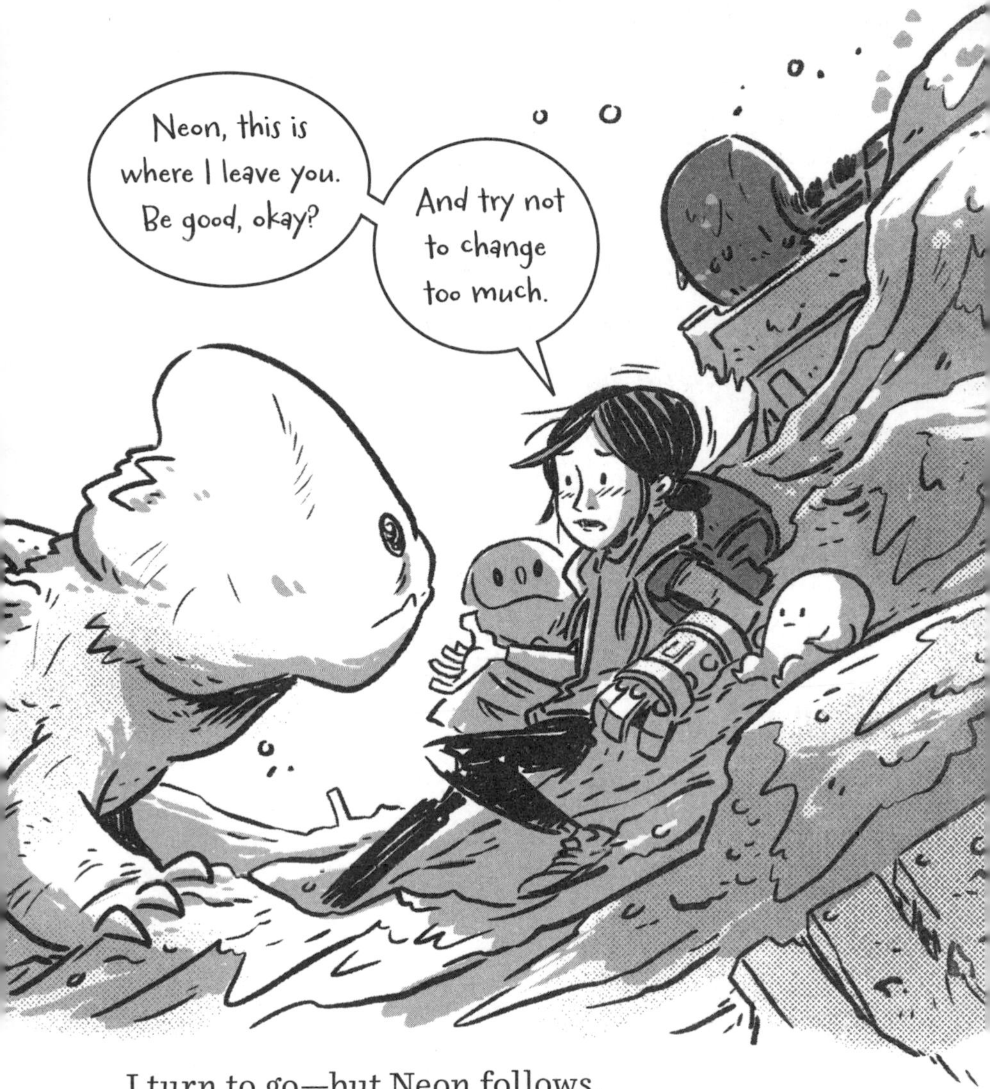
Neon, this is where I leave you. Be good, okay?
And try not to change too much.

I turn to go—but Neon follows.

"No, Neon. I go this way. You go that way," I say, pointing to the nest.

Neon's head cocks, then he makes a noise that sounds like Wretch laughter. Like he thinks all of this is a game.

And that makes this worse.

"GO!" I say. "You have to GO!"

Neon's shoulders draw up. He doesn't understand. He can't.

He takes a slow, apologetic step toward me, like he needs me—and it breaks my heart. *I can't do this any longer. I have to end this.*

"Fine!" I say. "If you won't go to them—I'll make them come to you."

I step past him, then—

*CRACK!* I bang a broken piece of my spear against the Thing-A-Ma-Blasty Gadget Blaster.

"WRETCHES!" I shout, using my best J. Jonah Jameson commanding newsroom voice. "COME TAKE THIS ONE! HE NEEDS YOU!"

A single Wretch swings its long neck toward me. Its cold, silver eyes lock on to mine—and I bang the spear harder and louder—

*CRACK!*

*CRACK!*

*CRACK!*

Finally, more Wretches turn—then beat their wings and lift off.

Neon is frozen. His talons dig into the ground. My sneakers push off the same ground.

And I run.

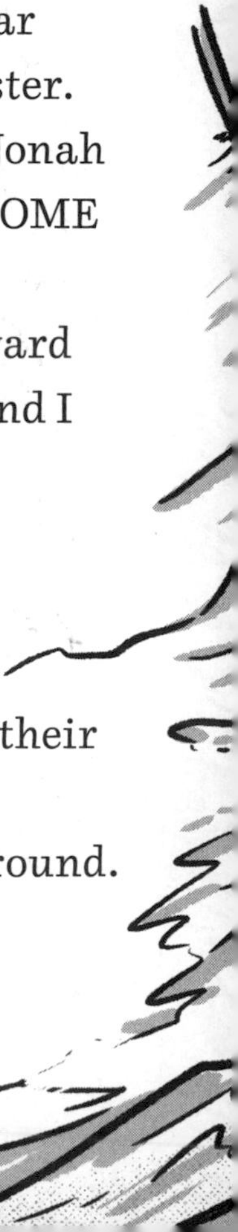

I'm racing, nearly tumbling, back down the nest hill. My feet go out from under me, and then I'm sliding, reaching out, grabbing on to an overturned Jeep. I pull myself behind it, out of sight.

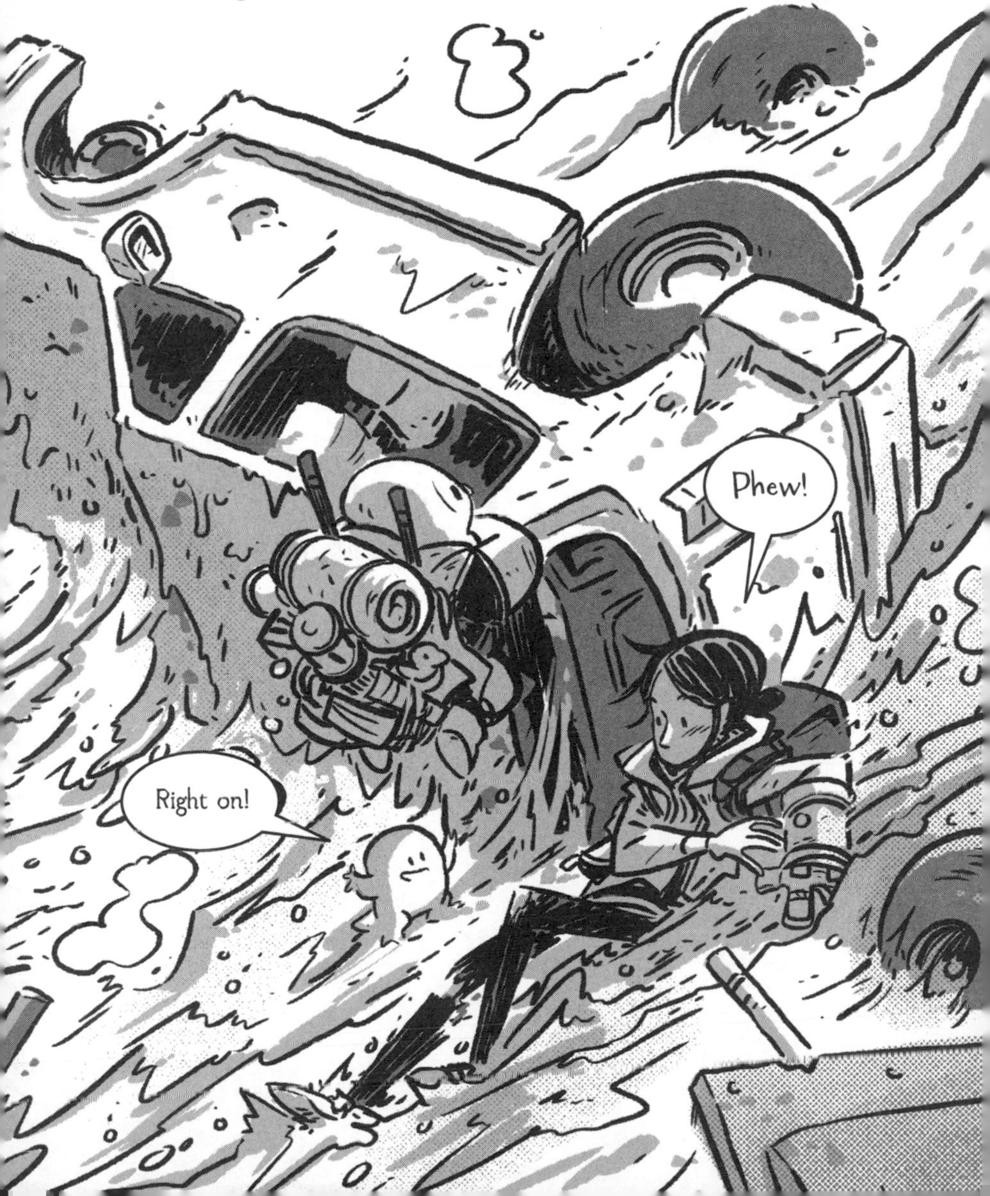
Phew!
Right on!

Peeking around the side, I see Wretches circling Neon.

One particularly large, scar-covered Wretch uses its snout to push Neon toward the nest.

Slowly, reluctantly he trudges upward. A crumbling billboard advertising a used car dealership looms over him.

He looks so very small and alone.

This is hard.

But that's what it means to be in charge of your own adventure. Sometimes you have to do the hard thing.

And I remind myself: the reason it's the hard thing is because it's the right thing.

That's what I was telling myself when I nearly ran out of breath, trying to save Neon underwater.

And that's what I'm telling myself now: I'm doing the right thing.

Or at least I thought I was. . . .

# chapter
# twenty-one

Neon looks back for me—slow at first, and then faster, frantic.

Globlet grabs my hand. "June, he looks scared. And I feel scared."

"I'm not sure this is right," Johnny Steve says.

Wretches crowd around Neon. One prods his back, where his wings used to be. And then, at once—

# KEE-AWWW!!

The Wretches attack! Neon whirls, trying to escape, but one enormous talon *snatches him*! The largest Wretch, some sort of den mother, *hurls* him into the horde!

Neon is writhing, twisting, flailing.

They're toying with him. Because they know he's damaged, they know he can't fly, they know he's not like them.

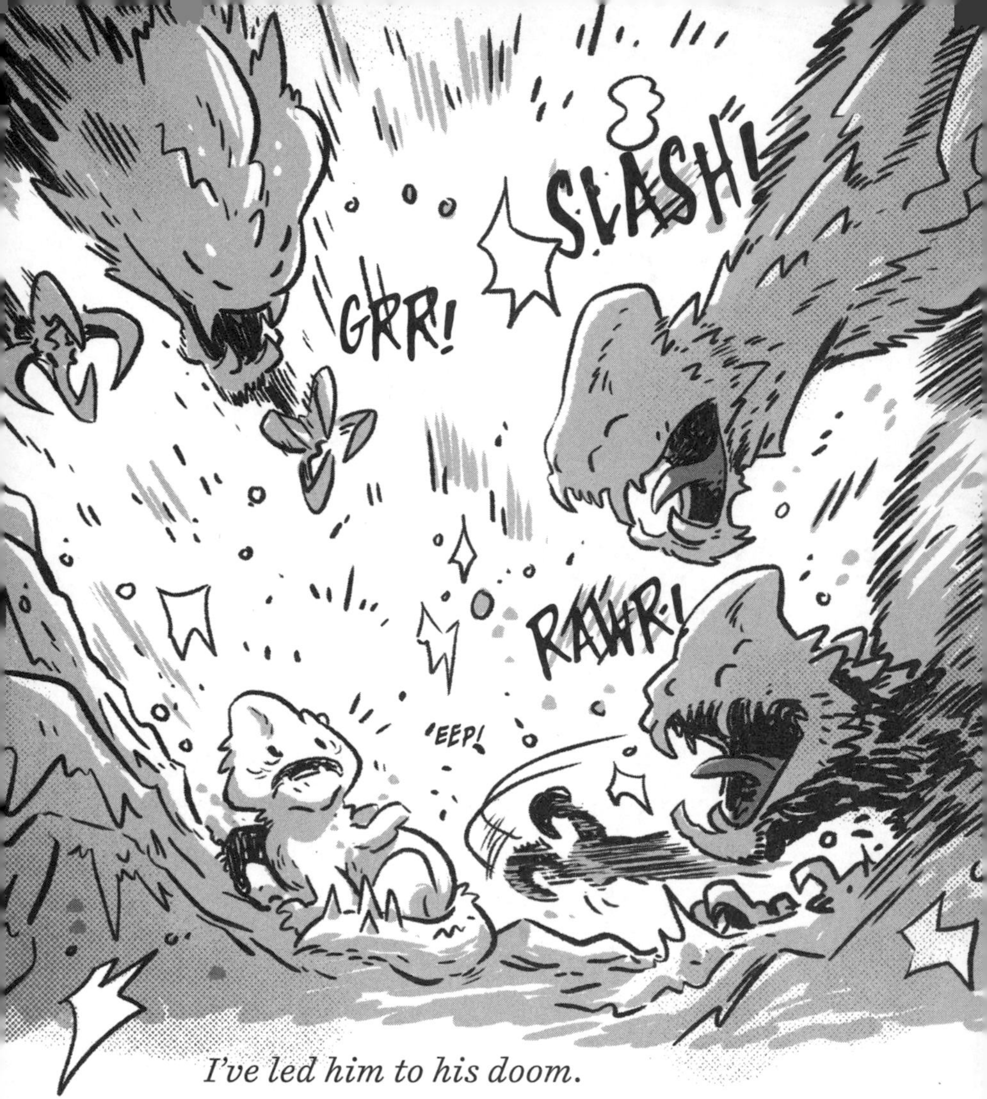
GRR!
SLASH!
RAWR!
EEP!

*I've led him to his doom.*

I burst out from behind the Jeep and race toward the horde of Wretches. I'm not thinking straight. Not even close.

Racing up the hill, I see Neon curled up into a little ball. It's so similar to what the Rifters did to him—like horrible déjà vu—that I want to puke. The Wretches are evil, yes—but I didn't think they'd be evil to their own kind!

Behind me, I hear Globlet and Johnny Steve screaming my name. Telling me to turn back. Telling me to get down.

But I don't, because in this moment I'm not scared of the Wretches.

However, it's not the Wretches they're warning me about. It's something else entirely. . . .

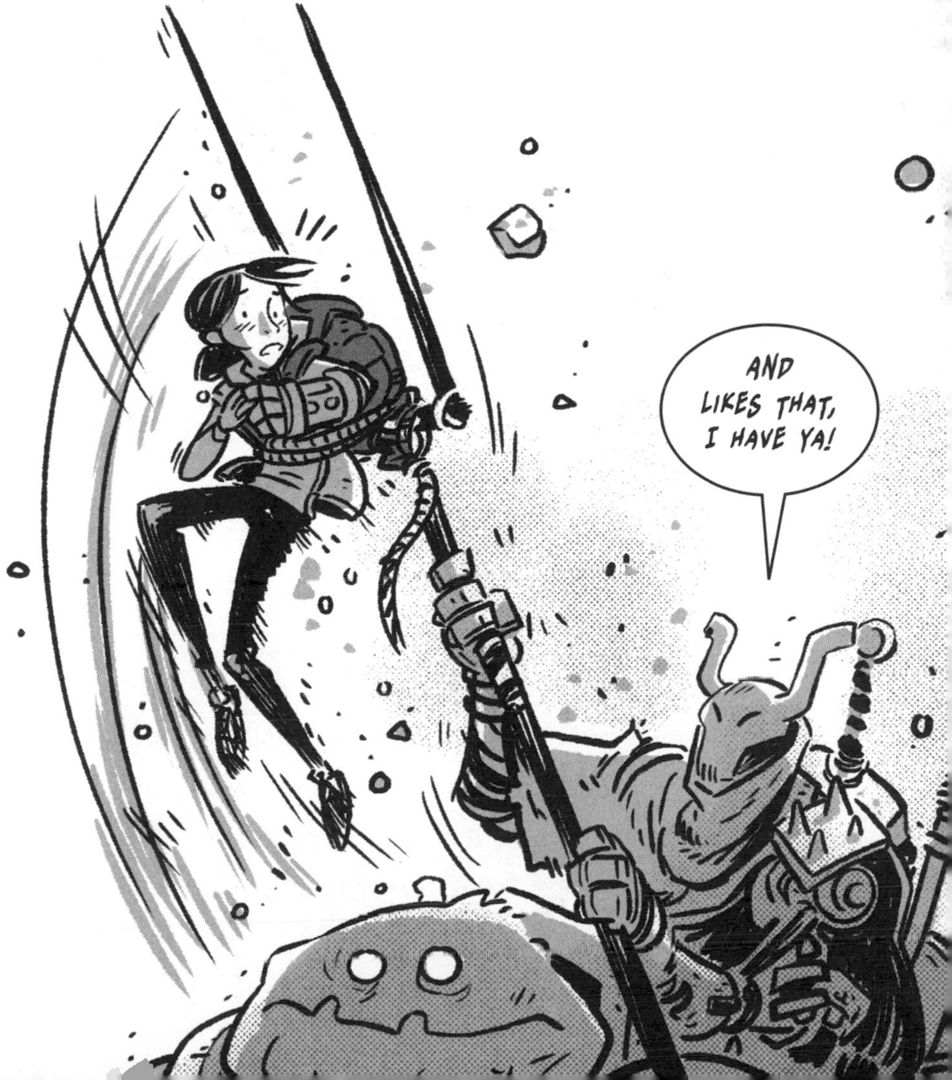
AND LIKES THAT, I HAVE YA!

"NO!" I cry out as I'm ripped upward, into the air.

"Yes," the Boss Rifter says, smiling cruelly.

I'm instantly clawing at the lasso, trying to use the Thing-A-Ma-Blasty Gadget Blaster to slice myself free. But the Ogre sweeps me across the ground. The Blaster bangs *hard* against a chunk of rubble and my entire arm goes numb.

"Leggo!" I cry. "Leggo!"

The Boss Rifter does *not* "leggo."

Instead, the lasso is swung up, over his shoulder. I'm suddenly weightless, tumbling through the air. This is like a surprise upside-down roller coaster—and I *hate* surprise upside-down roller coasters! If a roller coaster is gonna go upside down, I want *advance notice*!

I see Johnny Steve and Globlet, racing to catch me. But they won't make it.

And the last thing I see, as I'm carried away, is Neon. And a massive Wretch swinging a talon into his side.

It is a killing blow.

Neon cries out. Slowly, like it's a scene out of a movie, he sinks to the ground.

I open my mouth to scream, but blood rushes to my head, and everything goes black.

# chapter
# twenty-two

When I come to, my head aches, and I can't tell how much time has passed. Thick, heavy ropes bind my limbs. I crane my neck, and—

*What the . . .*

There's a giant *pirate ship anchor* next to me.

*Oh man—what dimension is this?*

There's a staticky buzzing sound—the lights overheard flicker, as some last, tiny bit of electricity shudders through them. In the dim light, I see a pirate. The real deal. Eye patch. Wooden leg. The whole thing.

Have these Rifters dragged me onto the set of a Pirates of the Caribbean movie? Oh no, am I *inside Davy Jones's locker?*

I spin my head wildly, before spotting a sign that explains it all—

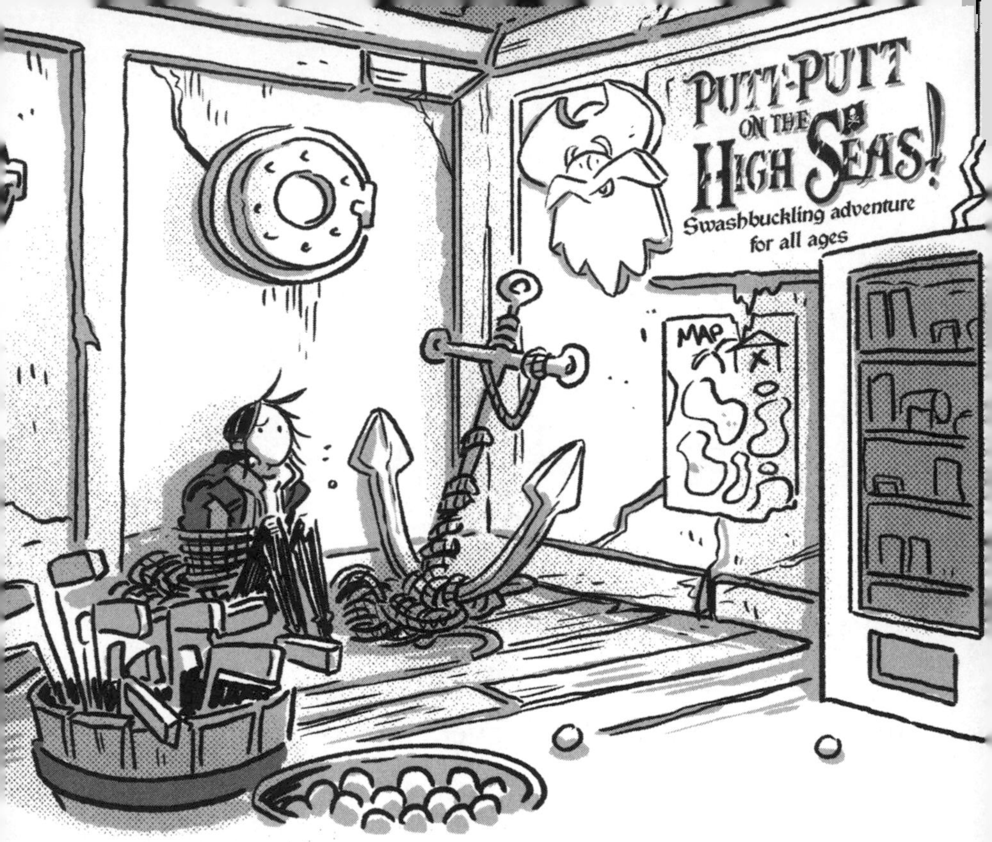
PUTT-PUTT
ON THE
HIGH SEAS!
Swashbuckling adventure
for all ages
MAP

Okay, so, *time to play catch-up, brain*. I've been taken prisoner by the Rifters. I'm inside, presumably—their *hideout*. And their hideout is a *mini golf course*, because, well, *the end of the world is the weirdest*.

*Think. Think. Need to escape*. My eyes dart left and right, searching for—

KRAK!

A door flies open. I shut my eyes, pretending to still be knocked out in case they spill the beans on anything worthwhile.

"When do we go back for the baby Wretch?" I hear a voice ask. It's the Rifter, Flunk, who struggled with the concept of a tire swing. "You said it was a gift for Thrull."

"S'right!" Boss says. "Ya see, Flunk, to prove our loyalty to Thrull, we needs to bring him a gift. A gift of value! Winged Wretches can bend minds; that gives 'em value. And a baby Wretch, that ain't been trained up? One Thrull can raise however he wants? That's even MORE value! And the big grand slam part is . . . it's got no wings! A Wingless Wretch! That goes and makes it the best gift of all, cuz it can't escape."

"Yep! A mighty good gift, Boss! Best gift I ever heard of! I bet no better gift exists, except maybe a coupon for—"

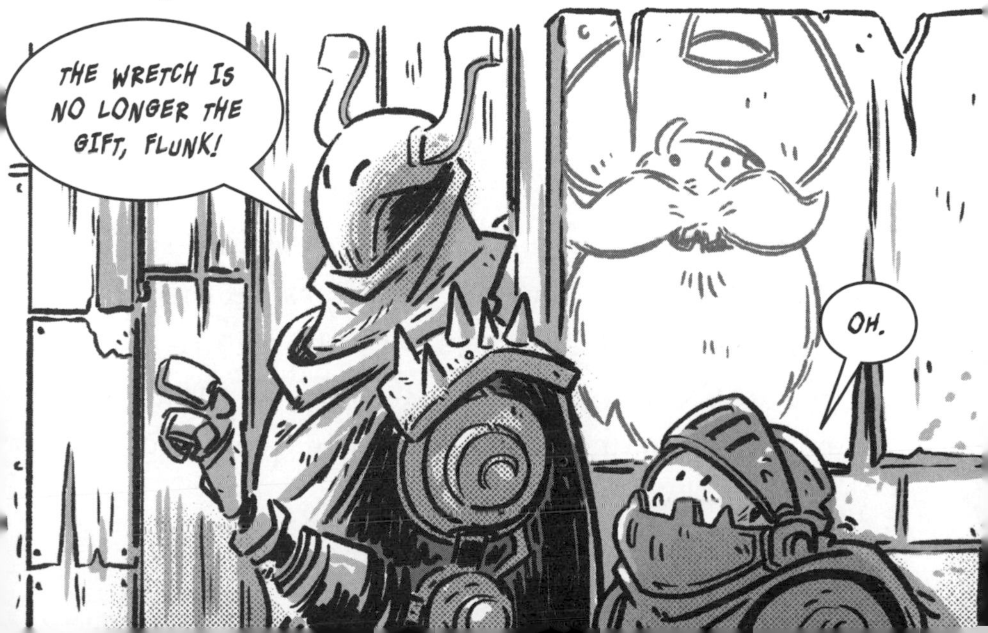
THE WRETCH IS NO LONGER THE GIFT, FLUNK!
OH.

I hear Boss and Flunk's scrap-metal boots on the floor.

"The baby Wretch would be a happy-makin' thing to Thrull," the Boss Rifter says. "But Thrull wields big power now. He's got lots a' happy-makin' things. We must do more. Lucky fer us, I know jus' what Thrull wants. . . ."

"A pizza party?"

"REVENGE!" Boss barks. "Think of how Thrull will reward our loyalty when we hand over one of his sworn enemies!" He *kicks* the anchor and my eyes fly open.

The Boss looms over me. "How lucky I am that we found each other," he says, with an ugly chuckle. "The one with the Multi-Hand. . . ."

Whoa, what?

"Back it up there a sec, pal," I say, squinting up at him. "The multi-*what*?"

The Boss Rifter's long, thick fingers tap the Thing-A-Ma-Blasty Gadget Blaster.

"Ohhhh, you mean the Thing-A-Ma-Blasty Gadget Blaster!" I say. "I used to call it the Gift. And, wait, you guys call it the Multi-Hand? Okay, we need to all get on the same page here, name-wise. I mean, just for ease of communication. Y'know what—how about we just call it Blasty? Simple, to the point."

The Boss Rifter snickers. "Soon, it'll belong to Thrull. Along with you. And then he can call it any name he likes. See, it's all goin' ta belong to him. Until Ŗeżżóch arrivens. . . ."

He makes a horrible laughing sound—choking as he cackles. Bits of spittle fly. I'm turning my head to avoid the shower of saliva when I see—

Blood.

A few tiny drops of magenta and teal on the Boss's boot.

It all comes rushing back. The moment *before* it all went black.

Neon.

Crying out.

Overwhelmed by that savage, sinister swarm of Wretches.

And that final, horrible blow.

I feel a lump in my throat. But I refuse to let this villain see me cry. I swallow it down, stiffen, and stare up at the Boss. "I'm going to ask you a question," I say. "And please. Just *please*—give me a real answer."

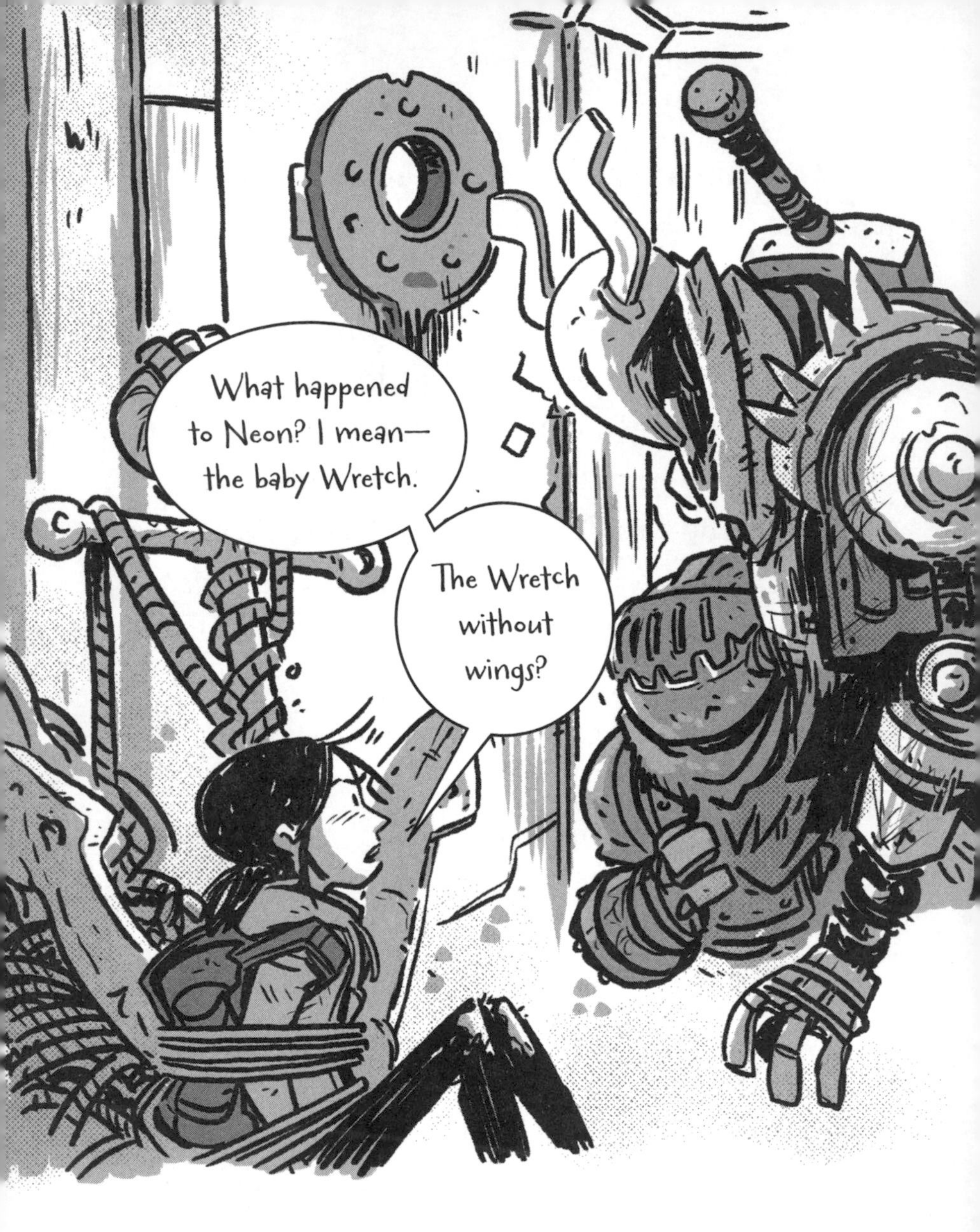
What happened to Neon? I mean—the baby Wretch.
The Wretch without wings?

Boss looks me over: torn hoodie, ripped backpack, and sneakers covered with mud and slime and grease. He considers me for a while. Then, finally, he seems to decide I deserve an honest answer. . . .

"Dead," he says. "The baby Wretch is dead. There were a dozen Wretches atop him when we left, with more on the way."

I manage to nod, then quickly look away.

I'm holding my breath, clenching my teeth, fighting back tears.

"I am sorry," the Boss says, kneeling down. "So very sorry, but—" He reaches out, his fingers tighten around Blasty, and then he yanks it off my wrist.

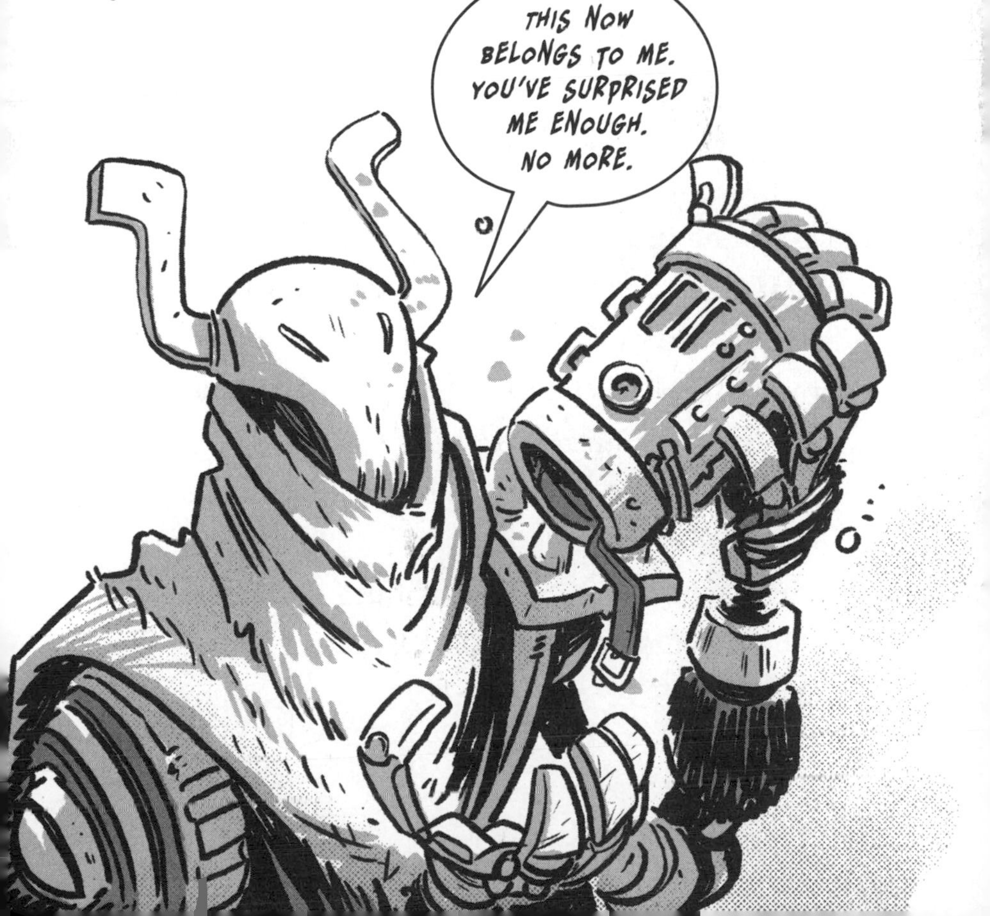
THIS NOW BELONGS TO ME. YOU'VE SURPRISED ME ENOUGH. NO MORE.

And then he's standing. "Flunk," he barks. "Guard the prisoner. We leave at dawn."

"You can count on me, Boss!"

Then the Boss leaves, slamming the door behind him so hard that a rack of golf clubs topples over and a bucket of balls spills.

"Ooh, roundies!" Flunk shrieks. He chases after the balls excitedly, shouting with glee when he finally grabs one.

I remember him on the tire swing, unable to figure out how it worked. And this is basically the same.

He lifts his faceguard, examining the strange, foreign sporting good.

Then he bites it. His teeth must be half metal, because he takes an easy chunk out of it. Then chews. And chews. Golf ball crumbs tumble from his mouth. "It's good," he finally announces. "But not *great.*"

I sigh. "Dude, it's a golf ball. For golf. You hit the balls."

"Hit—the balls?" he asks, but it comes out all garbled because he's choking down the last hunk of golf ball.

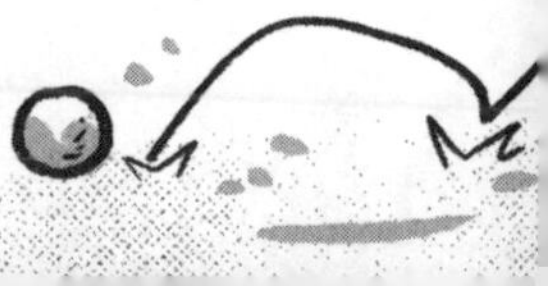

"With clubs," I say, nodding to the spilled pile.

He looks at the balls. Then at the clubs. Then back to the balls. Back to the clubs. Balls. Clubs. Balls. Clubs. Then, finally, a long "Ohhhhh . . . I get it!"

And a moment later—

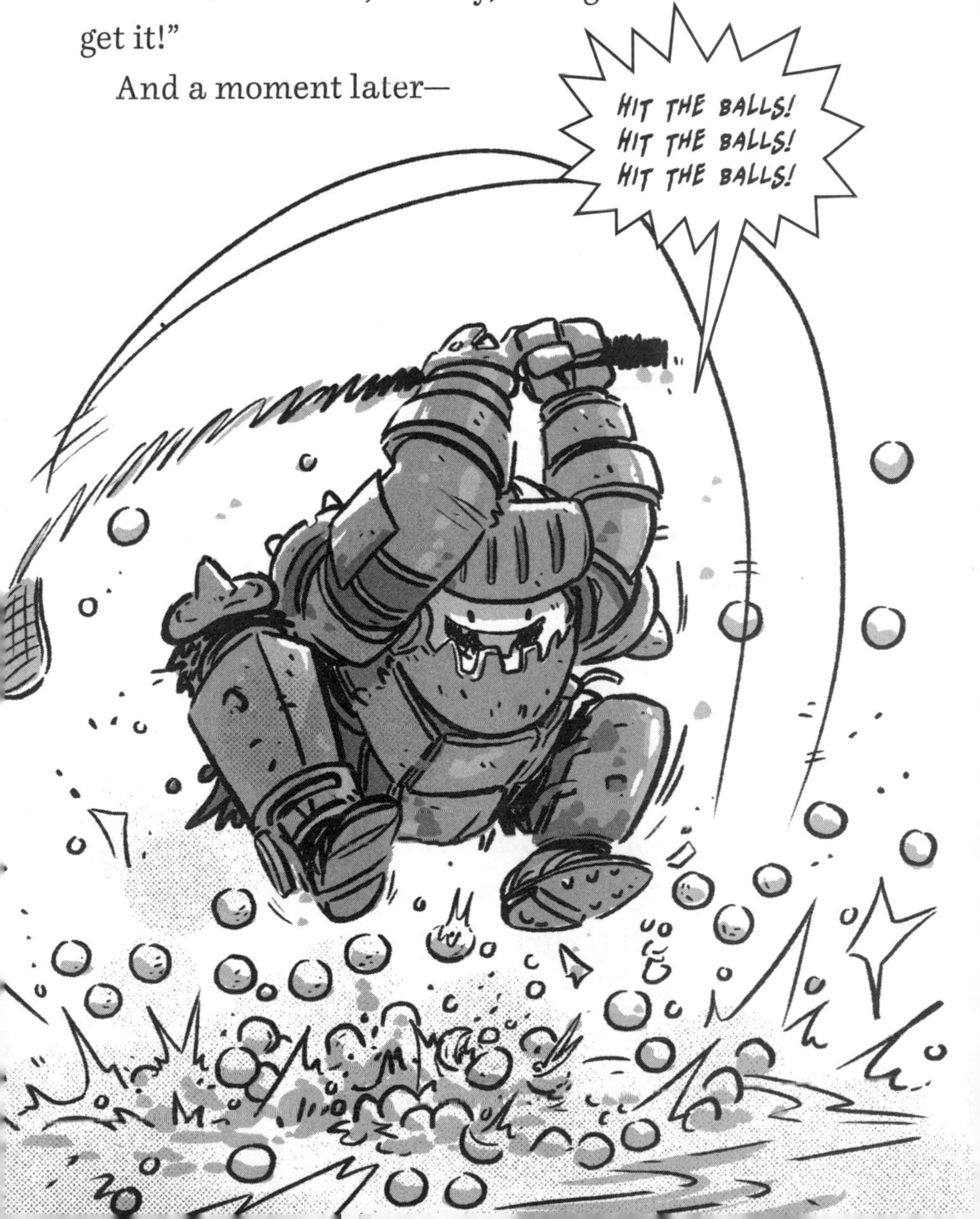
HIT THE BALLS!
HIT THE BALLS!
HIT THE BALLS!

Soon, he's out of balls—so he uses the club to *WHACK* the ball vending machine. It pops open and a tsunami of balls floods out, bouncing and rolling through the back door and out onto the driving range.

Flunk chases after them, giggling and shouting, "I'm gonna get you, roundies!"

And here I am.

Alone again.

I've messed everything up.

I'm being held prisoner by other-dimensional pirates inside a sprawling, tourist-trap mini golf course secret base. And soon, I'll be delivered to our arch-nemesis, who's constructing some sort of Tower thing to summon Ṛeżżőċh the Ancient, Destructor of Worlds.

Neon is dead, all because I stupidly tried to return him to his family.

Speaking of families, I'll never see *mine* again, not after Ṛeżżőċh turns our world into his own bottomless buffet of horrid delights. And I can forget about seeing my *other* family, too: Jack, Quint, Dirk, Biggun, Rover, Globlet, Skaelka, and all the monsters I call friends.

Even Johnny Steve.

And now—*ARGH*—I don't even have my

weapon. The one thing that might get me *out* of this mess.

I rest my head against the cold metal of the anchor. No hope. No path forward. No way out.

This is the most alone, the most lost, that I've ever been.

Actually, no.

That's not true.

I *have* been this alone before.

And it was not so long ago. . . .

# chapter twenty-three

I'm remembering the last time I felt this alone.
This memory, though—it feels *so real*. Like it's
more than just a memory. Like I'm *there*, back in
those middle school halls. . . .

I was at rock bottom. Crater city.

I remember clawing through my locker, looking for a bag of Fritos that I thought maybe I left in there, when—

## SMASH!

My framed Certificate of Merit shattered against the floor. I won it for being the first ever sixth-grade senior editor of the school paper.

I had hung it on my locker door.

And there it was on the floor, lying in a pile of broken glass. But I didn't care.

That dumb piece of paper didn't matter anymore, because NOTHING from my old life mattered anymore.

And the weight of that hit me like a cannonball.

Everything I'd envisioned for myself was *gone*.

I had a PLAN for my future. I always had clear-cut goals. I had my future mapped out by first grade, when half my classmates were still sucking Elmer's straight out of the tube.

I used to play it in my head, like a movie, during that ninety-nine-second sprint to the bus every morning. And then on the bus. And, well, all the time.

Youngest editor of the middle school paper: did that. Check mark.

Then, it would be first slow dance at the

eighth-grade formal, driver's license at sixteen, followed by starting midfielder on the Hounds lacrosse team, taking us to the state championship. Then an internship at the *Morning Horn News* in the *big city*.

Next, a scholarship to my first-choice college, graduate near the top of the class, then I'd move to the city, land my dream job at the *Morning Horn*, three years there and I'd be the paper's first female editor-in-chief—

And y'know what else? Y'know what the biggest, best part of my big plan was? I was going to do all of it with my family cheering me on, watching me become the person I was supposed to become.

But then the world was suddenly *shattered*. Just like the glass that held my dumb, useless Certificate of Merit.

I stared at it, on the floor—thinking about how my hopes and dreams were dead, done, destroyed—just like the rest of the world.

My hand tightened around the spear in my hand, and I knew what I would do.

I would break that too.

And once it broke, once my only weapon was gone—then I'd be able to truly, fully GIVE UP.

Anger rushed through me and I raised the spear and swung—

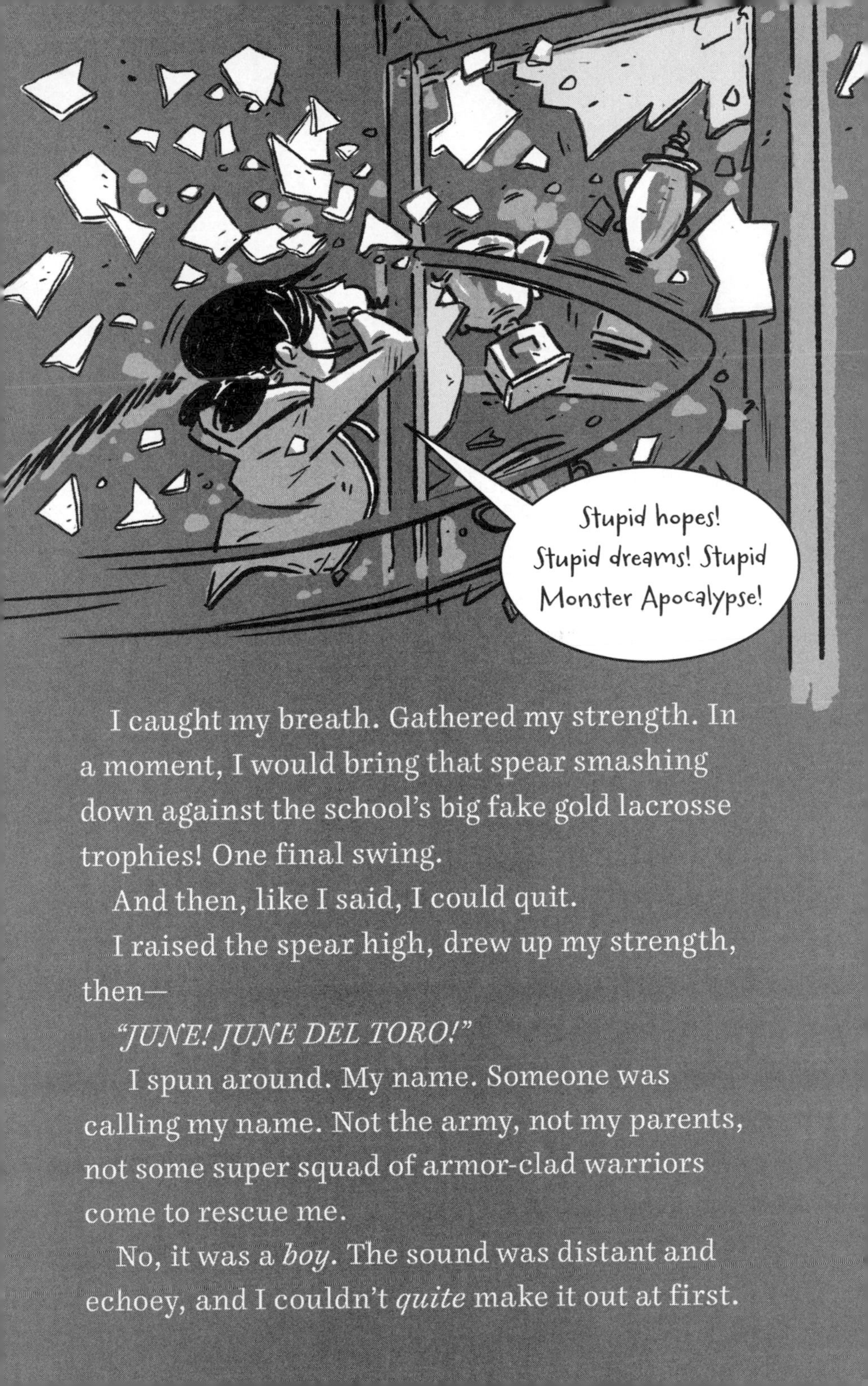
Stupid hopes! Stupid dreams! Stupid Monster Apocalypse!

I caught my breath. Gathered my strength. In a moment, I would bring that spear smashing down against the school's big fake gold lacrosse trophies! One final swing.

And then, like I said, I could quit.

I raised the spear high, drew up my strength, then—

*"JUNE! JUNE DEL TORO!"*

I spun around. My name. Someone was calling my name. Not the army, not my parents, not some super squad of armor-clad warriors come to rescue me.

No, it was a *boy*. The sound was distant and echoey, and I couldn't *quite* make it out at first.

I realized—with a mix of shock, horror, and wonder—that it was freaking *JACK SULLIVAN*. . . .

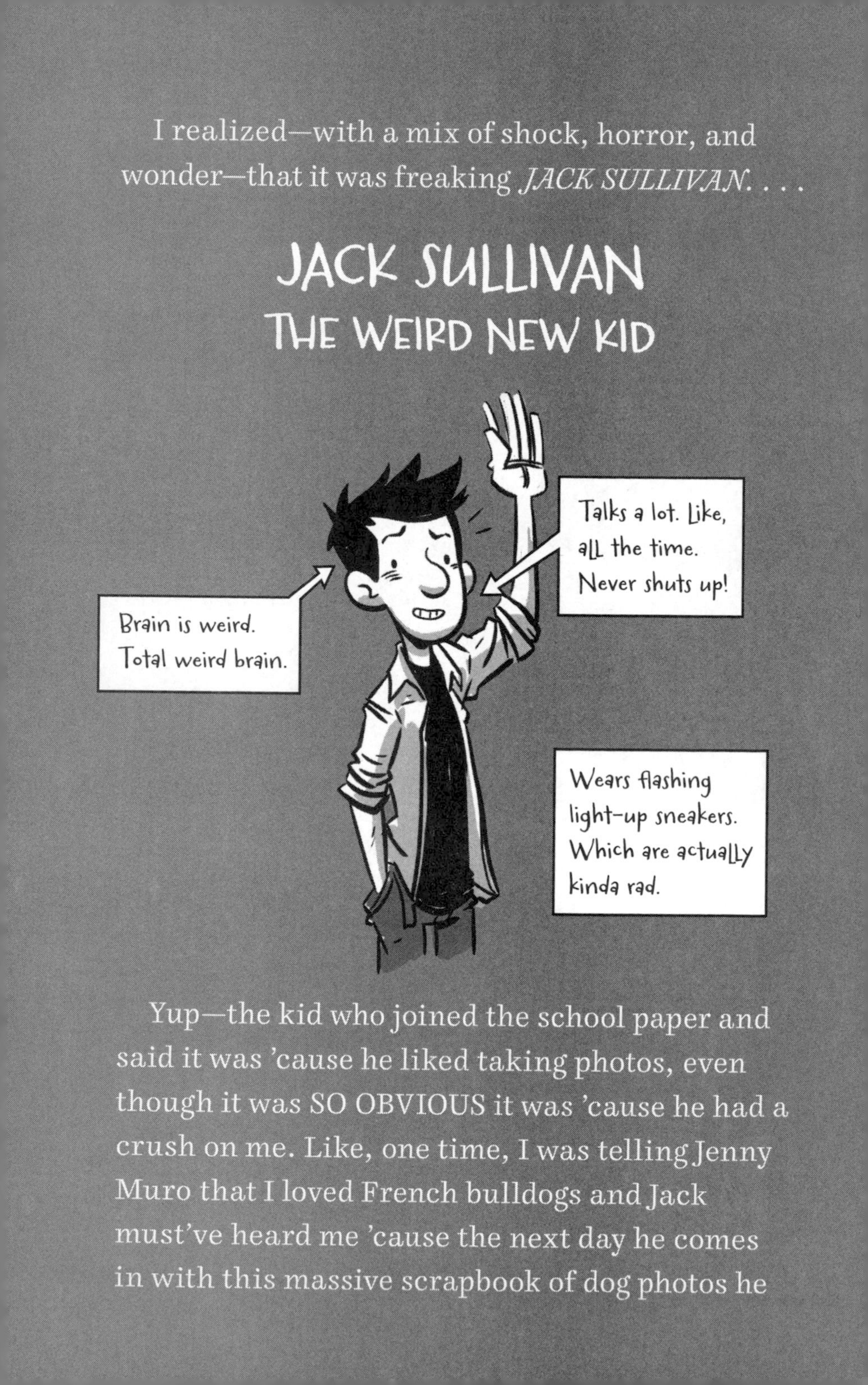
JACK SULLIVAN
THE WEIRD NEW KID
Talks a lot. Like, all the time. Never shuts up!
Brain is weird. Total weird brain.
Wears flashing light-up sneakers. Which are actually kinda rad.

Yup—the kid who joined the school paper and said it was 'cause he liked taking photos, even though it was SO OBVIOUS it was 'cause he had a crush on me. Like, one time, I was telling Jenny Muro that I loved French bulldogs and Jack must've heard me 'cause the next day he comes in with this massive scrapbook of dog photos he cut out of magazines. And he was all like, "Wait, whaaaat, *you like dogs, too*??! I had zero idea! I just always carry around this dog photo magazine scrapbook!! WEIRD! We're, like—CONNECTED!" And I just stood there, groaning and thinking, *Dude, freaking* everyone *likes dogs*.

And then, a few months later, he asked someone to ask someone to ask someone to ask someone if I liked him. But one of those people was Quint, and Quint is, well, Quint. So when it was Quint's turn to ask someone, he asked Mr. Burr, *my math teacher*, which led to *maybe* the single most uncomfortable moment of my life—

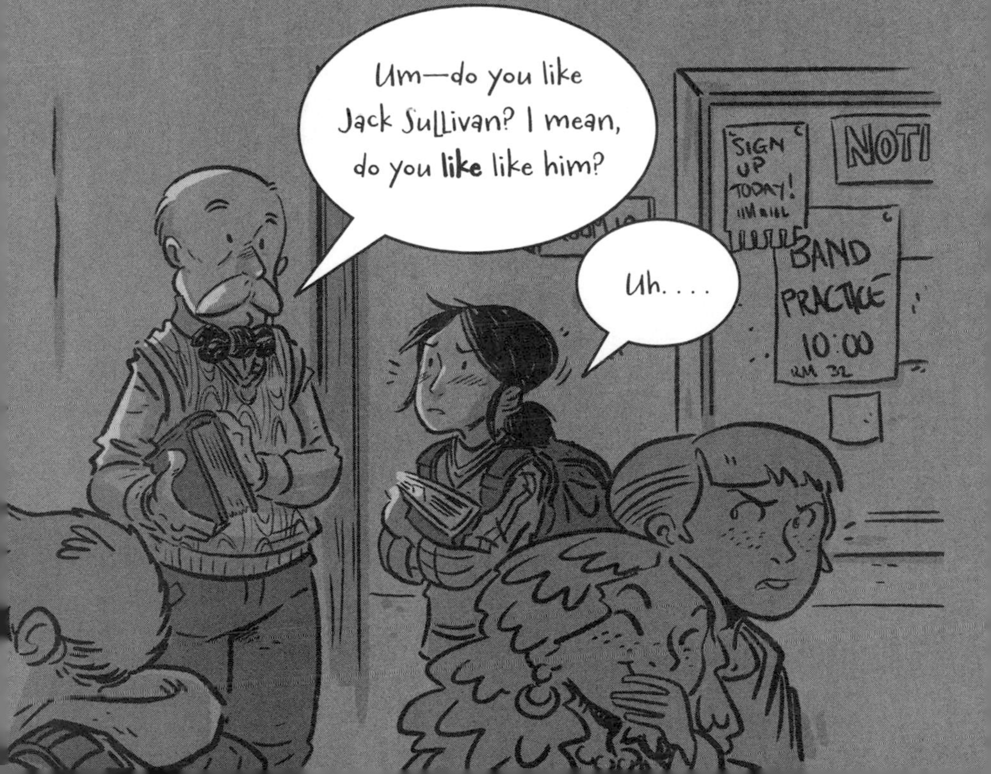
Um—do you like Jack Sullivan? I mean, do you **like** like him?
Uh. . . .
SIGN UP TODAY!
NOTI
BAND PRACTICE 10:00

Yep, Jack Sullivan.

And he was *in* the school.

His voice was coming from the end of the sixth-grade wing. I looked at my spear, suddenly glad I hadn't finished smashing it, and moved in that direction. Peering through double doors, I saw him *racing toward me*.

Flanked by Quint Baker and Dirk Savage (the Smart Kid and the Kid Who Can Grow a Beard and Never Comes to School).

They were being pursued by the Zombie Ball!

I had been living in the school with that Zombie Ball for MONTHS and it *never* came after me! It only tracked you if you stank like food. If you washed your hands and face every now and then, guess what? You'd be fine.

Clearly, nobody told these boys about washing their hands and faces.

I heard somebody shout something about "Indiana Jones!"

And then they were backed up against the doors. The Zombie Ball was going to *crush and devour* them!

Ugh. Those fools! Those dorky, reckless fools!

They had put me in a really dangerous position! I'd spent days reinforcing that door and over a month fortifying that wing of the school! And now it was ruined! All because of *JACK SULLIVAN?!*

*REALLY?!*

"I'm gonna regret this," I growled, then—

# YANK!

I quickly opened the door, and they crashed to the floor.

"GET BACK!" I shouted. The Zombie Ball was barreling toward us. At the last possible instant, I SLAMMED the door shut—

We were safe.

No thanks to the three boys who I did *NOT* want to see. I mean, *really*, world? I was *just* sitting there, thinking about all the things I had lost! My parents! My hopes! My dreams!

And what did life send me . . . ?

Three doofuses. . . .

Anger boiled up, building and building, until I slammed the spear against the floor and—

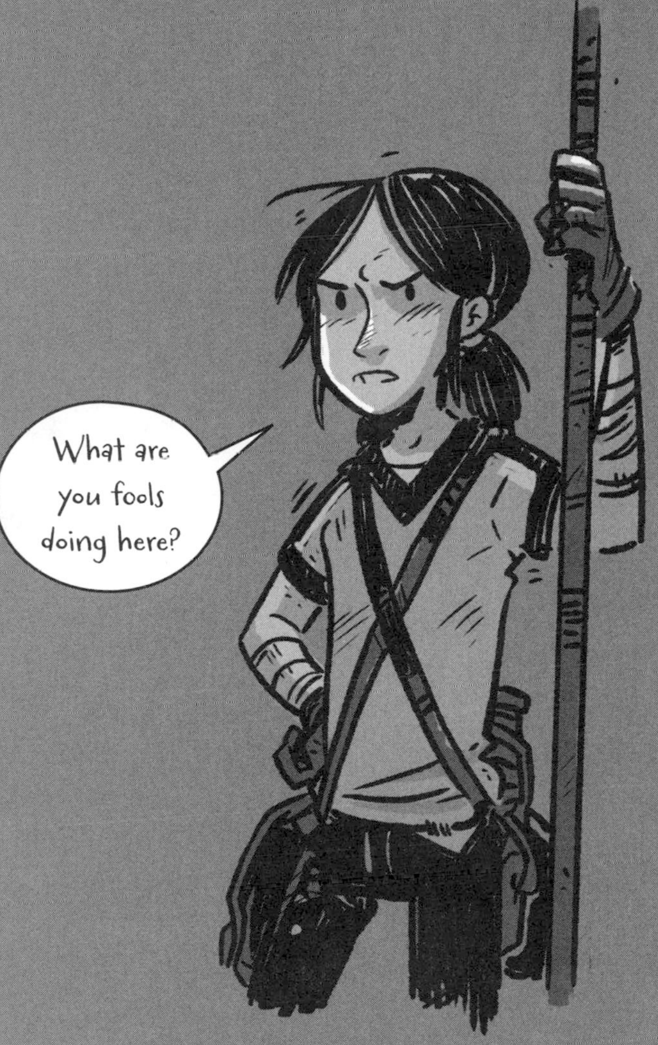
What are you fools doing here?

I was convinced that Jack, Dirk, and Quint were going to make things worse.

But here's the thing: I was totally wrong.

Because these guys made each other laugh. And they started to make me laugh, too. And make me WANT to laugh. Within five minutes of finding me, Dirk and Quint were having a legit

TICKLE FIGHT!

That night, on the rooftop, Jack and I tossed tennis balls at the zombie teacher down below. I didn't admit it then, but it was better—better

because I had someone else to do it with.

Jack and Quint and Dirk didn't magically fix everything. They didn't make me miss my parents any less and they couldn't put my plans and dreams back on track. But, as Jack said, "Life during the Monster Apocalypse is a whole brick-load better with buddies."

I knew my life wouldn't ever be the same as it used to be.

But I learned it could still be *good*.

That it was still worth *fighting for*.

The memory twinkles away. And suddenly I'm sliding back to the present . . .

. . . in the mini golf course, a prisoner. I feel like I've traveled a long way, when in fact I haven't moved an inch.

That wasn't just a regular old memory.

That felt *real*.

That was Neon. . . .

# chapter twenty-four

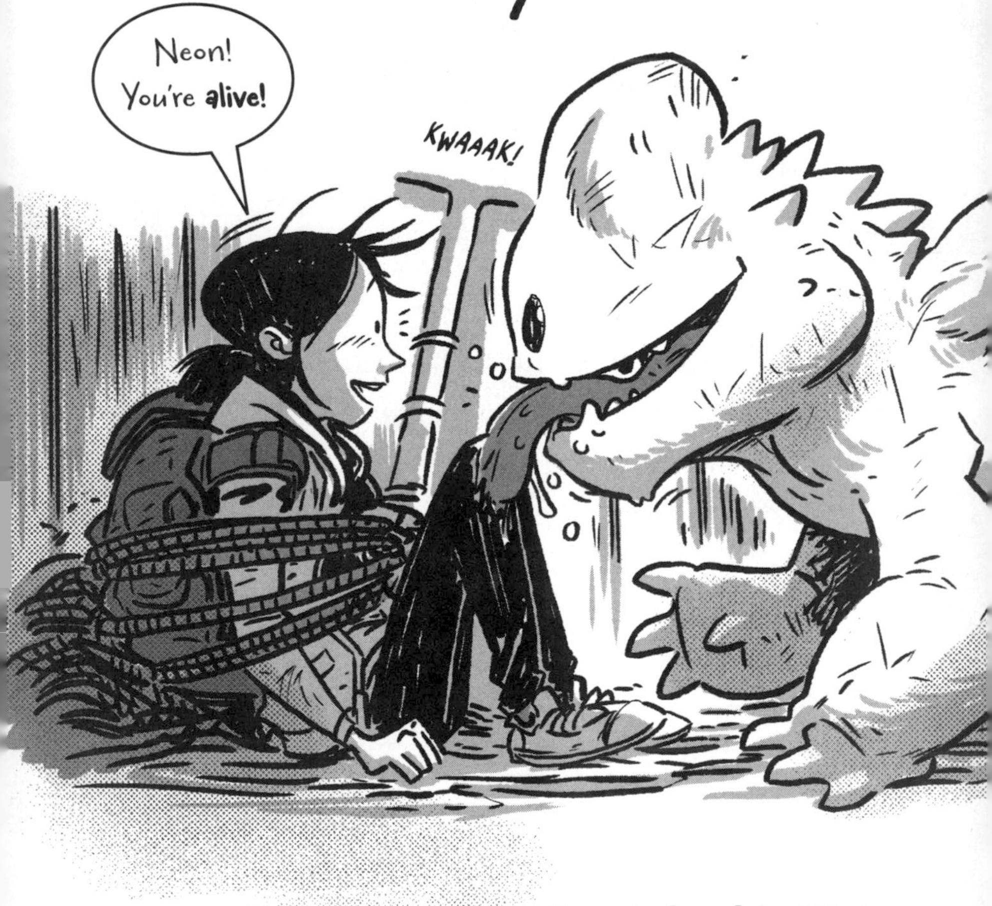
Neon!
You're **alive!**
KWAAAK!

I'm so happy to see Neon, I try to hug him! But my arms are tied at my sides, so he nuzzles his snout into my armpit. If that's how Wretches hug, I wholeheartedly approve.

"I thought you were dead!" I exclaim.

Neon huffs, as if to say, *How dare you doubt me?*

"But how did you find me?" I ask.

Just then, Johnny Steve walks through the door! "I suspected this particular band of Rifters used Putt-Putt on the High Seas as a hideout."

"But, Neon . . . Neon, you were . . . done for! The Boss Rifter even told me!" I glance at Johnny Steve. "How is he . . . ?"

Neon turns, striding to Johnny Steve and nuzzling against him. I gasp—Neon's left side is *absolutely* covered in bandages.

"It took a lot of Choco Taco wrappers," Johnny Steve explains. He lowers his hood, and I see he's plastered in napkin gauze and even has a waffle cone over one wounded eye. I have to choke back a laugh—it looks like a second beak.

Johnny Steve scratches Neon's neck while he fills me in. "After you were taken, I didn't know *what* to do. But I knew you were *trying* to save Neon. So I figured . . ." He suddenly looks very shy. "Well, I figured if that's what humans do for their friends, then I should do the same. Because—"

"Because you're a human expert," I say, grinning.

He smiles the widest smile I've ever seen.

"Oh, you and I should also do hugs now!" he says as he hurries over to cut me free. His walking sword is splashed with Wretch goo.

I shake my head in stunned awe.

A moment after he cuts me loose, I hear a squeaky voice say, "HELLO!"

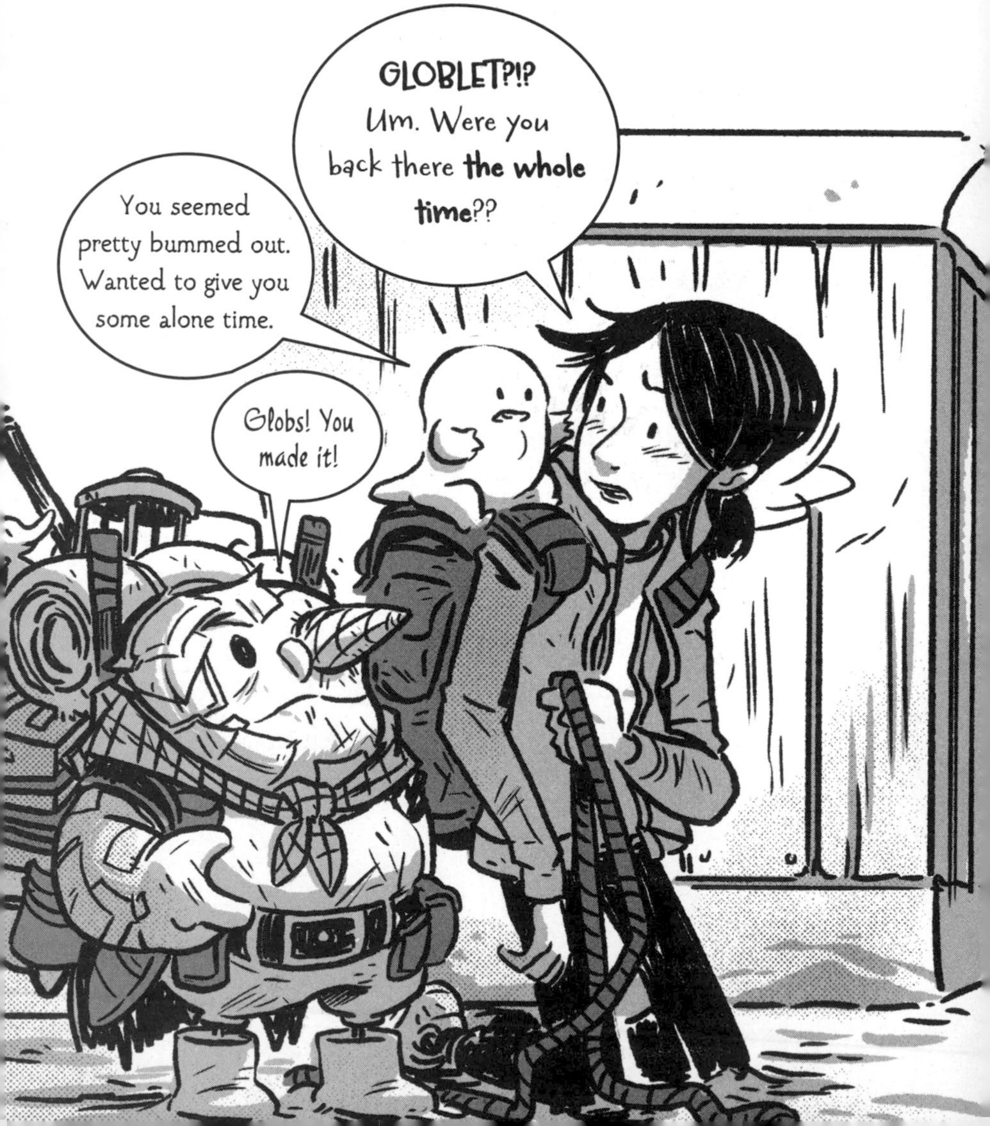
GLOBLET?!?
Um. Were you back there **the whole time**??
You seemed pretty bummed out. Wanted to give you some alone time.
Globs! You made it!

Just then, Neon slams into me so hard I practically flip over. I throw my arms around his neck, squeezing so tight that it hurts my bruised wrists. "Neon, I'm sorry," I say. "I'm so, so sorry. I never should have taken you there. . . ."

Neon slips out of my arms, then he looks at the floor.

"Hey, buddy—hey," I say softly, tilting my head so I can see him better. "Why did the Wretches attack you like that?"

Neon then pushes his head forward, so our nostrils are nearly touching. His eyes lock on to mine, and I feel his gaze creating bubbles in the back parts of my brain.

But I don't look away.

"It's okay," I say. "Show me."

Neon peers closer—so close that our faces touch. Looking *through* me. I hear a faraway *BOOM*, and then I'm not at the mini golf course anymore.

I'm not *anywhere*.

I don't see a vision of the future and I don't see a memory of the past. Instead, this time I see—

Neon.

He's a baby, even younger than he is today. But he doesn't look the same, and it's not just because he's smaller. He's happier.

He has his wings!

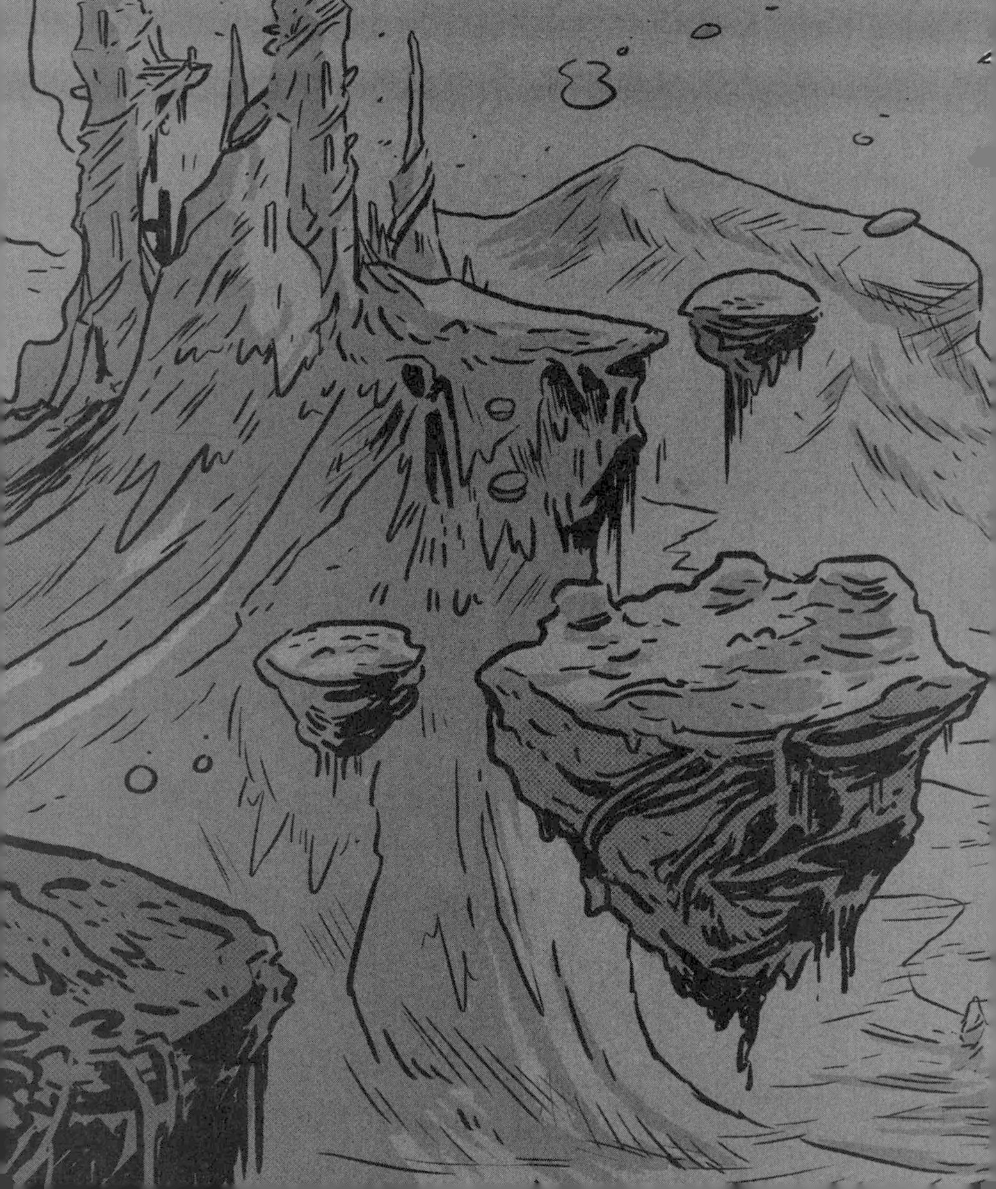

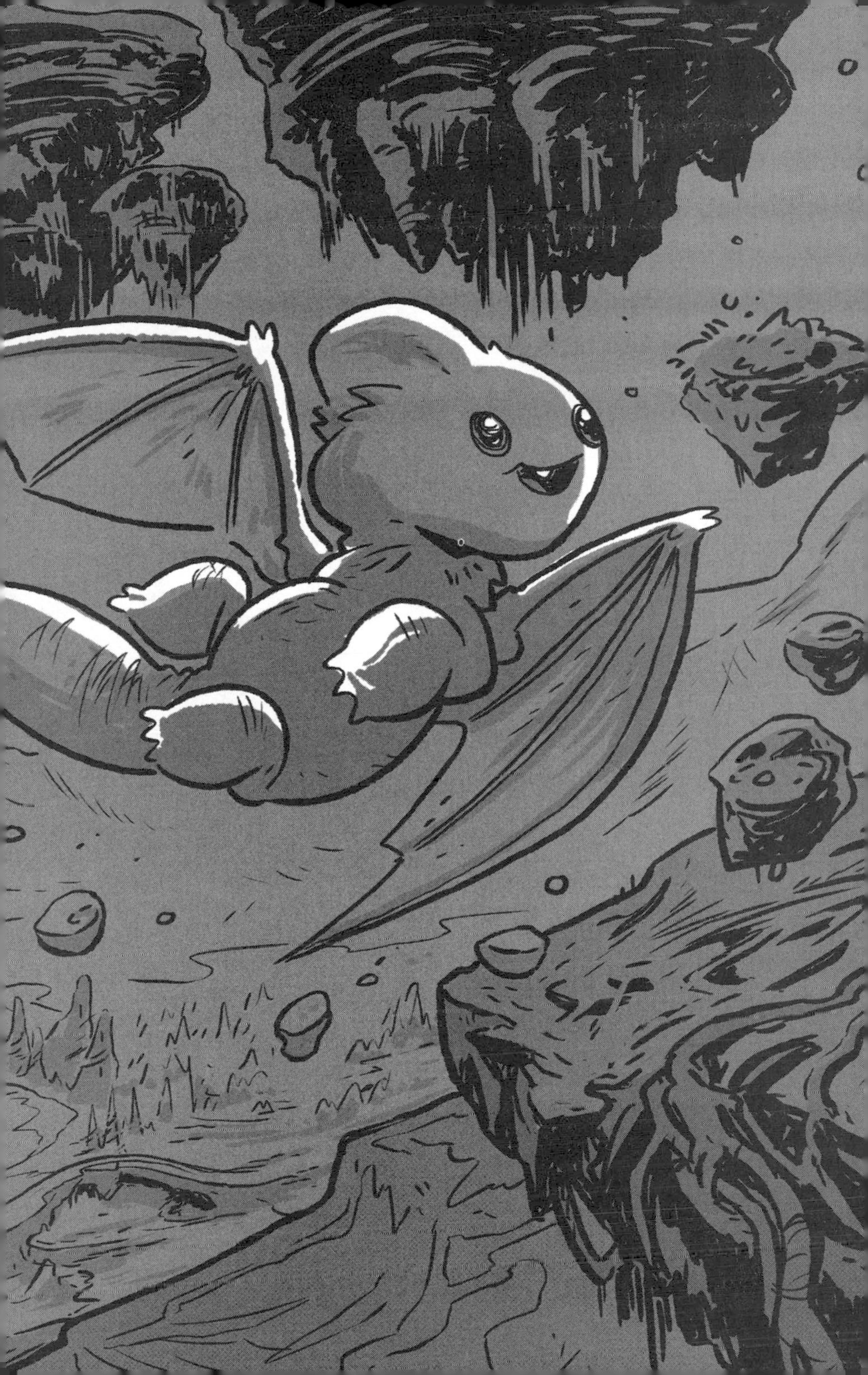

He's soaring through the sky, dipping and twirling and tumbling. He zooms around other baby Wretches and they play-wrestle in the sky. Everything looks different—the sky is pink and speckled, the ground seems to float, and water hangs in the air, unmoving.

I realize I'm seeing Neon in the *other dimension*. *His* dimension.

Then, suddenly—Neon's dimension seems to explode! The sky is sliced open and beams of light erupt from everywhere! Huge glowing holes appear: portals! I'm seeing portals, just like I saw that day at school—the day the Monster Apocalypse began. . . . Monsters, creatures, objects—*everything* is being sucked into the hole! It's like someone just flushed a cosmic toilet.

And Neon gets sucked in, too.

This is day number one of the Monster Apocalypse, and I'm seeing it up close—from Neon's point of view. It is an insane, swirling void—ablaze with color!

I realize now just how horrifying it all must have been for the monsters.

Neon howls and shrieks as he is dragged through the air, into the portal! It is twisting, shrinking—and Neon screams toward it. And then—

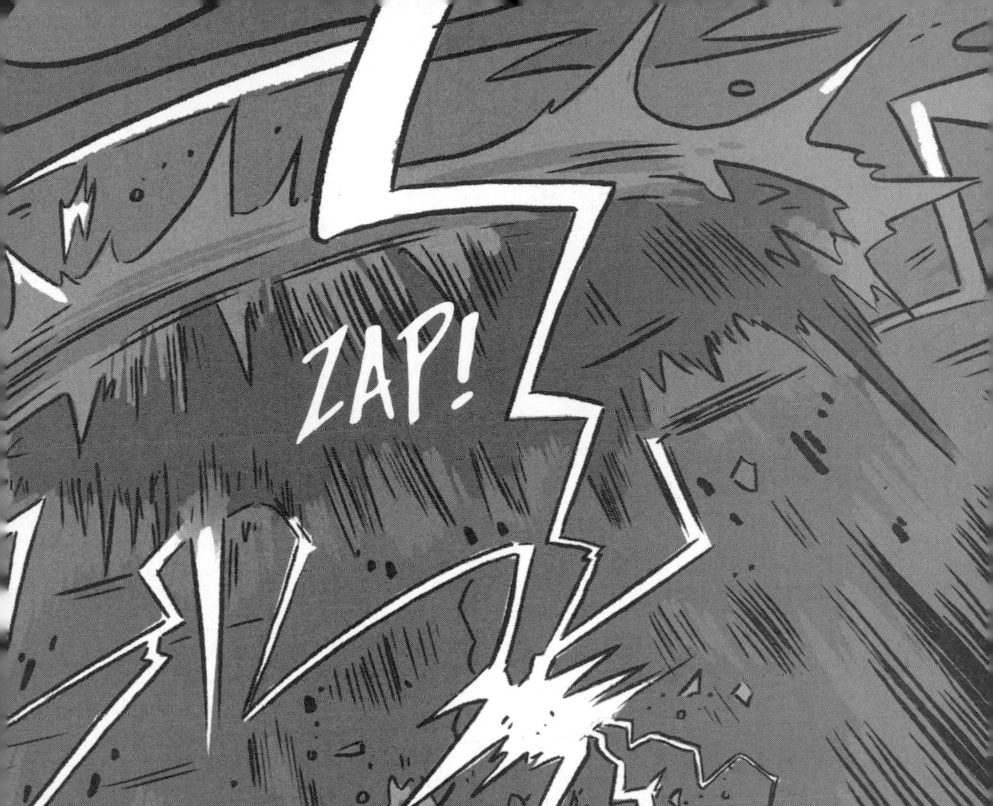
ZAP!

Neon passes through, into our dimension. Just as the portal is closing. He makes it.

But his wings don't. . . .

I hear him scream as his wings are clipped, and I feel—*really feel*—the pain he felt.

Neon crash-lands in this dimension.

He is hurting and he is scared. He hobbles across our changing world, alone. And then, at last, he finds a horde of Winged Wretches.

I *feel* the relief that he felt.

And then I *feel* the horror.

They reject him. The scaly beasts hiss and snarl and snap their teeth and pin him to the ground. Without his wings, this baby Wretch is no longer welcome with the rest of his pack. . . .

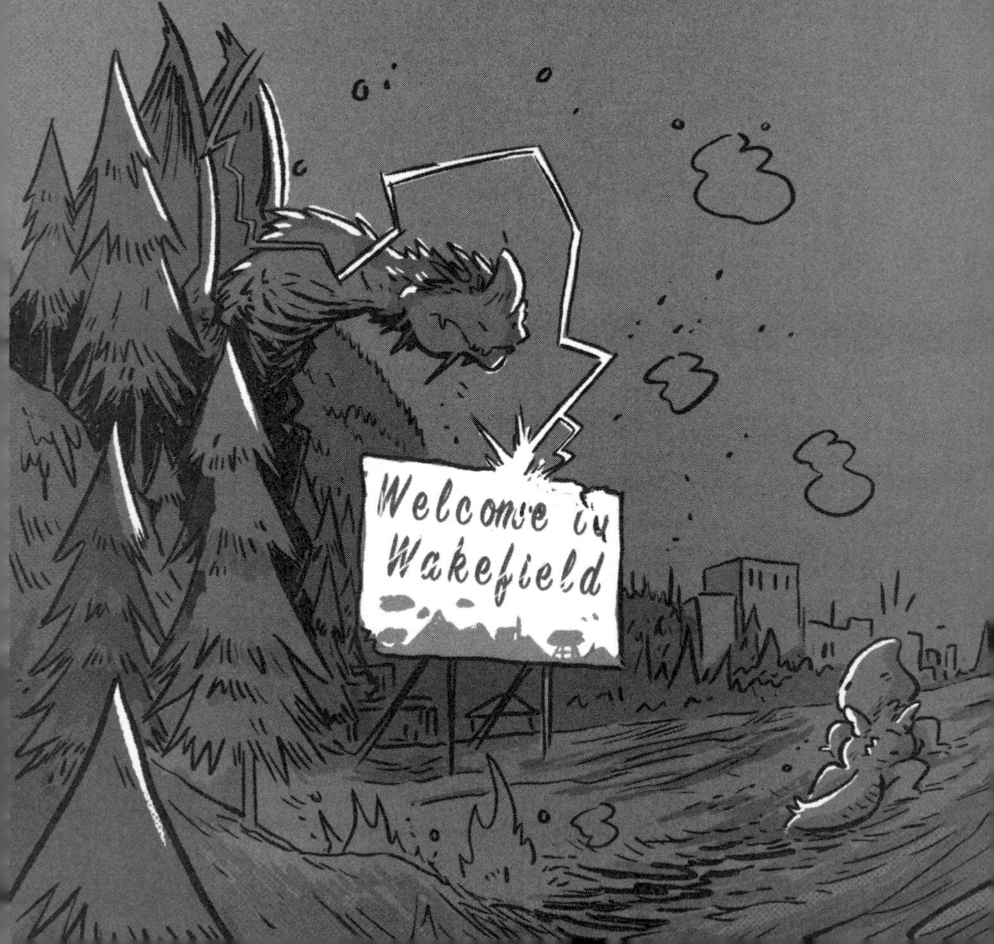
Welcome to
Wakefield

Everything shifts and changes and turns again.

I'm seeing my memories. My own life.

A flood of moments—the happy times, the good times, after I left the middle school for the tree house. Monster hammock hangouts, sugar-fueled stakeouts, and Ping-Pong tournaments—

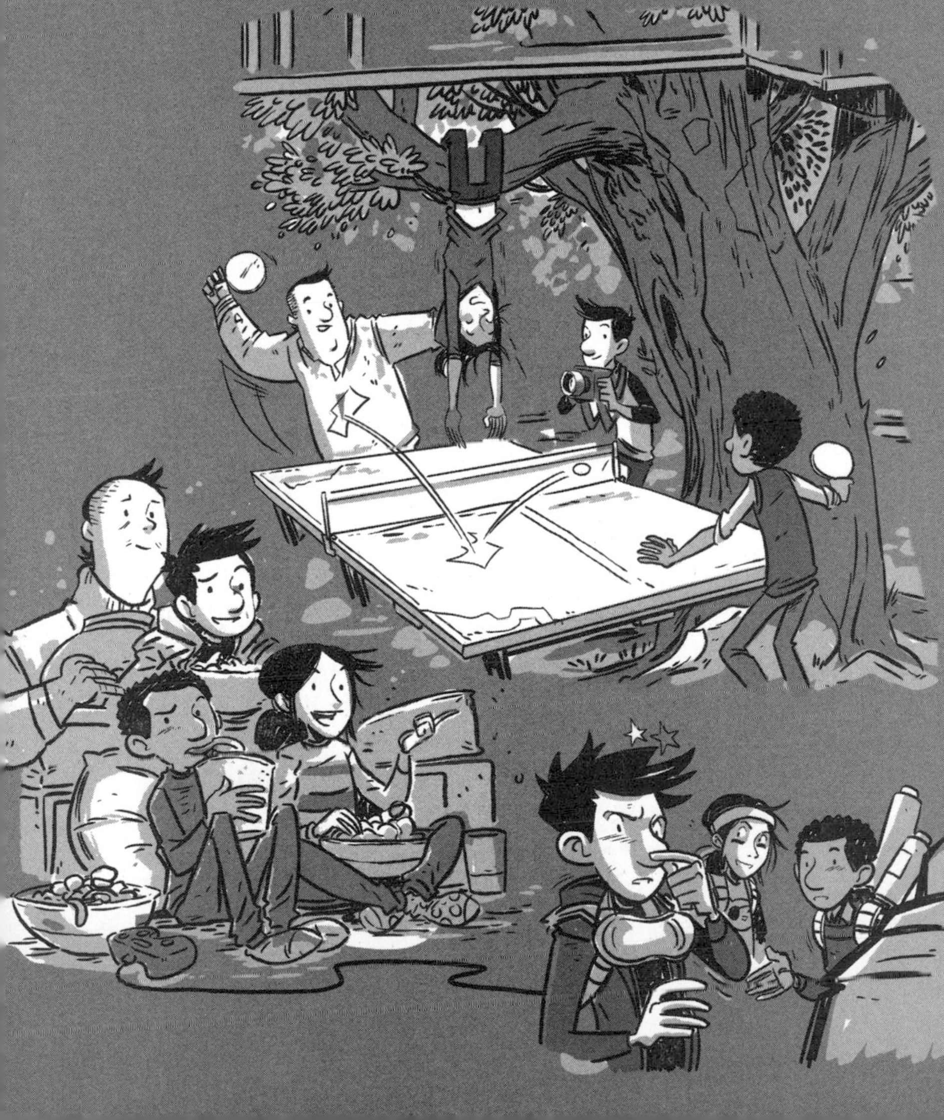

It is a giddy blur of happiness.
Happiness with friends.
And then, the visions and memories stop. . . .

I'm back at the mini golf course. And Neon is there.

And I get it.

We were both victims of this apocalypse. We were both lost and alone in a strange new world.

Earlier, when I saw a partial vision of Neon flying with the other Wretches, he wasn't trying to tell me *that he wanted to go back to them*. He was telling me that he wanted to *belong*.

We both lost everything—but I had friends to help me through it, and he didn't.

Neon is *me*, when I was in the school hallway, looking at my Certificate of Merit, crying over how useless it all was.

He's waiting for friends to come tumbling through *his* locked doors.

"Neon," I say. "Even without your wings, you're still whole and wonderful and awesome.

And you deserve to be happy. Neon, buddy, I am your—"

"FRIEND!" Johnny Steve says, totally jumping in and stealing my dramatic thunder. "I will be your BEST friend and we will travel THE WORLD together and learn all there is to know about this small, goofy land!"

"Ahem—" I say, giving Johnny Steve a little poke. "Neon, I am *also* your—"

"BUDDY!!!" Globlet squeals. "We're definitely buddies and for sure *BESTIES*!"

I smile and sigh. "Okay, okay, we're *all* your friends."

Neon blinks quickly.

"We'll always be there for you," I tell him. "No matter what. Just like Jack, Dirk, and Quint have been there for me. And like I've been there for them."

Neon's happy, but I see a hint of hesitation. Something in his eyes that I can't quite place . . .

He winces and curls his tail up beneath him. The makeshift bandages are peeling off his back, and I glance down to see the wounds where his wings had been are reopened. The Winged Wretches *targeted them*.

I pull my broken shield armor from my backpack. Tugging, twisting, I manage to pull off one large, curved piece of metal.

I set it over Neon's back, draping it over his wounds.

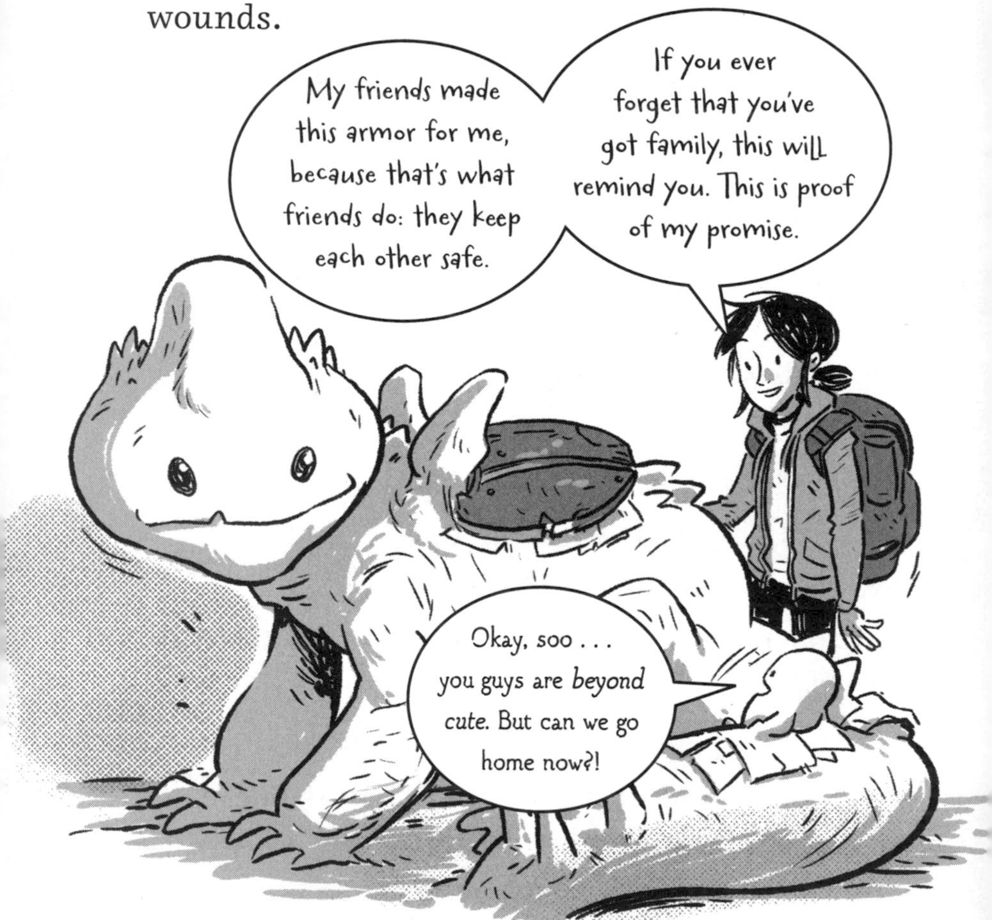
My friends made this armor for me, because that's what friends do: they keep each other safe.
If you ever forget that you've got family, this will remind you. This is proof of my promise.
Okay, soo . . . you guys are *beyond cute*. But can we go home now?!

"Nope. Not yet, Globlet."

"Say what now?" Globlet asks.

"Still one thing to do," I say. "I *need* Boss to tell me where Thrull is. We have a chance now, to get the information we need to stop Thrull and the Tower. And, while we're at it, make sure these Rifters never bother *any of us* again. Are you guys with me?"

"Yupper!" says Globlet.

"I'm supportive like a human buddy!" says Johnny Steve.

And Neon just purrs.

"Good," I say. "'Cause I have an idea . . ."

Then I crane my neck, toward the driving range, and call out, "FLUNK! CAN YOU COME HERE A SEC, PLEASE?"

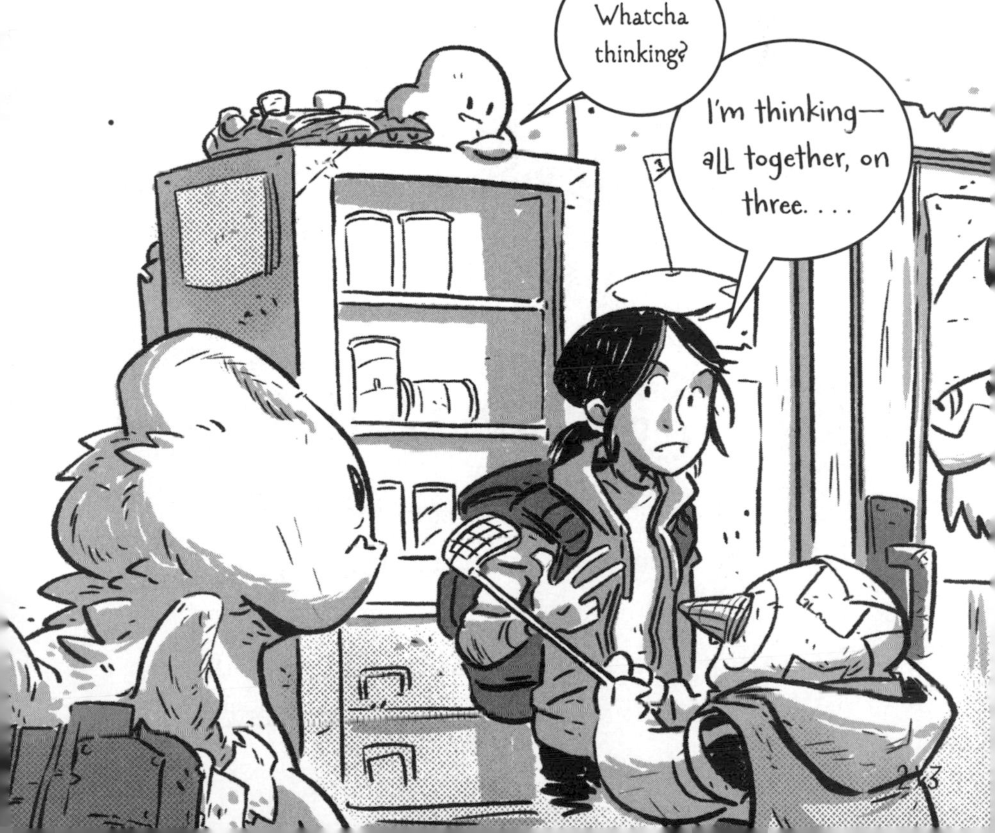
Whatcha thinking?
I'm thinking—all together, on three. . . .

# chapter twenty-five

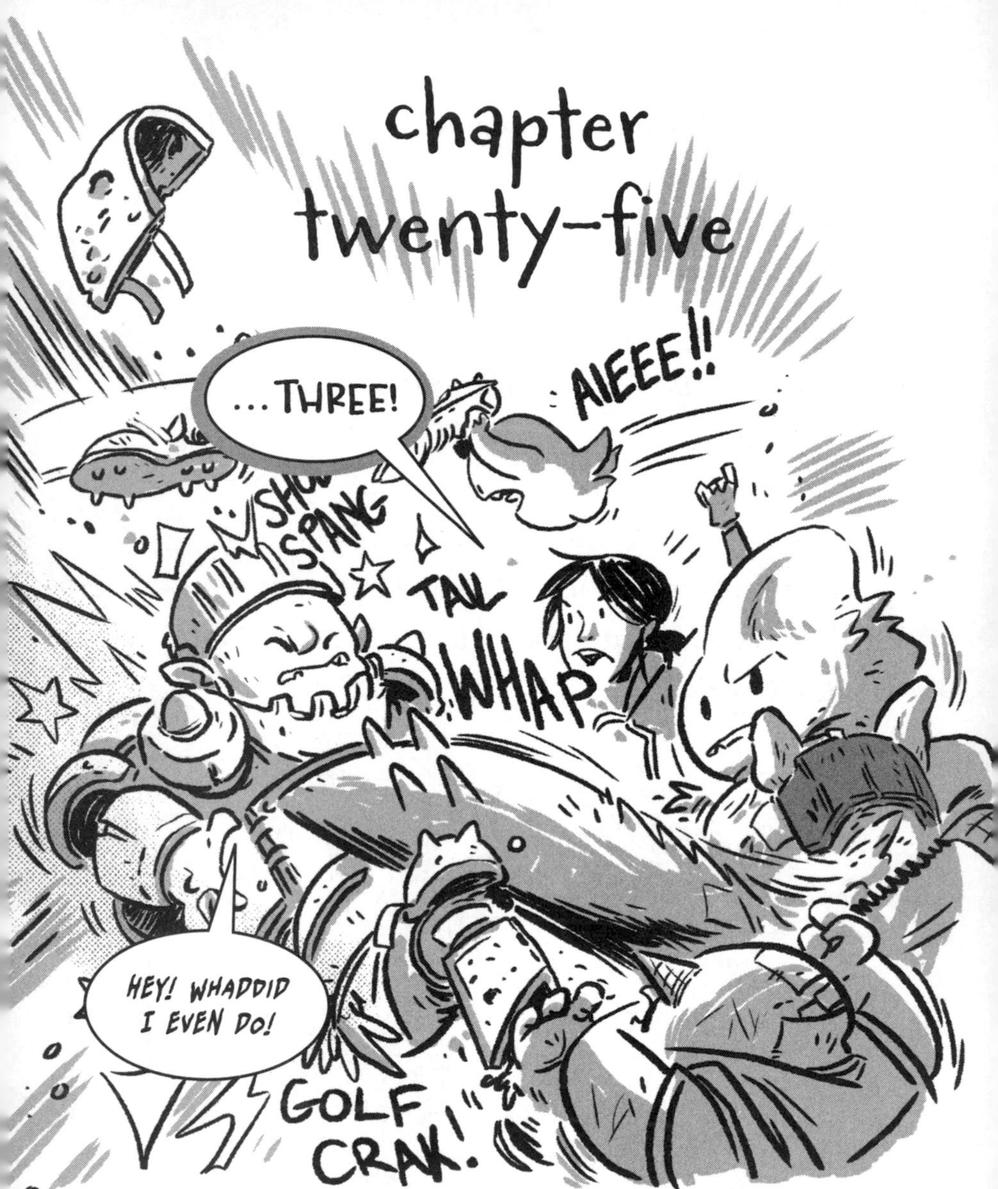
...THREE!
AIEEE!!
SPANG
WHAP
HEY! WHADDID I EVEN DO!
GOLF
CRAK!

In less than a second, we've tackled Flunk to the ground. The second after that, Flunk's practically *sobbing*.

"PLEASE!" Flunk cries. "TAKE ME ALIVE!"

"Well, obviously," Globlet says. "We're not *sickos*."

"We're just going to borrow your armor," Johnny Steve tells him.

"See, here's the deal," I say. "I'm gonna be you for a little while. Hope you don't mind. . . ."

Soon, we've removed his armor—and we discover a problem. Flunk is *long*! He's built like an other-dimensional grasshopper. There's no way I'll fit.

I glance around quickly, then, "Johnny Steve, grab me two putters! And a bunch of that tape that goes on the golf club handles. I've got an idea. . . ."

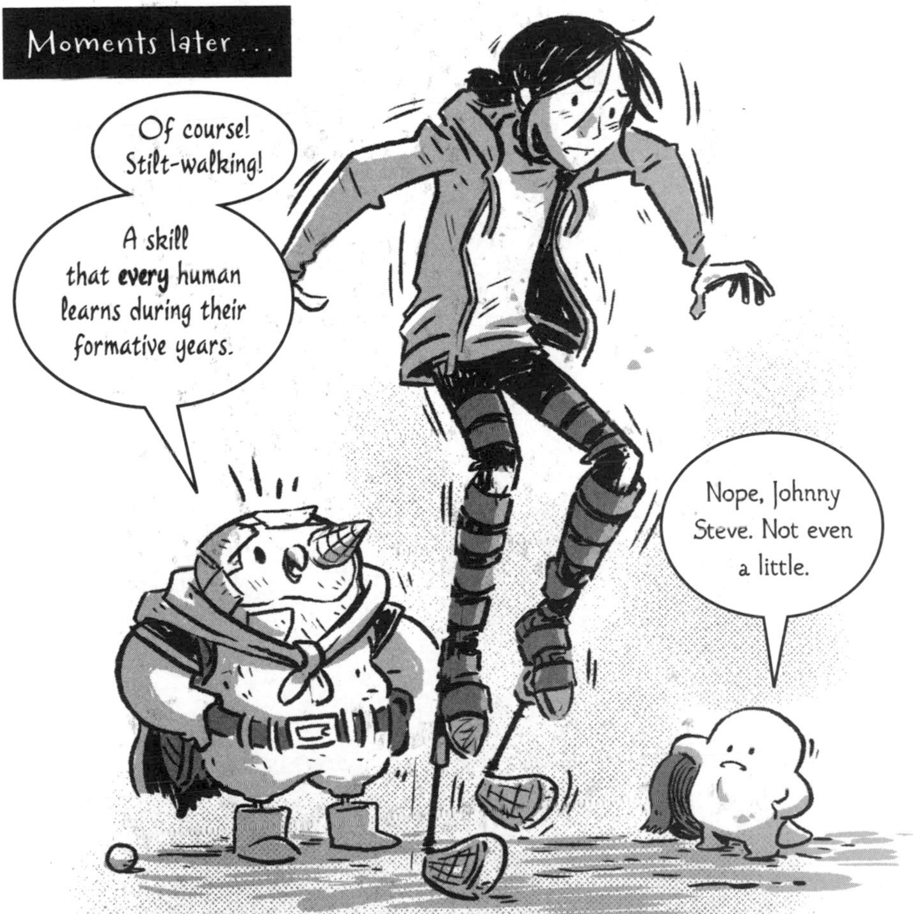
Moments later . . .
Of course! Stilt-walking!
A skill that **every** human learns during their formative years.
Nope, Johnny Steve. Not even a little.

"Holy stromboli, that actually worked!" Globlet exclaims.

"And I think I can actually walk, too," I say as I take a wobbly step forward. The armor is heavy, but the suit does half the work: all the joints are motor-powered. I manage to tramp all the way to the clubhouse mirror.

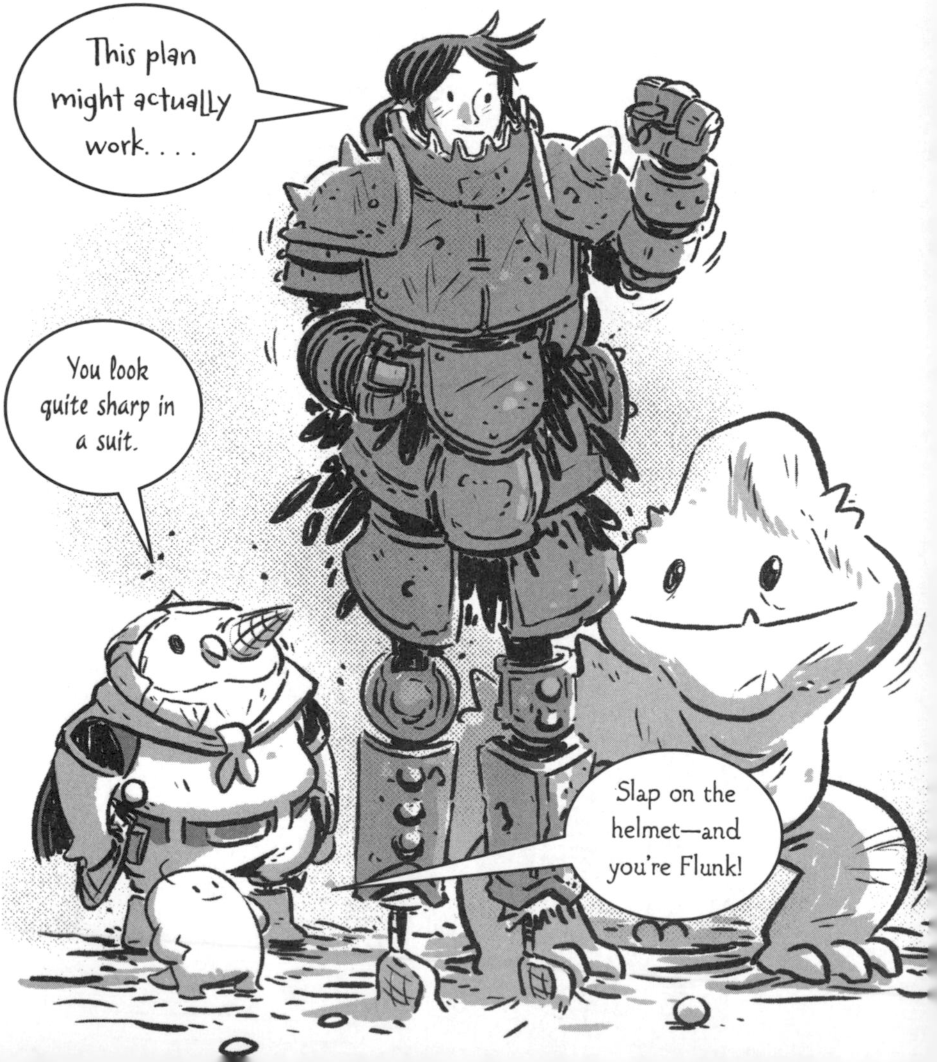
This plan might actually work. . . .
You look quite sharp in a suit.
Slap on the helmet—and you're Flunk!

Flunk, who we've tied to the anchor, watches us unhappily. I hear him murmur, "I look the coolest in it. The Boss told me so."

"Hush, you!" Globlet says.

Neon smiles as I stride past him. Each step is easier than the last. I'm walking like a real-deal Rifter by the time I reach the clubhouse door.

Slowly, carefully, I open it.

"Wait, wait! Lemme see! Lemme see!" Globlet says. She hops up the armor and slips beneath my shoulder guard. She peeks out from underneath, and we both peer outside.

First, I see the Ogres—they're in the parking lot, tied to old cars like horses in one of those old western movies Dirk loves so much.

Meanwhile, the Rifters are having a weird, celebratory party at the 18th hole. Rifters are chomping on raw meat and chugging very spoiled milk. One swigs from a carton—and I see it's curdled and thick and I can smell it all the way from the clubhouse.

"There he is!" Globlet says.

A cave sits behind the eighteenth hole and a waterfall splashes down. On top of the cave is the Boss Rifter. He sits on a giant plastic crocodile like it's some sort of throne, watching his Rifters down below like he's judging a contest.

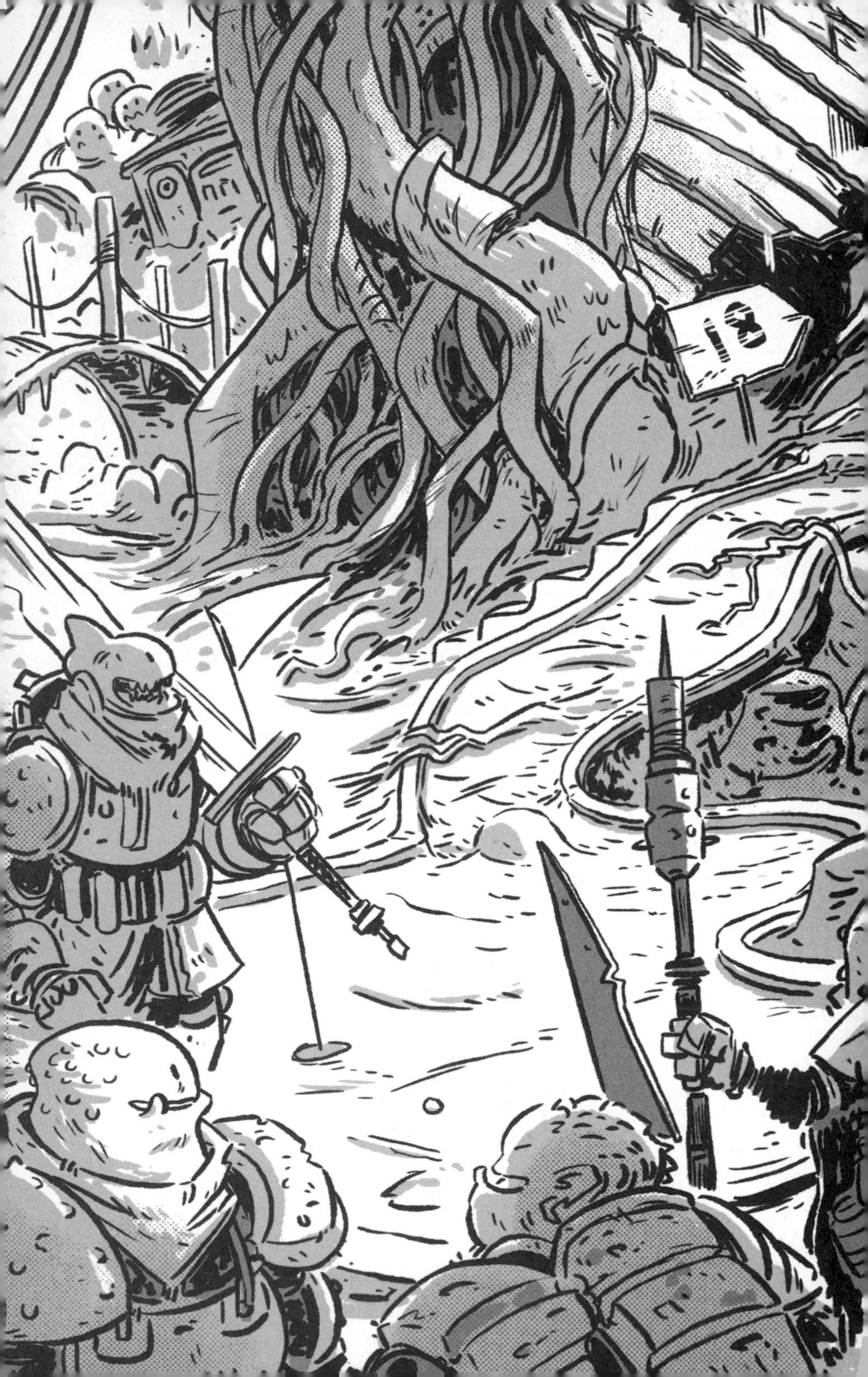

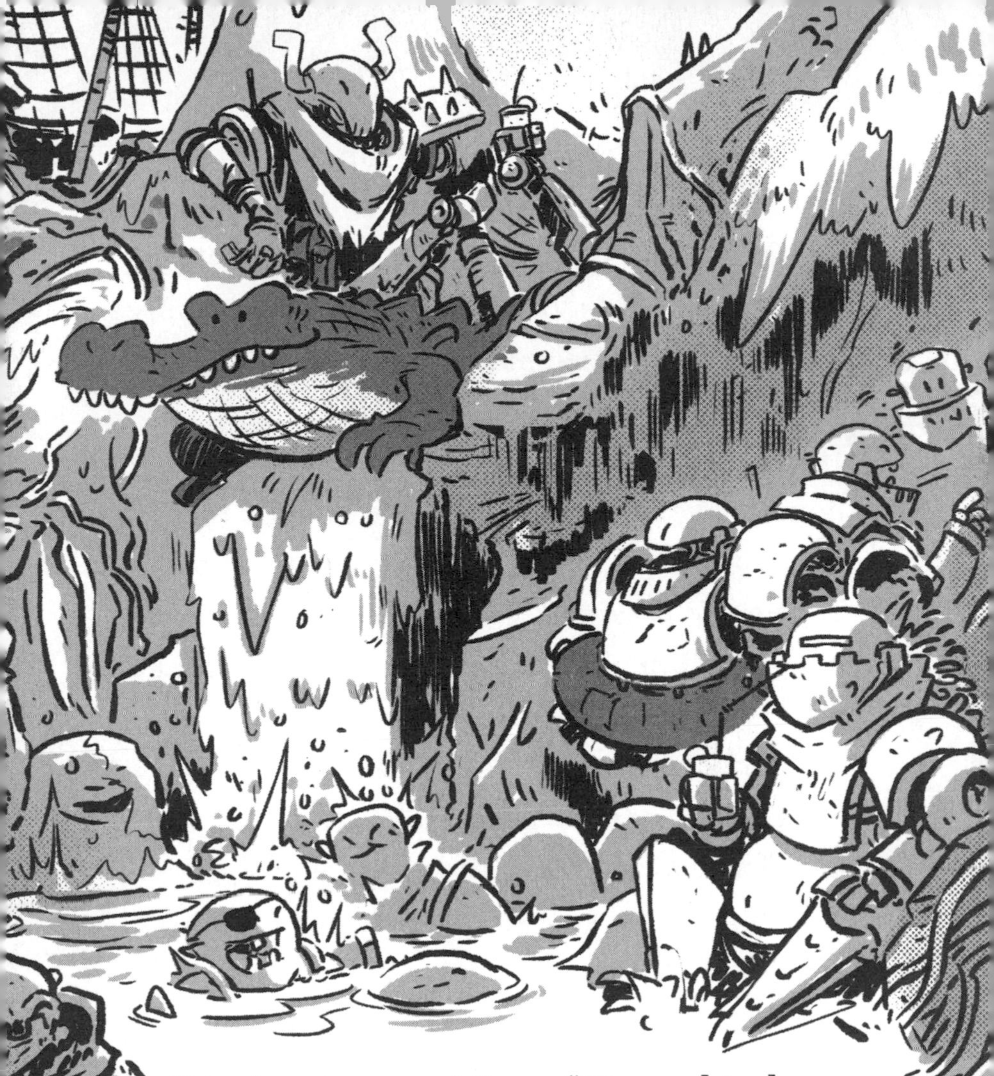

"It's time to move," I say. "We need to do this while the Boss Rifter is up there in his crocodile seat."

"I am quite ready!" Johnny Steve announces from across the clubhouse. He's cradling a karaoke machine we found in the birthday party room. "I will put *all* my human knowledge to use!"

I give him a thumbs-up. He doesn't *have* thumbs, so he grins. "See you shortly," he says, and he scurries out the back. I think, *He's got a big part to play in this plan. I hope he's up for it.*

"Let's goooo!" Globlet whines. "Enough dilly-dallying!"

"One sec," I say, and I glance at Neon. He bounds over. "Neon," I say. "I want you to swing around the back and just *wait. Do nothing.* You've been through enough. But if things get bad, then I need you to *run.* You understand? Run far and fast and don't look back."

I'm still not totally sure what Neon understands and what he doesn't, but when I say, "run" he wags his tail. Close enough.

"Then I'll see you when this is over," I say.

With that, Neon hurries out the back, and Globlet and I go back to watching the party on the eighteenth green.

Soon, it happens.

A small figure comes waddling across a wooden drawbridge from the seventeenth hole.

It's Johnny Steve. And, just like we planned, he's wearing the Mr. Shivers "brain freeze" headpiece. He actually did manage to take it from the ice cream truck!



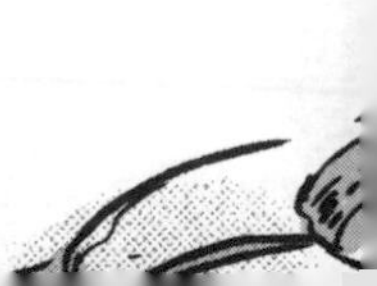

He strides past and beneath Rifters, waving and hollering. "Hello! Hello! I have just wandered in off the wasteland and I'd love some warm liquid and a high five!"

"How does he see out of that thing?" I wonder aloud. Then I get my answer—he doesn't. At least not well. Because next he trips, his walking sword gets hooked in the railing, he somersaults *over* the bridge, crashes onto the green, and then the karaoke machine smashes his foot—

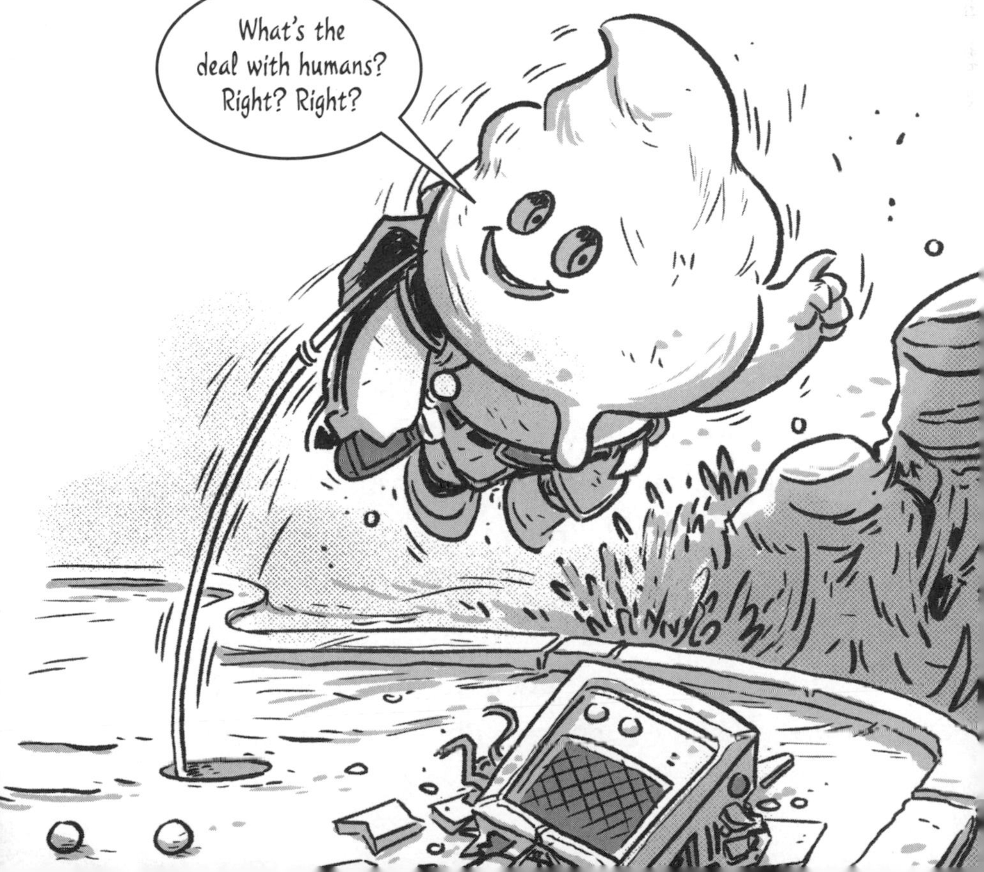
What's the deal with humans? Right? Right?

The Rifters erupt in laughter. I watch the Boss Rifter—it takes him a moment longer, but finally he laughs, too. Johnny Steve begins serenading the Rifters with human "facts."

". . . and that's not all you need to know about humans! Here's something: they drink water. WATER! Think about that! And they have fingernails. Now, raise your hand if you've ever eaten a fingernail. . . ."

Johnny Steve has the Rifters rapt!

"C'mon, Globlet," I say. "Now's the time."

We move around the rear of the course. The armor disguise is working—none of the Rifters even turn to look at me. Their eyes are glued to the Johnny Steve One-Man (Monster?) Show.

Coming around the back of the waterfall cave, I see the alligator's tail. The Boss Rifter's massive shoulder armor glimmers in the sunlight. I carefully walk up the sloping, green felted hill. When I get close to his throne, I gather my courage, lean forward, and break out my most villainous growl. "Hey, uh, Boss. Good show, eh?"

The Boss Rifter glances back and looks at me— *at Flunk*—right in the face armor.

I hear Globlet in my ear. "June, he's got Blasty!" she whispers. "I'm stealing it back. . . ."

I feel Globlet sliding down my armor, but keep my attention on the Boss Rifter.

"This guy," Boss says, gesturing toward Johnny Steve. "This guy makes me laugh."

I nod, thinking, *Great, he loves the show. Big fan of bad comedy. He's nice and distracted—now I just have to get him to talk.*

"Hey, Boss," I say, keeping my voice at a growl. "I got an idea—we should throw that little ice cream head guy in a burlap sack, bring him with us for the journey!"

The Boss Rifter chuckles. Then giggles. Then it's a full-on belly laugh! "I love it," the Boss Rifter says, smacking me on the shoulder. "We will do that, Flunk! We will throw him in a burlap sack! WHO HAS A BURLAP SACK?!"

Every Rifter instantly goes silent. They all nervously look up at the Boss Rifter. It appears that none of them has a burlap sack.

"I'll get one!" I say, smiling. Now I have the *in* I need. "We're gonna need entertainment on this long journey, right? SUCH a long journey. Hey, remind me—just, like, how long, exactly?"

The Boss Rifter catches his breath.

"Halfway across this massive land. Maybe more."

*Useful information,* I think. *Making progress.*

"All that trekkin' and we don't even get to see Thrull," he says with a sigh. "Just the Outpost. Then we find out *where* Thrull is."

I gulp. *WHAT?*

My mind is speeding. The Boss Rifter doesn't even know where Thrull is!

Globlet whispers, "C'mon—let's BEAT IT while we still can! What else do you need?"

*No,* I think. *I've come this far.* And the reporter in me is not totally satisfied. This interview is NOT over. I need to know more about this Outpost.

But the Boss Rifter is suspicious. I can practically see the gears turning. He glances down at the clubhouse, then back up to me. "Wait a second . . . Flunk, I told ya to guard—"

"The human?" I say, snapping up my face visor. I grin at the Boss. "Don't worry, I'm right here. And so is this. . . . "

Globlet inches forward on my shoulder and raises Blasty. "That's right," she chirps. "I'm a rubbery little pickpocket!"

He scowls. "My entire crew is here. And any ol' second now—"

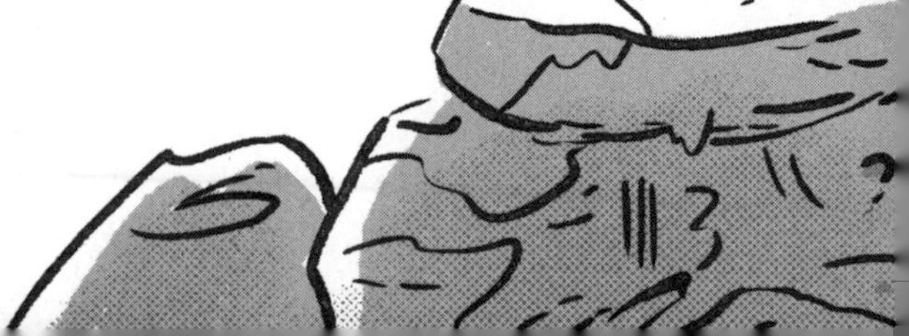

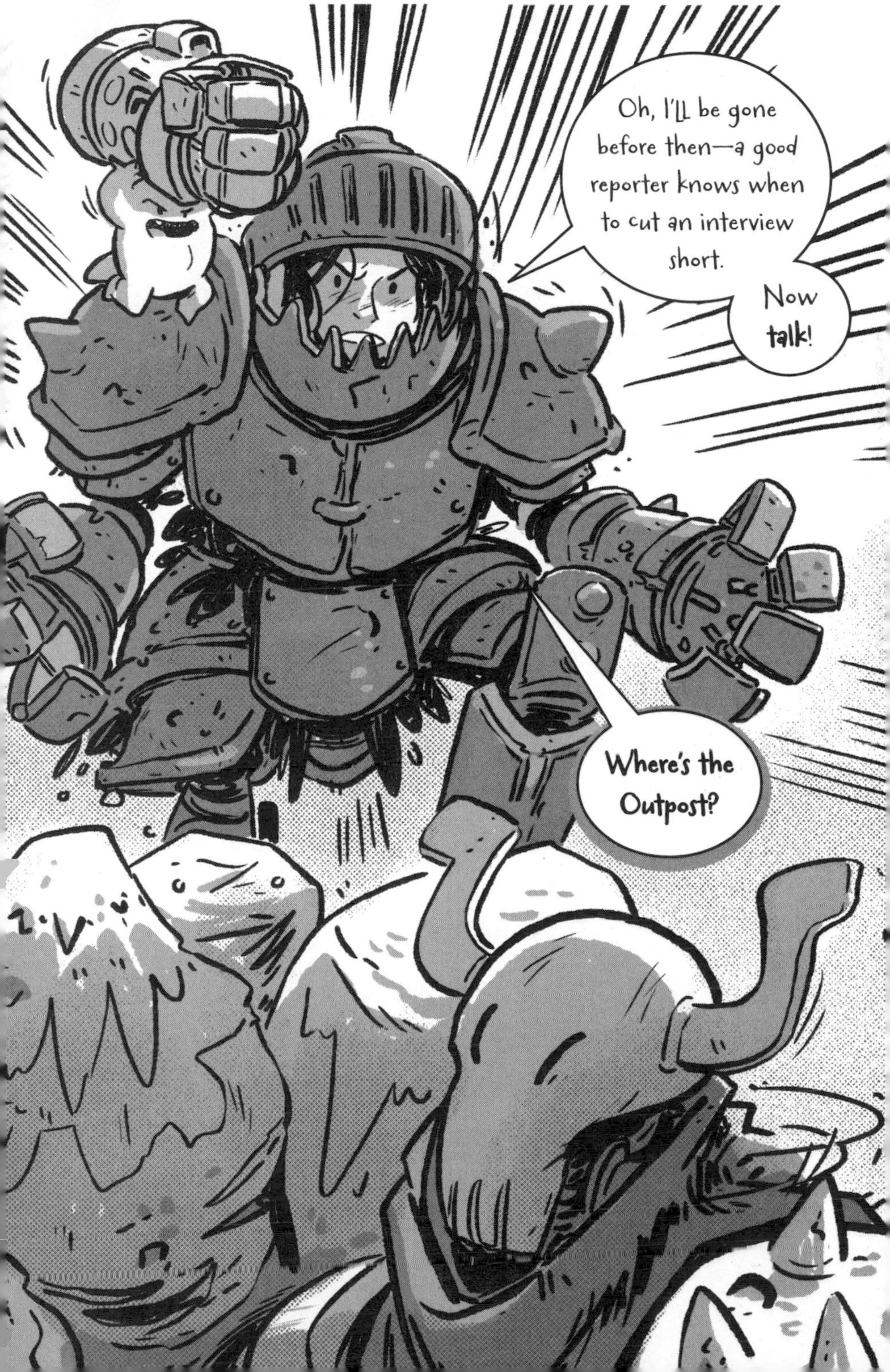
Oh, I'LL be gone before then—a good reporter knows when to cut an interview short.
Now **talk**!
Where's the Outpost?

He shakes his head. "You're tough, human girl."

"You haven't seen tough. Now tell me . . ."

And—I kinda can't believe it, but—he starts to tell me. He's about to spill it. And then, suddenly, from below—

"THE HUMAN PRISONER STOLE MY PANTS! AND ALSO ESCAPED!"

It's Flunk—bursting out of the clubhouse.

Globlet frowns. "He's really mad about his pants, huh?"

And that *very dumb question* reverberates, ringing in my ears, as the Boss Rifter reaches out, grabbing me by the armor, the helmet banging against my ears.

With one massive *heave,* the Boss Rifter *hurls* me to the waterfall's edge! My foot snags Globlet as I go, then we're smashing to the grass with a deafening, shattering—

**KA-KRUNCH!**

My helmet pops off. The armor bursts. My golf club stilts snap. Tumbling, end over end, I plow into Johnny Steve, and his mask pops off.

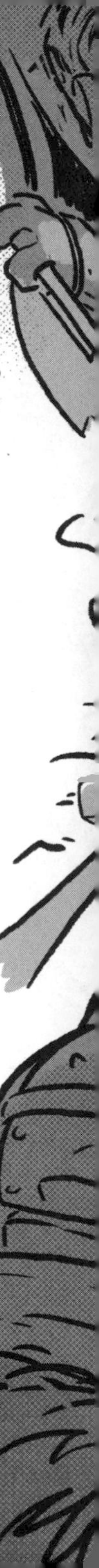

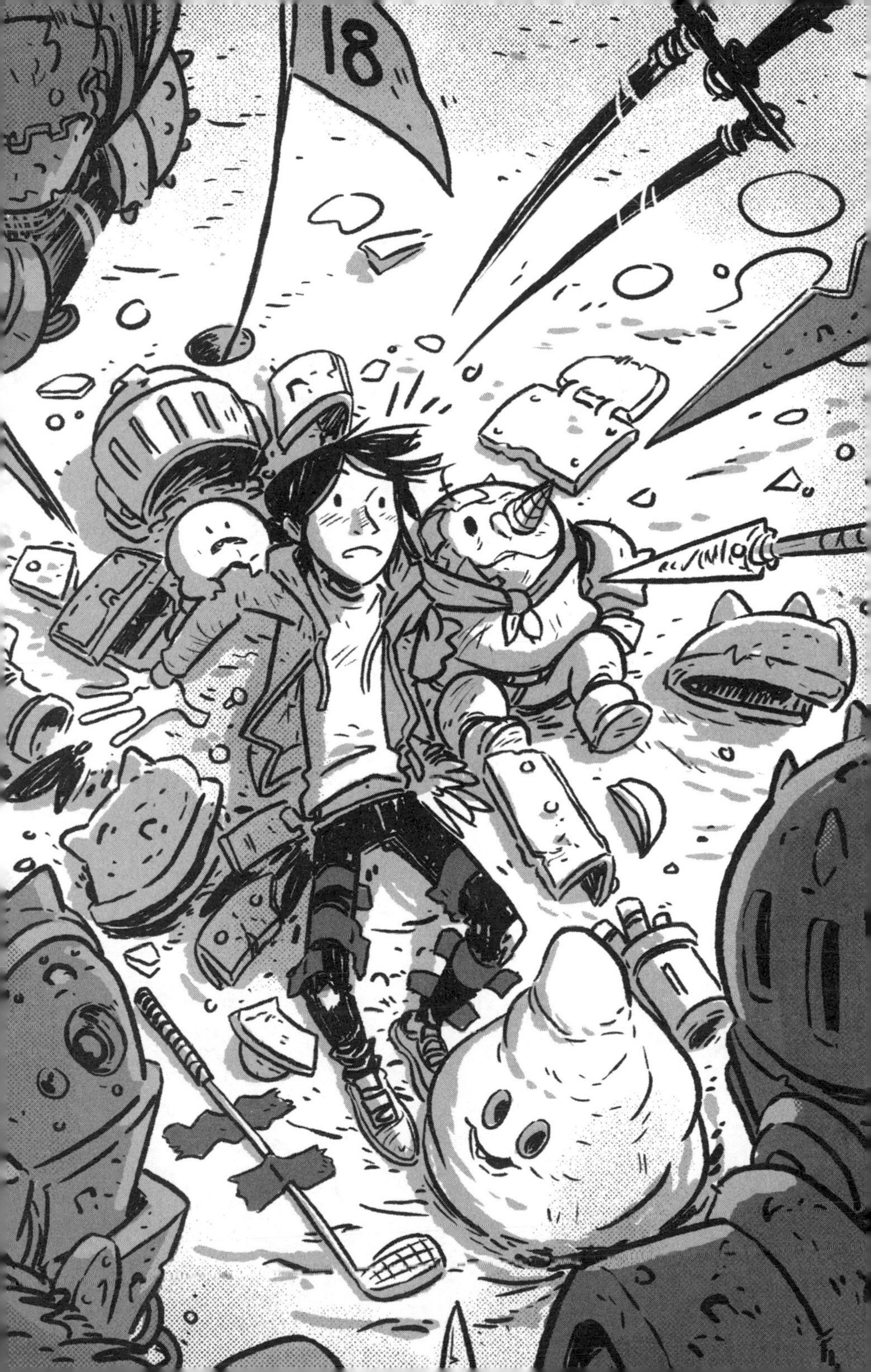
18

# chapter twenty-six

"Flunk!" Boss calls out, shouting down at the pantsless guard. "You was s'posed to be guardin' 'em!"

"I—I know," Flunk stammers. "But she tricked me! Her and her friends! The Wretch!"

The Rifters are suddenly shouting.

"The Wretch is alive?" one cries.

"WHERE?" another shouts.

Neon answers that question, exploding out of a huge plastic shark at the sixteenth hole.

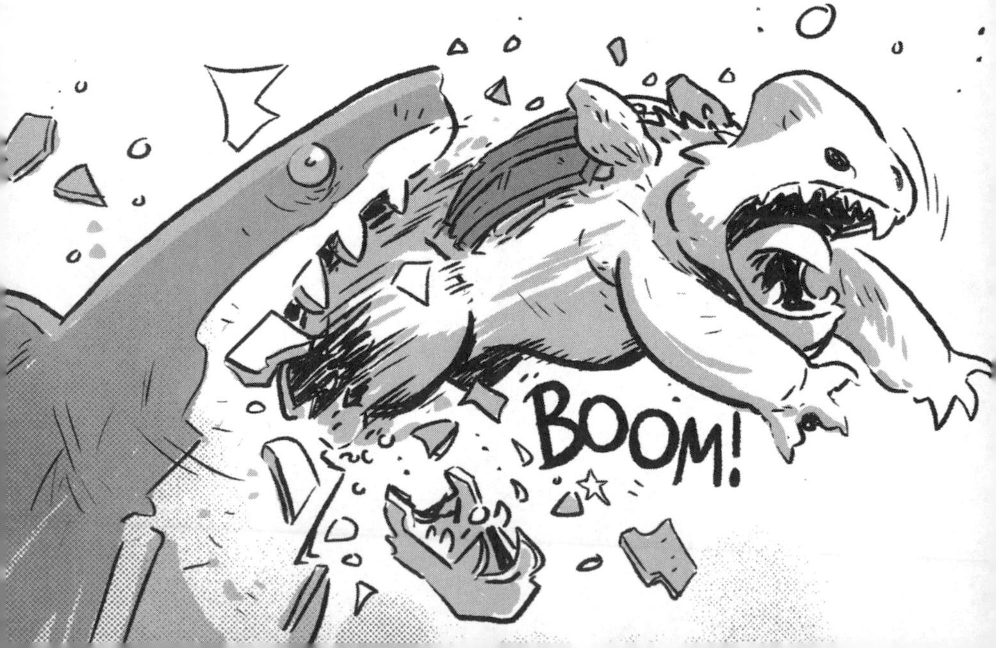
BOOM!

He comes crashing down beside us, talons slamming into the green.

The Boss Rifter scowls, then jumps off the waterfall ledge. He hits the green—and it quakes.

"Perfect." He sneers. "We'll bring Thrull his revenge *and* his Wretch . . ."

Neon snarls. These are the jerks who tortured him, chased us, and kidnapped me, his friend. Neon isn't going down without a fight.

He roars.

And his roar—usually soft and cute—is loud. I think *wow,* what a perfect time for him to grow into his roar! He's like Simba! But then I realize, it's the karaoke microphone, turning his *ROAR* into a—

# ROAR!

Johnny Steve has pressed it against the underside of Neon's throat. The sound is so epic that the Rifters leap back. I get chills. It's like Neon is proclaiming ownership over the Rifters' headquarters and everything in it.

The Boss Rifter takes a step back. He must be thinking that this baby has suddenly grown *full Wretch.* That's a scary deal, wings or no wings.

"Quickly!" Boss says, pointing to two Rifters in the back. "Untie the Ogres! Get them over here!"

The two Rifters run off, looking very happy to have an assignment that takes them away from the suddenly ferocious-sounding Wretch. They are unchaining the beasts of burden. I see it clearly, because they're lit up by a sudden bright light, almost like headlights in the distance.

I gulp. Oh no. Backup Rifters?

But no. Wait. Those are *actual* headlights.

And then I hear a new voice. This one booms, too. From Neon's stomach. . . .

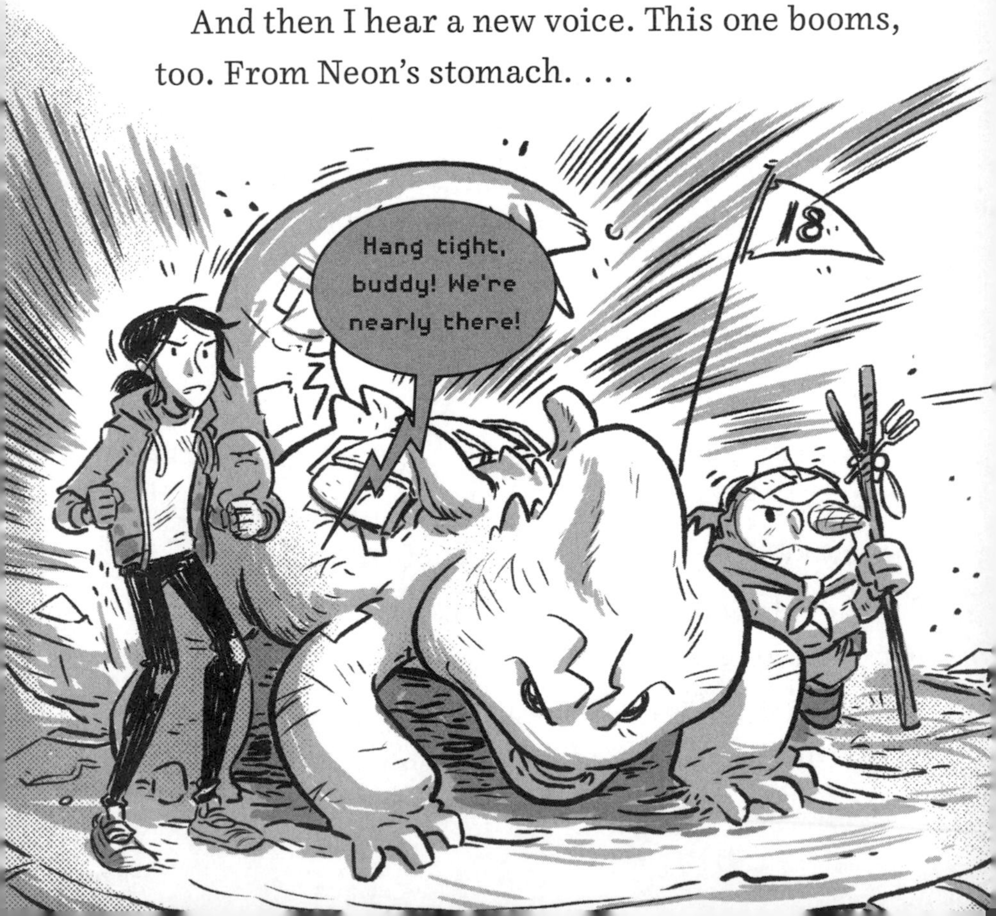
Hang tight, buddy! We're nearly there!
18

Globlet shrieks. "NEON ATE JACK!"

I do a double take. . . .

It takes me a split second to realize what's happening—

Neon ate the *walkie*! And the walkie is working again?!

"Jack!" I shout, pressing my head to Neon's belly. "Can you hear me!"

"Yes, friend!" It's Quint's voice now. "You came into range hours ago! We've been tracking you—and trying to talk to you. But YOU couldn't hear US!"

"I can now!" I say. "Johnny Steve, put the mic up to Neon!"

There's a long pause, before—

"Who's Johnny Steve? What's Neon?"

Before I can answer—

# KA-KLANG!

There's a metal smash and the gate enclosing the golf course BUSTS open! Then the sound of action-movie music blasting and Big Mama is suddenly there, exploding through the Putt-Putt sign and my friends are leaping into action. . . .

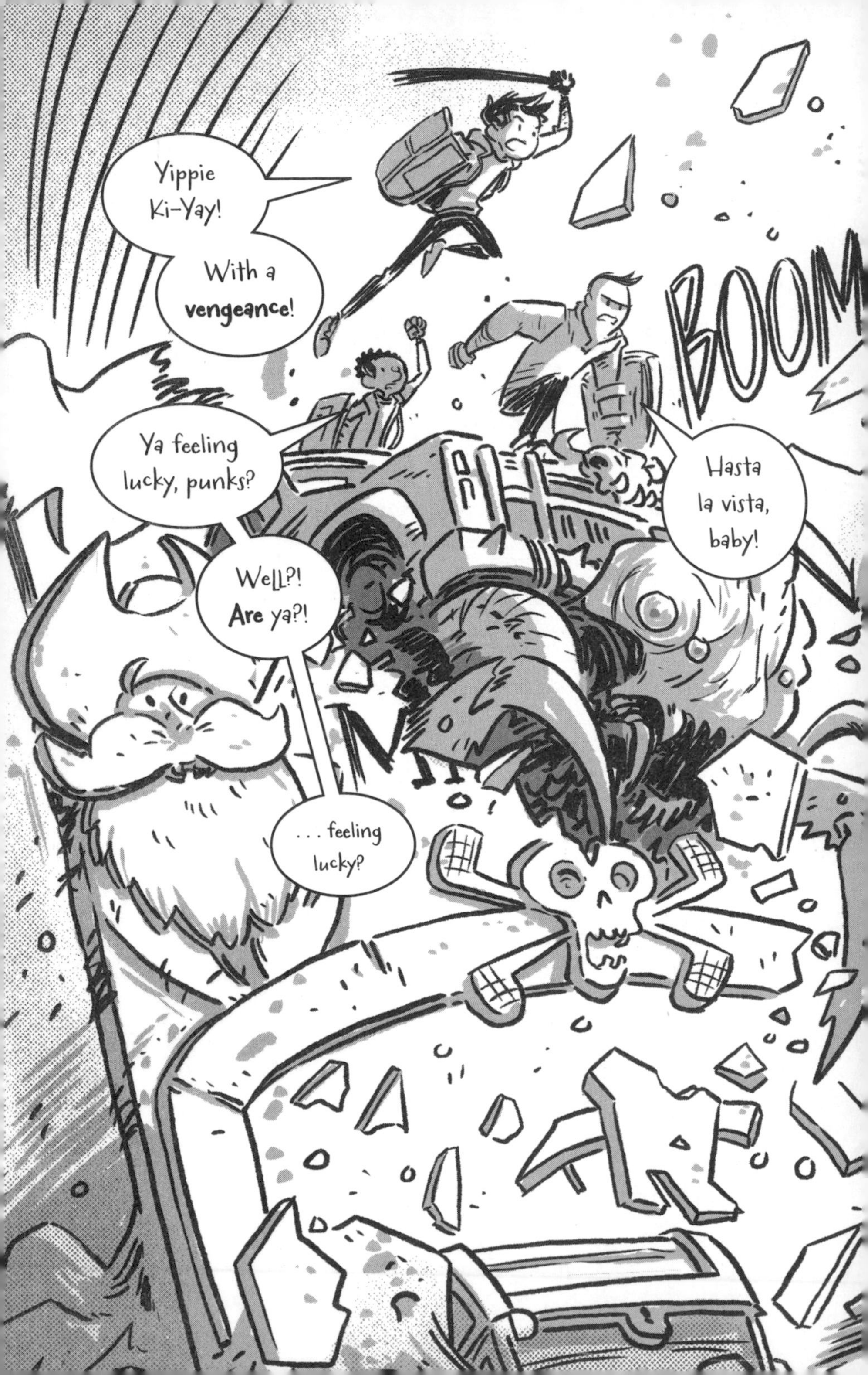

Yippie Ki-Yay!
With a **vengeance**!
BOOM
Ya feeling lucky, punks?
Well?! **Are** ya?!
. . . feeling lucky?
Hasta la vista, baby!

Big Mama smacks down onto the green, landing on a plastic pirate ship cannon. Green turf shreds as it spins and slides to a stop.

"I would say we're here to help," Jack says. "But it seems like you've got it under control."

"I never turn down my friends' help," I say. "Let's do this."

Big Mama is flanked by DoomKarts driven by Skaelka, Biggun, and the other Joe's Pizza monsters. Even Rover is here!

"Ax time!" Skaelka shrieks gleefully, chasing after the nearest Rifter. He gives a high-pitched squeal and flees—leaping a fence.

A Rifter runs at Jack, and Jack slashes out with his Louisville Slicer. Now we're *all* in the fight. Five Rifters dive at Dirk, but—

# KRAK!

Biggun sends the villians pinwheeling through the air with one massive slap.

I whirl, taking in the action—

It's a full-on Rifter versus everyone else battle! The Rifters have the numerical advantage, but we have our monster allies, our serious new armor, and we know how to battle *as a team.*

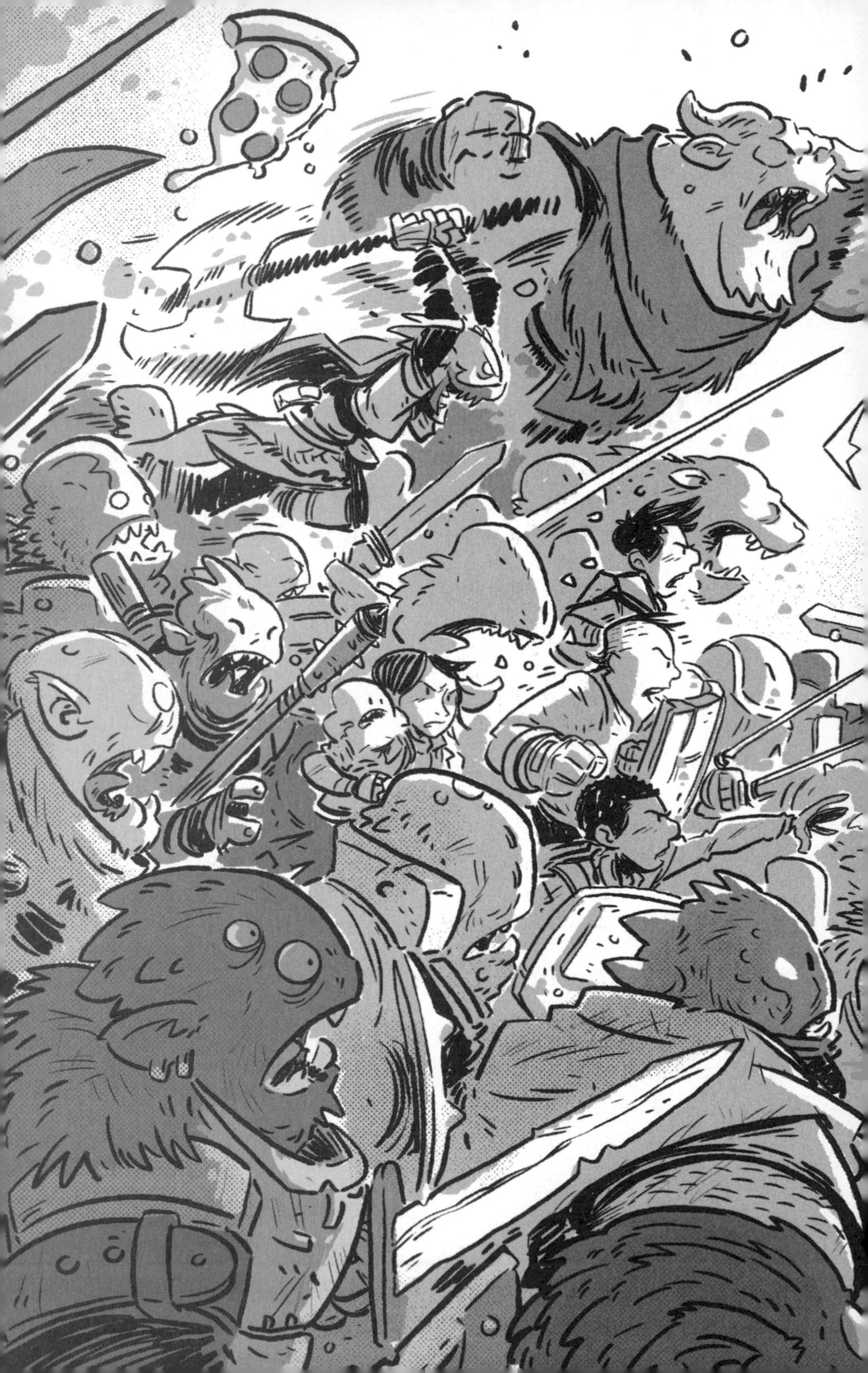

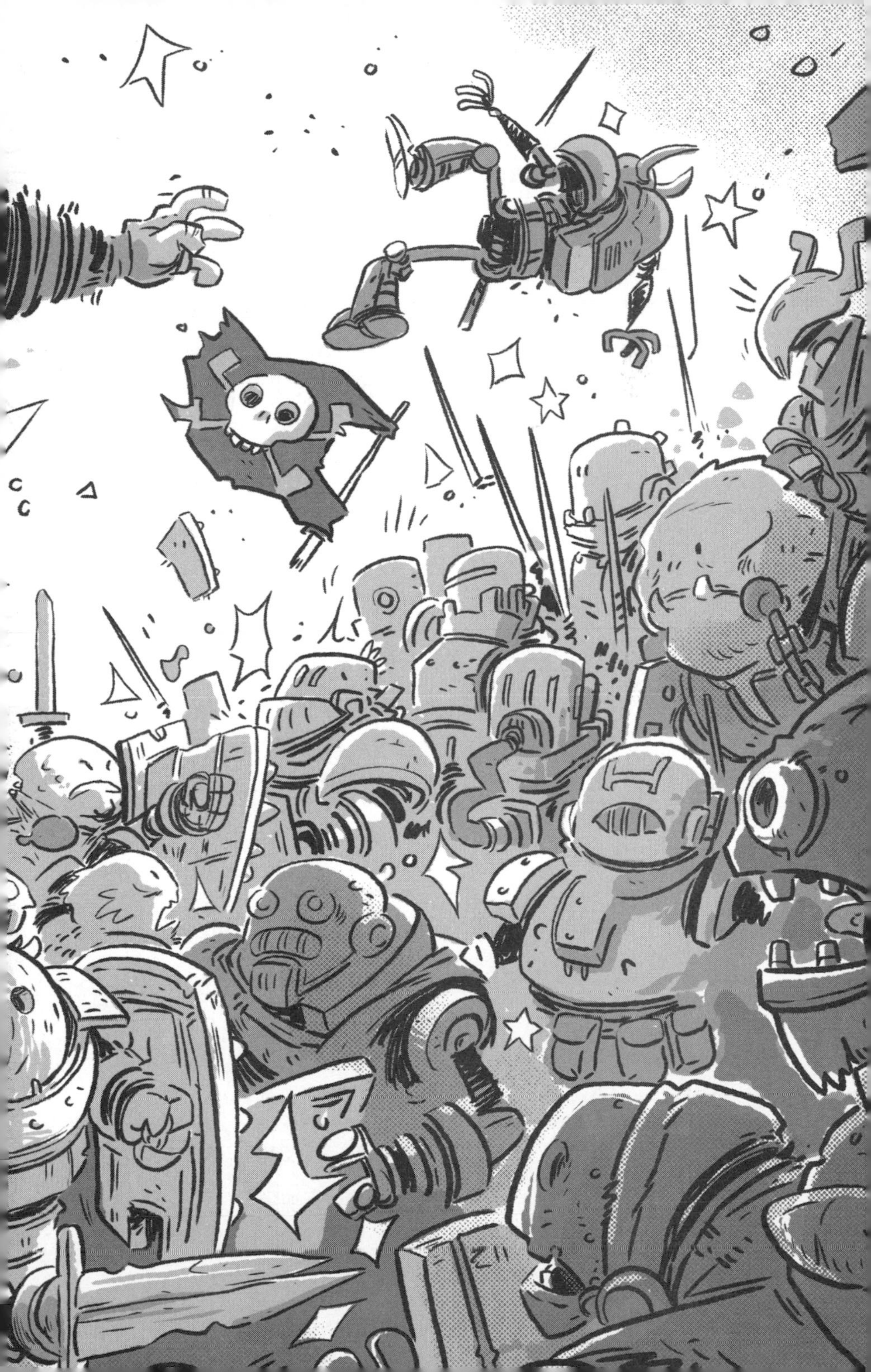

"Shields up!" Jack shouts as he grabs a small, scurrying Rifter with his octopus hand and *hurls* it toward Quint.

"Up and at 'em!" Quint says, swinging his shield *into* the Rifter.

The Rifter hits the ground, hard—then scrambles up and flees.

"ARE YOU FLEEING?!" the Boss Rifter screams. "IF YOU RUN, YOU ARE NOT WELCOME BACK!"

I spin, focusing on the Boss. Our eyes lock. He sees that things are not going his way. Snarling, he grabs a Rifter and hurls it at me, but misses.

In a flash, Neon is by my side.

I reach out toward him and touch the nubs where he once had wings, but now has armor.

And he doesn't pull back from my touch.

Neon leans into my hand, and it's like we're holding each other upright. We look at each other, and I see fear in his eyes. But I also see trust.

Tremendous trust—because he suddenly spins back, lunges low, and uses his snout to toss me up, and—

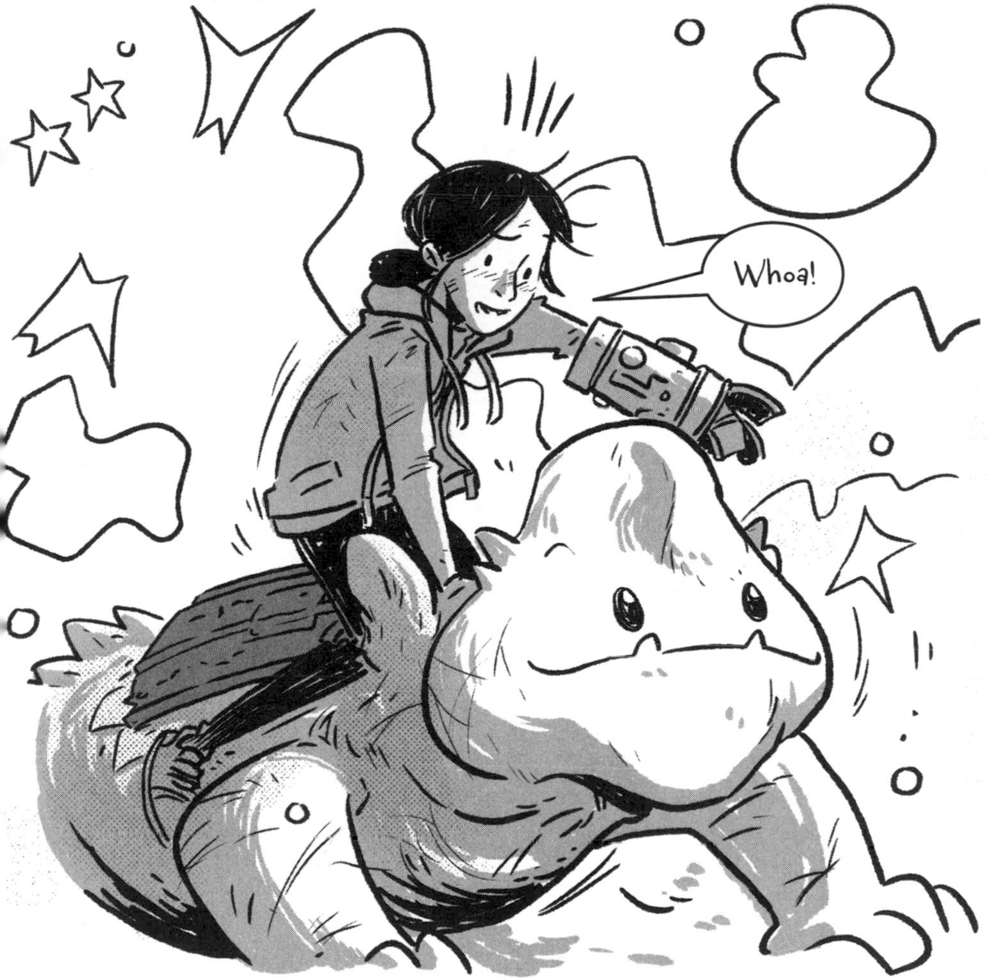
Whoa!

"I'm riding a Wretch!" I shout as I grab the armor and hold on tight. I can't help but call out to my friends. "Guys! I'm *riding a Wretch*!"

"Just like George Washington did, at the battle of Mars!" Johnny Steve exclaims. He has a golf club in one hand and his walking sword in the other and he's swinging them about like a whirling dervish.

A Rifter swings a heavy blade, but Neon reels around, knocks him aside, then dodges another Rifter and makes a flying leap onto the rope bridge where Johnny Steve had been performing.

"Neon!" I cry. "You're amazing!"

"DOUBLE AMAZING!"

I glance down and see Globlet on my shoulder. "Oh hello, fellow Wretch rider!"

"This is making me nauseous," Globlet says, "AND I LOVE IT!" I just laugh.

Neon pauses for a moment, staring out at the mini golf course turned battlefield—and the dozens of scattering Rifters. After a moment, he lets out a tremendous, triumphant *"RAWWWR!"*

He lost his wings, his home, and his family. He's been tracked all over town by bad guys who want to hand him over to Thrull.

But he's not broken.

Not at all.

"Neon," I say, leaning forward. "Let's go find that Boss Rifter. It's time."

I feel Neon's sides expand as he takes a deep breath, and then he bolts forward.

"Yeep!" Globlet cries out, clawing at my shoulder. We careen through the waterfall and into the cave. A Rifter is waiting for us when we come out the other side. His Ogre lunges for us, but Neon darts between its thick, clumsy legs.

I apply a little pressure to Neon with my left leg, and he instinctively knows that I'm asking him to turn. He picks up speed as we approach a bin of colorful golf balls.

"Swing me!" Globlet says, and I whip her around, into the bin, spilling it over on its side.

I twist around to watch with satisfaction as a pair of Rifters slip, trip, and flip.

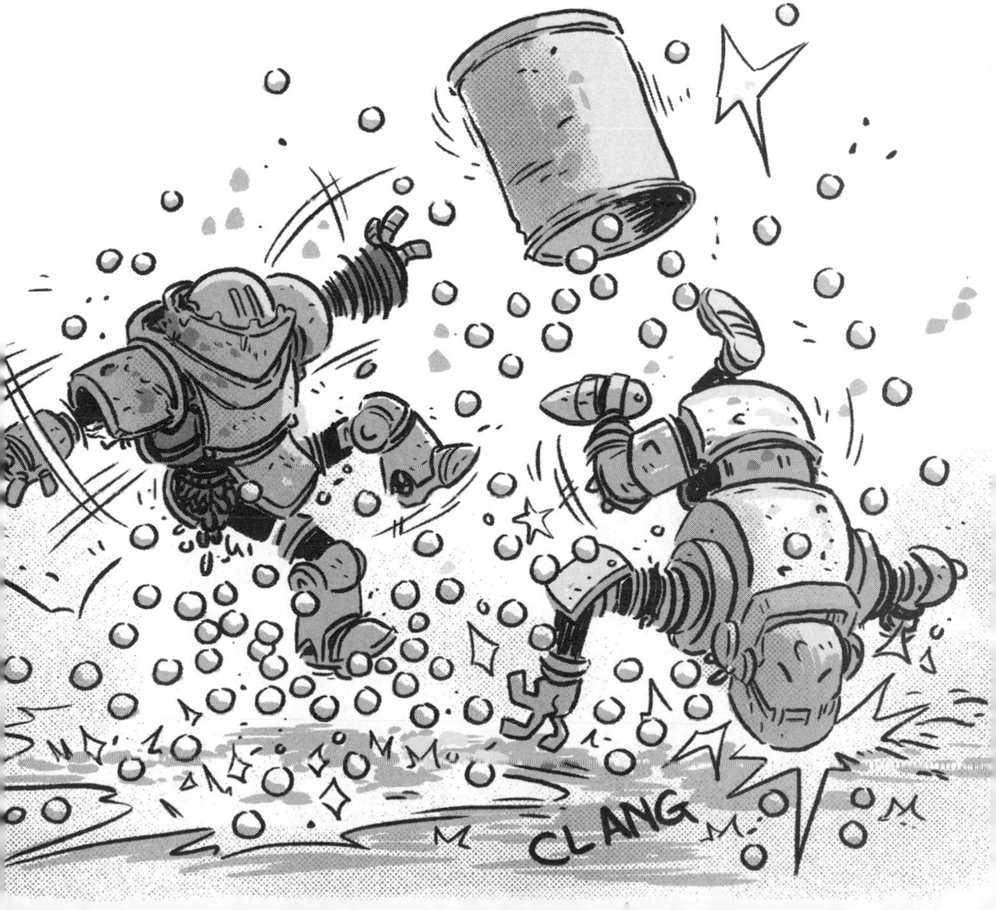
CLANG

I look around for the Boss Rifter.

Finally, I spot him and shout, *"THERE!"*

The Boss Rifter is scrambling up the fifth hole obstacle. It's one of those where you have to hit the ball really hard to get it to the top, because otherwise it just comes rolling back down toward you and it takes like fifteen swings and eventually you give up and just PLACE the ball in the hole because the laws of gravity just don't play fair.

But Neon makes it to the top in just a few big strides. From there, I see the Boss Rifter jumping onto a long rope ladder and sliding down to the course's bottom level.

"He's doing a getaway-type thing!" Globlet cries out.

"I don't think so," I say.

Neon growls softly—and I'm pretty sure that's his version of "I don't think so."

He charges.

He leaps.

And for a moment—

A long moment—

Neon IS flying.

# I rode a Wretch at PUTT-PUTT ON THE HIGH SEAS!

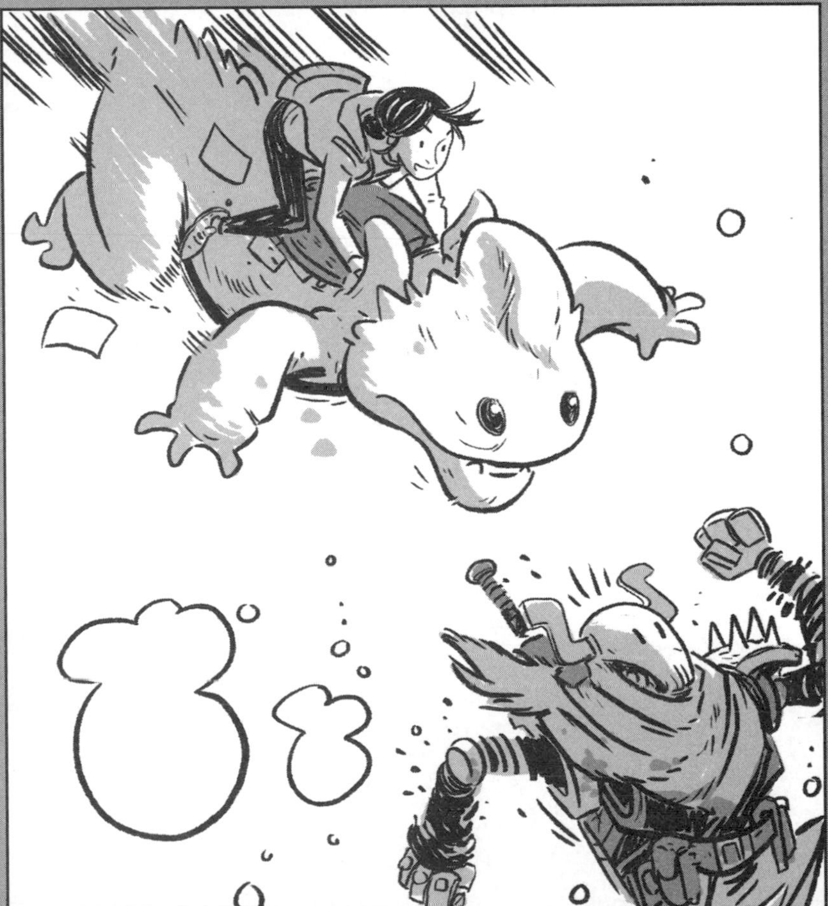

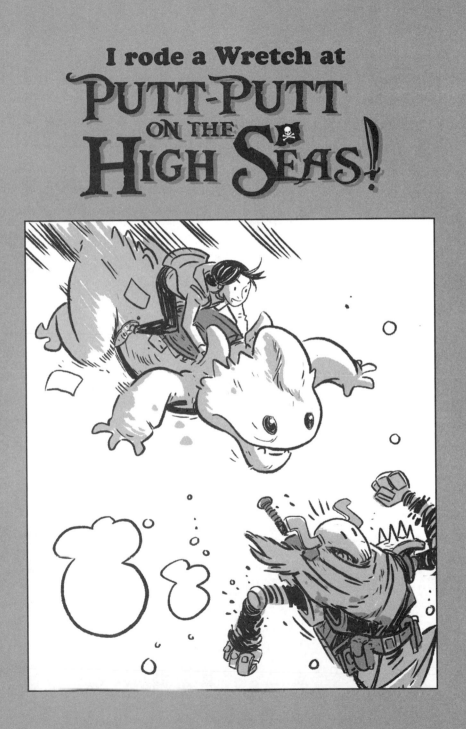

The first hole—a massive wooden pirate ship—nearly crumbles as we plow into the Boss Rifter.

Neon and Globlet both tumble off the deck, onto the putting green below. I'm thrown across the rough, rotted wood. Vines have twisted and broken it, so that the front juts out like a plank.

I try to scramble to my feet, but it's the Boss Rifter who rises first.

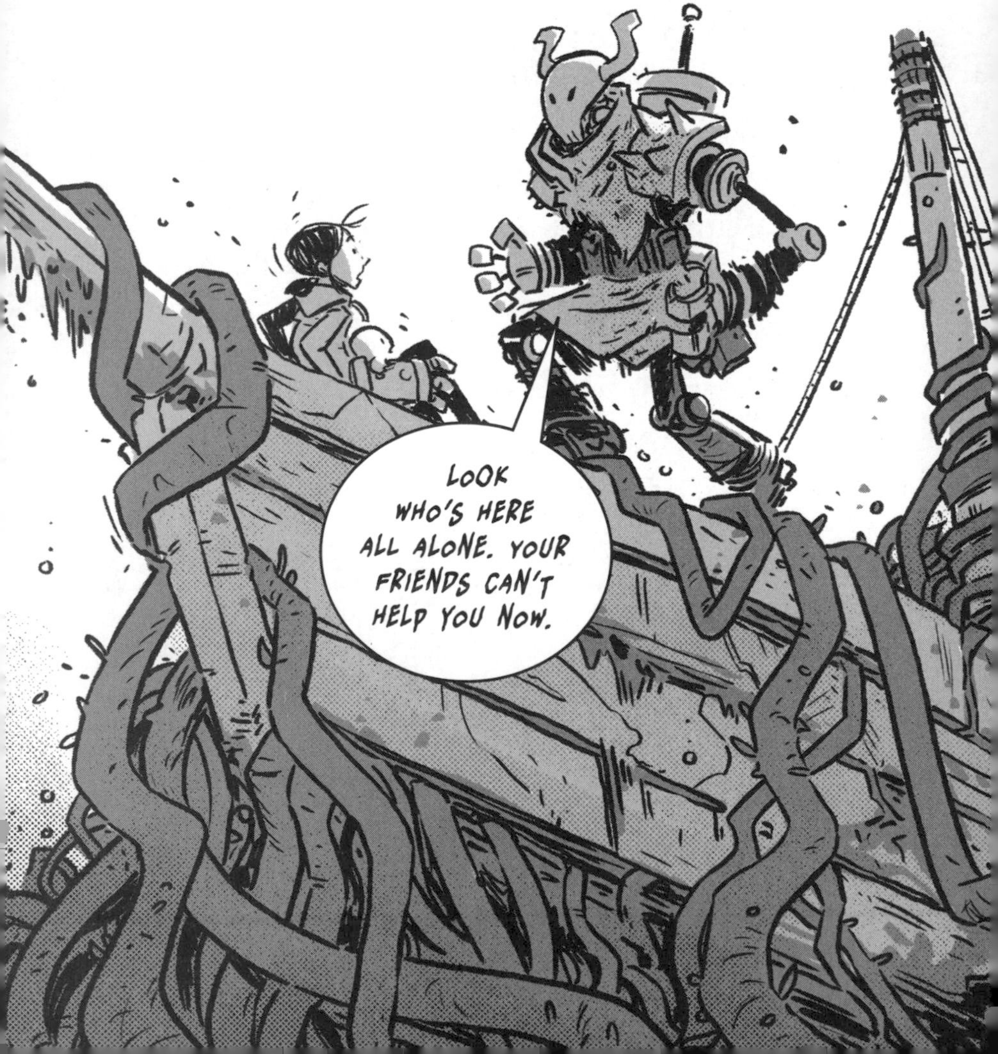
LOOK WHO'S HERE ALL ALONE. YOUR FRIENDS CAN'T HELP YOU NOW.

I almost laugh, because he couldn't be more wrong.

I'm not all alone.

And if he thinks he can scare me by saying that I am, then he doesn't know June Del Toro. My friends are always with me, helping me—even when they're miles and miles away.

"Where is the Outpost!" I demand.

He shakes his head. "Why should I tell you?"

"Because my friends and I—we are going to find Thrull. It's just a matter of time. And when we do, I'll have to decide what I say to him."

"What are you yappin' about?" the Boss Rifter asks.

"Ya know," I say with a cool shrug. "Do I mention the name of the Rifter who revealed to me that this Outpost even existed? The Rifter who couldn't manage to wrangle a single Wretch?"

Boss narrows his eyes at me. He hadn't thought about that.

"Or . . ." I say. "Do I forget your name altogether . . . ?"

"You wouldn' know how to find it even if I told yer. S'no place for a human—" he says "human" like it's a dirty word.

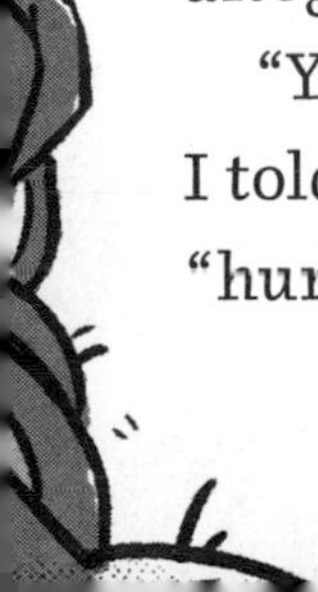

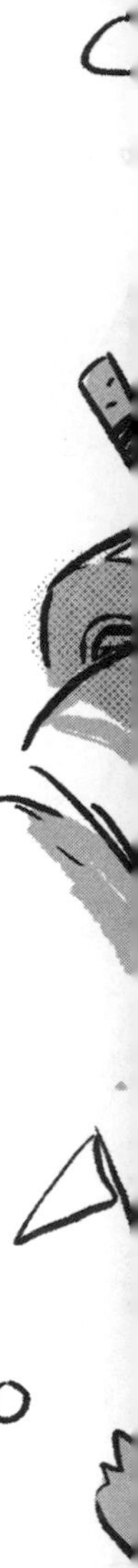

He's stomping forward and I'm picking up Blasty. Things are about to get ugly, when—

"JUNE! JUNE!!!"

It's Globlet, shrieking in terror. I glance over the side of the ship, at the putting green below us, and I see—

The Boss's Ogre! His Ogre has Neon pinned—and it's pressing him *into the ground*.

"Tell him to stop!" I growl. "Right now."

"Don't think I will," the Boss says.

I'm *this* close to learning what I need to learn, to getting information that will lead us to Thrull, lead us to the Tower, and *stop Ŗeżżőčh*.

I have to make a choice. Get the information I need. Or stop the Ogre from *crushing* Neon.

I make my decision.

And in a flash—

I slam Blasty onto my wrist and fire. Two bottle rockets shriek through the air and—

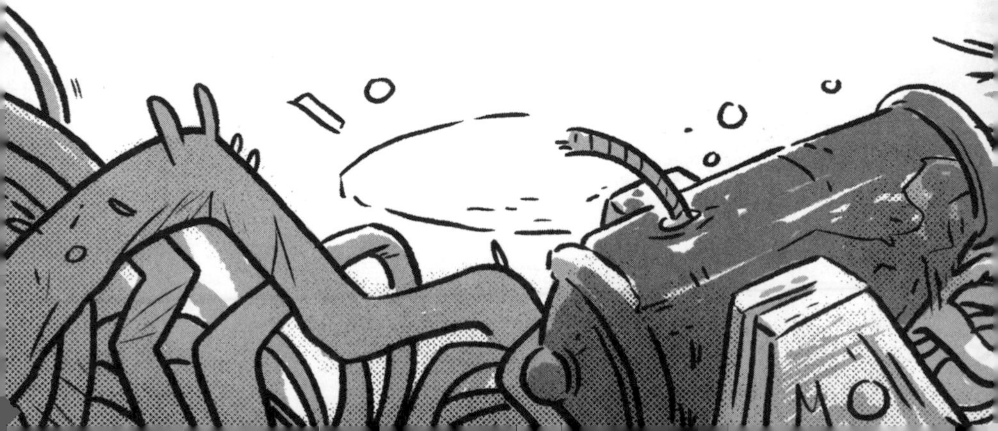

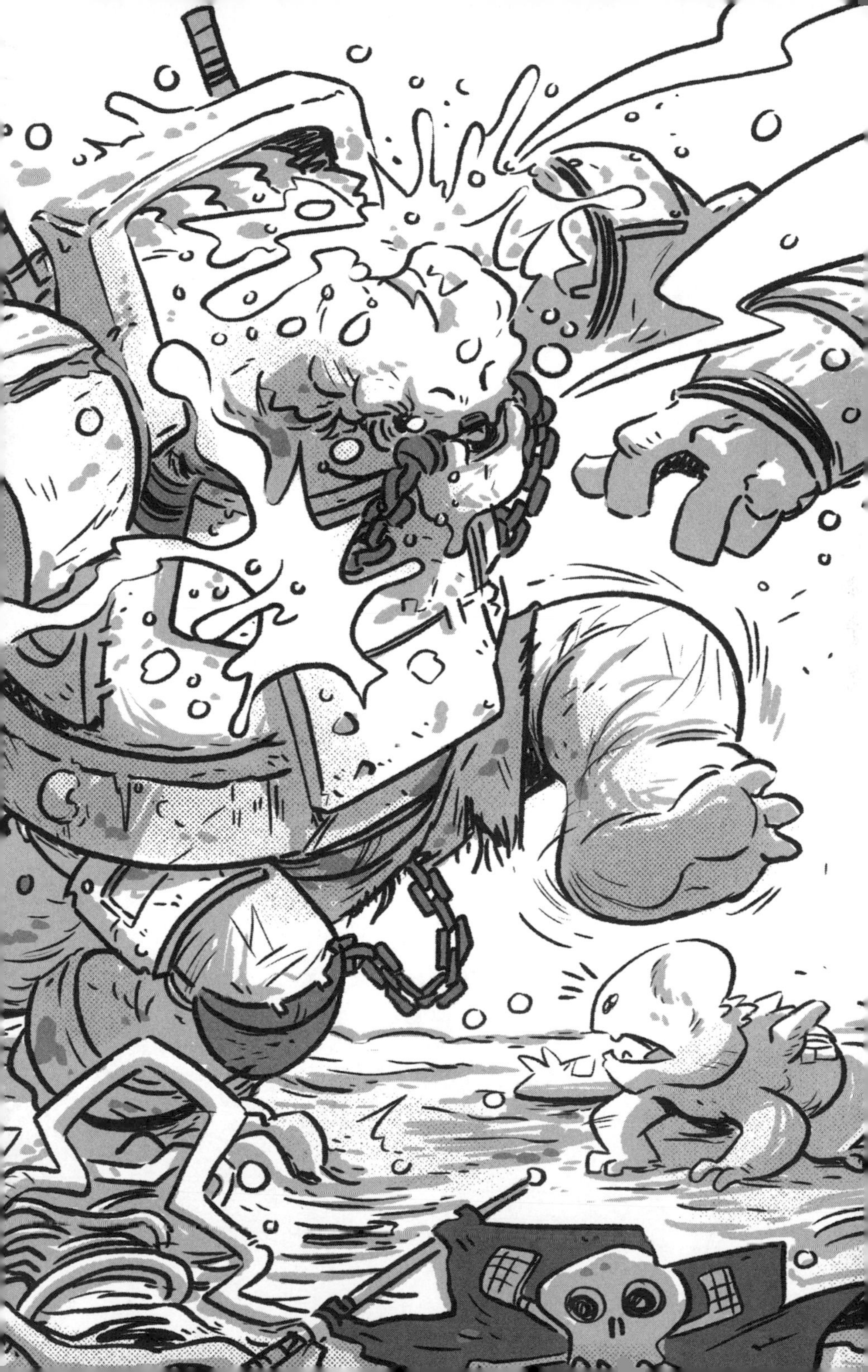

The pirate ship rocks and swings as the Ogre staggers away, howling. There's no more fight left in him. I spin back just in time to see the Boss Rifter *leap* off the bow of the ship.

I'm a step too slow—and I'm left watching the Boss Rifter land on the Ogre's back. Escaping.

And his Rifters go with him. Ogres pour out from the course with four or five Rifters apiece clinging on for dear life.

Maybe they'll look for some other gift to bring Thrull, to prove they can be an asset.

But they won't be bringing him any of us.

I grab hold of a coil of pirate rope—it's just decoration, but it holds me—and I slide down to the putting green.

I smile as I see—

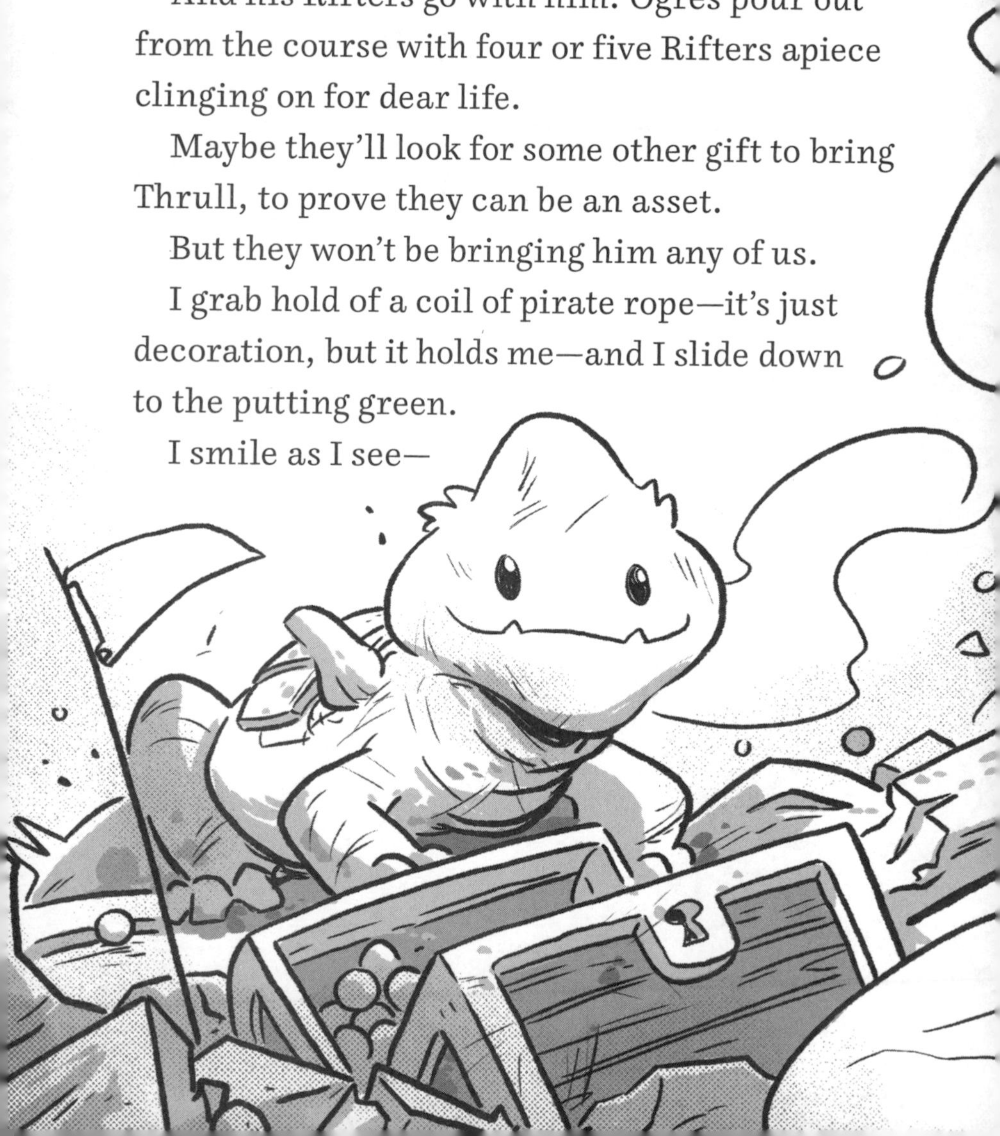

Neon goes down on his belly. Gently, I rub his wing armor. And he smiles.

I feel like I'm on a team. And it's a really good feeling.

I *can* go it alone. I got this far, after all. But it's way more fun to fight evil with my buddies by my side. I mean, that's what buddies are for!

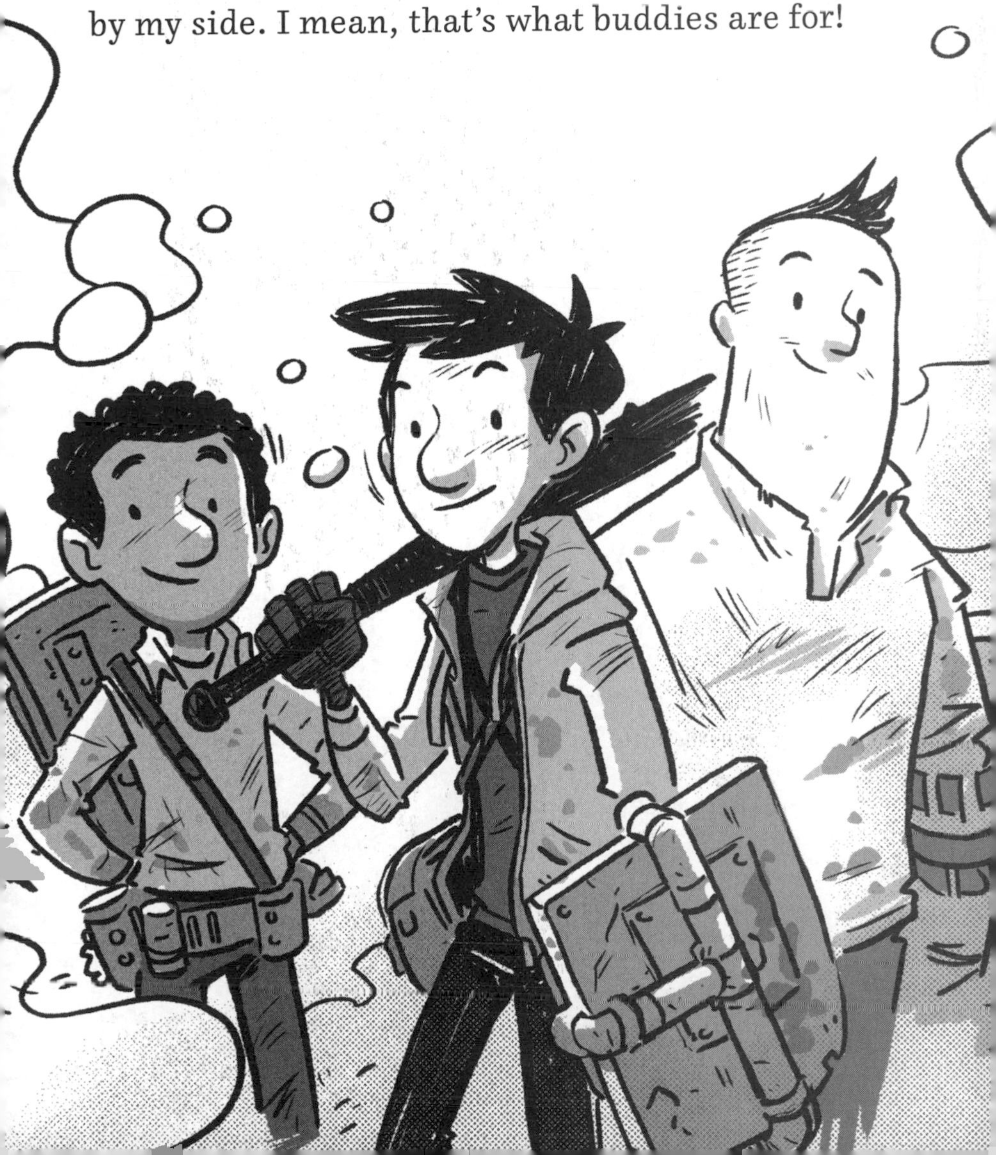

# chapter twenty-seven

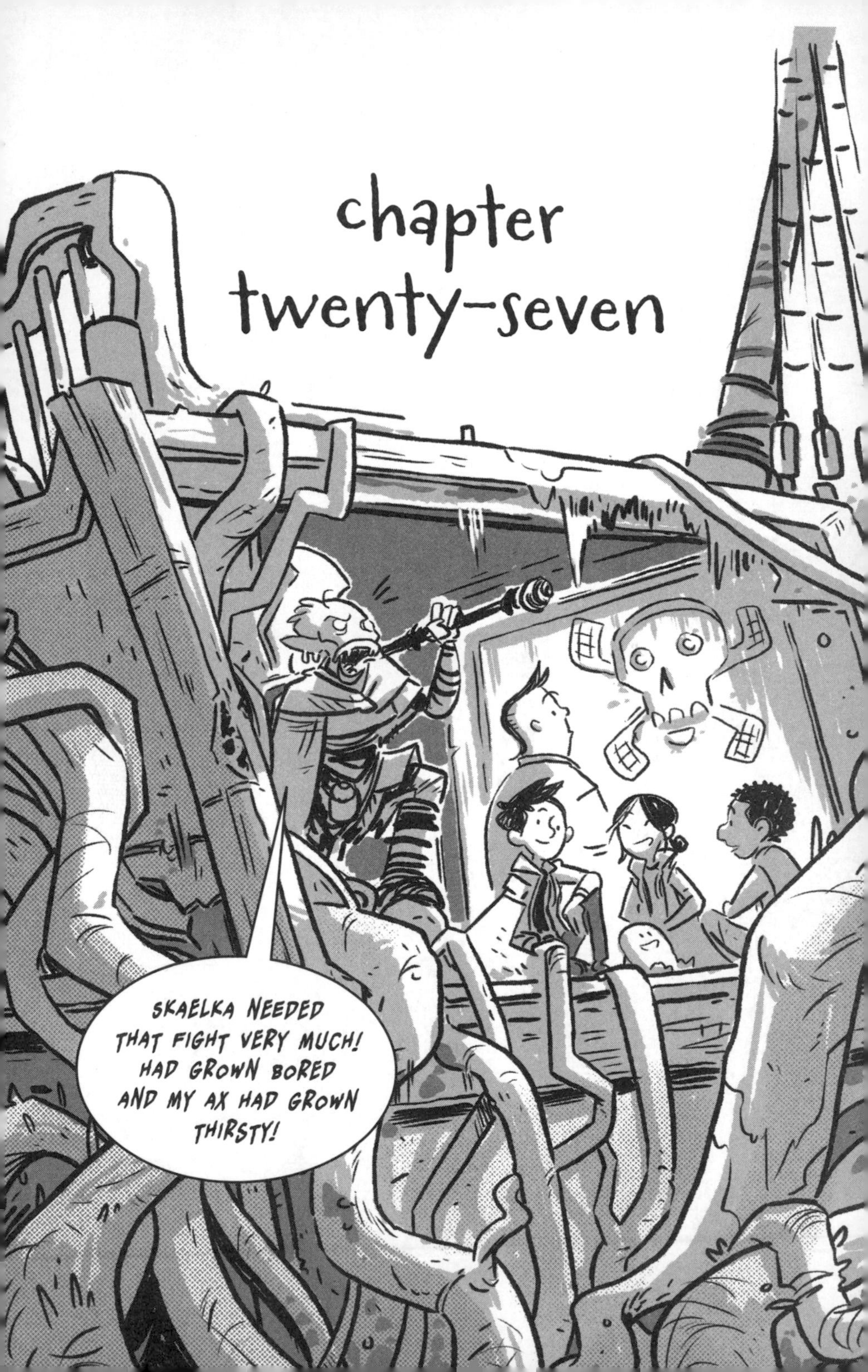
SKAELKA NEEDED THAT FIGHT VERY MUCH! HAD GROWN BORED AND MY AX HAD GROWN THIRSTY!

I'm on my fifth bag of Tropical Skittles Jack brought, because he figured I'd be hungry. Which I was. And I'm ALWAYS in the mood to taste the rainbow.

"Guys, should this be our new hangout?" Dirk asks, looking around. "I dig the skulls. I dig the crossbones. I dig the whole thing."

I shake my head. "Hard pass. Please."

Quint plucks an electric blue Skittle out of my hands. "June, next time you decide to get lost—could you *please* keep track of your walkie? I had to listen to hours of weird Wretch stomach grumbling before I could pinpoint your location."

I laugh. "Not surprised. Neon's diet is—well—unusual would be putting it lightly."

They all glance down at Neon. He's gnawing on a Rifter ax handle like it's a bone. My friends eye him warily. "And you *sure* he's not evil?" Jack asks again. "Like . . . *REALLY* sure?"

"I'm sure."

"I'm not worried," Dirk says. "Look, Rover loves the shiny dude. They're golf buddies already."

It's true. Now Rover and Neon are jumping and playing on the eighteenth hole like they're old friends.

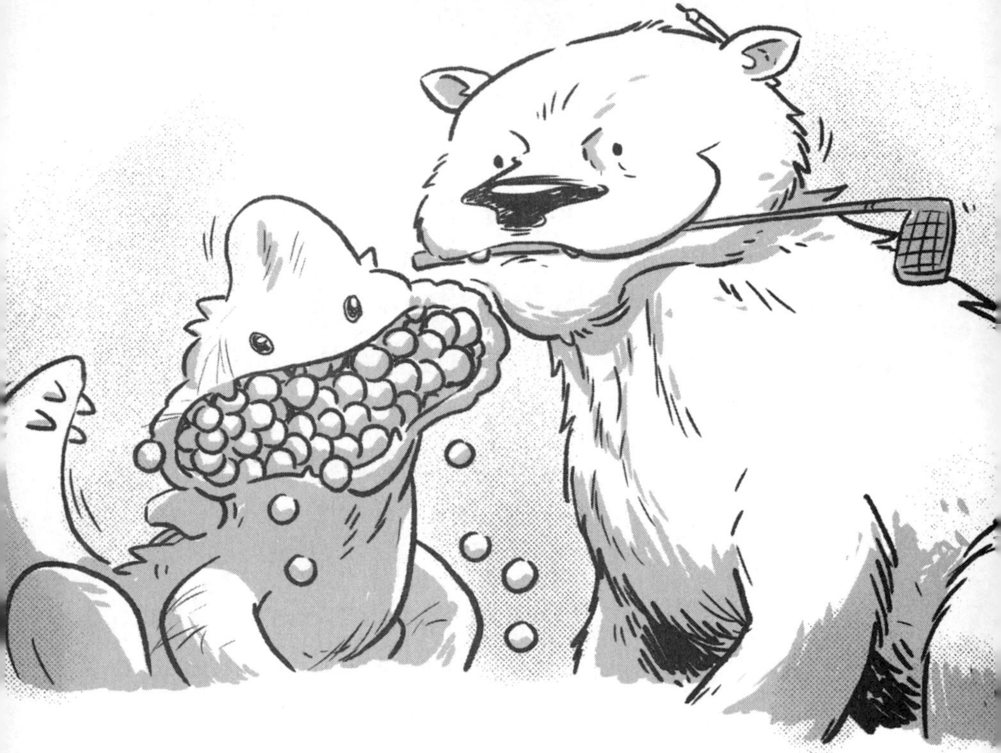

"Hey, Jack," I say, grinning. "Did you help Quint with the radio and the map?"

"Me?" he says. He sticks his hands in his pockets and looks embarrassed. "No, no, of course not. I was, uh, stargazing."

"Dude," I say, "you are the *worst* liar."

"He was just freaking out the whole time," Dirk says.

"No way!" Jack protests. "I was very cool. Very calm. I said, you know, June? She'll be fine on her own. Maybe she'll come back someday, maybe she won't, no big deal."

"Oh yeah?" I say, raising my eyebrows.

"Pretty much," he says with a shrug. "I guess, sure, I was *slightly* nervous. Medium nervous. Like, a four on a scale of one to ten."

Dirk erupts in laughter. "Medium nervous!!" he howls. "Oh man. The kid was having kittens! He calls it a four. You should've seen him. . . ."

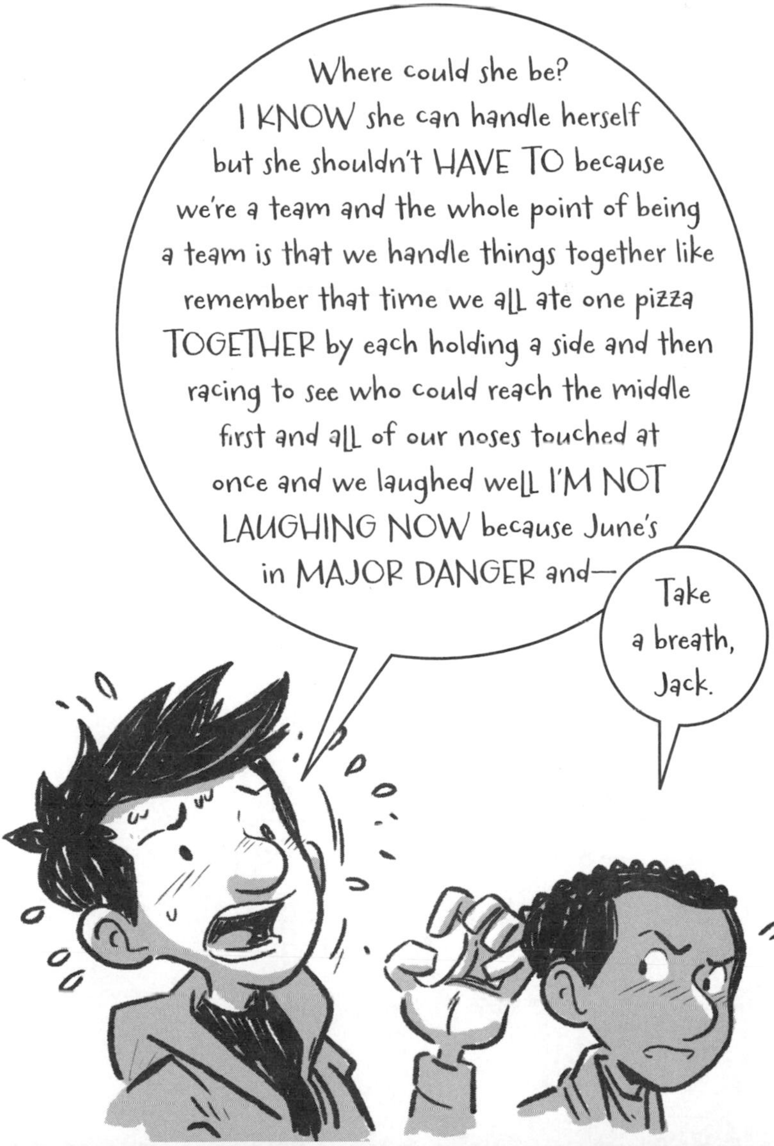
Where could she be? I KNOW she can handle herself but she shouldn't HAVE TO because we're a team and the whole point of being a team is that we handle things together like remember that time we all ate one pizza TOGETHER by each holding a side and then racing to see who could reach the middle first and all of our noses touched at once and we laughed well I'M NOT LAUGHING NOW because June's in MAJOR DANGER and—
Take a breath, Jack.

Jack blushes. His face is practically magenta. "I really *did* know you'd be okay out here on your own. I just . . . y'know. I wasn't sure *we'd* be okay without you."

"We'd all be okay on our own," I say. "But we're better together. Like peanut butter and marshmallow fluff."

I'm trying to find a free second to tell my friends the stuff I learned about Thrull and what the Boss Rifter revealed about the Outpost, but Globlet and Johnny Steve are sort of dominating the conversation. They're regaling everyone with the story of their epic journey and blowing the whole thing way out of proportion.

Dismantled seventeen Rifters—bare-handed! Of course, I do everything bare-handed.
And I'm taking it to Broadway!

When the sun comes up, we begin the journey back home. We take Big Mama most of the way—but then Neon starts to get fidgety in the backseat, and Skaelka keeps nagging us to drive, so we let the monsters take the truck.

And we walk.

Nobody asks where Neon will stay. . . . With me? With Rover? I'm not even sure. I'm thinking it over when Johnny Steve announces, "Well, human-folks—I must be on my way now."

"Whoa, what?" I ask, stopping dead in my tracks. "You're not really leaving . . . ?"

He nods his head. "I have business out there in the unexplored lands. I must meet with a monster. Our reunion is long overdue. . . ."

"Reunion?" Globlet exclaims. "I LOVE REUNIONS!"

"What kind of business?" Jack asks.

"I'm afraid I cannot say," Johnny Steve says. "But I promise you that Neon and I will keep each other fine company."

"Wait," I say. I look from Neon to Johnny Steve and back to Neon. "Neon's coming with you?"

"He has business as well," Johnny Steve says, patting Neon's hide.

After all that. After everything we've been through, they're just gonna pick up and leave? I crouch down next to Neon. "You don't have to go, you know," I tell him, my voice catching.

But then Neon puts something in my head. *One last vision.* It's like a replay—a flashback of what happened hours earlier.

It's me, letting the Boss Rifter escape so that I could save Neon. I'm making a sacrifice by *not learning* the location of the Outpost so that he could get away.

And it's like Neon's saying he'll make it up to me.

I run my hand over his back, about to tell him he doesn't owe me anything. But then I remember something Bardle once said. Some monsters are on the side of good—willing to make their own sacrifices to defeat Reżżóch.

Neon is my friend, but something out there is calling him. Something I can't be a part of. His own adventure, maybe. And this time, he'll have friends waiting for him when he gets home.

So I just stand there and watch Neon and Johnny Steve gearing up to set off.

"I hate saying good-bye," I tell him. "So I'm

just gonna say see ya next weekend. That's what I used to tell my cousins when we'd leave their house after a sleepover. Makes it easier."

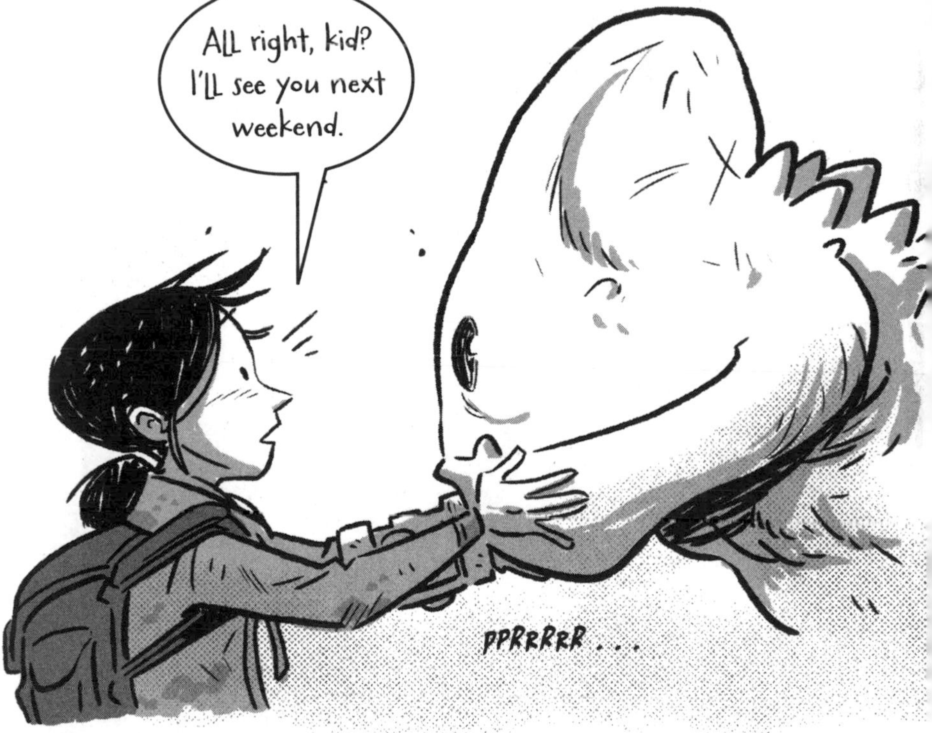
ALL right, kid? I'LL see you next weekend.
PPRRRRR . . .

A smile grows on Neon's face—then grows even larger as Johnny Steve climbs up on his back, using the armor I gave Neon as a saddle.

We continue our walk down the track. Soon, Neon and Johnny Steve are veering left.

I look straight ahead, because the tears are building and it's all I can do to stop them.

And then I hear Neon's feet, on the pebbles beside the tracks. Not daring to take another look, I wave at them as they go.

As we re-enter Wakefield, everything looks a little different. A little bit smaller.

The tree house is there, looking the same as it always does.

Tonight, I'm looking forward to hanging out and playing Monopoly and just enjoying things being back to normal.

But deep down, I know things can't stay normal for long. Not anymore.

"Guys," I say, finally ready to share my big news. "I learned something. About Thrull. There's a way to find him. A place we have to go. An Outpost, somewhere—way out there, in the wasteland. . . ."

Jack wheels around. "Are you saying . . ."

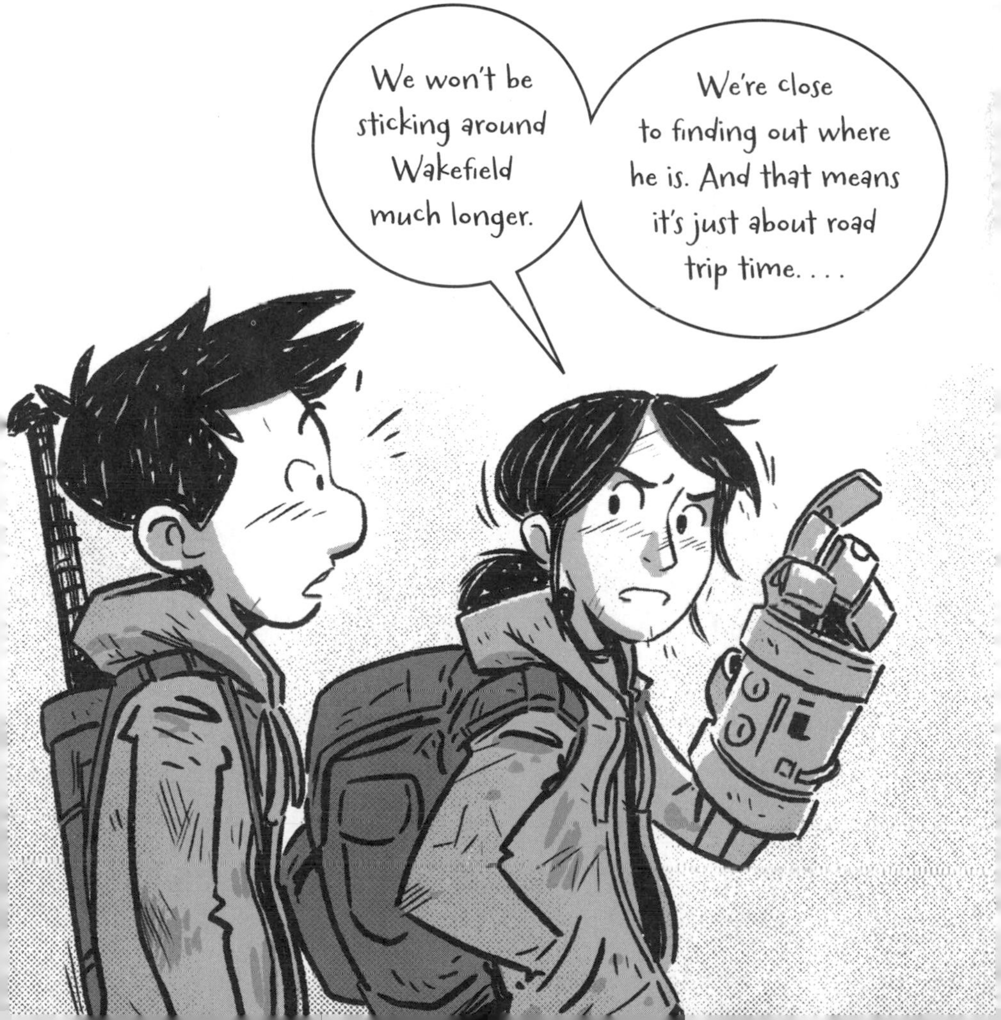
We won't be sticking around Wakefield much longer.
We're close to finding out where he is. And that means it's just about road trip time. . . .

# Acknowledgments

Douglas Holgate—the man with the million-dollar hips; thanks for joining me on this wild ride. Dana Leydig, for everything—and it was so, so much—along the way. Leila Sales, for helping bring June to life. Jim Hoover—if you're as patient with your son as you are with me, then that's one lucky kiddo.

Jennifer Dee—the real Captain Marvel. Josh Pruett, for endless help and late-night calls while shaping this thing—you're the smartest story maker I know.

Abigail Powers, Janet B. Pascal, Krista Ahlberg, and Marinda Valenti—thanks for catching and managing to fix my many, many, many typos and plot holes—and to the production team for creating extra time where there shouldn't logically be any.

Emily Romero, Elyse Marshall, Carmela Iaria, Christina Colangelo, Felicity Vallence, Sarah Moses, Kara Brammer, Alex Garber, Lauren Festa, Michael Hetrick, and all the other amazing people in Viking's marketing and publicity department—thank you for all that you do. Kim Ryan, Helen Boomer, and the PYR subrights team—a heartfelt thanks for all your work on the series from the very beginning. The entire PYR sales squad—thanks for getting these books out there! PYR audio—all of you—for bringing these stories to people who otherwise wouldn't have them. And Ken Wright, for being—well— Ken Wright; 'nuff said. Robin Hoffman and all the wonderful people at Scholastic—thank you for your endless support and for your endless dedication to getting books in kids' hands.

Dan Lazar—for all that you do, big and small and in between. Cecilia de la Campa and Alessandra Birch—thanks for helping Jack, June, Quint, and Dirk travel the world. Torie Doherty-Munro, for responding kindly to the dumbest emails anyone could ever receive. Addison Duffy—you are the absolute best, bar none.

Matt Berkowitz and everyone at Atomic Cartoons—thanks for taking June and making her so much more. Jane Lee and the entire Netflix crew—for bringing this world to an entirely new audience and doing it with care and enthusiasm. And the Jakks Pacific team—for making dreams come true.

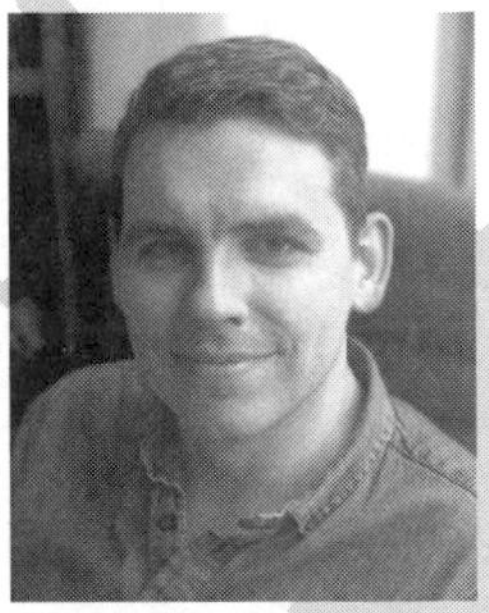

© Ruby Brallier

# MAX BRALLIER!

is the *New York Times* and *USA Today* bestselling author of more than thirty books for children and adults. His books and series include the Last Kids on Earth, Eerie Elementary, Mister Shivers, Galactic Hot Dogs, and Can YOU Survive the Zombie Apocalypse? Max lives in New York City with his wife, Alyse, who is way too good for him, and his daughter, Lila, who is simply the best. Follow Max on Twitter @MaxBrallier or visit him at MaxBrallier.com.

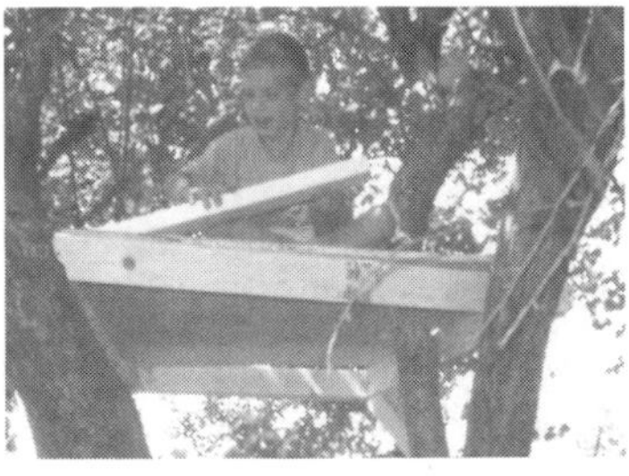

The author building his own tree house as a kiddo.

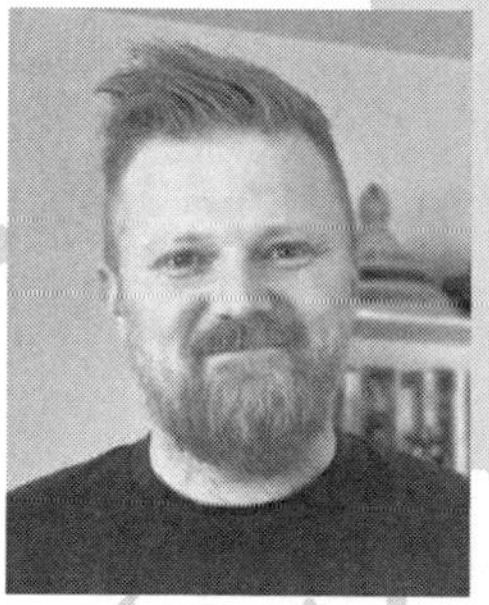

# DOUGLAS HOLGATE!

(skullduggery.com.au) has been a freelance comic book artist and illustrator based in Melbourne, Australia, for more than ten years. He's illustrated books for publishers such as HarperCollins, Penguin Random House, Hachette, and Simon & Schuster, including the Planet Tad series, Cheesie Mack, Case File 13, and *Zoo Sleepover*.

Douglas has illustrated comics for Image, Dynamite, Abrams, and Penguin Random House. He's currently working on the self-published series Maralinga, which received grant funding from the Australian Society of Authors and the Victorian Council for the Arts, as well as the all-ages graphic novel *Clem Hetherington and the Ironwood Race*, published by Scholastic Graphix, both co-created with writer Jen Breach.

Follow Douglas on Twitter @douglasbot.

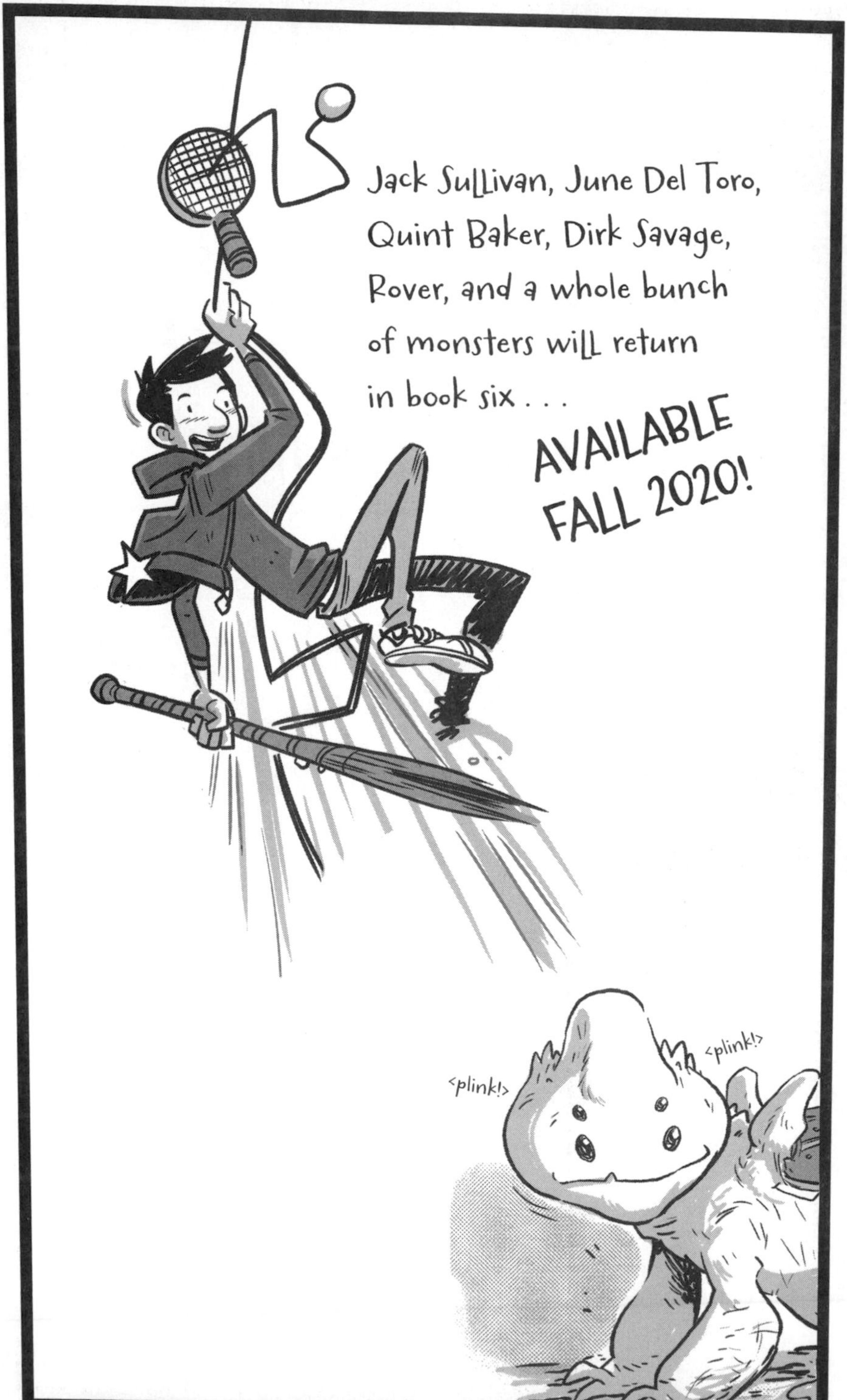
Jack Sullivan, June Del Toro, Quint Baker, Dirk Savage, Rover, and a whole bunch of monsters will return in book six . . .
AVAILABLE FALL 2020!
<plink!>
<plink!>

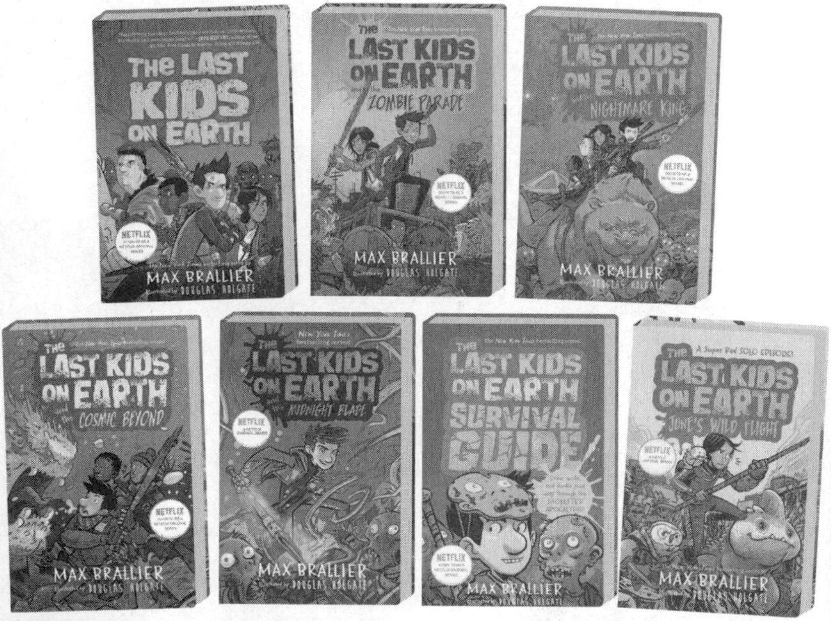
THE LAST KIDS ON EARTH
MAX BRALLIER
THE LAST KIDS ON EARTH and the ZOMBIE PARADE
MAX BRALLIER
THE LAST KIDS ON EARTH and the NIGHTMARE KING
MAX BRALLIER
THE LAST KIDS ON EARTH and the COSMIC BEYOND
MAX BRALLIER
THE LAST KIDS ON EARTH and the MIDNIGHT BLADE
MAX BRALLIER
THE LAST KIDS ON EARTH SURVIVAL GUIDE
MAX BRALLIER
THE LAST KIDS ON EARTH JUNE'S WILD FLIGHT
MAX BRALLIER



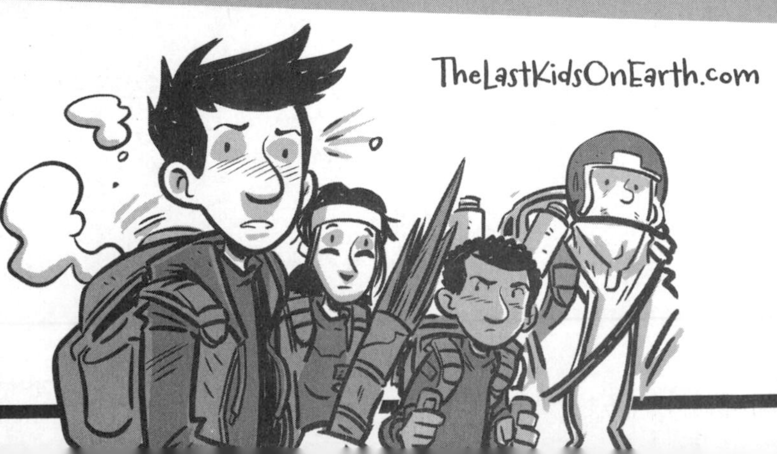

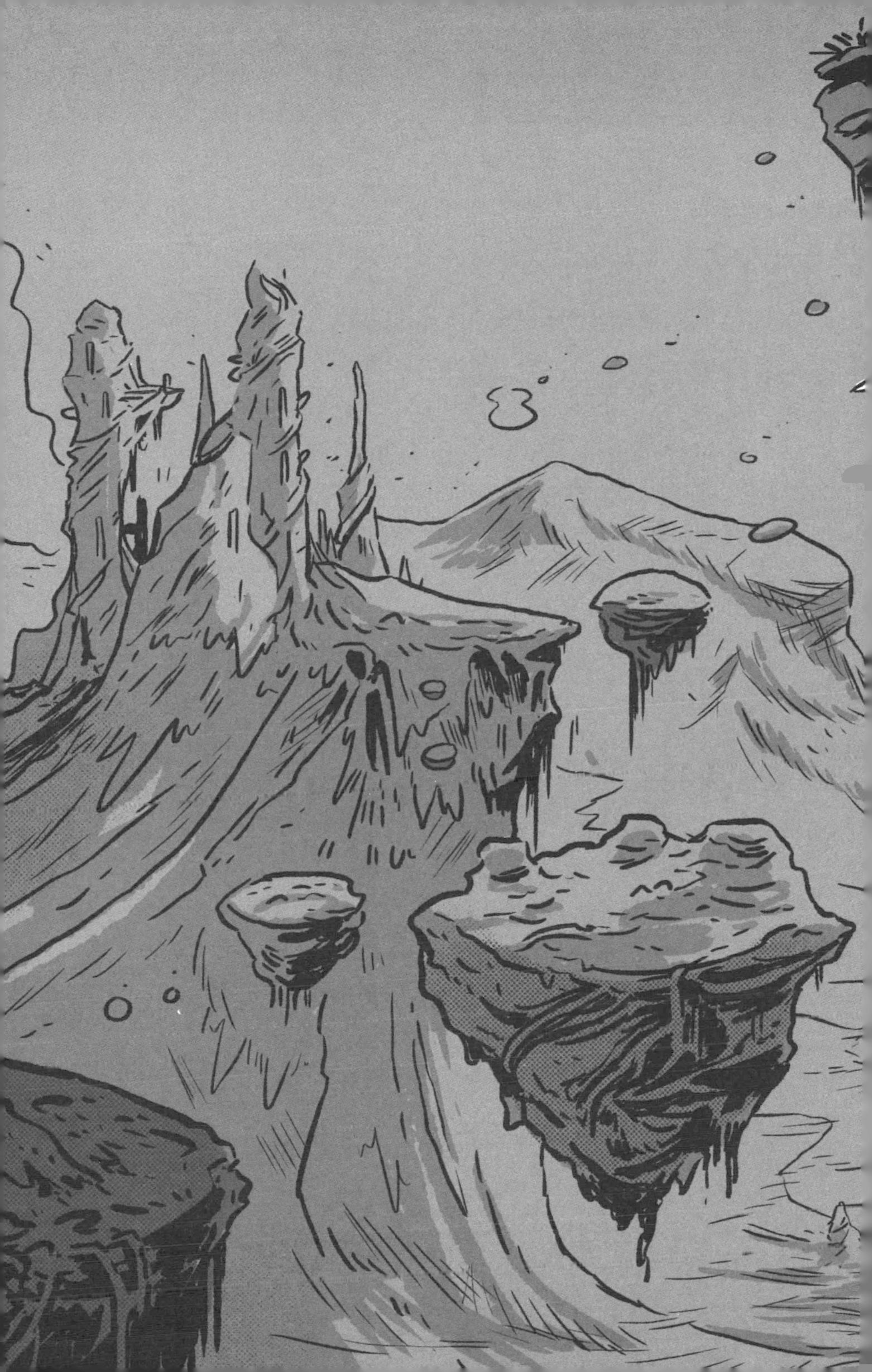

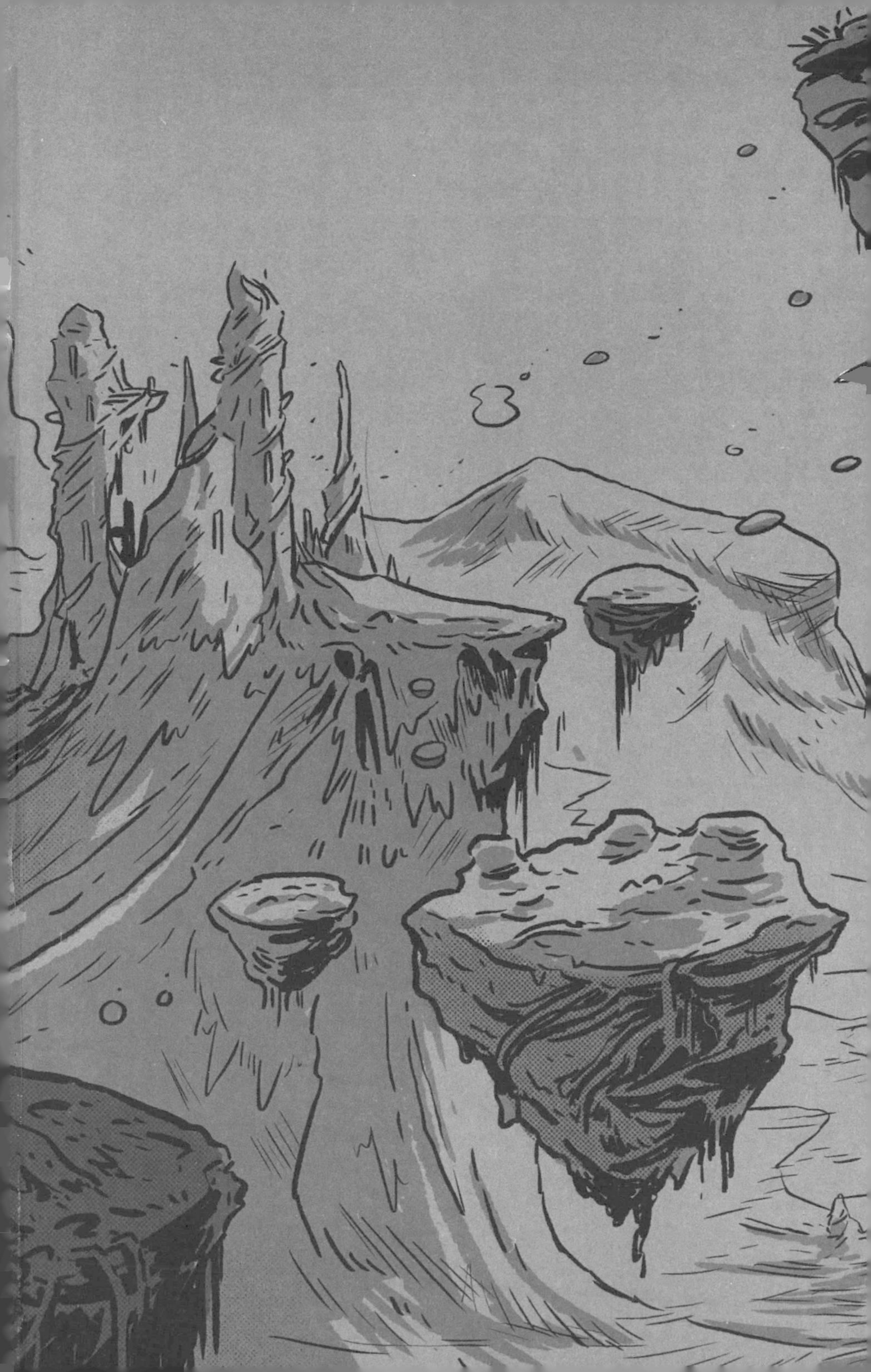